OUTSTANDING PRAISE FOR
THE OVERNIGHT GUEST

"*The Overnight Guest* is not only compelling, it's addictive.
I'll be thinking about this book for a long time."
—SAMANTHA DOWNING,
bestselling author of *My Lovely Wife*

"A tightly woven braid of a novel guaranteed to raise the hairs
on the back of your neck and keep you turning the pages deep
into the night. Atmospheric, fast-paced and perfectly plotted."
—CATHERINE MCKENZIE,
USA TODAY* bestselling author of *I'll Never Tell* and *Please Join Us

"Atmospheric and claustrophobic, tense and twisted,
this chiller will make you hold your breath as you turn
the pages. Cancel your plans when you start reading this
one because you won't be able to put it down."
—HANNAH MARY MCKINNON,
international bestselling author of *You Will Remember Me*

"Chilling, gripping, and gaspingly surprising.
The oh-so-talented Heather Gudenkauf has created
a modern-day *In Cold Blood*."
—HANK PHILLIPPI RYAN,
USA TODAY* bestselling author of *Her Perfect Life

"Scrupulously plotted and layered with multiple
narratives that culminate in some explosive surprises.
A chilling and heart-stopping stunner."
—KIMBERLY BELLE,
international bestselling author of *My Darling Husband*

THE OVERNIGHT GUEST

Also by Heather Gudenkauf

THE OVERNIGHT GUEST

HEATHER GUDENKAUF

PARK
ROW
BOOKS

PARK
ROW
BOOKS™

Recycling programs
for this product may
not exist in your area.

ISBN-13: 978-0-7783-1193-5

The Overnight Guest

This edition published by arrangement with Harlequin Books S.A.

Park Row Books
22 Adelaide St. West, 41st Floor
Toronto, Ontario M5H 4E3, Canada
ParkRowBooks.com
BookClubbish.com

Printed in Italy by Grafica Veneta

For Greg, Milt and Patrick Schmida—the best brothers in the world.

THE
OVERNIGHT
GUEST

1

On August 12, 2000, Abby Morris, out of breath with sweat trickling down her temple, was hurrying down the gray ribbon of gravel road for her nightly walk. Despite her long-sleeved shirt, pants, and the thick layer of bug spray, mosquitoes formed a halo around her head in search of exposed flesh. She was grateful for the light the moon provided and the company of Pepper, her black Lab. Jay, her husband, thought she was unwise to walk this time of night, but between working all day, picking up the baby at day care and then dealing with all the chores at home, 9:30 to 10:30 was the one hour of the day that was truly her own.

Not that she was scared. Abby grew up walking roads like these. County roads covered in dusty gravel or dirt and lined with cornfields. In the three months they'd lived here, she never once encountered anyone on her evening walks, which suited her just fine.

"Roscoe, Roscoe!" came a female voice from far off in the distance. Someone calling for their dog to come home for the night, Abby thought. "Ro-sss-co," the word was drawn out in a singsongy cadence but edged with irritation.

Pepper was panting heavily, her pink tongue thick and nearly dragging on the ground.

Abby picked up her pace. She was almost to the halfway spot in her three-mile loop. Where the gravel met a dirt road nearly swallowed up by the cornfields. She turned right and stopped short. Sitting on the side of the road, about forty yards away, was a pickup truck. A prickle of unease crept up her back and the dog looked up at Abby expectantly. Probably someone with a flat tire or engine trouble left the truck there for the time being, Abby reasoned.

She started walking again, and a feathery gauze of clouds slid across the face of the moon, plunging the sky into darkness, making it impossible to see if someone was sitting inside the truck. Abby cocked her head to listen for the purr of an engine idling, but all she could hear was the electric buzz saw serenade of thousands of cicadas and Pepper's wet breathing.

"Come, Pepper," Abby said in a low voice as she took a few steps backward. Pepper kept going, her nose close to the ground, following a zigzagging path right up to the truck's tires. "Pepper!" Abby said sharply. "Here!"

At the intensity in Abby's voice, Pepper's head snapped up and she reluctantly gave up the scent and returned to Abby's side.

Was there movement behind the darkened windshield? Abby couldn't be sure, but she couldn't shake the feeling that someone was watching. The clouds cleared and Abby saw a figure hunched behind the steering wheel. A man. He was wearing a cap, and in the moonlight, Abby caught a glimpse of pale skin, a slightly off-center nose, and a sharp chin. He was just sitting there.

A warm breeze sent a murmur through the fields and lifted the hair off her neck. A scratchy rustling sound came from off to her right. The hair on Pepper's scruff stood at attention and she gave a low growl.

"Let's go," she said, walking backward before turning and rushing toward home.

12:05 a.m.

Sheriff John Butler stood on the rotting back deck, looking out over his backyard, the wood shifting and creaking beneath his bare feet. The adjacent houses were all dark, the neighbors and their families fast asleep. Why would they be awake? They had a sheriff living right next door. They had nothing to worry about.

He found it difficult to catch his breath. The night air was warm and stagnant and weighed heavily in his chest. The sturgeon moon hung fat and low and bee pollen yellow. Or was it called a buck moon? The sheriff couldn't remember.

The last seven days had been quiet. Too quiet. There were no burglaries, no serious motor vehicle accidents, no meth explosions, not one report of domestic abuse. Not that Blake County was a hotbed of lawlessness. But they did have their share of violent crimes. Just not this week. The first four days, he was grateful for the reprieve, but then it seemed downright eerie. It was odd, unsettling. For the first time in twenty years as sheriff, Butler was actually caught up on all his paperwork.

"Don't go borrowing trouble," came a soft voice. Janice,

Butler's wife of thirty-two years, slipped an arm around his waist and laid her head against his shoulder.

"No danger of that," Butler said with a little laugh. "It usually finds me all on its own."

"Then come back to bed," Janice said and tugged on his hand.

"I'll be right in," Butler said. Janice crossed her arms over her chest and gave him a stern look. He held up his right hand. "Five more minutes. I promise." Reluctantly, Janice stepped back inside.

Butler ran a calloused palm over the splintered cedar railing. The entire deck needed to be replaced. Torn down to the studs and rebuilt. Maybe tomorrow he'd go to Lowe's over in Sioux City. If things continued as they were, he'd have plenty of time to rebuild the deck. Stifling a yawn, he went back inside, flipped the dead bolt, and trudged down the hall toward his bed and Janice. *Another quiet night*, the sheriff thought, *might as well enjoy it while it lasts.*

1:09 a.m.

The sound of balloons popping pulled Deb Cutter from a deep sleep. Another pop, then another. Maybe kids playing with firecrackers leftover from the Fourth of July. "Randy," she murmured. There was no answer.

Deb reached for her husband, but the bed next to her was empty, the bedcovers still undisturbed and cool to the touch. She slipped from beneath the sheets, went to the window, and pulled the curtain aside. Randy's truck wasn't parked in its usual spot next to the milking shed. Brock's was gone too. She glanced at the clock. After midnight.

Her seventeen-year-old son had become a stranger to her. Her sweet boy had always had a wild streak, which had turned mean. He'd be up to no good, she was sure of that. Brock was born when they were barely eighteen and barely knew how to take care of themselves, let alone an infant.

Deb knew that Randy was hard on Brock. Too hard at times. When he was little, it took just a stern look and a swat to get Brock back in line, but those days were long gone. The only thing that seemed to get his attention now was a smack upside the head. Deb had to admit that over the years, Randy had crossed a line or two—doling out bruises, busted lips, bloody noses. But afterward, Randy always justified his harshness—life wasn't easy, and as soon as Brock figured that out, the better.

And Randy. He'd been so distant, so busy lately. Not only was Randy helping his parents out on their farm, but he was also in the process of refurbishing another old farmhouse with half a dozen decrepit outbuildings, a hog confine, and trying to tend to his own crops. She barely saw him during the daylight hours.

Deb tried to tamper down the resentment, but it curdled in her throat. Obsessed. That was what Randy was. Obsessed with fixing up that old homestead, obsessed with the land. It was always about the land. The economy was probably going to tank, and they'd end up on the hook for two properties they couldn't afford. She wasn't going to be able to take it much longer.

One more bang reverberated in the distance. Damn kids, she thought. Wide-awake, she stared up at the ceiling fan that turned lazily above her and waited for her husband and son to come home.

1:10 a.m.

At first, twelve-year-old Josie Doyle and her best friend, Becky Allen, ran toward the loud bangs. It only made sense to go to the house—that's where her mother and father and

Ethan were. They would be safe. But by the time Josie and Becky discovered their mistake, it was too late.

They turned away from the sound and, hand in hand, ran through the dark farmyard toward the cornfield—its stalks, a tall, spindly forest, their only portal to safety.

Josie was sure she heard the pounding of footsteps behind them, and she turned to see what was hunting them. There was nothing, no one—just the house bathed in nighttime shadows.

"Hurry," Josie gasped, tugging on Becky's hand and urging her forward. Breathing heavily, they ran. They were almost there. Becky stumbled. Crying out, her hand slipped from Josie's. Her legs buckled, and she fell to her knees.

"Get up, get up," Josie begged, pulling on Becky's arm. "Please." Once again, she dared to look behind her. A shard of moonlight briefly revealed a shape stepping out from behind the barn. In horror, Josie watched as the figure raised his hands and took aim. She dropped Becky's arm, turned, and ran. Just a little bit farther—she was almost there.

Josie crossed into the cornfield just as another shot rang out. Searing pain ripped through her arm, stripping her breath from her lungs. Josie didn't pause, didn't slow down, and with hot blood dripping onto the hard-packed soil, Josie kept running.

2

Present Day

Because of how quickly the storm was approaching, Wylie Lark angled into the last open parking spot on the street where Shaffer's Grocery Store was tucked between the pharmacy and the Elk's Lodge. Wylie would have preferred to have driven to the larger, better-stocked grocery store in Algona, but already heavy gray snow clouds descended on Burden.

Wylie stepped from her Bronco, her boots crunching against the ice salt spread thickly across the sidewalk in anticipation of the sleet and two feet of snow expected that evening.

With trepidation, Wylie approached the store's glass windows, decorated for Valentine's Day. Shabby red and pink hearts and bow-and-arrow-clad cupids. She paused before yanking open the door. Shaffer's was family owned, carried off-brands, and had a limited selection. It was convenient but crowded with nosy townspeople.

So far, whenever Wylie made the drive into Burden, she had successfully dodged interactions with the locals, but the longer she stayed, the more difficult it became.

Once inside, she was met with a blast of warm air. She resisted the temptation to remove her stocking hat and gloves and instead inserted her earbuds and turned up the volume on the true crime podcast she had been listening to.

All the carts were taken, so Wylie snagged a handbasket and began walking the aisles, eyes fixed firmly on the ground in front of her. She started tossing items into her basket. A frozen pizza, cans of soup, tubes of chocolate chip cookie dough. She paused at the wine shelf and scanned the limited options. A man in brown coveralls and green-and-yellow seed cap bumped into her, knocking an earbud from her ear.

"Oops, sorry," he said, smiling down at her.

"It's okay," Wylie responded, not looking him in the eye. She quickly grabbed the nearest bottle of wine and made her way to join the long line of people waiting to check out.

The sole cashier's brown hair was shot through with gray and was pulled back from her weary face by a silver barrette. She seemed oblivious to the antsy customers eager to get home. She slid each item across the scanner at an excruciatingly slow pace.

The line inched forward. Wylie felt the solid form of someone standing directly behind her. She turned. It was the man from the wine aisle. Sweating beneath her coat, Wylie looked toward the cashier. Their eyes met.

"Excuse me," Wylie said, muscling her way past the man and the other shoppers. She set her basket on the floor and rushed out the doors. The cold air felt good on her face.

Her cell phone vibrated in her pocket and she fished it out. It was her ex-husband and Wylie didn't want to talk to him. He would go on and on about how she needed to get back to Oregon and help take care of their son, that she could just as easily finish her book at home. She let the call go to voice mail.

He was wrong. Wylie wouldn't be able to finish the book back home. The slammed doors and shouting matches with fourteen-year-old Seth over his coming home too late or not coming home at all frustrated her to no end. She couldn't think, couldn't concentrate there. And when Seth, glowering at her from beneath his shaggy mop of hair, told her he hated her and wanted to go live with his dad, she'd called his bluff.

"Fine. Go," she said, turning away from him. And he did. When Seth didn't come home the next morning or answer any of her calls and texts, Wylie packed her bags and left. She knew it was the easy way out, but she couldn't handle Seth's secrecy and anger a second longer. Her ex could deal with it for a few days. Except the days turned into weeks and then months.

She moved to shove the phone back into her pocket, but it tumbled from her fingers and struck the concrete and bounced into a slush-filled rut.

"Dammit," Wylie said, bending over to fish the phone from the icy puddle. The screen was shattered, and the phone was soaked through.

Once in her vehicle, Wylie ripped off her hat and shrugged out of her coat. Her hair and T-shirt were damp with sweat. She tried to wipe the moisture from the phone but knew that unless she got home in a hurry and dried it out, it was ruined. She futilely poked at the cracked screen, hoping that it would light up. Nothing.

The twenty-five-minute drive back to the farmhouse

seemed to take forever and she had nothing to show for it. No groceries, no wine. She'd have to make do with what she had back at the house.

Though it took Wylie only two minutes to put Burden in her rearview mirror, what laid before her felt like an endless stripe of black highway. Twice she got stuck behind salt trucks, but the farther north she traveled, the fewer cars she saw. Everyone was hunkered in, waiting for the storm to hit. Finally, she turned off the main road and bounced across the poorly maintained gravel roads that would lead her to the house.

Wylie had been staying in rural Blake County for six weeks, and the weather had been brutal. The cold went bone-deep and she couldn't remember seeing so much snow. As she drove, she passed fewer and fewer houses and farms until all she could see was a sea of white where corn and soybeans and alfalfa once stood. They gave no suggestion of the explosion of green and gold that was sure to come in a few months.

Wylie drove another several miles and slowed to a crawl to inch around the hickory tree that inexplicably grew in the middle of where two gravel roads intersected and then over the small pony trestle bridge that spanned the frozen creek below.

Two hundred yards beyond the bridge, the long, narrow lane, lined with shoulder-high, snow-packed drifts, would take her to the house. She drove past the line of tall pines that served as a windbreak and toward the red weathered barn, now covered in white. She left the Bronco idling while she pulled open the wide doors of the barn, which she used as a garage, drove inside, turned off the ignition, and shoved the keys in her pocket. She closed the wide wooden doors behind her and looked around at the open prairie.

The only sound was the rising wind. Wylie was alone.

There was no other human being for miles. This was precisely what she wanted.

Icy sleet fell from the sky. The storm was here.

Wylie slid the damaged phone into her pocket and headed for the farmhouse.

Once inside, she locked the back door, kicked off her boots, and replaced them with fleece-lined moccasins. Wylie rushed to the cupboards in search of a box of rice so she could dry out her phone. There was none. She would have to get it fixed or buy a new one. Wylie hung her winter parka on a hook in the mudroom but left her stocking cap atop her head.

At the beginning of December, Wylie had made a phone call, discovered that the remote farmhouse where the twenty-year-old crime took place was currently unoccupied, and decided to make the trip. The farmhouse was a hundred years old and was as creaky and contrary as an old man. The furnace chugged along but couldn't keep up with the cold air that snuck between the windowpanes and beneath the doors. Wylie had meant to stay for only a week, two at the most, but the longer she stayed, the harder it was to leave.

At first, she blamed her ex-husband, and the prickly patch she had hit with Seth. She was so weary of arguing with them. She needed to focus and finish her current book.

The house had only the basics—electricity and water. No Wi-Fi, no television, no teenage son to remind her what a bad mother she was. She'd be fifteen hundred miles away from any distractions. Now that she'd dropped and destroyed her phone, her only connection to the world was the landline. Her access to the internet, text, FaceTime was all gone.

She was working on her fourth true crime book and often traveled for research, but she had never been gone from home for so long. The longer Wylie stayed in Burden, she realized there was more to it, or she would have finished the book by now and been back home.

Tas, a geriatric coonhound mix, looked languidly up from his bed next to the radiator with his yellow eyes. Wylie ignored him. Tas yawned and lowered his long snout to his paws and closed his eyes.

Sunset was three hours away, but the storm cast a gray pall through the windows. Wylie went through the house, flipping on lights. She hauled the last of the cut wood from the mudroom, set it by the fireplace, and built a fire. She hoped the kindling would last through the night; she didn't relish the thought of having to go out to the barn to bring in more.

Outside, the sleet was picking up momentum, slashing at the windows and covering the naked tree limbs in an icy glaze. It would be pretty if Wylie wasn't already so tired of winter. The groundhog had seen his shadow, more snow was coming, and spring seemed far away.

Wylie began her routine just as she had every afternoon for the last six weeks. She went around the house, double-checking that the windows and doors were locked, and closed the shades. Wylie might have preferred to be alone, spent her life writing about horrifying crimes, but she didn't like the dark and what might be lurking outside after the sun went down. She opened the drawer of her bedside table to make sure that her 9 mm handgun was still there.

She showered quickly, hoping to beat the moment when the hot water turned tepid, and towel dried her hair. She pulled on long underwear, wool socks, jeans, and a sweater and went back down to the kitchen.

There Wylie poured herself a glass of wine and sat on the sofa. Tas tried to heave himself up next to her. "Down," she said absentmindedly, and Tas returned to his spot next to the radiator.

Wylie thought about using the landline to call Seth, but she ran into the chance that her ex would be nearby and insist on speaking with her. She'd heard it all before.

Inevitably, their conversation would collapse beneath a bevy of harsh words and accusations. "Come home. You're acting unreasonable," her ex-husband said during one of their last phone calls. "You need help, Wylie."

She had felt something crack inside her chest. Just a small fissure, just enough to let her know that she needed to get off the phone. She hadn't talked to Seth in over a week.

Wylie carried her glass up the steps and sat down at the desk in the room she was using as her office. Tas followed behind and lay down beneath the window. The room was the smallest of the bedrooms, yellow with Major League Baseball stickers lining the baseboards. Her desk sat in the corner facing outward so she could see both the window and the door.

The manuscript she printed the week before at the library in Algona sat in a stack next to her computer, ready for one final read through. But still, Wylie was hesitant to bring the project to a close.

She had spent over a year studying crime scene photos, reading through newspaper articles and official reports. She contacted witnesses and individuals key to the investigation including deputies and the former sheriff. Even the lead agent from the Iowa Department of Criminal Investigation agreed to talk to her. They were surprisingly candid and gave Wylie little-known insights into the case.

Only the family members wouldn't speak to her. Either they had died or flat-out refused. She couldn't really blame them. Wylie spent endless hours writing, her fingers flying across the keyboard. Now the book was finished. Had its resolution, as meager as it was. The murderer had been identified but not brought to justice.

Wylie still had so many unanswered questions, but now it was time. She needed to read through the pages, make any final revisions, and send the manuscript to her editor.

Wylie tossed her red pen on the desk in frustration. She stood and stretched and made her way downstairs to the kitchen and set her empty wineglass on the counter. Her hands ached with cold, but she was determined not to turn up the thermostat. Instead, she filled the teakettle with water and set it on the stove. While it heated, she hovered her hands over the burner.

Outside, the wind whipped and cried mournfully, and after a few minutes, the teakettle joined in with its own howl. Wylie took her cup of tea back to the desk and sat down again. She set aside the manuscript and her thoughts turned to the next project she might take on.

There was no shortage of grisly murders. Wylie had plenty to choose from. Many true crime writers chose their subject matter based on headlines and public interest in the crime. Not Wylie. She always began with the crime scene. This was where the story snaked into her veins, and she wouldn't let go.

She would pore over photos taken at the crime sites— images of the locations where the victims took their final breaths, the position of the bodies, the faces frozen in death, the frenzy of blood splatter.

The photos she was reviewing now were from a crime scene in Arizona. The first picture was taken from a distance. A woman was sitting propped up against a rust-colored rock, tufts of dusty scrub brush surrounded her like a wreath, her face tilted away from the camera. A black stain darkened the front of her shirt.

Wylie set aside the photo and looked at the next one in the pile. The same woman but up close and from a different angle. The woman's mouth was contorted into a pained grimace. Her tongue poked out black and bloated. Carved into her chest was a hole big enough for Wylie to stick her hand into, surrounded by a ragged fringe of skin, revealing bone and gristle.

The pictures were gory, disturbing, and the stuff of nightmares, but Wylie believed that she needed to get to know the victims in death first.

At 10:00 p.m., Tas nudged her leg. Together they went down the steps; Tas moved more slowly, his joints clicking rustily. It wouldn't be long, and Tas would no longer be able to manage the stairs.

She wondered what her ex-husband would say when Wiley told him she picked up an old stray she found sitting outside the farmhouse's front door. No matter how much she tried to get him to leave, the dog stuck around.

Wylie figured he was left behind by the people who had rented the place before she arrived. She named him Tas, short for Itasca, the state park where three young women's bodies were discovered and who were the subjects of Wylie's first true crime book.

Wylie didn't like Tas much, and the feeling was mutual. They seemed to have come to the understanding that they would have to coexist for the time being.

She unlocked the front door, opening it just enough to let Tas out, and shut it behind him. Still, cold air, snow, and sleet found their way into the house, and Wylie shivered.

One minute passed, then two. Tas, not fond of the cold, was

normally quick about doing his business and would scratch at the door to signal that he was ready to come back inside.

Wylie went to the window, but the panes were fogged over and lacquered with ice. She rubbed her eyes, gritty from staring too long at the grainy photos, and leaned her back against the door to wait. She wouldn't be able to sleep until the sun rose.

The lights flickered, and Wylie's heart flipped in panic. She stared at the lamp and held her breath, but the warm glow remained steady. She added more wood to the fire. If the power went out, the pipes could freeze, and she would have a real mess on her hands. Wylie opened the door a crack and peered out into a sea of white, but there was no Tas.

"Tas!" she called out into the dark. "Here!" The rain had transformed into hard pellets that hit the house with an incessant rodent-like scritch-scratch. Wylie couldn't see past the weak light that spilled from above the door. "Great," she muttered as she reached into the front closet for a spare set of boots, an old barn coat, and one of the many flashlights she kept stowed around the house.

Once bundled up, she stepped outside, careful not to slip on the steps leading from the porch to the front yard.

"Tas!" she called again in irritation. She hunched her shoulders to the biting wind and ducked her head to combat the sting from the tiny beads of ice striking her face.

Several inches of snow had already fallen, and now of all things, it was sleeting, transforming the yard into an ice rink.

Another flash of uneasiness went through Wylie. Heavy ice or snow on the power lines was sure to lead to their collapse and an outage and complete darkness. She wanted to find Tas and get inside.

Using the porch rail to steady herself and the beam from the flashlight to guide her, Wylie eased along, calling out to him. She squinted through the dark and aimed the flashlight toward the lane that led to the road. Two eerie red orbs flashed back at her. "Tas, you come here," she ordered. He lowered his head, ignoring her commands.

In resignation, Wylie began the trek toward the stubborn dog. She bent slightly forward and moved, flat-footed, trying to keep her center of gravity directly over her feet. Still, she slipped, landing with a thud on her tailbone.

"Dammit," she snapped as she got to her feet again. The sleet had worked its way into the gap between her coat and her neck. Her hands were bare, and she longed to shove them in her pockets but didn't dare. She needed them out, extended, in case she fell again.

Tas stayed put. As Wylie got closer, she saw that Tas's attention was squarely focused on something on the ground in front of him. Wylie couldn't tell what it was. Tas circled around the object, sniffing at it tentatively.

"Get away from there," Wylie commanded. As she shuffled forward, she could see that it was not an object but a living or once-living creature. It was curled in a tight ball and covered in a sheath of ice that glistened in the light from the flashlight.

"Tas, sit!" she shouted. This time, Tas lifted his head to look at her, then obediently sat back on his haunches. Wylie crept closer; her eyes followed the coil of the body. A scuffed shoe, the faded blue of denim, the downy gray of a sweatshirt, a shorn head of dark hair, a small fist pressed to pale lips. A thin, frozen river of blood branched out around its head.

What lay before them was no animal. It was a little boy, frozen to the ground.

3

"Maybe we can go outside and play?" the girl said as she peeked around the edge of the heavy curtain that covered the window. The sky was gray and soft drops of rain tapped at the glass.

"Not today," her mother said. "It's raining and we'd melt."

The girl gave a little laugh and then hopped off the chair she had dragged beneath the window. She knew her mother was teasing. They wouldn't actually melt if they went out in the rain, but still, it made her shiver thinking about it—stepping outside and feeling the plop of water on your skin and watching it melt away like an ice cube.

Instead, the girl and her mother spent the morning at the card table cutting pink, purple, and green egg shapes from construction paper and embellishing them with polka dots and stripes.

On one oval, her mother drew eyes and a pointy little orange beak. Her mother laid the girl's hands on a piece of yellow paper and traced around them using a pencil. "Watch," she said as she cut out the handprints and then glued them to the back of one of the ovals.

"It's a bird," the girl said with delight.

"An Easter chick," her mother said. "I made these when I was your age."

Together, they carefully taped the eggs and chicks and bunny rabbits they created to the cement walls, giving the dim room a festive, springy look. "There, now we're ready for the Easter Bunny," her mother said with triumph.

That night, when the girl climbed into bed, the butterflies in her stomach kept chasing sleep away. "Stay still," her mother kept reminding her. "You'll fall asleep faster."

The girl didn't think that was true, but when she opened her eyes, a sliver of bright sunshine was peeking around the shade, and the girl knew that morning had finally arrived.

She leaped from bed to find her mother already at the tiny round table where they ate their meals. "Did he come?" the girl asked, tucking her long black hair behind her ears.

"Of course he did," her mother said, holding out a basket woven together from strips of colored paper. It was small, fitting into the palm of the girl's hand, but sweet. Inside were little bits of green paper that were cut to look like grass. On top of this was a pack of cinnamon gum and two watermelon Jolly Ranchers.

The girl smiled though disappointment surged through her. She'd been hoping for a chocolate bunny or one of those candy eggs that oozed yellow when you broke it open.

"Thank you," she said.

"Thank the Easter Bunny," her mother said.

"Thank you, Easter Bunny," the girl crowed like the child on the candy commercials that she'd seen on television. They both laughed.

They each unwrapped a piece of gum and spent the morning making up stories about the paper chicks and bunnies they made.

When the girl's gum lost its flavor, and she had slowly licked one of the Jolly Ranchers into a sharp flat disc, the door at the top of the steps opened, and her father came down the stairs toward them. He was carrying a plastic bag and a six-pack of beer. Her mother gave the girl a look. The one that said, go on now, Mom and Dad need some alone time.

Obediently, the girl, taking her Easter basket, went to her spot beneath the window and sat in the narrow beam of warm light that fell across the floor. Facing the wall, she unwrapped another piece of gum and poked it into her mouth and tried to ignore the squeak of the bed and her father's sighs and grunts.

"You can turn around now," her mother finally said. The girl sprang up from her spot on the floor.

The girl heard the water running in the bathroom, and her father poked his head out of the door. "Happy Easter," he said with a grin. "The Easter Bunny wanted me to give you a little something."

The girl looked at the kitchen table where the plastic bag sat. Then she slid her eyes to her mother, who was sitting on the edge of the bed, rubbing her wrist, eyes red and wet. Her mother nodded.

"Thank you," she murmured.

Later, after her father climbed the steps and locked the door behind him, the girl went to the table and looked inside the plastic bag. Inside was a chocolate bunny with staring blue eyes. He was holding a carrot and wore a yellow bow tie.

"Go ahead," her mother told the girl as she held an ice pack to her wrist. "When I was little, I always started with the ears."

"I don't think I'm very hungry," the girl said, returning the box to the table.

"It's okay," her mother said gently. "You can eat it. It's from the Easter Bunny, not your dad."

The girl considered this. She took a little nibble from the bunny's ear and sweet chocolate flooded her mouth. She took another bite and then another. She held out the rabbit to her mother and she bit off the remaining ear in one big bite. They laughed and took turns eating until all that was left was the bunny's chocolate tail.

"Close your eyes and open your mouth," her mother said. The girl complied and felt her mother place the remaining bit on her tongue and then kiss her on the nose. "Happy Easter," her mother whispered.

4

August of 2000 was a tranquil month for crime in Blake County, Iowa, located in the north-central part of the state. With a population of 7,310 at the time, the rural, agricultural county wasn't known for its crime sprees. In fact, up until the events of August 12, 2000, zero murders had been reported in the entire county.

Despite its grim name, Burden, population 844, was known as an idyllic community to live and raise a family. Located in the southwest corner of Blake County, Burden boasted a crime rate of less than a fourth of the state average.

Though it was the dawning of a new millennium, Burden remained an agriculturally centered town. Corn and soybeans were the primary crops raised by families who had lived there for generations. Children ran barefoot through windflower, prairie larkspur, and yellow star grass just like their parents and grandparents before.

Summers were made up of hard work and hard play. Farm kids rode with their fathers high on tractors during planting season, played in haylofts, and went fishing after chores were done. Little girls spent nine months of the school year learning that they could grow up to be doctors and lawyers but still came home and helped mothers and grandmothers can butter pickles and rhubarb jelly. They hand-fed orphaned goats, read books behind the corncrib, ice-skated on Burden Creek, and played tag by leaping from hay bale to hay bale.

This was twelve-year-old Josie Doyle's existence when she awoke the morning of August 11, 2000, with giddy anticipation. She dressed quickly and pulled her unruly brown hair into a ponytail.

She needed to pack and make a list of all the most important attractions to show her best friend, Becky, a state fair first-timer. But first, breakfast and chores. Josie ate quickly and flew through her assigned tasks.

It was then that Josie noticed that their chocolate Lab, Roscoe was nowhere to be found. This wasn't unusual in itself.

Roscoe was a roamer. He'd take off for hours at a time, wandering around the countryside, but Roscoe always came home and never missed breakfast. Josie would lift the lid on the plastic bin that held the fifty-pound bag of dog food, and he'd come running with cobwebs of saliva dripping from his jowls.

That morning there was no Roscoe. Josie dumped a scoop of kibble into his bowl, filled his water dish with water from the hose, and then moved on to the chickens.

To help pass the time before Becky arrived, Josie went with her father as he mended fences along the northern section of their property. His gloved hands moved expertly as he stretched and wrapped and crimped the barbwire. Josie prattled on about the upcoming state fair and danced in and out of his line of vision, nearly tumbling into the rusty fence. Josie, small for her age, seemed to others to have endless energy.

While her father worked, Josie moved aimlessly along the edge of the road gathering wildflowers as she went. She heard the truck before seeing it. The popcorn snap of gravel. She turned and saw the truck's nose just around a curve in the road. Josie waited for the vehicle to drive past, but it just sat there, so she continued picking Black-eyed Susan and milkweed for her mother.

Again came the crackle of rock beneath tires. Josie turned, and the truck stopped. She moved, and it followed, slowly keeping pace. Josie squinted to see who was in the passenger's seat, but the sun was a shimmering gold disc in the east, making it impossible to know. She wasn't scared. Her brother's friends, she figured, teasing.

"Ha, ha," Josie called. "Very funny!" She reached down and picked up a small pebble and threw it toward the truck. It landed on the ground with an unsatisfying plink. Slowly, she walked toward the vehicle, and it began reversing.

Weird, she thought and took another few steps toward the truck. It backed up another twenty feet. A game of tag. Boldly, Josie trotted toward the truck, sure that it held her brother's obnoxious friends.

As she drew closer, Josie could see the silhouette of one person in the cab. A hunched figure, seed cap pulled low over his forehead. The truck rolled backward.

Just then, a shout came from across the field. Josie's dad beckoning her back to him. She gave the idling truck one final look, but by the time Josie reached her dad forgot all about it.

Back at the house, Josie dared to open her brother's bedroom door in hopes of getting him to help her look for Roscoe. "Leave me alone," Ethan said. He was sitting on the floor, his back pressed up against the bed.

"But Roscoe didn't come home last night, don't you care?" she asked.

"Not really," Ethan said flatly as he flipped through a magazine.

"What if he got hit by a car?" Josie asked, her voice rising. Ethan shrugged, not bothering to look at her.

"You'll feel bad if he doesn't come home," Josie said, grabbing a paperback book from the top of Ethan's dresser and tossing it to him, knocking the magazine from his hands. Josie couldn't help laughing.

"Get the fuck out of my room," Ethan snarled, reaching for one of his steel-toed work boots and hurling it at Josie. It struck just above her head, taking a small chunk out of the door frame.

Josie retreated quickly and ran into the bathroom, where she locked the door behind her. Ethan had been acting so bizarre lately. Getting in fights, drinking, calls from the school, calls from the sheriff. She never knew what to expect when they crossed paths, which wasn't very often since he stayed holed up in his room as much as possible. Josie waited until she heard Ethan's bedroom door open and his footsteps on the stairs before poking her head from the bathroom.

At four thirty, Becky and her mother, Margo Allen, pulled down the lane, and Josie ran outside to greet them, the screen door slamming behind her. Becky had long curly black hair that she constantly complained about and big expressive brown eyes. "I'll give you my hair, if I can have your name," Becky would always say.

Josie would have gladly made the trade. She thought Becky was beautiful, and so did everyone else. Soon after she turned thirteen, boys had been calling Becky's home and more and more she was begging off spending time with Josie to hang out with town kids. But this weekend was going to be different; Josie had Becky all to herself. They would talk and laugh and do all the things they did before life seemed so complicated.

Josie and Becky greeted each other with a squeal and a hug, and Josie relieved Becky of her sleeping bag and pillow.

"We'll drop Becky at your house Saturday night when we get back," Lynne Doyle, Josie's mother, said self-consciously, tucking a wayward strand of hair behind her ear. "I'm thinking around eight o'clock or so."

Margo asked that Lynne drop Becky off at her father's house.

"Oh, I didn't know," Lynne said as if surprised, then faltered. Josie hadn't said anything about Becky's parents splitting up. "Sure thing." Lynne dropped her gaze.

The two adults stood in awkward silence for a moment until Lynne finally spoke again.

"Another hot one today, but at least there's a breeze," Lynne said, looking to the sky stripped of clouds by a hot wind. When one ran out of things to say, there was always the weather.

"Have fun, Becky," Margo said, turning to her daughter and pulling her into a hug. "You be good and listen to Mr. and Mrs. Doyle, okay? I love you."

"I will, love you too," Becky mumbled, embarrassed by her mother's display of affection. The two girls darted into the house, up the steps to Josie's cheerful yellow room, where they dumped Becky's sleeping bag, pillow, and overnight bag on the floor.

"What do you want to do first?" Josie asked.

"The goats," Becky answered as an angry shout came from outside.

The girls moved to the open window to see what the fuss was about. Below them, Margo paused as she opened her car door, and Lynne pressed her hand against her forehead, salute-style, shielding her eyes from the afternoon sun. Both were looking toward the barn.

Ethan stormed out first, face set in the scowl that he seemed to wear all the time now. Close behind was their father, William. He clapped one large hand on Ethan's shoulder, whipping him around so they were face-to-face. Other angry words were swept away by the hot breeze, but *fucker* was clearly heard. Margo looked uneasily over at Lynne, who smiled apologetically and murmured something about teenage boys nowadays. She had been doing that a lot lately. Ethan ineffectually swatted at his father's hand.

"Honey," Lynne called out and, seeing that there was company, he let his hand fall from Ethan's shoulder. The sudden release caused Ethan to lose balance and drop to one knee. William reached down to help him up, but Ethan ignored it and got to his feet on his own. William looked over and raised his hand in greeting toward Margo. Ethan flinched as if about to be struck.

"Come on," Josie said, pulling Becky away from the window. "Let's go out back." She blinked back tears of mortification. This was just a snippet of the way her father and brother had been going at it lately.

Ethan had pulled away abruptly, his transformation sudden. He stopped talking, and when he did, it was in angry, resentful grunts. He was openly defiant and refused to help out on the farm.

"Your brother called your dad a fucker," Becky said, and just like that, the two began to giggle and couldn't stop. One of them would gather her composure and then the other would whisper *fucker*, and they would collapse in another fit of laughter.

After dinner, Lynne asked Ethan to run a pie she had made over to her parents' farm a mile down the road. "You go right over there and then come straight home," she ordered.

Ethan rolled his eyes. "Ethan," Lynne warned, "don't push it."

Before Josie could hear Ethan's smart-aleck response, she and Becky were out the door.

Josie's favorite spot on the farm was the big red hip roof barn. Eighty years old, it greeted Josie each morning with its broad red face. Its nose the hayloft door, its eyes the widely spaced upper windows, and its mouth the entry large enough to drive a truck through.

The barn smelled of sun-warmed sweet hay and tractor oil. It smelled of dust motes and goats. Josie filled the wooden feed bunks that ran down the center of the barn with feed. Josie filled a small bucket with pellets while Becky ran from corner to corner, searching for the mama cat and her kittens. They were squirreled away somewhere, nowhere to be found.

Josie and Becky walked back outside to where the barn opened up into a fenced area where the thirty-odd goats spent the day. When they heard the bucket bumping against her leg, the goats came running on their spindly legs. Josie and Becky reached into the bucket for the pellets and slid their hands through the fence, their palms laid flat. Becky laughed at their black caterpillar-shaped eyes and humanlike bellows.

"Hey, what's your brother doing?" Becky asked.

Josie looked up and spotted Ethan, walking toward his battered truck, a shotgun in one hand and the pie to be delivered to their grandparents balanced on the other. "I don't know, but he's definitely not supposed to be doing that," Josie said, hands on her hips.

"You are so lucky to have a big brother. He's so cute. Let's go see where he's going," Becky said, brushing the remaining pellets from her hands, and before Josie could stop her, she was running after Ethan.

"What are you going to shoot?" Becky asked breathlessly when they caught up with him.

"Kids who follow me around and won't shut up," Ethan said, barely glancing their way.

"Ha, ha," Josie deadpanned. "It's not even hunting season yet. Does dad know you're taking a gun to grandpa's?"

"I can hunt pigeons or groundhogs anytime, and no, Dad doesn't need to know every little thing I do. Besides, I'm just going to shoot at targets."

"Yeah, he'll never hear the gunshots. Good plan there, Ethan," Josie smirked, looking over at Becky, but she was focused on Ethan.

"Can we go with you?" Becky asked.

"Suit yourself," Ethan muttered as he carefully placed the shotgun in the gun rack in the back window of his truck. The girls climbed in and Becky commented on how clean it was. She poked around in his glove box, sorting through his things, pulling out a pack of gum and a tin of mints.

"You must really like fresh breath," Becky said with a laugh. Ethan blushed. Becky pulled out the Green Lantern figurine that Ethan kept in his glove box as a good luck charm and spoke in a low voice and walked the figure across his arm.

"Knock it off," Ethan said in a way that let Josie know he liked the attention Becky was giving him.

Becky chattered happily as Ethan sped down their lane and pulled right up to the porch and the red front door. "Run this in really fast and give it to grandma," Ethan ordered. "And don't hang around gabbing. I'm in a hurry."

Josie awkwardly climbed over Becky to exit the truck, the pie tipping dangerously. Not wanting to antagonize her brother, she did as Ethan said. Josie opened the front door without knocking and hurried to the kitchen where her grandparents, Matthew and Caroline Ellis, finished their own supper.

She said a hurried goodbye, and when she returned to the truck, she saw that Becky had moved so close to Ethan that their legs were touching. Josie climbed into the cab and the truck tires were spinning before she even shut the door. Instead of driving directly home, Ethan made a sharp right onto a dirt road that followed the creek's flow.

"What are you doing?" Josie asked. "Mom said to come right home."

"I'm just going to shoot for a few minutes," Ethan said as they approached a stand of Black Hills spruce on the west side of their grandfather's property and pulled up next to a rusty silver truck that was parked next to the road. "Cutter," Ethan said through the open window.

"Hey," the boy responded with a lift of a pimply chin. Cutter was one of the boys that Ethan was forbidden to hang out with anymore.

"Stay here," Ethan ordered.

Josie and Becky ignored him and climbed from the truck.

"Josie," Ethan said, his voice heavy with warning.

"What?" Josie asked innocently, her eyes wide. Next to her, Becky stifled a laugh.

"Why'd you bring them?" Cutter asked, nodding toward Josie and Becky. Cutter had a first name, but no one called him by it. He was tall and broad chested with straw-colored hair and deeply tanned skin from his hours spent working outside on the family farm. He had round, full cheeks and an easy smile that at first glance made him appear mild tempered and jovial, but upon closer inspection, his eyes were hard and held more mean than mischief.

"We're not kids," Becky said.

Cutter gave a little laugh that matched his eyes and looked the girls up and down, pausing when his eyes landed on Becky's chest. "Maybe one of you isn't," he said.

"Come on, I only have a few minutes," Ethan said, pulling his shotgun from the gun rack.

"That the one your grandpa gave you?" Cutter asked.

"Yeah," Ethan said and grabbed an old bucket from the truck's bed and walked about fifty yards away. They watched as he flipped the bucket over and set it on an old stump, then walked back. "Now, stand back."

Cutter stayed put, but Becky and Josie took three steps back while Ethan fished a shell from his pocket, slid it into the loading chamber, and gave it a pump. He raised the gun snugly to his shoulder, staggered his feet, pressed his cheek to the stock.

"Cover your ears," Josie advised, and Becky clapped her hands to her head. There was a loud bang, and the clatter of metal against metal as the bucket was knocked to the ground.

They dropped their hands, and Ethan smiled triumphantly as he lowered the gun from his shoulder.

"Cool," Becky exclaimed.

"Pretty good!" Cutter conceded, reaching for the gun. "My turn." He pulled the weapon from Ethan's hands.

"Come on," Josie said, pulling Becky toward the truck, "this is boring."

"No, I want to try it," Becky said. A flash of jealousy rippled through Josie. Becky was her best friend. The idea that she would rather spend time with her brother and Cutter than with Josie sent a flood of envy through her.

"You can't," Josie said. "It's dangerous."

"Come on, Cutter," Ethan said. "Go ahead and shoot. We have to go in a minute."

"Yeah," Cutter interjected. "Little girls shouldn't be playing with such big weapons." He held the shotgun at crotch level and waggled his tongue suggestively.

"Gross," Becky said with a laugh.

"Yeah, gross," Josie echoed.

"That's okay, you're scared," Cutter said. "We should get you back home. It's probably your bedtime."

"I'm not scared," Josie mumbled.

"Okay, then do it." He held the gun, barrel down, toward her.

Josie was tempted. She wasn't one to turn down a dare, but guns were different. Her dad had drilled into their brains how guns were not toys. How accidents happened by careless show-offs or novices who didn't respect the power a firearm possessed.

"I don't want to," Josie said casually.

"You're scared," Cutter taunted.

"I'm not," Becky piped up. "Can I try?"

"Sure, come here. I'll show you," Cutter beckoned Becky toward him. She took the gun from him and, surprised by its weight, nearly dropped it.

"Watch it," Cutter cried. "You want to shoot somebody?"

"Sorry," Becky said, flustered.

"Here, I'll show you." Cutter moved in behind Becky, reaching for the gun. He pressed his hips into her back and slid his arms around her waist, his inching fingers creeping beneath the fabric of her shirt. Becky tried to sidestep his grasp, but Cutter had her boxed in.

"I want Ethan to show me." Becky lightly elbowed her way free. Cutter's lips pursed into a sullen pout.

Ethan shrugged and showed her how to hold the rifle and peer through the sight.

"It's heavier than I thought it would be," Becky said, squinting at the bucket, now lying on the ground.

"You better not do that," Josie warned. She looked around, afraid that someone might see. They would get in so much trouble.

"I just want to hold it," Becky said in a voice that made it clear that she thought Josie was acting like a baby.

"Go ahead," Josie said, "shoot your foot off. I don't care." She turned her back on them and strode to the truck to wait for the sound of more gunshots. A boom erupted, and an excited squeal came from Becky.

Cutter snatched the shotgun from her hand. "My turn." He loaded the gun and lifted it to his shoulder, but instead of aiming at the bucket, he pointed toward the trees, slowly moving the gun from left to right. His jaw tightened, his eyes narrowed just before pulling the trigger. There was a bang, a rustle of leaves, and then the dull thud of something hitting the ground.

"Eww," Becky said. "You shot a bird. Why'd you do that?"

They were too far away to see exactly what kind of bird the bullet struck, but it was good-sized and black. Maybe a crow or a turkey vulture.

"Trash bird, anyway," Cutter said. "Hey, you coming out later?" he asked.

Ethan cut a glance toward his sister. "Naw, I'm grounded."

"When did that ever stop you?" Cutter laughed. He turned to Josie and Becky. "How about you? You want to come out and play tonight?"

"No, thank you," Josie said, rolling her eyes. Becky blushed. Cutter laughed, but his face reddened beneath his brown tan.

Becky rubbed her shoulder where the butt of the gun recoiled.

"Now that's going to leave a bruise," Cutter said. "Maybe Ethan will kiss it all better for you."

"Shut up, Cutter," Ethan said, grabbing the gun back from him.

"Can I try again?" Becky asked.

Again, Ethan positioned himself behind Becky, and she cast a shy smile back toward Ethan. He rested his chin on her shoulder and helped her take aim. That's when William Doyle slowly drove past them in his truck.

"Oh, fuck, it's my dad," Ethan said, grabbing his shotgun from Becky.

"Gotta go," Cutter said, jogging toward his truck. "I'll see you later."

As William made a sharp U-turn, Cutter pulled away and sped off down the road. William pulled up next to Ethan's truck, stepped from his vehicle, and slammed the door. "What the hell are you doing?" he asked.

"We were just coming back to the house," Ethan said as if there was nothing wrong.

"Jesus Christ," William said through gritted teeth as he strode toward Ethan. "What the hell were you thinking?"

"It's no big deal," Ethan said. "We were careful."

"Careful?" William repeated, a red flush creeping up his neck. "I've told you about letting others shoot your gun. It's not safe. Josie, Becky," he said, turning to the girls. "Get in my truck."

"I'm sorry," Becky said, tears filling her eyes. Josie clutched her hand.

"Jesus, Dad," Ethan said. "You're scaring her."

"Give me the gun," William said, lowering his voice.

"No," Ethan said, clutching more tightly to the shotgun. "It's mine."

William looked as if he wanted to rip the gun from Ethan's hands but knew that was how misfires happened. Instead, William strode to Ethan's truck, opened the door, yanked the keys from the ignition, and stuffed them in his pocket.

"Josie, Becky, get in my truck, now," William ordered, and the girls rushed to climb inside. Ethan shook his head and began to follow, but William held up his hand to stop him.

Ethan laughed and then realized his father wasn't joking. "You want me to walk all the way home?" he asked.

"That's the only way you are going to get anywhere for a very long time," William said.

"We have to leave my truck here?" Ethan asked in disbelief. "Damn right," William said. "Your mom and I will pick it up later. Buckle up," William said to the girls.

Ethan lifted his chin in defiance and looked his father square in the eyes. William's fingers twitched, and for a moment, it looked as if he was going to hit Ethan. Instead, he brushed roughly past his son and stepped up into the cab of his truck.

William put the truck into Drive and drove about fifty feet down the road when an explosion filled the air. He hit the brakes and leaned his head out the window. Ethan was looking directly at them. In his hand, he held the shotgun, a grim smile on his face.

William swore under his breath and began driving again. Ethan cradled the shotgun in his arms and started walking. Josie and Becky turned to look out the back window and watched Ethan as they drove away, getting smaller and smaller until he was just a speck on the gravel road and then disappeared.

Less than eight hours later, William and Lynne Doyle were dead, and Ethan and Becky were missing.

5

Wylie clapped a cold, chapped hand to her face and bit back a scream. A child. A child was lying in her front yard. She trudged through the snow toward him and instantly lost her footing, pitched forward, and broke the fall with her right arm. She felt the bone give and waited for the snap. It didn't come.

The flashlight slid across the ice, spinning like a roulette wheel until it finally stopped, its beam illuminating the unmoving child. He glistened like an ice sculpture.

Wylie lay there, just a few feet from the child's face, momentarily stunned. His eyes were closed, his thumb in his mouth. A small river of blood trickled from his head. She couldn't tell if he was breathing.

With a groan, Wylie pushed herself to her knees using only her left hand. She flexed her fingers and bent her elbow, quickly scanning her right arm for any major damage. It hurt, but Wylie didn't think it was broken. She crawled forward until she was right next to the child.

She wasn't sure what to do. Should she try to move him? He obviously had a head injury, but what if he had a spinal injury too? She needed to call for help but would an ambulance be able to get all the way out here in this storm? She didn't think so.

"Hey," she said, wiping a film of ice from his pale cheek. He didn't react. She pressed her finger beneath his nose. Was he breathing? She couldn't tell. Wylie inhaled deeply, tried to gather her wits. She had no medical training but knew that she had to get the boy inside and warm, or he would freeze to death.

She slid her arms beneath him and was relieved when his body shifted easily. He wasn't frozen through. She began to slowly get to her feet. He weighed thirty pounds maybe, much lighter than she thought he would. She positioned him so that they were chest to chest, his head on her shoulder, his thumb still firmly between his lips.

Her sore arm supported the back of his head while her healthy one held the bulk of his weight. The trick would be getting him back to the house without falling.

She was only fifty yards from the front porch, but it felt like a million miles. Inch by inch, she moved her feet forward, clasping the boy's cold body against her, pausing each time she felt the ground shift beneath her. Tas crept along at her hip, stopping when Wylie did.

Wylie looked over her shoulder. The road was no longer visible. The miles of fields beyond the road, swallowed by the storm. Where had the boy come from? Nothing could survive out here for long.

Wylie tried to push the thought away and focused on the earth below her. Despite his slight frame, the boy was dead weight, and Wylie's uninjured arm began to ache. She resisted the urge to sprint toward the house. She would never make it without falling. Instead, she focused on taking a step with each breath.

The welcoming twinkle from the house was a guidepost. The snow was coming down now in dizzying whorls and frosting them white.

"Hang on," she whispered into his ear. "We're almost there." Did he move? Or was that just Wylie shifting his weight a bit as they trudged forward?

Dreadful thoughts kept creeping into her head. The boy's cold cheek was pressed against her neck, and she feared she was holding a dead child in her arms. What if help couldn't come? She could be snowed in for days. How in God's name could she sit in a house with a child's body until help arrived?

Only ten more yards, and they would be at the front door. The instant Wylie's foot transitioned from gravel to the concrete walkway, she knew they were falling. With a cry, she pressed the boy to her, clasping his head tightly in hopes of protecting it from the impact.

Somehow, she was able to land on her knees and kept the boy from hitting the ground. The concussion of bone on cement sent spasms through her legs. Tears of pain and frustration sprang to her eyes. She didn't know how she was going to be able to get to her feet.

Tas looked at her, his eyes laden with judgment. *Hurry up*, he seemed to be saying. *You're not going to give up when we're so close, are you?*

The boy's head lolled against her shoulder, and a small gasp escaped from his lips. Wylie nearly cried with relief. He was alive. Wylie repositioned his weight and got back to her feet, her muscles screaming with exhaustion. Her lower back protested beneath the weight of the boy, but she kept going inch by inch until she was finally at the red front door.

Carefully lowering her hand from the boy's head, she reached for the doorknob and twisted. It swung open, and Tas muscled his way inside first. Breathing heavily, Wylie laid the child over the threshold and onto the colorfully braided floor mat. The boy emitted a soft moan. Using the doorjamb, Wylie pulled herself to her feet, staggered inside, and slammed the door behind her.

She ran to the kitchen. Her broken cell phone lay on the counter, useless. Wylie turned to the landline, picked up the receiver, and was met with silence.

That was one of the drawbacks of living in the middle of nowhere. One ice storm and you were guaranteed to lose phone and internet service. "Dammit," she growled. No one would be coming to help them tonight.

Wylie needed to get the child warm and see how extensive his injuries were. She rushed up the steps and to the bedroom, rummaged through her suitcase for socks and a sweatshirt. Thinking that she would be staying in the farmhouse for only a short time, Wylie hadn't bothered to unpack. But days had turned to weeks and here she still was. She yanked the comforter from the bed, and headed back down the stairs.

The boy was still lying in the entryway. His eyes were closed, but his thumb was back in his mouth, and his chest was rising and falling rhythmically. Wylie breathed a sigh of relief and moved toward him, her wet boots squeaking against the hardwood. The child tried to open his eyes, but they kept fluttering shut. He lifted his hand to the gash on his head and began crying upon seeing his fingers wet with blood.

Wylie moved forward cautiously and began speaking in low, gentle tones. "My name is Wylie, and I found you in my yard," she said to the boy. "You bumped your head. Here, let's put this right here," she carefully pressed one of the socks she grabbed to his temple. "Can you tell me your name? Do you know how long you were out there? Let me see your hands."

The boy shoved his hands behind his back. He probably had frostbite, and Wylie wasn't sure what to do about that. Was she supposed to run his hands and feet under hot water? That didn't sound right. She thought it was the opposite— she was supposed to rub the affected area with ice. But what if she was wrong and made things worse?

"We have to get you out of those wet clothes and get you warmed up," Wylie explained.

The child continued to cry. Wylie laid the sweatshirt on the floor next to him. "Take off your wet clothes, and I'll put them in the dryer for you, okay?"

The boy abruptly sat up, looked around, eyes darting around, for an escape route. His gaze landed on the front door. "You don't want to go out there," Wylie said in a rush. "It's still snowing and really slippery. Is that what happened to your head?" Wylie nodded to the gash at the boy's temple. "Did you hit it on the ice?"

The boy didn't respond but got unsteadily to his feet. He looked to be about five years old with thin, pinched features made more pronounced by his ragged buzz cut.

"Can you tell me your name?" Wylie asked. "Where you're from?" He remained silent. "Once the phone lines are up again, I can try and call your mom and dad for you."

The boy continued to look around like a trapped animal. She wasn't even sure if he understood her. He trembled inside his baggy sweatshirt and too-short jeans.

"You must be freezing," Wylie said, stating the obvious. "You need to get out of those clothes." Wylie took another step toward him, and he reared back as if burned. "It's okay," Wylie said in a rush. "I'm not going to touch you if you don't want me to."

Wylie didn't know what to do. She couldn't force the child, and she didn't want to frighten him any more than he already was.

"I know you're scared, but I promise you I'm here to help you. Dry clothes are right there, and I'll put the blanket here on the couch." Wylie retrieved the comforter from the floor and laid it over the arm of the sofa. "When you're ready, you can change and sit here and get warm."

Wylie paced the floor. A strange child was sitting in front of her. Distressed and injured. What the hell was a kid doing out in this kind of weather, and where were his parents?

"I really need you to tell me your name," Wylie said, her voice rising with panic.

The boy shivered, but he didn't answer. The skin on his face was an unnatural grayish-yellow. She had visions of his fingers turning black or his heart stopping due to hypothermia.

Wylie needed to get the boy out of the wet clothes. She slowly advanced on him. She reached out to lift his damp sweatshirt, and the boy emitted a blood-curdling scream that bounced off the walls. Wylie managed to snag the elbow of the shirt and started to pull him toward her.

"You have to get out of those wet clothes," Wylie said through her teeth. "You're shivering. You'll get sick. Let me help you change your shirt."

The boy lashed out. His elbow landed squarely on Wylie's cheek, and she fell backward, releasing her grip.

"Dammit, I'm trying to help you," Wylie said, pressing her fingers to her bruised face. The boy scrambled behind a wing-back chair and peeked around the corner at Wylie.

Why was she so bad at this? She could never find the right words for Seth and could never seem to make things better for him. And now, here was this strange child, and once again, she was making things worse. Hot shame filled her chest.

"Fine," Wylie said, getting to her feet. "Stay in your wet clothes, but you're going to be miserable."

She turned her back on the boy and walked into the kitchen. She tried the phone again. Still dead. She needed to get him warmed up. She rifled through the cupboard until she found a box of hot chocolate mix.

As she filled the kettle with water and placed it on the stove, she realized she blew it. The kid was still in his wet clothes, and now he trusted her even less. Wylie understood, though. She was a complete stranger; of course he was terrified.

Making the twenty-five-mile drive to the emergency room in Algona was impossible in this weather. Wylie would have to figure out a way to care for the boy at home. She'd clean his cuts and make sure he was covered up and close to the fire, and she would keep him hydrated and fed. It wasn't much of a plan, but it was a start.

She ripped open a packet of hot chocolate and poured it into a mug and added the hot water. Hot chocolate was good, right? All kids loved cocoa. She'd use it as a peace offering.

Hot liquid sloshed over her hand. "Dammit," she muttered. She couldn't give the boy scalding cocoa. She reached into the freezer, scooped out a few ice cubes, and dropped them into the cup.

Wylie carried the steaming mug to the living room and glanced to the spot by the front door where she had last seen the boy. He wasn't there. Her eyes swung to the couch. Tas lay there, sleeping, but there was no boy. Wylie scanned the room. The boy wasn't there. She checked the dining room and opened the closet doors. She checked the bathroom and even went back into the kitchen.

He was gone.

6

Small flowers grew at the base of the window, casting a purplish glow into the room. They were so pretty, and she imagined they smelled like grape jelly. The girl wished she could pick them for her mother. She wasn't feeling well and the girl thought flowers might cheer her up.

Instead, she colored a picture of the flowers. The only problem was she had lost her orange crayon, so she couldn't draw the spiky pieces poking up through the middle. "What are these called?" the girl asked.

"I don't remember," her mother said from the couch. She had been lying there for a long time and she fell asleep a lot on and off throughout the day. The girl was careful to be extra quiet and spent the time coloring and looking at the books from the small bookshelf that sat next to the bed.

At dinnertime, the girl rifled through the cupboards in search of something they could eat. She found a loaf of bread and pulled two slices from the bag and dropped them into the toaster.

"Oh, God," her mother said, staggering from the bed to the bathroom.

Her father walked in to find the girl waiting for the bread in the toaster to pop up and to her mother retching in the bathroom.

"What's the matter?" he asked, plucking the bread from the toaster and taking a bite. The girl wanted to snatch it back. It was for her mother. It helped her stomach feel better.

Her mother stumbled from the bathroom, pale faced and weak.

"Pregnant?" her father asked when her mother told him the news. "How is that even possible?" He was shocked but also a little angry. The girl moved closer to her mother.

Her mother rolled her eyes. "The same way I got pregnant the first three times," she said crossing her arms in front of her midsection.

Her father had banged out of the house angrily. The girl put another piece of bread in the toaster.

"I had two little boys before you, did you know that?" Her mother asked with that faraway look in her eyes that she had been getting so often lately.

The first, a baby boy, was born too early. Her mother was home alone and all of a sudden, her stomach felt like someone was stabbing at it with sharp knives. "I didn't know what to do," her mother said. "I lay in bed for hours, not sure what was happening and then all of a sudden he was coming. It was like my body was being turned inside out. And then he was here. He was so small."

Her mother held her hands about ten inches apart. "And blue. His skin was the strangest color of blue—like an old bruise. I was so weak and sore I couldn't get out of bed. I fell asleep, and when I woke up, your father was back. He took the baby away."

The girl had asked her mother what happened to the baby and she pursed her lips together and shook her head. "He died. He was too small. Your dad named him Robert. And then a year later, another boy, this one even smaller. His name was Stephen."

"And then came me?" the girl asked.

"Yes, then came you," her mother said. "And I told him that this time, the baby was going to live, and I was going to pick the name. And I gave you the most beautiful name in the world."

The girl smiled. It was a beautiful name.

7

Josie was mortified at the scene between her brother and father and once back at the house, to distract Becky from her family drama, Josie suggested that they search for the missing dog.

Josie and Becky walked slowly up the dusty lane. The farm rested in a dip at the bottom of a valley and when they reached the top of the lane, they could see for miles. Fields of alfalfa, soybean, and corn were yellow and green patches in a never-ending quilt that blanketed the earth. Narrow gravel roads were gray seams and Burden Creek was a ragged tear through the fabric.

They took turns calling for Roscoe. Their voices were harsh, momentarily silencing the chirp of crickets and the high-pitched buzz of the grasshopper sparrow hiding in the butterfly milkweed and partridge pea. Josie was getting nervous. Roscoe never stayed away for this long. She had visions of him lying by the side of the road, struck by an unaware farmer in his truck or on his tractor.

"I wonder where Ethan is?" Becky asked, looking up and down the gravel road. Josie wondered the same thing. He should have been home by now.

"Who cares," Josie said, still miffed at him for nearly ruining the night. Becky shrugged.

Unhurriedly, they walked up and down dirt and gravel roads past the Cutters' new hog confinement operation, past the old Rasmussen farm all the way to Henley farm. The sun, matching their pace, was still a few hours from setting.

Describing the Henley property as a farm was being generous. The cropland was sold off long ago, and all that remained in the Henley name was a wind-scrubbed two-story farmhouse that stood on a hardscrabble yard along with dozens of rusted-out vehicles. A half-collapsed barn and several outbuildings were bursting with broken-down washing machines, farm equipment, and lawn mowers.

The girls approached a woman holding an unlit cigarette in one hand and a bucket in the other as she crossed the weedy yard.

Sixty-one-year-old June Henley, all tendons and sinew, wearing a housedress, flip-flops, and a pink, rolled brim cloche to cover her bald head, was a curiosity to the girls. Though most neighbors knew one another, to date, Josie had never actually met June nor her adult son, Jackson, who lived with her. Josie shyly introduced herself and Becky and explained how they were looking for a lost dog.

June relayed that they had stray dogs hanging around the yard all the time and they could walk through the property and take a look. "My son is tinkering about, so just stay away from the outbuildings."

The girls thanked her and began to explore the five-acre property. Filled with what looked like garbage to most, it was surprisingly organized. The mangled steel and rubber collections were sorted into long, weedy rows.

One row was dedicated to antique farm equipment—tractors, hay rakes, manure spreaders, and seed drills; one row to old pickup trucks; another row to stacks of old tires.

"Look at all this junk," Becky marveled. "What do they do with all of it?"

"Probably sell it," Josie shrugged. "My grandpa likes old stuff like this."

They called out for Roscoe but managed only to summon a mangy tabby cat and rouse a sleeping possum. The possum bared his sharp teeth at the girls causing the girls to squeal and clutch at each other.

Laughing nervously, the two watched as the possum scurried off into the brush with his long tail dragging in the dirt behind him.

The two girls parted ways briefly. Becky turned down the row that held all the antique farm equipment while Josie veered off behind the mountain of stacked tires.

Minutes later, the girls reunited at the end of the row. Josie looked back and saw a tall, thin man staring back at them. Uneasiness coiled in her stomach.

"Who's that?" Josie asked.

Becky shrugged. "I think it's that lady's son. He just wanted to know what we were doing."

"He looks creepy," Josie observed.

"He did smell kind of bad." Becky wrinkled her nose and the girls laughed.

Josie and Becky made their way back toward the Henley house. They waved goodbye to June Henley, who was sitting on her front porch steps. Josie looked over her shoulder to find the man still staring after them. She walked faster.

As they left the property, Josie noticed a wadded-up cloth in Becky's hand. "What's that?" she asked.

"Nothing," Becky said and dropped it to the ground. The girls made the two-mile walk back toward the Doyle house, stopping along the way at Burden Creek. They carefully picked their way down the steep bank to the edge of the water. Because of the lack of rain, Burden Creek was much lower than usual and the smell of dead fish was strong.

It did stink, but that was just part of living out in the country. The sweet scent of mown hay intermingled with cow manure. The clean, crisp smell of laundry just pulled from the line suddenly smothered by the sharp, acrid smell that came from the nearby hog confinement.

Josie and Becky walked along the bank, yelling for Roscoe and pausing to catch the small spotted brown frogs who croaked and hopped about in the shallow water. Becky giggled as the slimy creature squirmed in her hands.

It was nearing 8:00 p.m., and though the sun was finally sliding behind the trees, the temperature still hung in the mid-eighties, and the air was heavy with humidity. Mosquitoes buzzed around their ears and harassed them until they climbed back up to the bridge, wiping muddy hands on their shorts.

When the girls got to the top of the bank, there was a truck pulled off to the side of the road. Josie thought it was white but behind the glare of the setting sun, it could have been any light-colored truck.

"Who is it?" Becky whispered.

"I don't know, but I think I saw that same truck earlier

today." Josie looked up and down the gravel road. It was empty. Through the grimy windows, she could see the shadow of a figure wearing a dark-colored jacket and a hat pulled down so low that it shielded his forehead and eyes. It was much too hot to be dressed that way.

For the first time, a ripple of fear coursed through her. "Let's go," Josie said, pulling on Becky's arm.

"Who is it?" Becky asked again. "Is it that creepy Cutter?"

"I don't think so, but I couldn't really tell," she said. "Come on, it's starting to get dark."

Behind them, the truck engine suddenly roared to life, and the girls screamed, grabbed hands, and started running, casting glances over their shoulders as their feet kicked up dust, leaving a gray cloud in their wake.

When Josie and Becky came running down the lane, Lynne was bringing in the laundry from the clothesline. Seeing the look of fear on their faces, she dropped the basket onto the grass and hurried toward them. "What is it?" she asked with concern. "What happened?"

"A man. In a truck," Josie said, trying to catch her breath. "Down the gravel road."

"Was he bothering you?" Lynne asked, taking in the girls' bright red, sweaty faces. "Are you okay?"

The girls nodded. "He was just sitting there, staring," Becky said.

"But he didn't say anything or do anything?" Lynne asked.

"No," Josie admitted, "but it was weird."

"It's probably nothing. Just one of the neighbors checking their crops," Lynne assured them. "Now come on inside and get something cold to drink."

They trooped into the kitchen and Lynne pulled a pitcher of lemonade from the refrigerator. "You didn't happen to see

Ethan while you were out there?" Lynne asked as she poured them each a glass. She was trying to be casual, but there was a lilt of worry in her voice.

"Not since earlier," Josie said, taking a big drink.

Lynne pressed her hands against the counter and craned her neck to look out the window above the sink. "That boy," she let out a weary breath. "Do you know what's been going on with him?" she asked, turning back to face Josie. Her eyes were troubled.

Josie shrugged.

"It's that jerk Cutter probably," Becky said and Josie kicked her beneath the table.

"Yeah," Lynne murmured.

"We're going to go upstairs," Josie said, taking her glass to the sink.

"I know you'll probably end up talking all night but don't stay up too late," Lynne reminded them. "We want to be on the road by six tomorrow."

"Okay. 'Night, Mom," Josie said, but Lynne stopped her by tugging gently on her ponytail. "Not so fast," she said. "Don't tell me you're too big to give me a hug and kiss good-night too, are you?"

Josie peeked over at Becky, who was waiting in the doorway, intently examining her fingernails. Looking back, Josie wished that she would have given her mother a long embrace. That she would have taken the time to remember the tickle of her mother's curtain of hair tumbling over her as she pulled Josie close. But she didn't. Josie gave her a quick hug and slipped away before her mother could kiss her forehead like she usually did each night.

"Good night, Dad," she hollered as they hurried past the living room and tromped up the stairs.

"G'night," he called groggily. Later, Josie would say she wished she would have taken the time to go to him, leaned into him as he lay back in his shabby recliner, felt his evening whiskers rasp against her face and said good-night.

The girls unfurled their sleeping bags and lay atop them. The heat pressed down on them like a thick quilt.

From below, there was canned laughter from the television and soft footfalls in the kitchen, then the rev of a truck and the crackle of tires on gravel. They talked about the fair, about the upcoming school year, about boys. Becky asked if Ethan had a girlfriend. Josie said he did, though this wasn't true. There had been trouble with a girl and no one since, but Becky didn't need to know that.

The conversation turned to music and movies and the box fan blew recycled air across their bodies. Words slowed and eyes grew heavy.

A slam of a door made Josie startle and Becky gave a frightened gasp.

A jumble of voices rose and fell.

"Where have you been?" William snapped. There was a muttered response and tromping on the stairs. "You don't get to just come and go as you please," William went on. "Especially carrying a shotgun around. Hand it over now."

"You made me leave the truck," Ethan shot back. "Like I'm going to leave it in there. Besides, we're stuck out in the middle of nowhere out here," Ethan yelled.

"I asked you where you were," William said tightly. There was silence then, and Josie imagined that her father and Ethan were staring each other down.

Ethan finally spoke. "I was at the pond, okay? Where else would I even go?"

"Nowhere for a very long time," William shot back.

"Like I go anywhere now," Ethan snapped. They were outside Josie's bedroom door now.

"Shhh," came Lynne's voice. "You'll wake the girls."

"Kara Turner's father called again," William said, lowering his voice, but it was impossible not to hear him.

Kara Turner was a girl that Ethan dated for a while. She was a pretty, quiet fifteen-year-old, but the romance didn't last long. Kara's father didn't like Ethan. Didn't like his attitude, didn't like the things he heard about the sixteen-year-old who kept calling, kept showing up at his door. But Ethan persisted. Making an appearance in the rare moments William allowed Ethan to run an errand into town. The girl's father called the house, telling them he wanted Ethan to stay away.

"You need to leave Kara alone, Ethan," Lynne said, her voice filled with weariness.

"It's none of your business," Ethan yelled. "Why can't you just leave me alone."

"We can't leave you alone. We can't," William said in exasperation. "This is serious. Stay away from her. Now the Turners are getting hang-up calls."

"That's not me," Ethan insisted.

"Someone is doing it, and the Turners think it's you," William shot back. "They're threatening to call the police."

"That's bullshit," Ethan hissed. "And you know it."

"What I know is you have had a serious lack of judgment lately," Lynne said. "Kara, driving on the baseball field..."

"That was Cutter," Ethan interrupted. "I wasn't even driving."

"And until you can show me you've grown up," William continued, "there are going to be some changes around here. Give me the gun."

"What? You think I'm going to shoot someone?" Ethan scoffed. "It's my gun. Grandpa gave it to me," Ethan countered.

"That's not even funny," Lynne said. "Don't joke about things like that."

"When you can show me that you can handle it responsibly, I'll give it back to you. Until then, it's mine."

"No," Ethan said defiantly.

"Give it to me," William said, and there was the rustle of a struggle.

"Get off," Ethan snarled, and the picture above Josie's bed shook with the impact of bodies striking the wall. "Don't touch me," Ethan said, breathing heavily. "It's my gun." There was the slam of a door. The quiet click of another. The hushed voices of William and Lynne arguing.

"I'm sorry," Josie whispered.

"That's okay," Becky said. "My parents fight too."

Outside the window, fireflies blinked and cicadas roared. She heard her mother calling for Roscoe. Josie thought of Ethan in his bedroom, seething with anger. She wondered what he had been up to all evening, why he had been so secretive as of late. What did her brother have to hide?

8

Wylie pounded up the steps and did a cursory search of each of the rooms. As she threw back the shower curtain, a horrible thought hit her. "Shit," she hissed and rushed back down the stairs. She threw open the front door and cold air and a swirl of snow swept in. She squinted into the wall of white. The storm had increased its fury. She couldn't see beyond the front step. "Oh, Jesus," she whispered. The child would never survive out there for very long.

Wylie took a deep breath and tried to get her wits about her. He had to be somewhere around here. She started over and retraced her steps, rechecking the closets and behind doors. Finally, she peered behind the sofa and wedged next to the wall was the boy. Dressed in the sweatshirt she had given him, he was fast asleep, thumb in his mouth. On the floor next to him was his pile of wet clothes.

Wylie strode over to the front door and flipped the dead bolt. She pulled the sofa a few feet away from the wall, giving the boy a little more space, and knelt down next to him.

His head rested at an awkward angle on the hardwood floor. Wylie reached for a throw pillow and slid it beneath his head. He barely stirred. His skin was alarmingly pale, and a strange, angry red rash encircled his mouth and crept toward his cheeks. The cut at his temple had stopped bleeding but was a bit bruised and swollen. The tips of his toes that peeked out from beneath the blanket looked waxy and hard. Small blisters had erupted on the curved edges of his ears. Frostbite.

He shivered in his sleep, and Wylie pulled the comforter from the sofa and tucked it around his small body. He was thin. Too thin.

Wylie still had so many questions. How did he end up here? Who did he belong to? She had to wait for those answers. At any rate it looked like she was going to have an overnight guest.

Wylie gathered up the boy's wet clothing. She winced at the musty, moldy smell that emanated from them. She checked his pockets in hopes of finding something that might help identify him. There was nothing but a small figure of an action hero. She set the toy on the kitchen counter and then tossed the clothes into the washing machine.

Wylie added a few more logs to the fireplace. The wood crackled and popped and the flames danced. The wind howled and buffeted the house; the lights dimmed and then brightened again.

Wylie sat down next to Tas on the sofa. She was exhausted but the thought of how the boy got there nagged at her. In this weather, it seemed impossible that a child, dressed as he was, could walk a mile from the nearest house to the front yard of the farmhouse. He had to have come from the road. Maybe there had been a car accident.

Wylie went upstairs to a window that overlooked the front yard. She wanted to see if she could spot any hint of what might have happened. The hackberry trees were otherworldly, their sharp limbs shimmering, bending beneath a heavy glaze of ice. The lane that led to the gravel road beyond the property disappeared into white mist.

How far did the boy have to walk before collapsing in front of the house? It couldn't have been that great of a distance. Visibility was terrible, and he was such a small boy; he couldn't have walked that far on his own. Perhaps a vehicle went off the road somewhat nearby.

Wylie returned downstairs and pulled on her down parka and boots with cleats that would hopefully anchor her to the icy ground and keep her from falling.

She looked down at the sleeping child and considered waking him to let him know she was going outside. He was sleeping so soundly, she decided to just let him rest. Hopefully, he wouldn't wake up while she was out and panic.

Wylie grabbed a flashlight and her hiking sticks with sharp points that could penetrate the ice. Once outside, the frigid air instantly took her breath away but at least the wind had died down a bit.

The ice was an inch thick and Wylie took a tentative step out the door and let out a breath of relief when her feet didn't fly out from beneath her. It was only half a football field to the top of the lane, but it would be slow going, hopefully with the help of the ice cleats and the hiking sticks, she would be able to stay upright.

She moved methodically; the tap, tap of her pole tips sinking through the snow and striking the ice was like a drumbeat urging her forward. Holding both a flashlight and the hiking sticks was awkward. The light's beam dizzily bobbed up and down with each step. She passed the spot where she found the boy. It was as if he was never there. The tracks and body-shaped indentation were already covered with fresh snow.

By the time Wylie was halfway up the lane, she was breathing hard and sweating beneath her coat. She resisted the urge to remove her stocking cap and turned back to look at the barn and the house through the gauzy veil of snow.

From this vantage point, they looked almost magical. The eaves were dripping with silvery icicles and a frosting of snow covered the roofs. Smoke puffed from the chimney and the windows glowed with warm light—no wonder he had tried to make it there.

She scanned the iron-gray sky above. Soft snowflakes fell in lazy circles to the ground. No rough-legged hawks circled the area in search of rodents in the empty fields. No black-masked horned larks with their high-pitched, delicate song. The air was quiet except for the sound of her own heavy breathing. All the creatures were hunkered in for the next round of storms. Wylie needed to hurry.

Once at the top of the lane and past the windbreak of pines, Wylie spotted the tire tracks, a vehicle had traveled this road recently. Deep ruts that zigzagged back and forth across the field were already filling with new snow. Whoever was driving was having a hard time staying on the road. Wylie swung the flashlight from side to side as she searched the ditches half-filled with snow and ice. No vehicle. The wind lifted, and a piece of dingy, white fabric tumbled toward her and clung to her pant leg.

Wylie peeled the cloth from her pants. It was the size of a hand towel, grimy and frayed and covered in faded bunny rabbits. It reminded her of the blanket she had as a kid. She dragged that thing around until it was as thin as tissue paper. She pressed it to her nose. It smelled musty and like wood smoke. Maybe it belonged to the boy or maybe it was wayward garbage. She shoved it into her pocket.

A flash of red in the snow caught her eye. Her breath quickened. Was it blood? Wylie focused the beam of light on the ground in front of her. More red speckles shining through a thin layer of snow. She bent down to get a closer look, ran her gloved hand through the snow, expecting it to smear pink. It wasn't blood. Shards of what looked like a broken taillight dotted the snow. Next came a trail of unidentifiable pieces of broken plastic and more broken glass.

It had to be a car accident, Wylie thought as she fought against the wind. Every time she tried to catch her breath, a blast of air would snatch it away.

A few steps farther, more detritus. Wylie reached down and picked up the remnants of a side-view mirror. She examined her face, numbed by the cold, in the cracked glass. Her distorted reflection, as frightened as she felt, looked back at her.

The blizzard winds had arranged the newly fallen snow into tall dunes. Wylie picked up her pace, walked a few yards and came to the spot where it looked like a vehicle first left the road: undisturbed snow where it must have gone airborne for a moment after striking a telephone pole, then a violent gash in the ground covered in a mosaic of broken glass.

Ten feet farther, Wylie found what she was looking for. A black truck flipped upside down in a deep furrow next to a field.

Using the hiking sticks to keep her balance, Wylie picked

her way down into the ditch and circled the mangled steel and rubber tires now encased in a glaze of ice. She rubbed at the rear window using her gloved fingers, but a lacy film of ice and snow covered it, making it impossible to see inside.

The driver's side door was wedged open. The faint impression of small shoes led away from the truck. Wylie held on to the truck's undercarriage to maneuver around to the other side, and her legs plunged through the icy crust up to her knees.

"Dammit," she muttered and tried to brush away the snow that had fallen into her boot but only made it worse. She waded through the snow and bent down to look through the open door. The front window was shot through with a spiderweb of cracks and what looked like specks of blood.

Wylie twisted her neck to see if anyone was in the back seat. It was vacant except for some empty cans of beer. Had the driver been drinking with a child in the car? Was this why the tire tracks had been all over the road? At first, Wylie thought it was just the icy roads, but it looked like there could be more to the accident.

Wylie finished her search around the truck. The snow must have been able to hold the boy's weight as he made the trek to Wylie's house in his tennis shoes. How cold his feet must have been. If Wylie had stepped outside even an hour later, she surely would have found the boy's dead body.

Where could the driver have gone? Would a parent really leave their son alone in a wrecked car even if it was to go find help? Or had the boy been the one to go for help first?

Wylie looked toward the farmhouse and spotted a soft glow through the gloom. From the child's viewpoint, the lights must have seemed like a welcoming beacon after not knowing where the driver had gone.

She backtracked the way she had come looking for any

sign of the truck's driver, this time staying in the ditch and the upturned ground that marked the truck's path. The ditch protected her somewhat from the now rising wind, but still her face tingled with cold. She stepped over more debris half-buried in the ice and snow. A nearly empty package of sunflower seeds, more beer cans, broken glass and fast-food wrappers snagged on frozen prairie sage. Wylie kept walking.

And that's when she glimpsed it, poking out of the snow in the empty field—a red swath of fabric. Wylie struggled through the knee-deep snow, her legs burning with the exertion. She stopped short when the rest of the figure came into view. The truck's driver or another passenger, thrown from the vehicle as it careened off the road.

The woman was lying on her stomach at the edge of the snowy field, entangled in a web of barbwire fencing pulled from its post. Her forehead rested on one bent forearm; the other arm was outstretched as if reaching for some sort of lifeline. The woman's long hair, dusted with snow as fine as sugar, spread out like snakes, frozen in midstrike. She was deathly still.

Wylie hurried toward the woman, her breath coming in raspy, white puffs. When she was about thirty feet away, Wylie could see just how ensnared the woman was. The fencing coiled around her legs and the sharp prongs bit deeply through the woman's pants into her skin, leaving bloody skin exposed.

"Shit," Wylie muttered. She had to step down into the ditch, cross the basin filled with snow and climb up the other side to get to the woman. Wylie moved carefully, knowing one wrong step could result in a broken ankle or twisted knee.

By the time Wylie crossed the ditch, the woman still hadn't moved, and Wylie feared the worst. She dropped to her knees and set the flashlight down so it illuminated the injured woman. Wylie lay down next to the prone woman. She gently brushed the newly fallen snow from the woman's face to find a large gash across her forehead and one eye completely swollen shut. She was in bad shape. Wylie had to get her out of there.

Wylie saw no way of turning the woman without inflicting further injury. The best Wylie could do was pull as much snow away from the woman's face as she could.

"Can you hear me?" Wylie asked as she pulled off her gloves and pressed her fingers to the woman's neck in hopes of finding a pulse. "I found the little boy. He's safe." Nothing. "Please," Wylie repeated, "Please don't be dead." Wylie tried to silence the roaring in her ears, to steady her trembling fingers.

Then there it was, a barely perceptible thump beneath her fingertips. "Oh, thank God," Wylie breathed.

The woman gave a soft groan. "I'm here," Wylie said. "My name is Wylie, and I'm going to help you. I found the boy, he's okay. Is there anyone else?"

The woman seemed to hesitate a moment too long before shaking her head no.

So was it just the woman and the child in the accident? Wylie wasn't sure she believed the woman, but why would she lie? Wylie thought again of the strange way the boy had acted when he first regained consciousness at the house. He reminded her of a trapped animal—desperate to escape. Was this woman his mother or someone else?

"Okay, I'm going to help you get out of this," Wylie said as she put her gloves back on, carefully pushed down the razor-sharp fencing and climbed over. She dropped to her knees and began to frantically try and free the woman from the barb-wire. The spiked hooks from the fence dug into the woman's pants, tearing her jeans and the skin beneath. Bright red drops of blood marred the newly fallen snow.

The barbs bit through Wylie's gloves, but she couldn't free the woman. The woman cried out weakly in pain. "I'm sorry, I'm sorry," Wiley said in a rush. "I just have to get you untangled from the fence."

The woman tried to inch away from Wylie and the spikes dug even more deeply into her skin.

"Try not to move just yet," Wylie urged. "You'll just get caught up worse." The woman continued to moan softly, her uninjured eye looking at Wylie with pain and something else. Defiance.

Wylie sat back on her heels, snowflakes catching on her eyelashes and melting against her sweaty face.

"I'm going to go back to the house and get some wire cutters," Wylie told her. The woman reached out and grabbed Wylie's wrist as if begging her not to leave. Wylie easily slipped from the woman's grasp.

"I'll be right back," she assured her. "I promise. It's the only way I'm going to be able to get you untangled." The woman reached for her again, this time holding on to Wylie more tightly. Wylie understood the woman's fear. Once Wylie left, the flashlight would go with her. The woman would be left behind in total darkness. The cold and wind were relentless and it was snowing even harder. The woman was slowly being buried alive.

Wylie unzipped her coat and wriggled out of it. Immediately the cold punched through her clothing and she gasped. Shivering, Wylie tucked the coat around the woman, covering her up as much as possible. Next, Wylie removed her hat and carefully placed it on the woman's head, pulling it gently over her ears. At the last moment she remembered her car keys in her coat, fished them out, and stuffed them into her back pocket.

Wylie knew it was a risk exposing herself to the elements, but she would be able to get another hat and coat back at the house. On the other hand, the woman didn't stand a chance without some kind of protection and wouldn't last much longer.

Wylie unwound the yellow scarf from her neck and wrapped it around the barbwire fence just above the woman's head. Its fringe blew in the wind like a grim flag, but when Wylie returned, it would help her locate the woman more quickly.

Something was completely off about this entire scene. Why would anyone dare to drive in the storm? Neither the woman nor the boy was dressed for the weather. No coats, boots, hats, or gloves. Did they live nearby? Were they trying to get home or trying to get away?

Wylie turned back toward the house. She had to hurry.

9

August 2000

Josie lay in the dark, her muscles tense, waiting for the next outburst of anger between her parents and Ethan. Instead came the usual sounds of the house at bedtime—the groan of pipes and running water, the flush of a toilet, the squeak of bedsprings. And finally, silence.

"Are you awake?" Becky whispered.

"Yeah," Josie answered. She lifted her head and looked at the clock on the bedside table. 12:07. "I can't sleep," she said. The argument between her brother and parents made her feel sick. More so than usual. Her stomach swayed.

"Come on," Becky whispered, getting to her feet.

"Where are we going?" Josie asked.

"Shhh," Becky answered. She slowly opened the bedroom door and peered into the darkened hallway. All was quiet.

The girls tiptoed to the staircase, covering their mouths to stifle any laughter.

This would be the most difficult part of sneaking out. The maneuvering down the stairs without alerting the entire house of their antics. Each step had its own tone and timbre when touched—a squeak, a sigh, a groan. Finally, they just held their breath and scurried down the steps. At the bottom, Josie and Becky stood, hearts racing, waiting for someone to come to the top of the stairs and order them back to bed.

The remainder of their escape was easy—through the kitchen, into the mudroom and out the back door. The Doyles never bothered to lock their doors. Why would they? They knew their neighbors, were miles from town, and had nothing of real value to steal.

The wind had died down, and while still hot, the air smelled sweetly of clover. The sky was brightly lit by the moon and from stars set deep into the black sky.

"What are we doing?" Becky whispered as Josie led her to the trampoline and together they scrambled up. They held hands, the ones they scored with a paring knife when they were ten so they could be blood sisters, and began to bounce.

"Sisters forever," Josie called out as they jumped higher and higher until the rest of the world fell away. The air was humid and velvety against their skin. Sweat slid down their temples and into their eyes, but still they jumped, the rhythmic thump, thump of their feet hitting the rubber of the trampoline filled their ears like a heartbeat.

"I can almost grab them," Becky cried, lifting her free hand toward the sky.

Josie pressed her lips together to keep her laughter inside, but she'd never felt so free as she did in that moment, soaring into the air, the fingers of her left hand interlocked with her best friend's, the fingers of her right hand extended to the sky.

The stars felt so close. Like a pile of jacks to be scooped up in her palm. A fistful of stars. In that moment, such a thing didn't seem impossible.

Josie and Becky leaped and snatched at the sky until their breath came in hitches and they could no longer keep the laughter tucked inside. They collapsed to the floor of the trampoline and lay on their backs sweaty and out of breath until the world stopped swaying. "How many did you get?" Josie asked, glancing at Becky's left hand still clasped tightly shut.

She brought her fist to her eye as if peeking inside. "A million," she whispered. "How about you?"

"A million and one," Josie said because she always had to win. It was as if they were little again when nothing mattered except for that very moment when being with your best friend was enough. There were no worries about boys and family arguments and growing up. Josie smiled and let the easiness of it all flow over her.

A popping sound interrupted their stargazing and Becky sat up on one elbow. "What's that?" Becky asked.

"I'm not sure," Josie said uneasily. They scanned the farmyard. Everything was still. The goats were snug within the confines of the barn, the hens perched inside their coop.

"Probably just a truck backfiring." Josie brushed away her concern and lay back down.

Another pop rang out and this time, Josie recognized it. Living out in the country, living with hunters, Josie knew the sound intimately. Gunfire.

This was the only thing that made sense to Josie, so instead of running away from the noise, she was drawn toward it. She crawled over the side of the trampoline and dropped to the earth below. "What's going on?" Becky asked, following close behind. A cloud eased in front of the moon and the light curdled behind it leaving the girls in darkness.

"Maybe someone is shooting at a fox or coyote," Josie said, but even as the words left her mouth, she knew that wasn't likely. An uneasiness settled into her chest. Her dad wouldn't shoot blindly into the dark like that. Besides, the blast sounded a little muffled, too far away. Maybe it was the neighbor a mile down the road. Sound carried out in the country.

"Let's go back inside," Josie said. The carefree feeling of earlier was gone, and the girls moved toward the house, hobbling over the rocky earth on their bare feet. From the barn, the noise had woken the goats. They bleated anxiously. Josie could hear their restless pacing in the barn.

A third blast came just as they rounded the barn. A brief flare of light filled her parents' window like the flash of a camera. Then silence. Next to Josie, Becky cried out.

Josie thought of her brother and his anger and the sly, mean way he looked at their father earlier, the way he refused to hand over his shotgun. No, Josie told herself. Ethan would never do this.

Three more explosions came from within the house—one after the other. Becky covered her ears with her hands and screamed. Josie grabbed Becky's hand and led her to the barn door. Josie tried to open the door but it was too heavy and worn from age. The bottom edge dragged slowly against the ground and got caught. She lifted the handle and yanked harder and the door squeaked open a fraction before getting stuck again. "Hurry!" Becky scrabbled at Josie's arm.

There were dozens of hiding places in the barn: the hayloft, the goat stalls, behind a pile of lumber. Josie wedged through the door and was plunged into darkness and immediately understood she made a mistake. The goats, startled by her entrance, began to stir with an alarming cascade of bleats. Within the splintered walls of the barn they would have nowhere to go. They would be trapped. Josie quickly squirmed back out. "We can't hide in here," Josie whispered.

Josie looked around frantically. They needed a phone, but Josie was too afraid to go into the house. Her grandparents were a mile away. The cornfield. They could move through the cornfield and it would eventually lead to her grandparents' house. They would know what to do. In the shadows, the stalks of corn stood tall, like gangly sentries.

Did they dare? One of Josie's earliest memories was of her mother scolding her not to go into the fields alone. "You'll get lost in there and we'll never, ever find you," she warned. For a long time, her mother's warnings worked, but as time passed, the more daring Josie became, and venturing into the corn was a common occurrence.

A dark figure emerged from the house. Josie couldn't tell who it was but the shotgun in his hand was unmistakable. Like a wolf, he walked slowly, methodically toward them.

Josie reached for Becky's hand and they started running, their bare feet pounding against the ground, sharp rocks and twigs pierced the soles of her feet, but Josie barely noticed. Next to her, Becky's breath came in frantic hitches.

If they could make it to the corn, Josie was confident that they would be okay.

"Josie," came a male voice. Had she heard right? Had someone called her name? She dared a glance over her shoulder, and the figure was picking up speed and gaining on them. Was it her brother? Josie couldn't tell and didn't want to slow down to find out.

"Faster," Josie breathlessly urged Becky. "Hurry." Josie stumbled and fell to the ground but quickly got to her feet. Almost there. The thunder of footsteps approaching prodded them forward. Screams punctured the air. Josie managed to stay upright but Becky lost her footing, and try as Josie might to hold on, Becky's fingers slid from her own.

"Get up, get up," Josie begged, pulling on Becky's arm. "Please." Once again, she dared to look behind her. The figure raised his hands and took aim. Josie dropped Becky's arm, turned, and ran.

Josie stumbled into the field and was immediately swallowed up by the corn. Becky's desperate cries followed her but still she kept running. The crack of the shotgun exploded in her ears and searing pain ripped through her arm. *He shot me,* she thought in disbelief. *I've been shot.* The world pitched and tilted but using the cornstalks, Josie somehow kept her balance, kept moving. She wanted to go back for Becky, but her feet could move only forward.

The coarse leaves whipped against Josie's face leaving red welts and the hard-packed soil gouged her feet. When she could run no more, she stopped, bent over, hands on knees, and tried to hold completely still. Her arm was throbbing and her ears rang painfully. Was he coming? Her instinct was to keep going, but she had no idea where she was.

Josie had torn a path through the corn and knew that the gunman would only have to follow the flattened stems to find her. Josie began to sidle through the rows, zigzagging as she went, holding her arm, slick with blood, close to her body. Josie knew what a shotgun shell could do to pheasants and deer. She'd seen it time and again. Gaping holes, blood gushing. A few inches over and the bullet would have struck her in the heart. She'd be dead.

Gradually, Josie's breath steadied and the clanging in her ears subsided. She kept her eyes on the corn above, looking for a ripple or sway that might alert her to another presence. Josie's mind whirred. Maybe the shooter thought she was dead. She considered lying on the ground in a heap and playing dead just in case he was still looking for her, but that was too scary.

She thought of Ethan and her father and the ugly words exchanged between the two of them. Her father's terse words kept replaying in her mind: *Ethan, give me the gun.* And Ethan's defiant refusal.

Was it Ethan? No. Josie refused to believe it. It couldn't be her once-sweet brother who taught her how to bait a hook and how to ride a bike.

Josie needed to get her bearings. She had been in this field a thousand times. She could do this; she could find her way out and get help.

A scratchy rustle of leaves came from off to Josie's right. Josie stopped and stood erect, holding completely still, listening. Clouds curtained the moon and stars, and the field's shadows bled into one another until Josie couldn't even see her hand in front of her face. Still, she felt a presence some twenty feet away. She hoped, prayed it was her father or mother coming to look for her but deep down knew that whoever was in the corn with her wasn't there to help.

The dry, whispery sound came closer and Josie pressed her fingers to her mouth to keep from crying out. Blood dripped down her arm and into a puddle at her feet.

Josie fought the urge to bolt. *Stay still,* she told herself. *You can't see him, so he can't see you.* But then the dark shifted—just slightly. The shadows darkened, and he was right there, just a few feet away, his back to Josie. So close that if she reached out, she could touch him, so close that she could smell the heat coming off his skin—the not so unfamiliar scent of sweat and body odor. Was it Ethan? Could her brother have been the one who shot her and chased her into the field?

A small grunt of impatience came from the figure and Josie held her breath. The shape began to drift away but then paused and slowly turned around. After what felt like an eternity, the shadow slunk deeper into the corn and disappeared.

Josie let out a shaky breath. He was gone for now.

10

The flowers' delicate purple petals shriveled and dropped one by one to the ground, then blew away. Now prickly green nettles sprouted in front of the window.

Her mother was still sick, pinballing from the bed to the bathroom, hand covering her mouth.

"You have to get her to eat and drink something," her father said one evening when he stopped by.

The girl would pull the chair over to the wooden shelf where they kept the food so she could reach the jar of peanut butter and a loaf of bread. The girl would try to make her mother eat, but she wouldn't. She would resolutely keep her mouth shut, and the girl would end up eating the sandwich all by herself and wash it down with a cup of water from the bathroom sink.

Her father started bringing thick shakes for her mother to drink. He would prop her mother up in the bed and cajole her into drinking. "Just a little bit more," he'd urge. "You have to stay strong for the baby."

Her mother would try and please her father. Would take a few sips and then vomit into the bucket she kept by the bed.

"Come on," her father would snap in frustration. "Keep trying." Her mother would push the drink away and curl up into a little ball as if trying to disappear.

One day, after her mother refused to drink what he had brought her, her father went into a rage. "You're worthless," he said, grabbing the girl's mother by the arm and wrenching her from the bed. "Don't you care about her?" he asked, flicking a hand toward the girl. "Don't you care about the baby?"

He dragged her mother to the table and forced her into a chair.

The girl pulled a book from the shelf, went to her spot beneath the window, and faced the wall.

Her father pulled a spoon from a drawer and dipped it into the cup. "Eat," he ordered. Her mother tried to turn her head, but he held her chin and poked the spoon into her mouth. She gagged wetly and her breath came in hitches.

The girl turned the page of her book and recited the story to herself. It was the one about the princess and the pea. Though she knew how to sound out some of the words, she had the story memorized.

After a while, the retching stopped, the crying faded. Her father spoke in low, soothing tones. "See, that wasn't so bad, was it? You ate almost all of it."

The girl looked up from the pages of her book and watched as he gently wiped her mother's mouth with a washcloth and led her back to the bed. Soon she heard her mother's soft, rhythmic breathing. She had fallen asleep.

Her father tugged on the girl's ponytail before he opened the door to leave. "She's okay. Just let her rest."

Once the girl heard the click of the door and the rasp of the lock falling into place, she returned the book to its spot on the shelf and walked over to the kitchen table. She lifted the cup that held the ice cream. She could smell the chocolate and her stomach rumbled. There were still a few spoonfuls left. Her mother wouldn't mind.

The girl brought the cup to her lips and drank. The sweet creaminess filled her mouth and slid down her throat. She scraped out the last drops with a spoon and licked it clean.

The girl turned on the television but set the volume to low. Hours passed. Her mother slept. The pain in her stomach came fast and hard. The girl doubled over and barely made it to the bathroom before getting sick. Her intestines twisted and her stomach heaved.

She lay on the bathroom floor—the cracked tile was cool against her skin. Night eased into the room until there was only the soft blue light from the television. The cramps eased, her muscles relaxed. The girl felt wrung out and empty. She fell into an uneasy sleep until her mother gently shook her awake and led her back to the bed.

11

Present Day

The sharp wind was gaining momentum, sending showers of grainy snow pummeling against Wylie with each gust. She needed to hurry to the barn to retrieve the wire cutters.

She figured she had no more than twenty-five minutes to get to the barn and back to the accident site before the woman was seriously in danger of hyperthermia. Even then, it might be too late. Once Wylie freed the woman, she still had to get her back to the house.

Agitated, Wylie looked to the dark sky and the snow pelted her face. She needed to get back to the woman before the weather got worse. Her face and ears, now exposed to the cold, burned painfully. She couldn't imagine how the woman had survived this long lying in the snow.

Once at the top of the lane, Wylie paused to catch her

breath, but the wind was whipping itself into a frenzy, creating cyclones of snow that twisted and convulsed about her. She had to keep moving. She pointed her flashlight toward the barn and the silos disappeared behind a veil of white. The soft light coming from the house urged Wylie forward. The hiking sticks helped keep Wylie upright, but her legs felt heavy and ached with the effort of stepping through the high snow.

As she approached the house, the ice-laden trees were further weighed down by the new snowfall and threatened to snap with each blast of wind.

She had been gone too long. The fire may have gone out, the boy's injuries may have been worse than she thought, and she still needed to get back to the woman. Wylie's chest tightened, and she picked up her pace as she powered through the final fifty yards to the front door.

She pushed through the door bringing a flurry of snow inside with her. Wylie shut the door behind her and dropped the hiking sticks with a clatter to the floor. Ignoring the gouges her ice cleats were making in the hardwood floor, Wylie went straight to the sofa where she had left the boy. He was there, still asleep, with Tas curled up next to him.

Next, Wylie checked the phone, knowing that the chances of making a call were slim. She was right; no maintenance workers would be sent out in weather like this.

Wylie added another piece of wood to the fire and fought the urge to stay and warm herself next to the flames. Her ears and nose burned painfully. She had to keep moving. Wylie went to the closet and grabbed another coat and scarf. She had given the woman her stocking cap, so she pulled the fur-lined hood attached to the coat over her head and tied it into place.

Wylie dreaded stepping back into the storm, but the clock was ticking.

With renewed determination, Wylie left behind the warm house. The storm continued to rage. It felt as if the wind was coming at her from all directions.

Wylie passed the rickety henhouse and the toolshed that had been reclaimed by earlier renters as a dumping spot for their unwanted furniture and household items. Once inside the barn, Wylie shook the snow from her coat and checked her watch. It had already been about twenty-five minutes since she left the woman. She scanned the rough walls in search of what she needed.

Hanging from nails and hooks were rakes and hoes and all matter of farm tools. She located the wire cutters, a rusty shovel, and an old-fashioned wooden toboggan with steel runners. A musty horse blanket hung from a bent nail, and she laid it atop the sled with the other supplies securing them with an old rope.

She held on to her flashlight but abandoned the hiking sticks, didn't dare bring anything else. It was going to be hard enough to lug what she had through the snow and back, hopefully with the woman in tow.

Though the snow was blinding, and the wind was scrubbing away any sign of her earlier tracks, Wylie at least had a good sense as to where she was headed.

She kept the flashlight and her eyes focused on the ground in front of her. Wylie's plan was simple in theory. She would snip away the tangled barbwire, freeing the woman, who would hopefully be still alive. If the woman couldn't walk on her own accord, Wylie would do her best to pull her to the house on the toboggan. The shovel just seemed like a good idea.

By the time Wylie was halfway to the wreckage, despite her warm layers, cold permeated her body, and she questioned the wisdom of this rescue mission. One wrong step and Wylie could end up with a broken leg and find herself in an icy grave. Wylie wasn't known for her decision-making skills as of late, and what good would it do if they both froze to death? What would the boy do then?

Wylie considered backtracking. She was good at leaving. That was something she knew how to do. This was different, though. No one was dying back home. Her teenage son, Seth, was still furious at Wylie for trying to lay down the law and wasn't missing her one bit. He was in good hands with his father.

Finally, through the eddy of snow, she saw a glint of metal, and the wreckage came into view. Wylie picked up her pace. She was almost there.

Wylie left the road and crossed down through the ditch to the barbwire fence that skirted the field, searching for the yellow scarf left behind as a place marker. As she drew closer to the truck, there was no sign of the yellow scarf. Chest heaving, she stopped short. She must have made a mistake. Wylie dropped the shovel and the rope connected to the sled and turned around in a slow circle. Everything looked the same— a stark, barren, snow-covered wilderness.

She had to have passed the spot where the woman was located. There was no way the scarf could have blown away in the storm; she had been sure to wrap it securely several times around the metal barbs.

The scarf and the woman could be buried beneath one of the chest-high snowdrifts that pressed against the fence. In frustration, Wylie backtracked along the fence and, this time, moved even more slowly until she reached the first large drift. Using her gloved hands, she began brushing the snow aside until the fence was visible. No scarf appeared.

Wylie kept moving. The cold snaked its way through her layers of clothing. She couldn't stay out here much longer. Just when she was ready to give up and head back to the house, her eyes landed on a clump of yellow fabric snagged around a fence barb. She dropped her eyes to the ground, expecting to see the woman's frozen, broken body ensnared in the fencing. But it was gone. The scarf was gone.

Wylie dropped to her knees, peering closely at the metal fencing. Minute drops of blood and what looked to be bits of frozen flesh clung to the fence. She ran her fingers across the ground.

Wylie got to her feet and examined the ground for any new footprints, but the heavy snow and wind had already swept the frozen canvas clean. There was no sign of the injured woman. Why would she have left in this brutal storm when Wylie had promised to come back to help her?

Wylie wandered around the wreckage and field searching for the woman until the cold forced her in the direction of the house. What was the woman running from and where could she have gone? A new unease settled in Wylie's chest. She had so many questions and now there was only one person left to answer them and he wasn't talking.

12

Sheriff's Deputy Levi Robbins cruised the highways and back roads in search of trouble. Any kind of trouble. A ten-year veteran of the Blake County Sheriff's Department, he normally wasn't on nights, but Frazier was on vacation, so Levi volunteered to take his shifts thinking a change of pace might be good.

It was after 1:00 a.m., and there wasn't one call so far. Try as he might, he couldn't even find a reason to pull anyone over for a traffic violation. The hours crept by and Levi passed the time by listening to country music on the radio. He drove along Meadow Rue and slowed as he approached the scarred bitternut hickory that rose from the middle of the road. It was an unexpected landmark to those who didn't know the area.

No one really knew how the eighty-foot tree sprouted

where two gravel roads intersected, and no one knew why it was never cut down. Those who needed to drive past were forced to slow down to maneuver around the nature-made traffic circle.

Once past the bitternut, Levi turned south on County Road G11. He'd make one more loop and then swing by Casey's General Store to grab a pop and some gas. Maybe if he was lucky, someone would be trying to rip off the station. It'd been a long time since he'd dealt with a robbery. And he couldn't remember the last time he unholstered his gun. At least that would be interesting.

A hot breeze swept through his open windows. There had been high hopes for rain that night. The sky had clouded, and the air had that damp, electric smell of an oncoming thunderstorm. It didn't last long though, and the moon and stars made a reappearance. Too damn bad. The farmers needed the rain.

Levi spat a sunflower seed out the open window. As hot as it was, the fresh air helped keep him from falling asleep while on his route. He worked the cruiser up to sixty, then seventy, then eighty miles per hour. One of the perks of working nights. Wide-open road.

Suddenly, a pickup truck, with its headlights turned off, came roaring out from a gravel road tucked between two cornfields. Levi slammed on his brakes, causing the back of his cruiser to fishtail. The scream of tires on asphalt drowned out the radio, and the smell of burning rubber filled his nose.

"Son of a bitch," he muttered as he struggled to keep the car on the road. Once he straightened out the cruiser and his heart settled back into its rightful spot, he peered through the windshield and pressed his foot on the gas. "Light 'em up," he said to himself and flipped on his lights and siren.

The truck ahead of him briefly sped up and then slowed as

if the driver realized there was no chance of outrunning the cruiser. "That's right, motherfucker," Levi said as he pulled off to the side of the road behind the truck.

Illuminated by his headlights, Levi could see that the driver was the only person in the truck. He tried to get a look at the license plate, but the numbers and letters were concealed by dried mud. Could be intentional, but most likely not. Farm trucks got dirty out here. The mood he was in though, Levi wasn't planning on letting this transgression ride.

He stepped from his car and slowly approached the silver 1990 Ford Ranger with a vinyl truck bed cover. Before Levi could speak, the truck door opened.

"Hey, now, stay in your vehicle," Levi warned, his hand drifting toward his sidearm. "Put your hands on the steering wheel."

"I'm sorry," a young, shaky voice came from within the truck. "I didn't see you. I looked both ways before I turned and all of a sudden you were there. You were coming so fast."

"So you say," Levi said as he stopped next to the driver's side window and directed his flashlight on a young man with shaggy blond hair clutching the steering wheel.

The inside of the truck smelled like body odor, tobacco, and fear. An overturned pop can lay on the floor, tobacco spit spilling out on the passenger side rug. Levi almost smiled. He loved scaring the shit out of knucklehead teenagers.

"You know your headlights are off? You almost killed me back there. Where you going in such a hurry?" Levi asked. "You been drinking?"

The boy squinted up at him. "No, sir. I'm just heading home. I'm late." The boy's face was shiny with sweat, and dark stains ringed the neck of his shirt and beneath his arms.

"Where you coming from?" Levi asked as the boy handed

over his driver's license. Levi noted that the boy's name was Brock Cutter. There were a lot of Cutters in the county. Big family of farmers.

"I was at a movie over in Spencer," the boy answered. "With my cousin."

"So you're a Cutter kid?" Levi asked, looking up from the license.

"Yes, sir," the boy said, trying to see past the beam of light. "Brock Cutter."

"You have a cousin named Brett?" Levi asked. The boy nodded, his eyes darting around nervously.

"I don't think I've seen you since you were yay high," Levi said, holding his hand about four feet above the ground. "I graduated with your cousin, Brett. You look just like him. How's he doing?"

"He's good," Cutter said, his voice quivered. "Lives over in Perry, works at the pork plant there. He's married and has two kids."

"Two kids, wow, that's wild. God, we had some good times back in the day. He coming back for our reunion next summer?" Levi asked, removing his hat and wiping the perspiration from his forehead.

"Probably," Cutter said. "Listen, like I said, I'm really sorry. I didn't see you. It won't happen again. I'll be more careful next time."

Levi stared down at Cutter. He didn't know why he didn't check the kid's driving record. Levi never gave people a break. Maybe he was nostalgic for the good old days when he and Brett Cutter drove around these back roads drinking Everclear and Dr Pepper. He knew he was at least a bit at fault, going eighty mph in a fifty-five zone. Maybe there was a part of him that didn't want to be the one to break the quiet streak they'd had in the department.

If he had run the license plate, he would have seen that Brock Cutter had a suspended license and a bench warrant for a failure to appear for a court date related to a harassment case over in Kossuth County. He would have learned that Brock Cutter wasn't as innocent and good-natured as his cousin, Brett.

"How about you tell that son of a bitch cousin of yours to give me a call next time he's in town, and I'll give you a break," Levi said with a grin. "But you gotta promise me to be more careful. I don't want to have to pull you over again. Got it?"

"Thank you," Cutter said with relief, finally releasing the steering wheel and wiping his wet palms on his jeans. "I promise."

Levi waited until Cutter pulled carefully back onto the road, drove slowly away, his taillights fading to red pinpricks in the dark. He shook his head. Brett Cutter. Damn, he hadn't thought of him in years. Good guy.

He got back into the cruiser and turned the ignition. On the radio, country music was replaced by some talk show program.

Levi continued his rounds, stopping at the gas station for that pop and a slice of pizza. The rest of the night remained calm, uneventful.

The sun slipped into the hazy sky, bringing a new wave of heat. Levi had one hour to go before his shift was over. He was exhausted. He was going to go home, take a shower, and go to bed.

Sixty minutes later, Deputy Levi Robbins was summoned to the bloodiest crime scene in Blake County history.

13

Once back at the house, Wylie dropped the shovel and sled on the front steps and went inside. She wearily pulled off her boots. What was she going to tell the boy? Simply armored with Wylie's hat and coat, there was no way that the woman was going to survive out in the elements.

There was no sign of the woman. Any footprints left behind in the snow were swept away by the harsh wind. It was as if she had simply disappeared.

Now the living room was empty. The boy and Tas weren't where she left them. The fireplace had dimmed to orange embers and the room was chilly.

She moved from room to room with increasing worry. She made her way up the steps, the cold from the wood floor seeping through her socks. The second-floor landing was dark.

Her bedroom door was shut tight and Wylie turned the knob and nudged the door open. Standing in the dim pool of light from her bedside lamp was the boy, his back to the door with Tas lying at his feet.

"There you are," Wylie said, and the boy swung around, startled. Clutched in his hands was Wylie's 9 mm gun. Wylie gasped. Wide-eyed, the boy stood frozen; the gun was aimed directly at Wylie's chest.

"Put it down." The words came out raggedly, like fabric caught on barbwire.

He just stared, his mouth agape.

"Put it down, now!" Wylie ordered.

Tas began barking and the boy dropped the gun as if burned. It clattered to the floor and Tas scrambled away. Wylie closed her eyes and covered her ears, waiting for a bullet to discharge and rip through her. When it didn't come, she pounced on the gun, throwing herself atop it, the cold metal digging into her midsection.

Above her stood the boy, frozen in terror, with Tas yapping wildly.

"What were you thinking?" Wylie snapped as she staggered to her feet, gun in hand. With shaking fingers, she removed the bullets. "Never, ever pick up a gun. You could have shot yourself, or Tas, or me. Do you understand?"

The boy didn't answer, couldn't answer. His breath snagged in his throat, and he tried to gulp in air.

"This is not your house," Wylie snapped. "You could have killed someone. You shouldn't be going through other people's things." Wylie moved to the closet and shoved the gun as far back as it would go on the top shelf. As she turned back around, she saw the boy crawl beneath her bed.

Wylie felt like she was going to be sick. She never worried

about locking the gun away here because she was the only one in the house. She had no guests; no one came to visit.

"Tas, hush!" Wylie shouted, and Tas's barks faded to soft whimpers. He looked up at her with trepidation.

Wylie lowered herself to the edge of the bed and tried to calm her thumping heart. When she trusted her voice again she spoke. "I shouldn't have yelled. I didn't mean to scare you." There was no response, just the soft snuffling hitches of the boy's breath from beneath the bed.

"It wasn't your fault. It was mine. I should have had the gun locked away. Come out," Wylie urged.

The boy remained beneath the bed. "I was scared," Wylie tried to explain. "Have you ever been scared? Really, really scared?"

What a silly thing to ask, Wylie thought to herself. Of course, the boy had been scared. He was just in a terrible car accident and had wandered alone through the storm and nearly froze to death. The boy knew what it was like to be scared. To be terrified.

Wylie waited. The boy's frantic breaths eased. Minutes passed. Wylie felt a gentle tug on her pant leg like a tiny sunfish pulling on a night crawler. She bent over, head between her legs so that she could peer beneath the bed. The boy's tearstained face looked back at her. "Will you come out?" Wylie asked.

The boy eased himself out from beneath the bed and got to his feet. Though he didn't speak, Wylie knew what questions he wanted to be answered.

"I found the truck," Wylie said carefully. "No one else." A blatant lie, but why add to his anxiety? The boy's shoulders sagged with disappointment. "Was your mom in the truck with you? Or someone else?" she asked. "Someone you cared about?" The boy didn't respond.

Wylie reached for the boy's hands. His skin was cold, and

the bones beneath felt like they could break within her grasp. He pulled away at her touch as if burned.

"Once the storm passes, I'll look more," Wylie promised. She reached into her pocket and pulled out the dirty white scrap of fabric she found near the wrecked truck. "I found this. Does it belong to you?" Wylie asked.

The boy's eyes lit up and he smiled before reaching out his hand tentatively. Wylie handed the piece of cloth to him and he pressed it to his cheek.

Why hadn't the woman waited for Wylie to come back for her? Where could she have possibly gone? Wylie couldn't help thinking that maybe she was into some bad business and was running away. Her mind raced with possibilities: She was running from the law or from an abusive husband. Maybe it was as simple as the woman being disoriented from the accident and she wandered off into the storm.

They came back down the stairs and Wylie fed another stick of wood into the fireplace. The boy had a funny way of turning his body to the side and watching what was going on around him out of the corner of his eye as if trying not to be noticed. Wylie straightened the blankets on the sofa, Tas jumped up, turned around three times, and settled into one corner. This time she didn't reprimand him.

Wylie went to the kitchen to get the boy a glass of water. He had to be hungry too. She dug through the cupboards and found a box of Cheerios and filled a bowl. She took the dry cereal and the glass and found the boy curled up next to Tas on the sofa, thumb in his mouth.

"You should drink something," Wylie said, holding the glass of water toward him, but tight-lipped, he turned his head away. "Okay," Wylie said, setting the glass and bowl of cereal on the coffee table. "Help yourself when you're ready."

The boy's eyes grew heavy, and soon his breathing matched Tas's; they were asleep.

Wylie checked her watch. How could it be only midnight?

Outside, the storm had worked itself into a frenzy. The wind bayed angrily, and the snow scoured the windows. Wylie kept looking outside, hoping to see the woman coming toward the house, but all she could see were froths of white. After a while, she gave up. The woman either found help on the snowed-in road, which was unlikely, or she succumbed to the weather.

Wylie retrieved her manuscript and folder filled with crime scene photos from upstairs and considered pouring herself a glass of wine but settled on coffee. She tried to read but kept looking at the sleeping form nestled on the sofa. Who was he? Someone else had to be out there looking for him.

Periodically, she checked the landline but was met with the same silence. For the first time in a long time, she wanted to talk to someone.

Not to just anyone. Wylie wanted to talk to her son. She wanted to apologize for just taking off. She had been so frustrated with him, so tired of the arguments, of Seth pitting her ex-husband against her. And when he took off that night and didn't come home—that was pure torture. She didn't know where Seth was, who he was with, didn't know if he was alive or dead.

Wylie had taken the easy way out as a parent. Seth's words had hurt her so much. He hated her, wanted to go live with his father. Wounded, she used finishing her book as an excuse, came to this sad, lonely place. Wylie left her son and only God knew what it would take to mend their relationship.

At that moment, she would have been content to talk to Seth about school and his friends, but that was impossible.

Now Wylie was the lone caretaker of another child—one she was ill-equipped to tend to.

The storm raged, the shadows shifted, darkened. She checked her watch; 1:00 a.m. Wylie hated these quiet moments. It felt like the entire world was asleep except for her. The moment the dove-colored light peeked between the edges of the curtains, she would relax. She would close her eyes, and for just a moment, she would be like everyone else.

Wylie awoke to the creak of floorboards. She blinked sleepily to find the child sitting on the floor next to the fire, his back to her.

Something fell from the boy's fingers and fluttered to the floor. Photos of throats slit open, broken teeth, empty eye sockets. Oh, no, Wylie thought. He had found the crime scene photos. The boy stumbled to his feet and he ran from the room. Wylie jumped from the sofa to follow him. He barely made it to the bathroom before his stomach tilted and heaved and bile, hot and sour, erupted from his mouth.

The boy retched until there was nothing left in his stomach.

"You shouldn't have seen those," Wylie said from just outside the darkened bathroom. "I'm so sorry. They're for my work. I'm a writer."

The boy climbed into the small space between the wall and the toilet and covered his face with his hands.

Wylie lingered in the doorway for a moment, and when it was clear that the boy wasn't going to come out of the bathroom, she returned to the living room.

How could Wylie adequately explain what those awful images were for? There were no words. He thought she was a monster, and any chances of getting the boy to trust her were now lost.

14

August 2000

From her hiding spot in the field, Josie fought the urge to run. He could be lying in wait, poised to pounce the minute she moved. So Josie waited. She waited for something to happen, for someone to help, to come to find her. She kept willing her father or mother to push their way through the stalks, but they didn't appear.

The clouds evaporated, and the moon stared garishly down at her. Josie kept time by its slow crawl across the sky. She fought back nausea, afraid that if she vomited, the person with the gun would hear her retching and discover her location. She couldn't keep the tears from falling though, her body convulsed with silent sobs until her head pounded and jaw ached from forcing back the screams.

Josie shivered despite the heat of the night. The wound in

her arm had stopped bleeding, but she could feel the nubby buckshot embedded in the fleshy part of her tricep.

She had stayed on her feet for as long as she could, but her muscles began to seize. The mosquitoes feasted on her bare skin, their bites like a thousand pinpricks. She finally crouched down, sat back on her heels, pulled her arms into her T-shirt and over her knees. The pain in her arm was a drumbeat. Miserable, Josie sat there like a plump corn flea beetle waiting for daylight.

With every soft rustle of the corn, her heart would boomerang from terror to hope. Someone had to have heard the gunshots. Sound traveled for miles through the countryside. Surely, someone would have heard the pop of gunfire, become alarmed and called the police. She half expected her father to appear, hold out his hand to help her up and take her home. But he never came. No one did.

Hours passed. The stars faded, and the sky above was slowly stripped of its nightclothes and replaced with gauzy veils of pink and tangerine. Josie's mouth was dry and her tongue heavy with thirst. Every time she moved, a jolt coursed through her arm, and she whimpered with pain.

She had broken her ankle once when she was ten. She and Becky were hopping across the maze of round hay bales in her field when she misjudged the distance to the next bale of hay and tumbled six feet to the hard-packed earth.

That pain was intense—but nothing compared to being shot. When Josie could no longer stand the fullness of her bladder, she unfolded herself from the cocoon of her T-shirt and stood. Using only one hand, she awkwardly pulled down her shorts and relieved herself, urging the unending stream of urine to hurry up.

Josie was so thirsty that she was tempted to step out of the field to get a drink of water but couldn't bring herself to leave the camouflage the corn provided. She tried to keep time by the movement of the shadows. She wanted to lie down and sleep but was afraid that the gunman would find her.

A dry, papery crackle moved through the field, and the corn shivered and swayed above her. Someone was coming. Panic clutched at her throat. She wouldn't be able to outrun him; she had no weapon, no protection. Josie braced herself for what was coming.

But instead of someone crashing through the crops, a large black cloud swept over her head and dipped and rose and fell and rose again. Red-winged blackbirds, thick as smoke, making their annual migration through the fields, gathered on the stalks above her.

Josie's father would be irritated to no end. It happened every year; the glossy black birds with red and yellow shoulder patches swooped through the fields to feast on their corn. She expected to hear the loud bangs of the propane exploders, a device that her father relied on, to scare away the pesky birds. The cracks never came, only the flapping of wings and the chatter of the redwings.

Josie couldn't stay hidden in the field forever. No one was coming to rescue her. She needed to save herself. Josie struggled to her feet, and the cloud of birds noisily rose and moved on to another section of the field. Her leg muscles screamed in protest, her arm pulsed and was swollen and hot to the touch. Another wave of nausea washed over her, and Josie closed her eyes and conjured up their farmyard at dawn.

It calmed her, the thought of the big red barn and her mom and dad drinking coffee at the kitchen table. The morning sun gliding up from behind the barn meant that if she headed in the opposite direction of the sun, she would come out of the field somewhere near the house.

Step by step, Josie made her way through the canopy of green, the hot morning sun burning the top of her head. She quickly found the path she took the night before. Stalks lay flat, leaving a crumpled, frenetic trail. Josie's heart hammered in her chest.

She was so close to home. She wanted to run toward the house, fling open the front door and find her parents, Ethan, and Becky sitting at the kitchen table, irritated because she made them late getting on the road to the fair, but Josie was too scared. Instead, she hovered on the edges of the field, peeking between the thick stems.

At first glance, everything looked just as it should. The yard and house looked the same as always. Her father's truck and her mother's car sat in the drive. Ruby-throated hummingbirds hovered above the bright orange butterfly weed next to the house. The copper weather vane rooster atop the barn spun in the hot breeze.

But still, Josie couldn't bring herself to step out into the open. The screen on the back door swung on its hinges. Maybe everyone overslept, Josie thought hopefully, though she knew it wasn't likely. The outdoor goat pen was empty, and human-like cries came from the closed-up barn. Josie knew it was just hungry bleats coming from the goats, but their desperate calls caused the hair to stand up on her arms. Her father never forgot to feed and milk the goats.

She wanted to sprint to the house and find her family and Becky waiting for her, but the soles of her feet, chewed up by rocks and parched earth made it impossible. She cringed with each step.

The chickens in the coop clucked at her approach, harassing Josie to feed and water them. Please let everyone still be asleep, she begged silently.

Josie looked up at the house. She remembered the bangs and the flash of light she saw in her parents' bedroom window the night before. Nothing moved behind the curtains, but they were a bit askew, as if someone was peeking out from behind them.

It was just a bad dream, Josie told herself; she had been walking in her sleep. The more she thought about it, the more it made sense. She'd had an awful nightmare.

Once past the barn and the henhouse, the goats and chickens grew quiet. She passed the old shed where her mother kept her gardening tools and passed the trampoline where she and Becky had jumped with so much joy the night before. It felt like a million years ago.

Josie cocked her head in hopes of hearing her mother and father chatting at the kitchen table. All was quiet except the creak and bang of the screen door opening and closing with the hot breeze.

Josie caught the screen door midswing, stepped into the mudroom, and closed it behind her. She'd get a talking-to for leaving the door open all night too. Josie spotted her father's dusty work boots on the mudroom floor and another surge of anxiety rushed through her.

The kitchen was empty. There was the hum of the refrigerator, the whir of a ceiling fan. In the living room, a pair of Ethan's tennis shoes lay on the floor and the paperback book her mother had been reading lay open on the arm of the sofa.

Josie moved to the bottom of the stairs and looked up.

"Mom? Dad?" she called out. No answer. She couldn't lift her left hand to place it on the banister so she hugged the right side, her shoulder grazing the wall to steady herself.

She should have turned around and gone right back down the steps, but she couldn't stop her hand from pushing open her parents' bedroom door and stepping over the threshold. The room was dim, the sun diluted by the curtains that covered the windows. The air smelled out of place but familiar. A prickle of fear buzzed through her.

"Mom, Dad," Josie whispered, jiggling the bed. "It's time to get up." There was no answer. It was too quiet.

Her eyes drifted to the right where a sunburst of blood tattooed the wall next to the bed. She followed the scarlet spray downward to where a figure was slumped in the corner, eyes wide, a fist-sized hole in her chest. Josie couldn't tear her gaze from the horror in front of her. It vaguely resembled her mother, but how was that possible? The twisted grimace on her face was one out of a horror film. Her blood-soaked nightgown clung to her skin.

The cord to the powder blue telephone next to the bed was ripped from the wall and lay in a jumbled heap beside her mother.

A strange numbness spread through Josie's limbs and her ears filled with the thrum of her heartbeat. She stumbled from the room.

"Dad?" she cried out. "Daddy?" She careened toward her bedroom but stopped abruptly. On the floor, peeking from the doorway, was a hand, closed as if trying to make a half-hearted fist. Josie didn't want to see what that hand was attached to, but she knew. Her father. But she didn't want to see what he had become. Still, she moved forward. The glint of a gold wedding ring winked up at her.

Josie let out a tremulous breath and looked around the door frame. Her father's face was gone, replaced with an unrecognizable canvas of blood and bone and gray matter. A scream lodged in her throat, she turned, and in her hurry to get away, Josie felt the give of soft flesh as her bare foot struck her father's hand. In terror, she ran down the stairs, her feet barely touching the steps. She flung open the front door and stepped out into the unrelenting sunshine and started running.

At half past seven in the morning, Matthew Ellis was heading past his daughter and son-in-law's farm just a mile from theirs down on Meadow Rue. He was on his way to town to meet up with some of the other old-timers for coffee at the feed store.

Matthew saw it weaving back and forth across the road from about a hundred yards away. Behind the shimmer of heat rising from the asphalt, Matthew, at first glance, thought it was a deer that had gotten hit by a car.

As he drove closer, he realized that the battered, bloody figure was no animal, but a person, hunched over with pain careening from one side of the road to the other.

Matthew later told investigators that *it was like coming across a zombie from one of those old movies. It was dead eyed and lurching, and my heart nearly stopped when I saw who it was.*

If Josie was aware of the truck approaching, she gave no indication. Her grandfather pulled off to the side of the road and leaped from his truck.

"Josie?" he asked. "What happened? What are you doing?" Josie acted as if she didn't hear him, just kept walking. Not knowing what to do, Matthew finally grabbed Josie by the shoulders and forced her to look at him.

"Josie," he said, staring into her red, unfocused eyes. "What happened? Where are you going?"

"To your house," Josie managed to croak. It was an odd response, Matthew thought, since Josie was heading in the wrong direction. Josie's arm was swollen and caked with dried blood and her arms and legs were slashed with scratches that were too many to count. He led Josie to his truck and helped her inside.

"What happened, Shoo?" Matthew asked, using the nickname he had given Josie as a toddler when she would follow him around everywhere. "Shoo fly, shoo," he'd tease, and Josie would giggle and buzz after him. "What happened?" he asked in alarm. "Was there an accident?"

"I thought there must have been an accident at home," Matthew told the deputy when he arrived on the scene. "It was the only thing that made sense at that moment. They were leaving for the state fair early that morning. They should have been on the road already. I decided to take Josie back to her house. I never imagined I'd find what I did."

When Matthew and Josie pulled down the lane and parked behind two vehicles in the drive—his son-in-law's Chevy truck and the minivan that Lynne drove. The only vehicle missing was Ethan's truck.

This was where Matthew took another look at his granddaughter. A bright red rash feathered her cheeks, her hair was tangled and unbrushed, her eyes swollen and bloodshot as if she'd been crying. She was barefoot and dirty and it looked like someone took a switch to her legs. It was a closer look at Josie's arm that caused Matthew's throat to close up. He'd seen injuries like this before. "Josie, what happened to your arm," Matthew asked.

Next to him in the truck, Josie forced her eyes open and looked down. Her arm was bloody and swollen and dimpled like a golf ball where the buckshot had embedded her skin.

Despite the hot morning, Josie began to shiver.

"Where is everyone?" Matthew asked.

Josie looked out the window toward the second floor of the house.

"Up there?" Matthew asked, his voice filled with fear. Josie nodded. "Do I need to call for help?"

Josie nodded again and then turned her head away, resting it against the car window.

Matthew stepped from the truck. The yard was silent except for the insistent tick of the engine cooling down. "Stay here," he told her as he moved toward the back of the house.

Josie's grandfather entered the house through the screen door, which creaked and banged shut behind him. Josie remembered screwing her eyes shut as if this could protect her grandfather from what he was about to see.

And even though she covered her ears, Josie still heard his strangled cry, the thumping on the steps, and the crash of the back door being thrown open. She heard the gasp of her grandfather trying to draw air into his lungs and then the wretched sound of gagging and the rush of liquid hitting the ground.

Matthew's anguished cries filled the air and Josie pressed her hands more tightly against her ears to block out the sound, but it did no good.

Deb Cutter, who was in her yard, a mile away as the crow flies, reported she heard the cries. She looked up from her weeding when the shrieking didn't stop, and thinking it must be an injured animal, Deb wished to herself that someone would put the poor creature out of its misery. Frightened, Deb gathered up the sheets hanging from the clothesline and took them inside.

Gradually Matthew's cries turned to a soft keening and then to silence. Josie remembered hearing the screen door creak open again. He was going back inside? Why? she wondered. Why would he do that?

He wasn't inside for long. Josie heard the truck door opening and the soft snick of it closing again as her grandfather climbed back into the truck. She dared to take a peek at him. He sat slumped in the driver's seat with his head bent and his weathered, age-spotted hands gripping the steering wheel. They sat that way for what felt like a long time, the temperature in the truck rising as each second passed.

In the distance, a faint, persistent wail bloomed. Sirens. Help was coming.

"Shoo," Matthew croaked. "What happened here?" He raised his head and his red-rimmed eyes found Josie's.

"I think they're dead," Josie whispered. "Did you find Ethan and Becky?" she asked.

"No, just your…" He let out a shuddery breath. His hands wouldn't stop shaking.

"I let go of Becky's hand," Josie said as if in a daze. "I'm sorry, I didn't mean to." The sirens were getting louder.

"It's time to get out," Matthew said as he opened the truck door. The blare of the sirens peaked and then abruptly stopped as two Blake County sheriff's cars turned into Josie's driveway and parked. "Stay behind me, Shoo," he said and Josie held on to his belt loop as two men climbed out of their police cars, guns drawn. Once out in the open, Matthew held his hands up.

"They're upstairs," Matthew said, nodding toward the house. "They've been shot."

15

The little girl sat on floor while her mother braided her hair. "When I was little, I had hair like this," her mother said. "My mom used to braid my hair into a fishtail, but I never learned how to do that kind of braid."

The girl liked hearing stories about when her mother was young, but it was a rare occurrence. Her mother's parents were dead, and it made her sad to talk about them, so when they were mentioned, the girl savored every word.

The girl was just about to ask what a fishtail braid was when her mother suddenly gave a soft groan. "What's wrong?" the girl asked, twisting around. Her mother stood and swayed. A bright red stain bloomed between her legs and blood oozed down her thighs.

"It's the baby," her mother murmured as she staggered to the bathroom.

"Is she coming?" the girl asked because she was sure the baby was going to be a girl.

"It's too soon," her mother cried as she peeled off her shorts and then shut the bathroom door.

The girl stood on the other side of the closed door and listened as her mother moaned and cried out. She was so loud. Too loud. The girl looked anxiously to the door at the top of the steps and hoped her mother's cries weren't disturbing her father. He'd be so angry.

"Shhh," the girl said through the door. "Shhhh." But her mother's groans continued, rose and fell like waves. She sat down on the floor, back against the door, and waited, praying for help but also praying that her father wouldn't come.

Was this what dying sounded like? the girl wondered. What would she do without her mother? Who would take care of her? Her father barely paid her any mind. It was her mother who sang her to sleep, braided her hair, and painted her nails, the one who held her close when she had bad dreams.

The room grew dark, and still, her mother remained on the other side of the door. There were so many things to be afraid of, but the dark wasn't one of them. The girl didn't mind the dark one bit. There were three kinds of dark. In the morning, there was the gray-edged dark that gradually slid into blues and pinks and meant that most likely, her father would be going to work soon. It was always better when her father was away though it made her mother more anxious. Her mother worried that he wouldn't come back, and then what would they do? They wouldn't have money for food and clothes. Her mother fretted, but the girl felt more relaxed in the long hours that he was away.

Then there was after-dinner dark. This was the time after she washed her face and brushed her teeth. She would sit on the sofa between her mom and dad and watch one of the movies that they pushed into the little machine that sat beneath the television. After-dinner dark was made up of hazy purples and navy blues and gave her an all-is-right-with-the-world feeling. Watching TV together, sometimes sharing a bowl of popcorn, told the girl that her family wasn't all that different than the ones in the movies.

But after-dinner dark was also the most unsettling time of day. If her father was in a bad mood or her mother sad, there was nowhere for her to go. She had to listen to the angry words, the tears, and the sharp slaps and punches. In these times, she would go to her favorite spot beneath the window and look at books in the fading light peeking through the gap between the shade and pane of glass.

The blackest dark came in the middle of the night. It was warm and velvety and sounded like her mother's breathing right next to her.

It isn't the dark you should be afraid of, the girl thought, it's the monsters who step out into the light that you need to fear.

16

Present Day

While Wylie waited for the boy to come out of the bathroom, she opened the front door to let Tas outside. The storm had picked up steam again, the cold burrowing through the folds of her clothing. This time, Tas quickly returned.

The boy couldn't stay in the bathroom the entire night. It was too cold. Wylie tapped on the door. There was no response.

"Are you okay in there?" Wylie asked. Still no answer. She turned the knob and the door swung open. The boy sat there, fists pressed to his eyes.

The child was as skittish as a frightened deer, and Wylie knew she would need to carefully choose her next words. "I know you're scared. I know those pictures were scary. I write books about people who get hurt—I try to tell their stories.

But I would never hurt anyone. Do you understand that?"
The boy still refused to meet her gaze.

"I want to help you. I want to get ahold of your family, but
I need your help to do it."

She beckoned to the little boy to move toward her, but he
remained fixed to his spot.

She couldn't blame him.

Though it was the middle of the night, Wylie doubted
the boy would sleep again after what he saw in those photos.
She moved to the kitchen, and after a minute, she heard the
boy's soft steps behind her. "I bet you're hungry," Wylie said.
"Would you like something to eat?"

The boy didn't respond. "Well, I'm starved." She opened the
refrigerator. "Let's see, what do we have in here? How about
eggs and pancakes?" Wylie set the egg carton on the counter
and pulled the pancake mix from the cupboard. "What would
you like to drink?" Wylie asked. "I've got milk, juice, and
water. Or coffee. Do you drink coffee? I bet you take it black."

Wylie looked over to see if her little joke made the boy
crack a smile, but his face remained inscrutable, and he rubbed
a small hand across the top of his shorn head. "How's your
head?" she asked. "It must hurt."

The boy fingered the bruise on his temple but didn't speak.

"Oh, your clothes should be dry by now," Wylie said. "I'll
be right back." Wylie darted to the laundry room, retrieved
the boy's clothes from the dryer, and set them on a kitchen
chair. "You can go on into the bathroom and get dressed. By
the time you come back the first batch of pancakes will be
done."

The boy snatched the clothes from the chair as if expecting to be swatted and hurried from the room. Wylie cracked

the eggs into a bowl and poured the pancake batter into a hot skillet.

Wylie flipped the pancakes and set the butter, syrup, and a bowl of grapes on the kitchen table.

"Do you like pancakes?" she asked as the boy sidled back into the room.

Wylie set a pancake on a plate and handed it to him. "You sit right on down and get started. I'll join you in a second."

Wylie brought a plateful of pancakes and the skillet of scrambled eggs to the table, scooped some onto the boy's plate, and then added some to her own. She sat across from him at the round, oak table. "Go ahead and eat," she urged, "you don't have to wait for me." The boy stared uncertainly up at her.

"Do you want me to cut your food for you?" Wylie asked, but the boy pulled his plate close and picked up the pancake with his fingers.

She watched as the boy dragged it through a puddle of syrup, brought it tentatively to his lips, and took an experimental lick. Deciding that it was okay, the boy ate the rest of the pancake and then started in on the second one that Wylie slid onto his plate. He ate without pause, barely taking time to chew and swallow.

"Slow down," Wylie said. "There's plenty more where that came from."

The boy bent over his plate to sniff at the scrambled eggs and then wrinkled his nose.

"That's okay," Wylie assured him. "You don't have to eat anything you don't want to."

The boy looked longingly toward the door.

"Remember the storm?" Wylie asked. "It's not safe to go outside right now. The roads are very bad." The boy shifted in his chair as if ready to bolt.

Wylie didn't want to panic the child, but she didn't want to lie to him any more than she already had. "I promise I'm going to do my best to get you home," she said. "It can't snow forever." The boy seemed to think about this as a few tears escaped and slid down his cheeks.

"Don't cry," Wylie said in alarm. "How about we play a game?" Wylie asked, hoping to distract him.

The boy looked at her suspiciously.

"It's called First You, Then Me," Wylie said, standing up from the table. She picked up her plate and carried it to the sink. "First, you ask me a question, and then I ask you one. Do you want to start? All you do is ask me a question like what my favorite things are, and I answer it."

Wylie rinsed the plates and placed them in the dishwasher. "Okay, then. I'll start," Wylie said when the boy didn't answer.

Wylie looked up at the ceiling and tapped her chin as if deep in thought. She wanted to come up with an easy question. One that wouldn't be too personal. "What's your favorite color?" Wylie asked. No answer.

Wylie decided to try a different tack. "Well, Wylie," Wylie said with a childish lilt to her voice. "My favorite color is blue. How about you?"

Wylie returned to her regular voice. "Now isn't that a coincidence? My favorite color is blue too."

Wylie looked at the boy for some kind of reaction but he just stared back at her blankly. Maybe he didn't speak English, or maybe there was a physical reason he couldn't talk. Or he was just scared shitless.

Wylie sighed. "Well, I can tell you about me, I guess. You've met Tas. Do you have a dog?" Wylie paused for just a moment, not expecting an answer, and then launched into her next question.

"My favorite TV show is *Dateline*. What's yours," Wylie asked as she refilled the boy's glass with milk.

The boy snatched a grape from the bowl and took an experimental nibble. Had he never eaten a grape either? Wylie wondered.

The boy wouldn't even look at her.

Wylie threw up her hands. The boy flinched at the movement. "I just wish you would tell me your name. That's it, your name. Why is that so hard?" she asked.

The boy considered this and looked as if he might speak but instead clamped his mouth shut.

More alarms began to go off in Wylie's head. She knew that she gave the boy very little reason to trust her, but she had saved him from freezing to death. What could be so bad that he couldn't even utter his name or his parents' names? What kinds of secrets was this child keeping and why?

17

"It's Matthew Ellis," Matthew called out with a shaky voice.

"We got a call about a shooting," Sheriff Butler said, lowering his weapon warily. At his side was Deputy Levi Robbins, who'd pulled down the lane just after the sheriff.

"That was me," Matthew said. His next sentence was unintelligible, and the sheriff had to ask him to repeat it. "My daughter and her husband are dead," Matthew repeated, his voice strangled with tears. "There's blood everywhere," he cried, looking at the sheriff desperately. "Everywhere."

Josie, still behind him, pressed her face into his back. "They shot Josie too," Matthew said, wiping his eyes with a handkerchief he pulled from his back pocket.

"We've got help coming. Let me take a look," Butler said. Josie remained behind her grandfather.

"It's okay, Shoo," Matthew said, moving aside so that the girl came into view. "They're here to help."

Levi gave a low whistle. He didn't understand how the girl could still be standing. Josie swayed on her feet, and her grandfather grabbed her uninjured arm and guided her to the truck's running board where she sat.

"Don't worry, honey, an ambulance is on its way," the sheriff assured her. "You said *they shot Josie*. There was more than one person?"

Matthew leaned against the truck to steady himself. "I don't know. I don't know who did this."

"You think they're gone?" The sheriff's eyes scanned the property.

"I didn't see anybody else in the house," Matthew said. "Aww, Jesus, it's bad. It's really, really bad."

"You went inside?" Butler asked.

Matthew nodded. "I found Lynne in her bedroom and William in Josie's room. I don't know where my grandson is." A new wave of tears overtook him.

"We have to make sure the house is clear before we send the EMTs inside," the sheriff said apologetically. "You understand that, don't you, Matthew?"

"Not much you can do for them now," Matthew whispered.

Josie reached up and tugged on his shirtsleeve. "Don't say that, Grandpa. They have to try," she insisted. "They can take them to the hospital and make them better." Josie cried, her tears carving a path down her dirty face.

"You let us take care of things now, darling," Sheriff Butler said in a low soothing voice.

"I need you to move away from the house now," the sheriff said. "Let us do our job now." He and Levi needed to view the crime scene then secure it. For all they knew, the perpetrator was still inside the house. And there was the outside chance that one or more of the victims was still alive. Precious seconds were being lost. Seconds that could never be retrieved.

The sun had already burned away the morning moisture. With a sweat-slicked hand, Matthew held Josie by the elbow as she limped over to the old maple tree and sat beneath its green canopy to wait. The sheriff and Levi moved cautiously through the back door, weapons drawn.

The next moments passed in a hazy blur. More deputies arrived, and Matthew once again told them what he knew.

The cry of an oncoming ambulance filled the air and Matthew joined Josie beneath the maple tree. He wrapped his arms around his granddaughter, being careful to avoid her injured arm, and Josie buried her face in his shoulder, inhaling the scent of tobacco mixed with the harsh detergent used to wash his work clothes.

"We'll have them check you out, Shoo, while they look for Ethan, okay?" Matthew said, wiping Josie's tears from beneath her eyes with his thumbs.

The ambulance turned down the lane and came to a stop just beyond the crime tape. Out stepped two paramedics, a man and a woman. They opened the back doors, scanned the scene in front of them, and waited for direction from one of the deputies.

Matthew waved the EMTs over. "My granddaughter was shot," he told the paramedics, who quickly grabbed a gurney and rushed toward them. They transitioned Josie to the stretcher and carried her to the ambulance's back deck where they could get a better look at her injuries.

"You won't leave just yet, will you?" Matthew asked the female paramedic.

"We'll check her out, but by the look of that arm, we'll need to take her to the hospital in Algona. We need to get going soon, but I'll let you know before we leave," she said, giving Matthew a reassuring smile.

"I'll be right back, honey," Matthew said, and Josie clutched at his hand, not wanting him to go. "I won't go out of your sight," he promised. Josie reluctantly released his grip.

Once through the unlocked front door, Sheriff Butler made a mental note to ask Matthew Ellis if he had just walked into the home or used a key.

The house was dim and quiet and had the feel of being empty. Butler and Levi started in the living room, looked behind the heavy drapes and in the closet, cleared it, and then moved on to check the first-floor bathroom.

"No one in here," Levi declared, "but it looks like we've got some blood in the sink."

Sheriff Butler stuck his head in the room. The bottom and sides of the white porcelain sink were covered with a pinkish film. Butler nodded. The two moved on to the dining room. In the middle of the room was a large wide-planked wooden table surrounded by six chairs. An arrangement of dried flowers sat in the center of the table.

"Clear," Butler called, wiping sweat from his face. The room was hotter than a Dutch oven though he noted that there was an air-conditioning unit in the window. It was odd that the unit wasn't running in this heat, especially since the windows were shut tight.

Levi took the lead and entered the kitchen first. It too was empty. A coffee maker was filled with black liquid. Levi reached out to touch the glass pot—it was cool to the touch. Hanging on a key rack next to the back door were two sets of keys that probably went to the vehicles parked outside.

"Should we check downstairs?" Levi asked, nodding toward the basement door.

Butler checked the slide lock near the top of the door. It was in place. "Door's locked from outside," he said. "We'll clear it after we go upstairs. That's where Matthew said the victims are."

Butler led the way up the stairs. The heat was stifling. Beads of sweat dripped into his eyes. Butler could smell fear emanating from the younger deputy's skin. Levi had seen plenty of dead bodies before, the casualties from motor vehicle accidents, two suicides, and the corpse of a man who tripped over his own gun and shot himself while turkey hunting, but never the victim of a murder. Levi had no idea what they were walking into. The sheriff had seen it all, but it didn't make it any easier to step into a crime scene. Was it a murder-suicide? Had an intruder entered the home and started shooting? If so, what was the motive?

On the staircase, there was a blind turn coming up. They had no idea who or what was around the corner. Butler tried to listen for any sound above them, but all he could hear was his own breathing. They needed to stay alert. The sheriff signaled for Levi to stop, took a deep breath, and quickly rounded the corner with his firearm at the ready. No one there. He paused to steady his breath and continued upward.

When Butler reached the second-floor landing, the smell hit him in the face. Rust intermingled with the scent of fecal matter. Blood and the bowels relaxing soon after death.

"Jesus," Levi said.

"Breathe through your mouth," Butler ordered as he moved down the hallway. He pushed open the first door. A bathroom. He pulled aside the shower curtain. No one there. "Clear," Butler called over his shoulder. They were getting closer.

Levi stood in front of a closed bedroom door. He was afraid

to touch the knob. What if he wiped away fingerprints? He didn't want to see what was behind the door. He glanced back at the sheriff who nodded at him. Trying to touch as little surface as possible, Levi twisted the knob, nudged the door open, and stepped into the room with his gun drawn. The smell was overwhelming, and Levi resisted the urge to cover his nose.

The morning sun seeped through the edges of the blinds. At first glance, the room looked like any other bedroom. A dresser sat against the wall topped with framed family photos, an unmade bed, a stack of books, and a scattering of coins on a bedside table. But the carnage next to the bed was unmistakable. A woman. Her body already decomposing in the sweltering heat of the room.

Behind him, Levi heard Butler's voice. "Room clear?" he asked.

It took a second for Levi to react, but he bent down, lifted the lace-edged bed skirt, and looked beneath the bed. He half expected someone to peer back at him. No one there. He checked the closet, also empty.

"Clear," Levi breathed, running a hand through this damp hair. "First victim," he said as the sheriff squeezed through the doorway behind him.

"Ah, man," Butler said. "That's Lynne Doyle. Looks like a gunshot to the chest at pretty close range."

"Mr. Ellis said that there were two bodies," Levi said as they backed out of the room.

"Yeah, you cover me this time," Butler said. "I'll go first. You okay?" he looked at Levi with concern. His face was pale, eyes wide.

"I'm good," Levi answered.

The sheriff led the way, pausing at the next bedroom on the left. This door stood wide-open and the male victim lay face-up on the hardwood floor. He was barefoot and dressed in boxers and a T-shirt, but where his face should have been was a great yawning wound that exposed bone and gray matter.

"Damn," Levi breathed. "That the husband?" he asked, his heart pounding.

"Looks like it, but we'll have to confirm that," Butler said.

Levi looked around the room. It was clearly a young teen's room. The girl sitting outside beneath the maple tree. On the wall, there was a poster of a horse galloping through a yellow meadow and another of NSYNC. The baseboards were decorated with baseball stickers.

There was a single bed covered in a purple comforter and piled with stuffed animals. Either the bed was made earlier or wasn't slept in. There was a white wooden dresser with a softball glove and a bottle of pink nail polish sitting atop it. Above the dresser was a bulletin board covered with 4-H ribbons. Next to the bed were two unrolled sleeping bags.

"Come on," Butler said. "We have one more room to check out."

The final room, a typical teenage boy's room with piles of dirty clothes, pop cans, and car magazines. It smelled like sweat socks and Axe body spray. No dead bodies.

The men returned to the hallway stood in the doorway where the male victim was. "What do you think? Murder-suicide?" Levi asked. "He offed the wife and killed himself in here?"

"Doesn't look like a suicide to me," the sheriff answered. "No weapon."

"Right," Levi said, nodding. "Now we talk to the girl downstairs and find the brother?"

"And find the other girl," the sheriff said grimly.

"Other girl?" Levi asked. "What do you mean?"

"There are two sleeping bags on the floor," Butler explained. "The gym bag filled with clothes next to it. It was a sleepover." The sheriff shook his head. "What the hell happened to the other girl?"

In the ambulance, paramedic Lowell Steubens was trying to distract Josie Doyle from the frenzy of activity just beyond them. Lanky and long limbed, with basset hound brown eyes and an easy smile that put his injured charges at ease, thirty-nine-year-old Lowell had gone to elementary school with Lynne Doyle and remembered her as a shy, quiet girl but they hadn't said more than a few words to each other in passing. Despite the small community, Lowell and Lynne ran in different circles.

"You look cold," Lowell observed. "Let's check you out quick and then I'll get you a blanket." Josie didn't respond. She closed her eyes but couldn't mute the deputies' chatter, the click and buzz of their radios. Sounds so foreign to the farm. The back of the ambulance smelled like a hospital room. Like rubbing alcohol.

There was the snap of latex gloves and Josie flinched.

The female paramedic gently brushed a stray lock of hair from Josie's eyes.

"My name is Erin," she said. "And this is my friend, Lowell. We're going to check you out, and then once Sheriff Butler says we can leave, we'll take you to the hospital so the docs can take a look at your arm. How about you let me look at your other one so I can take your blood pressure?" she asked.

Josie held up her right arm so the woman could wrap the blood pressure cuff around her biceps. Josie winced as the pressure in her arm built and then eased. "Did I hurt you?" Erin asked. "I'm sorry."

"No," Josie said dully. "It doesn't hurt. Just feels weird."

There was a flurry of activity next to the house. Josie tried to sit up to see what was happening. Lowell eased her back down on the stretcher.

"Can you tell me what happened to your arm?" he asked. A bloody ragged notch had been taken out of the fleshy part of Josie's tricep, and buckshot was embedded in the skin.

"We were playing on the trampoline and we heard the bangs. We went to see what was going on and someone came after us and we ran. I made it to the field but Becky didn't. Then he shot me. Is Becky okay? Did you find her?"

Lowell and Erin exchanged a look. "I'm sure a deputy is going to talk to you soon," Erin murmured. "I'll go see what's happening."

"Do you know where my brother is?" Josie asked Lowell. "I couldn't find him or Becky."

"Try not to think about that now," Lowell said soothingly. "I'm going to leave your arm for the doc to take a closer look at," Lowell smiled encouragingly.

"This might sting a bit," Lowell said, lightly swiping the soles of Josie's feet with a with cold liquid. "It's alcohol," he explained. "To clean your cuts." Josie winced at the burning sensation. "They aren't too deep. We'll clean them up and get you to the hospital where the real docs will check you out."

"Can't I stay with my grandpa?" Josie asked. "My arm really doesn't hurt that bad."

"Sorry, kiddo," Lowell said. "We have to take you to the hospital, doctor's orders."

"I don't want to go," Josie said and tried to slip past Lowell.

"Whoa now," he said, catching Josie around the waist. "Hold up there. You don't want to get me in trouble, do you?"

Matthew, seeing the ruckus, came over to the ambulance. "Come on, Shoo," he said. "You stay put now. Let them help you."

Josie reluctantly sat back down. "You're going to come with me, aren't you?" she asked her grandfather.

Instead of answering, Matthew took her hand. "Listen," he

said. "The police will want to talk to you for a few minutes before they take you to the hospital. Do you think you can do that, Josie? It's really important. We need to do all we can to help find your brother and friend."

All Josie wanted to do was to forget. Forget the blood and her parents' broken bodies and the terror of being chased into the field, but the images were seared into her brain. She would never be able to forget but she could try and help. She would hold on to every detail and tell them to the police, so whoever did this would be caught and so that her brother and Becky would come home to them.

In Burden, Becky's mother, Margo Allen, had just started her shift at the grocery store and was pulling her green apron over her head and signing into her cash register when her first customer of the day approached her checkout lane. "How are you today, Bonnie?" Margo asked when Bonnie Mitchell laid her items on the counter.

"Oh, just fine," Bonnie said. "Did you hear what happened west of town?" she leaned in with a conspiratorial whisper.

"No, what?" Margo asked as she handed Bonnie her receipt.

"Big to-do near the old bitternut. All kinds of police out there, and that must have been why I heard the ambulance scream down the street a little while ago."

"Bitternut?" Margo repeated. "On Meadow Rue?" A brief flash of concern swept over her, but she quickly dismissed it. The Doyles lived on Meadow Rue. But they were supposed to leave for the fair in Des Moines a few hours ago. If something was wrong, surely she would have been contacted by now.

"Bet it's one of those meth houses," Bonnie said, shaking her head.

Margo handed the woman her bagged items and wished

her a good day. How many homes were actually on Meadow Rue? She replayed the drive over in her mind. At least four, probably more. Chances were it had nothing to do with the Doyles.

Margo looked around the store. There were only a few customers. "Hey, Tommy," Margo said to the boy placing freshly picked ears of corn on a display, "can you watch the front for a few minutes?"

Margo went to the break room and pulled her purse from the cupboard where she stored it during work hours. Inside was the little red notebook where she kept important numbers. She picked up the phone and dialed the Doyle house. It rang and rang. She hung up. Of course there was no answer. She checked her watch. It was just after 9:00 a.m. Margo fiddled with a strand of hair that escaped its clip.

The owner of the store, Leonard Shaffer, wouldn't mind if she stepped out for a bit. Tommy could cover things for a while. Her husband, almost ex-husband, she amended, would think she was silly, overprotective. Becky was growing up so fast, but she was still her little girl. A niggle of doubt kept poking at her. *Something's wrong, something's wrong.* Margo looked at her watch. She'd be there and back in about forty minutes. And what could it hurt? She'd just drive past the Doyle farm and then come right back.

Oblivious to the gathering crowd of law enforcement and paramedics, Levi burst out the front door and stumbled from the house. Hands on his knees, he gulped in the fresh air, trying to clear his nose and throat of the smell of blood and death. Close behind came Sheriff Butler, grim faced and drenched with sweat.

"Sheriff?" a young deputy stepped forward, his face shining with anticipation.

"Seal off the property," Sheriff Butler ordered. "No one comes or goes without my permission." The deputy nodded and ran off to spread the word and retrieve the yellow crime tape from his cruiser.

"Levi," Butler said.

Levi stood up straight and willed his stomach to settle.

"Sir?" he asked.

Butler looked over to where Matthew Ellis was standing beneath the maple tree, watching them carefully, hat in his hand. Butler gave a little shake of his head and Matthew's face fell.

"I need you to put a call in to the state police," Butler said, turning his attention to Levi. "Tell them we need some agents here ASAP." He mopped his sweaty forehead with his sleeve. "And tell them to bring the search dogs. We've got two dead bodies, two missing kids, and we're going to need all the help we can get."

18

Present Day

After eating, Wylie and the boy returned to the living room and sat in front of the fire. Wylie couldn't stop looking at him. The rash around his mouth seemed to be calming down a bit. It was still red but not as inflamed. Wylie leaned in more closely. Something silver and shiny glinted back up at her. Wylie lightly touched his face and rubbed. Surprisingly, the boy didn't pull away. His skin clung momentarily to Wylie's fingers, then pulled away.

Wylie carefully picked the small, silver fragment from the boy's bottom lip and rolled it between her fingers. It was gummy and sticky. Duct tape? It couldn't be.

"Did someone put tape over your mouth?" Wylie asked in a whisper.

The boy blinked up at Wylie. He wasn't shocked by the question and didn't react with indignation. He simply nodded.

"Who?" Wylie asked, her chest constricting with something she couldn't quite name. Horror, anger, sadness. All three, probably. "Your dad?" Wylie asked. "Your mom?"

Before the boy could respond, there was a thunderous crack. And then another and another. Wylie jumped to her feet, smacking her shin against the cedar chest.

"Dammit," she muttered at what sounded like breaking glass coming from outside. The windows were fogged over and Wylie rubbed her fingers over the glass to clear them. From this vantage point, she couldn't find the source of the noise. It was still snowing, the wind had whipped itself into a frenzy, and she could barely see beyond a few feet in front of her.

Another crack splintered the air. Tas whimpered.

"The trees," Wylie said. "Tree branches are snapping because of the weight of the ice and the snow. First the trees, next it will be the electrical wires."

The boy looked at her questioningly.

"It means it's going to get very dark and very cold fast," Wylie said, moving from the window to the closet. She pulled open the door and reached for a heavy-duty flashlight on the top shelf and set it on the cedar chest. Then she opened the drawer in the end table next to the sofa and found another, smaller flashlight.

"Here," Wylie said, handing it to the boy. "You push this button here to turn it on. Give it a try." The boy slid the black switch upward and a beam of light appeared. "Now turn it off. Only turn it on if the lights go out." He slid the button to the off position. "Stay here," Wylie ordered. "I'm going to go get the other ones."

Wylie ran from room to room, grabbing flashlights. On her

arrival at the farmhouse, she had stowed several throughout the house for just such an occasion. Wylie had never needed them before, and her pulse quickened at the thought of being plunged into blackness even in a place she knew so well. If there was light, everything would be okay, she thought.

Wylie carried the flashlights back to the boy and dumped them on the sofa. "I'm going upstairs to get some more; I'll be right back."

Upon seeing the uncertainty on the boy's face, Wylie paused. Wylie didn't want to scare him any more than she already had. The dark was her issue, not his.

"Just a few more, and I'm going to grab some extra batteries," Wylie said. Snatching one of the flashlights from the pile, Wylie hurried up the steps. She should be more worried about having enough wood for the fireplace. Rationally, Wylie knew that the dark couldn't really hurt them, but the cold could. Once she had all the flashlights in place, she would get more wood from the barn.

Once upstairs, Wylie went to the room she used as her office. It was where she spent most of her time, so that was where she kept her storm lantern. It could last for a hundred and forty hours on one set of batteries.

Outside, the pop of fracturing tree limbs continued. Wylie watched in awe as an ice-encased limb stretched across her window, swayed and splintered like a toothpick, and crashed to the ground below. Wylie reached into the bottom desk drawer and scooped up several packs of batteries when a glint of orange shone through the storm.

Wylie leaned over her desk, pressing her face to the window to get a better look. The wind sent billowing clouds of snow across the fields. Again, another flash of orange. Was it headlights from a car or maybe an emergency vehicle? Wylie couldn't tell.

She turned off her desk lamp in hopes of getting a better look. The light outside disappeared, and for a moment, Wylie thought she must have imagined it, but then the air stilled as if the storm was taking a deep breath. The snow parted, and a ball of fiery orange lit up the sky at the top of the lane.

It was the wrecked truck engulfed in flames.

Maybe a power line came down atop it, igniting the gas tank? That's what had to have happened.

There was nothing to do but let it burn.

The storm exhaled, obscuring the road and enveloping the fire in a whorl of white.

Another flash of orange broke through the dark. Wylie could hear the crackle of flames through the wind. She thought of the glove box and any paperwork that might have been stored inside that could have told her the truck's owner's identity, literally now up in flames. She should have taken the time to check when she first found the wreckage.

Above her, the lights blinked. Wylie held her breath, but the lights stayed on. She needed to get more flashlights, more batteries.

There was nothing that Wylie could do about the truck now. She had to worry about the things she could control. Like keeping herself and the boy warm and keeping the darkness at bay.

Wylie turned away from the window and juggled the lantern and a handful of batteries as she moved through the hallway to the stairs. Just as her foot hit the first step, the house was plunged into darkness.

Wylie froze. Her fingertips tingled and her heart raced. A wave of dizziness rolled through her and she dropped the batteries. They clattered down the steps, disappearing into the dark as Wylie stared down into the black abyss below her. Her rational mind knew that she had nothing to fear, but she couldn't think. Beads of cold sweat popped out on her forehead and a low hum filled her ears.

Unsteadily, she sat down on the top step. She couldn't catch her breath; the air wouldn't fully enter her lungs. It was blocked by something that had lain dormant for years. Something black and oily slid into place and took hold.

Wylie pressed her fingers to her throat as if she could pry away its cold grip. Night had finally found her unprepared, and Wylie felt she might suffocate.

Until now, she had learned to control light and dark. She couldn't outrun it any longer. She squeezed her eyes shut.

A stream of coughing, sharp and harsh like seals barking, scattered the buzzing bees in her head and Wylie opened her eyes. "Hey?" she called out. "Are you alright?" Wylie asked, trying to keep her voice steady, even.

A beam of light bounced against the walls, filling the stairwell with an eerie glimmer. The dizziness subsided and the world righted itself. There was light. Everything was going to be okay.

"I'm coming," Wylie managed to say, waiting until her breath steadied before getting to her feet. Feeling came back into her limbs and she felt the smooth wooden banister beneath her fingers. Her legs felt heavy, but with the gleam from the boy's light, she was able to move slowly downward.

Seeing the worry on the boy's face, Wylie murmured, "I'm fine, I just don't like the dark very much."

The boy reached over and flipped the switch on the lantern in Wylie's hands, and the room was flooded with a soft light.

Tas, unconcerned, was stretched out in front of the fireplace. The black knot in Wylie's throat slid away.

Wylie set the lantern on the cedar chest. "It could take a few days for crews to get the power back on, but we'll be okay. We've got light and food and wood," she said with weak conviction.

Wylie glanced at the dwindling pile of kindling next to the fireplace and her heart dropped. Wood. They needed more wood for the fire, but there was none in the house. She would need to go out to the barn. This was the last thing she wanted to do, but what choice did she have? They needed logs for the fire. "We need more wood. Do you want to help me?"

The boy looked down at his shoes.

"My arms are going to be filled with wood, so maybe you can open and shut the back door for me. But first, we need to make sure you're warm enough. It's going to get cold in here fast, especially when the door opens. How about it?" Wylie asked.

Finally, the boy nodded, and Wylie gave him a grateful smile.

Wylie was tempted to turn on every single flashlight she had gathered but knew that would be a waste of batteries. She would have to make do with her lantern. Together, each holding a light, Wylie and the boy made their way to the mudroom. First, Wylie tested the outdoor lights hoping the back yard would suddenly become illuminated. Nothing happened.

Wylie found an old sweatshirt and pulled it over the boy's head. It fell below his knees, and Wylie had to roll up the sleeves several times, but it would do the trick. She rifled through a basket filled with outdoor gear, found a stocking cap, and pulled it down over his ears.

"There," Wylie said, stepping back to survey her work.

"Keep your hands tucked inside your sleeves and you'll be ready for business."

Wylie pulled on her own gear and stepped outside to retrieve the sled that she had dropped off on the front step. She'd use it to help transport the wood back to the house.

"Hey, you okay down there?" a man called from the top of the lane. "I saw the fire from the house and got on my snowmobile to see what was going on."

He stopped halfway down the drive and removed his helmet. Through the falling snow Wylie recognized him as one of the neighbors to the east, Randy Cutter. From her research for the book, Wylie knew that Randy and Deb Cutter divorced and he moved to another residence not far away.

"Came upon the wreck," he said breathlessly. Randy's salt-and-pepper hair peeked out from beneath his stocking cap and snowflakes clung to his eyelashes. "Anyone injured? It's a bad one."

"Yeah," Wylie called back. "It was crazy. I found a boy. He's shaken up but fine. It's the woman who was in the truck with him I'm worried about. She disappeared."

"What do you mean, disappeared?" Randy asked.

"After I found the boy I went to see if I could figure out where he came from," Wylie explained. "Found the truck and a woman. She was caught up in some barbwire and I couldn't get her out. I went to get some tools and when I came back she was gone."

"Gone?" Randy repeated. "Damn. Where would she have gone to?"

"Good question," Wylie said. "It makes no sense. She looked like she was banged up really good. I can't imagine she went far, I just couldn't find her. This is a hell of a storm."

"Yeah, it is," Randy agreed. "I'd offer you and the kid a

ride on my snowmobile back to my house to wait out the storm, but it's getting worse by the minute. You might be better off staying put."

"I think you're right. We're doing okay here," she assured him. "We have wood, water, and food. We'll be fine—I'm more worried about the woman. Any way you can go look for her?"

"I can do that," Randy said. "I can't stand the thought of someone stranded out in this weather. I'll ride around and see what I can find. How about I stop back tomorrow and check on things, let you know what I find. Hopefully, the snow will be done by then."

"That would be great. Thanks," Wylie said, hesitant to send him on his way. "Be safe," she said, as Randy turned and trudged to the top of the lane.

Back inside, Wylie shook the snow off her and carried the sled toward the mudroom. She debated telling the boy about Randy's visit but thought the mention of the injured woman in wreckage might upset him. Better to wait and see if Randy found her.

Once at the door, Wylie realized that if she carried a flash-light outside with her, she wouldn't have her hands free to haul the toboggan, heavy with wood back to the house.

Plan B. Wylie had a headlamp stowed away in her car. At the barn she'd retrieve the lamp and would have hands-free access to light.

"Okay," Wylie said, pulling her gloves on, "you and Tas wait here, and when I get to the door, turn the knob and let me in."

The boy nodded and Wylie opened the door. The frigid air hit them with a blast. Wylie stepped outside and bent her head to the wind. The air smelled like gasoline. The truck fire.

★ ★ ★

The flashlight she carried lit the way allowing Wylie to see a few feet in front of her. The new snow covered the ice, reached nearly to her knees, and provided some traction so that she was able to move at a faster clip.

When Wylie reached the barn, she tugged on the door. It opened only a few inches, the bottom edge getting caught up in the snow. She kicked at the snow with her boot, trying to clear a path, then wedged her hip into the opening and pushed open the door just enough so that she could squeeze inside.

Though the cattle that were once housed here were long gone, old farm equipment remained: a bale spearer, chain harrows, a loader bucket, and more.

She made a beeline for the Bronco and dug around until she found the headlamp. She pressed the on button and a bright beam of light appeared. She secured the lamp over her stocking cap and looked down at the pile of wood stacked in the corner.

It would take several trips to bring in enough wood to outlast the storm. Wylie piled the logs atop the sled and then covered it with a plastic tarp.

Above her, Wylie heard a noise. A dry, shuffly sound. Something was in the hayloft. "Hello," she called out tentatively. Maybe the woman from the wreck had found shelter in the barn.

She had mixed feelings about the woman from the accident. The remnants of duct tape on the boy's face disturbed her. Was the woman the boy's kidnapper? Could she be his mother?

Wylie climbed the rickety ladder up to the hayloft and peered over the edge. The light from the headlamp filled the space. The loft floor was covered in straw, and in the high corners, frozen cobwebs laced the wooden crossbeams. She ascended the top rungs of the ladder and stepped onto the floor of the loft.

Bits of dust rose as Wylie shuffled through the loose straw. From a corner, two small golden eyes blinked up at her and then scurried past Wylie. A raccoon seeking shelter for the winter.

Wylie made a cursory search of the loft. The woman wasn't there. She approached the latched hayloft door once used to transport bales of hay and looked out the small, grimy window next to it. From this high vantage point, if not for the blizzard, Wylie would be able to see for miles across the countryside. The heavy snow had extinguished the flames from the truck fire, and now her view was limited to what she could see through the beam of her headlamp.

Through the heavy curtain of snow, Wylie got a glimpse of the soft halo from the boy's flashlight from within the house. He was waiting for her return.

For a moment, the wind stilled, the snow rearranged itself into a steady, glittering shower of white, and the beam from her headlamp bounced off a dark shape emerging from the shadows of the old garden shed. The figure was lurching toward the house. Toward the boy.

It had to be the woman from the truck. She must have found shelter in the old toolshed. But why didn't she come straight to the house? Wylie had told the woman that the child was safe, that she was there to help her. Wylie couldn't shake the thought that the woman was up to no good.

She hurried down the ladder, pushed on the barn door, and for a moment, it didn't move. *Someone locked me in*, was her first, panicked thought. Wylie threw her shoulder against the door and it groaned open a few inches. In the short time she'd been inside, the snow, gathered up by the wind, had blocked her exit.

Wylie pushed on the door until it opened far enough for her to sidle out of the barn. The blizzard whirled, and the wind blew fiercely into her face making her eyes water. Squinting through the storm, Wylie could see the figure still moving slowly toward the house.

Wylie fought the urge to sprint toward the woman, but they still needed wood for the fire. It would be crucial to get the woman warmed up after hours spent in snow and in the uninsulated garden shed. Wylie forced the barn door open as far it would go, stepped back inside, and pulled the sled, piled with wood, into the storm.

Wylie's boots sank into the snow with each step, it was like slogging through mud but she was gaining on the woman. From the light of the headlamp, Wylie could see that it was the woman from the accident. She had Wylie's hat atop her head and was wearing Wylie's coat.

"Hey," Wylie called out, but the woman didn't pause, just kept lumbering forward.

As they came closer to the house, the boy's face appeared in the window, a pale moon in the dark, and then it vanished. When the wind settled, there he was again. His hands were pressed against the glass, a look of fear stamped on his face. The stranger was almost to the door and Wylie was still thirty yards behind.

Wylie dropped the sled's rope and started running toward the house. "Hey," Wylie called out. "Lock the door!" But the boy just stood there, mesmerized by the shape moving toward him. The back door opened, and the woman slipped inside. Through the roar of the wind, Wylie thought she heard Tas's frantic barks.

The wind lifted, bringing with it a billowing cloud of snow and obscuring the entire house. At that moment, not even the blaze from her headlamp could pierce the storm. Wylie pushed forward.

When she finally reached the back door, Wylie fumbled with the knob and twisted. The door didn't open. It was locked. She thumped on the door with a fist.

"Hey," she called out. "Open the door!" Wylie pressed her face to the window, her headlamp lighting up the mudroom.

Inside, Tas barking and dancing in excited circles around the woman who kicked out at the dog. Tas gave a sharp squeal of pain and slunk away.

The woman's back was to Wylie, but she could clearly see the boy's face. Tearstained and frightened. But it was what dangled from the woman's hand that caused Wylie to gasp. A long smooth wooden shaft ending with a triangular wedge of steel that glinted in the glare of the headlamp—a hatchet.

The woman held the weapon in her hand and pulled the boy from the mudroom and into the shadows.

19

When the girl's mother finally emerged from the bathroom she murmured, "It's gone," and moved as if in a daze toward the bed, leaving faint red footprints in her wake.

The girl ran into the bathroom. The floor was covered in towels soaked in blood. The girl understood. Her baby sister had died and was lying somewhere beneath one of the bloody towels. She gagged and quickly closed the door.

The heat in the basement was becoming unbearable. The air was heavy and wet and the hot sun killed the grass that tried to grow up around the window. Now it lay in limp, brown clumps. Once in a while, a bird with a bright yellow breast and black wings would land at the window to choose the perfect strand of dead grass for his nest. The girl and the bird would stare at each other through the filmy glass. The bird was always the first to look away. He had things to do, places to visit.

Her mother slept and cried. The girl had to go to the bathroom but couldn't bring herself to open the bathroom door. She tried to distract herself by looking at books, by looking out the window for the yellow bird, by watching television, but the urgency became too much to bear.

The girl pushed open the door in hopes that, in some kind of miracle, the bloody towels had disappeared. They hadn't. She tiptoed across the floor trying to avoid the red sticky spots to the toilet.

Her father would come soon, and what would he do when he saw the mess? He'd be angry. He'd swear and yell and then hurt her mother, who lay in the bed too weak to move, too sad to eat or drink. She wouldn't be able to take it.

The girl found a black garbage bag and began to stuff it with the soiled towels. "Don't think about it," she told herself.

The girl used paper towels to scrub away the remaining blood and added them to the garbage bag until it bulged. "Don't think about it," she said over and over. When she finished, and all remnants of the baby were gone, she climbed into bed next to her mother and slept.

When her father finally came, he was carrying a shake for her mother. The overflowing garbage bag sat in the middle of the room. "What happened?" he asked.

"It's gone," her mother said from beneath the covers.

"Are you going to be okay?" her father asked, but her mother didn't answer. "It was probably for the best," he said, sitting on the edge of the bed and resting a hand on her mother's hip. She rolled away from him.

"You cleaned this up?" her father asked the girl.

The girl nodded.

"Huh," her father made the noise as if impressed. He went over to the garbage, peeked inside, tossed in the shake he brought for her mother to the mix, and carried the bloody bag from the room.

20

In the front yard of the Doyle house, a half dozen deputies still milled around, waiting for Sheriff Butler to tell them what to do next. After the quiet month they'd had, crime-wise, Butler shouldn't have been surprised that it would return to Blake County with a vengeance. He expected a breaking and entering or a meth bust or a drunken bar fight maybe, but not this. William and Lynne Doyle were good folks. No trouble at all. Sure, their teenage son got into a few dustups, but nothing too serious.

The only available witness was a twelve-year-old girl with a gunshot wound. The girl needed to get to the hospital, but Butler wanted to talk to her first. It looked like there was a guest spending the night with the family and he needed to figure out who it was.

"Christ," he muttered to himself. Two dead and two missing. He had to talk to the witness before they whisked her away in the ambulance.

Sheriff Butler strode toward the ambulance where two paramedics tended to the girl. Matthew Ellis stood on the perimeter, watching anxiously. "She's still shivering," Matthew said. "Can you get her another blanket?"

The female paramedic tucked another blanket around Josie. "You hanging in there, honey?" she asked. Josie nodded, jaw clenched as if trying to keep her teeth from chattering.

"Hi, Josie, I'm Sheriff Butler," he said, leaning into the ambulance. "Are Erin and Lowell taking good care of you?" he asked and lightly touched her shin. Josie jerked away as if burned. "Whoa, sorry about that," Butler said, pulling his hand away. "Are you in a lot of pain?" he asked.

"A little," she admitted.

"We gave her a little something to help with that," Lowell said and moved more deeply into the ambulance.

"I only have a few questions for you," Butler said, giving Josie a sympathetic smile. "And I'm sorry to be so blunt, but we want to get you to the hospital. Did you see who hurt your parents?"

Josie looked to her grandfather who nodded. "I never really saw," Josie said in a small voice. "We were outside. Becky and me. We heard the gun but didn't see who did it."

"What's Becky's last name?" Butler asked.

"Allen," Josie said. "Becky Allen."

"Her mother works at Shaffer's Grocery," Matthew filled in, and Butler turned to a deputy. "I need you to find the Allen parents and fill them in on what's going on. Just the basics," Butler cautioned. "Tell them there was an incident at the Doyle house and we're trying to locate Becky. No more than that, got it?" The deputy nodded and rushed off.

"Okay, you're doing a great job, Josie," Butler said. "Did you see who shot at you?"

Josie shook her head. "It was too dark. I just saw someone coming toward us. He had a gun. He chased us."

"So it was a he?" Butler asked.

"I think so," Josie said.

"Was he young or a grown man?" the sheriff asked.

A ripple of doubt crossed Josie's face. "I think it was a man, but I'm not sure," she said thickly, her eyes fluttering shut. "I couldn't see how old he was."

"Okay, Josie." Sheriff Butler sighed. He didn't get to her before whatever pain medication the paramedics gave her. "Did you see or hear anything else strange last night?"

"A truck. There was a truck," Josie said groggily.

"Last night? You saw a truck on your property?" Butler asked. This was something.

"No," Josie said. "On the road. I saw it on the road earlier. Twice. It was white."

The sheriff let out a breath. White trucks were a common sight in Blake County. Always had been. It wasn't exactly helpful.

Levi Robbins approached the sheriff. "State police are on their way. Said it might take some time to get the dogs here."

The sheriff nodded and returned his attention to Josie. "Anything else you came across recently that was unusual. Any strangers hanging around?"

Josie rubbed her head as if it hurt to think. "Not really. We saw Cutter right after supper."

"Cutter?" Levi asked in surprise.

"Brock Cutter. He's my brother's friend," Josie told them.

"Anyone else you see?" the sheriff asked. "Anyone at all?"

"My grandma and grandpa when we dropped off the pie at their house and then Becky and I went looking for Roscoe. We stopped at that house, the one with all the junk."

Sheriff Butler knew who Josie was talking about. June Henley and her son, Jackson Henley, lived about two miles away over on Oxeye Road. Word was that June Henley was very sick. Cancer.

Jackson ran a hodgepodge operation selling vehicle parts, scrap metal, and farm collectibles. Jackson was a Gulf War vet with PTSD and a drinking problem. He lost his license sometime back and took to driving an ATV around the back roads. Jackson was odd for sure but not known to be violent.

The sheriff jotted the name down in his notebook.

"One more question for now," Butler said. "Becky Allen. When did you last see her?"

Josie closed her eyes trying to remember. They heard the gunshots. Heard someone call her name. Who was it? Ethan? Her dad? No, that wasn't right. They grabbed hands and ran. More explosions rang out. Becky's hand was ripped from hers. But she kept running.

Josie's face was wet with tears. "I don't know," she cried, looking to her grandfather for help. "I'm so sorry."

"Hey, now," Lowell said. "I think that's enough for now." He laid a cool hand on Josie's forehead. "There will be plenty of time later for questions. We really need to get that arm looked at by a doctor. We don't want an infection to settle in. Is there someone who will be meet us at the hospital?"

"My wife. Oh, God, I have to call my wife," Matthew covered his eyes. Dry, silent sobs shook his shoulders.

"Why don't you go with Josie?" Sheriff Butler said. "I'll stop by later and we can talk more."

Matthew shook his head and ran a shaky hand across his gray whiskers. "I can't leave," he insisted. "Not until we find Ethan and the girl and not until they bring my daughter out." Sheriff Butler flicked his eyes toward Josie. Her eyes were closed. "They'll be brought out once the scene is processed and the county medical examiner arrives."

Two deputies stepped from the barn, and along with them came the impatient bleats of the goats, eager to be fed and milked. "Barn's clear," one of the deputies called out.

"Do we know how many vehicles should be here?" Butler asked.

"Two," Matthew said. "Lynne's car and William's truck." Matthew looked around the yard. "Three, actually. Ethan has a truck. An old Datsun. It's not here."

Two teenagers missing along with a truck. Parents dead, sister shot. Butler pulled Levi aside, out of earshot, his mouth set in a grim line. "Put out a BOLO for Ethan Doyle's truck."

At the ambulance, Matthew kissed Josie's forehead. "Be good. Listen to the doctors," Matthew said, wiping his eyes, his voice raw. "Your grandma will be there soon."

"Hey," came a shout from the edge of the cornfield. "We found something!"

All eyes swung toward the cornfield. Matthew didn't know whether to be hopeful or terrified. He found he was both. Before anyone could move a breathless voice came from behind them. "What happened? What's going on?" Matthew stepped aside and a woman came into view.

"Ma'am, you can't be here," Sheriff Butler said.

"Is my daughter here? Becky Allen?" Margo reached for Butler's arm.

"You're Becky's mother?" Butler faltered. "Why don't you step over here and we'll talk?"

"Sheriff, we need you," a deputy called again. "We found something." Butler was torn. He needed to find out what was found in the field but couldn't abandon the missing girl's mother.

"Where is she? I heard something happened." Margo looked around, bewildered. Lost. "Where is she?"

Josie lifted herself onto her elbows, the blanket covering her slid to the ambulance floor. No one spoke.

Margo looked from face-to-face. A cold knot formed in her chest, spread through her limbs. "Please," she said weakly, "you have to tell me what happened."

She set her gaze on Josie. She took in Josie's bloody arm and clothing. "Oh, my God," she breathed. "What happened? Where's Becky?"

Sheriff Butler laid a hand on her elbow, but she shook it away. Josie stared up at her wide-eyed. "Where's Becky!" she shouted.

"I don't know, I don't know," Josie whimpered. The words came out in short gasps.

"Josie, where's your mother?" Margo asked. She looked around as if Lynne Doyle would suddenly materialize. "You tell me where she is. I want to talk to her right now."

"Come along now, ma'am," Butler said, reaching for her arm again.

"No," Margo said, clutching the side of the ambulance for support. "Josie, where is your mother?"

The rumble of tires on gravel caused everyone's eyes to shift. A black SUV with the words *Blake County Medical Examiner* stenciled in white across its side bounced down the lane.

"Oh, God," Margo's legs buckled beneath her and she nearly dropped to her knees before Sheriff Butler steadied her. "No, no, no, no," she said over and over again.

"We're not sure what happened here just yet," Sheriff Butler murmured and guided Margo away from the ambulance as the paramedics closed the doors.

"Try not to think about it, Josie," Lowell said soothingly. "They'll take care of her. Everything is going to be okay. Right now, we're going to start an IV and get some fluids in you. You're going to feel a little pinch, okay?" Josie closed her eyes as Lowell slid the needle into her arm. The whoop-whoop of the siren intermingled with Margo Allen's cries as they pulled from the lane.

It was a thirty-minute drive to the hospital in Algona and Josie knew these roads with her eyes closed. Knew every curve, turn, pothole, and dip of the road. But riding in the back of an ambulance was different than riding in her dad's truck or mom's van. She became disoriented and kept asking where they were going.

"The hospital," Lowell said. "The docs are going to check you out there."

"Will they bring my mom and dad there too?" Josie asked. If they got them to the hospital, then the doctors could fix them, she thought. That's what doctors did. Put people back together again. She tried to push away the bloody, broken images of her parents that kept flashing behind her eyes.

"Everyone is going to do all that they can to help your parents," he assured her.

"Will my grandma be there?" Josie locked on to Lowell's bright brown eyes for reassurance. "Do you think they found Ethan and Becky?"

"Shhh," he soothed. "Don't worry about those things right now. Your grandma is going to meet us at the hospital. I promise, Josie. You're safe now."

Josie floated away on his words and thought of the night sky filled with white gold orbs, thought of her and Becky leaping toward them trying to snatch them up.

Before she knew it they arrived at the hospital. The back doors of the ambulance opened and the gurney that she was lying upon was lifted. Above her, Josie briefly saw a shard of hard blue sky and heard Lowell say, "GSW to the left arm. Cuts and contusions to her feet and arms. Blood pressure and heart rate are below normal. Watch for possible shock."

"This the girl from the farm out near Burden?" a woman wearing yellow scrubs asked.

"Yes," Lowell said, squeezing Josie's hand. "Her grand-mother should be here any minute."

"Any other incoming from the scene?" the woman asked.

The air was cold and a sharp antiseptic smell bit at Josie's nose as they moved down the hallway.

Josie looked hopefully to Lowell; a small spark of hope fluttered in her chest.

"Not sure," he said shortly.

"I'm Dr. Lopez," the woman said, leaning over Josie. "I'm going to take care of you. Can you tell me what happened?"

"I got shot," Josie said. Again, she looked to Lowell. "Can you stay with me?" she asked him as she was wheeled into an examining room.

"'Fraid not, Josie," he said apologetically. "I have to get back to work, but I'll peek back in later to see how you're doing. Sound good?" Josie nodded and Lowell disappeared from the room.

The doctor and nurses took over then. "Looks like you've got some buckshot embedded in there. You're a lucky girl, though," Dr. Lopez said as she probed the wound gently with gloved fingers.

Josie didn't feel lucky.

"It just grazed you, thankfully. There doesn't appear to be any tendon or bone damage, but we'll take some X-rays and get you cleaned up," Dr. Lopez said.

Josie was wheeled to X-ray and then taken back to an examination room. Dr. Lopez bathed the wound in saline, all the while telling Josie precisely what she was doing. "We'll numb up your arm really well, and then I'll debride the wound, give you a few stitches, and you'll be as good as new." When Josie looked at her nervously, she smiled. "That just means I'll remove the remaining buckshot from your arm. Don't worry, you won't feel a thing."

She was right, except for the initial prick from the local anesthetic, Josie didn't feel anything, but still, she kept her head turned and eyes screwed shut so she wouldn't have to see what was happening. Dr. Lopez then examined the cuts on Josie's feet and the scratches across her arms. "These are just superficial. Nothing to worry about, but they'll be sore for a while. Keep them clean and we'll give you some antibacterial cream to put on them."

Josie dozed and when she opened her eyes, she was in a different room and her grandmother was sitting in a chair in the corner. Her long gray hair was pulled back in a ponytail. She wore what she called her *around-the-house jeans* and a short-sleeved collared shirt and was nervously kneading the strap of her big black leather purse that was perched on her lap.

"Grandma," Josie whispered.

"Josie," Caroline Ellis said, leaping to her feet. "How are you?" Her voice trembled.

Josie scanned her body. She felt no real discomfort. Her tongue was thick and heavy in her mouth and she wanted a drink of water. She tried to sit up but a jolt of pain went through her left arm.

"Mom, Dad?" Josie whimpered. Her grandmother stood over her, raw grief etched across her face.

"I'm sorry, honey," Caroline said. "I'm so, so sorry."

Josie moaned and tried to turn over on her side and curl up into a ball but moving hurt too much. Instead, she lay on her back and cried. Hot tears rolled down her cheeks and mucous filled her nose and throat. "Why?" she asked thickly.

"I don't know, honey. The police want to talk to you about what you remember. I know it's scary," Caroline added quickly, seeing the fear on Josie's face. "But they have some questions. Do you think you can do that?"

"But I already talked to someone," Josie protested.

"I imagine they'll want you to go over it several times, Josie," Caroline said, reaching for her hand.

Josie could go over things a million times, but it didn't change what she knew. She didn't see anything. Not really. Already the events of the night before were dissipating into a nebulous fog, but a few details remained clear: the sharp barks of a shotgun, the figure in the dark coming toward them, Becky falling behind.

"Ethan? Becky?" Josie asked. Her grandmother shook her head, and for a moment, Josie thought she meant that they, too, were dead. She inhaled sharply and the air snagged in her dry throat and she dissolved into a coughing fit.

Josie raised her hand to cover her mouth and felt the pull of the IV against the tender skin in the crook of her arm and quickly laid it back down.

Her grandmother sprang into action. She reached for a cup of water next to Josie's bed and placed the straw between her lips. Josie took a sip.

"They haven't found Ethan or Becky yet," Caroline explained. "Your grandpa thinks they might be hiding in the field like you did. They have searchers looking now."

The cool water soothed the fire in her throat. "Can I help?" Josie asked. "Can I go look for them too?"

"Not right now," she said apologetically. "Your job right now is to rest and answer any questions the police have for you. That's the most important thing you can do." Caroline scraped her teeth across her lower lip and let out a shaky breath. "Do you have any idea who might have done this?" she asked.

Once again, tears gathered in Josie's eyes. "I think," she began in a barely perceptible whisper, "at first, I thought it might have been Ethan."

Seeing the horror on her grandmother's face, Josie quickly backtracked. "But I know it wasn't him. He would never hurt us."

"No, of course he wouldn't," Caroline said, clutching her granddaughter's hand. "He's a good boy," she murmured as if trying to convince herself. "He's a good boy."

21

The girl's father kept promising to bring her a puppy one day but never did. He did that a lot—made promises. "One day we'll go to the ocean. We'll walk on the beach and pick up seashells and sea glass." The girl had talked about it for days. She drew pictures of the seaside and read about the Pacific Ocean and all manner of sea creatures from the set of World Book Encyclopedias *on the bookshelf.*

"Did you know that the blue whale is the biggest animal in the world, but its throat is smaller than my hand?" she said, holding up her fist in demonstration.

"He's lying, you know," her mother said, flicking through a magazine. "He does this all the time. It's never going to happen."

When the girl thought about it, she knew her mother was right. Her father was always saying things like this. Two years ago, he promised to take them to Disney World but balked when she kept bringing it up. "Do you think I'm made of money?" he snapped. "I don't want to hear another word about it."

And last year, he started talking about taking a trip to the Wisconsin Dells that had a hotel with a water park right inside. It seemed like this time they might really go, but then her father came home and said, "Sorry, I've gotta work."

But still, the girl was hopeful that he'd bring her a dog—a cat even. She started standing on the chair beneath the window so she could hear the rumble of his truck's tires. Each time her father came through the door, she stared at his jacket pockets hoping to see movement. That happened sometimes on television—the dad would come home with a puppy tucked in his pocket. But there was never a dog.

She had finally given up when one day her father came home carrying a big cardboard box. The girl's heart soared. Finally, she thought. He set the box on the table and the girl rushed over in anticipation.

"Brought you something," he said.

"Can I open it?" the girl asked, and her father nodded. Even her mother was intrigued and came over to see what he brought.

The girl lifted a flap on the box and expected to see a tiny nose poke out. Instead, a musty, dry scent filled her nose. She lifted the second flap. Inside were books. Dozens of books. Old ones based on the smell and the shabby covers.

The little girl looked up at her father and did her best to hide the disappointment. Books were nice. The girl loved books, but there wasn't a puppy in the box and these books were dog-eared and not well cared for.

"What?" her father asked sharply. "You don't like them? I made a point to stop to pick these out for you and I don't even get a thank-you?"

The little girl sniffed and rubbed her eyes. "Thank you," she said blinking back the tears and reaching into the box. She pulled out one with a coffee-colored stain across the front of it.

"I don't even know why I bother," her father said knocking the book from her hand. The girl shoved her fingers into her mouth to take away the sting. "Ungrateful little shit," her father muttered pushing

the cardboard box from the table. The books spilled to the floor with a crash and the girl watched as her father stomped up the steps and locked the door behind him.

Later, after he left, her mother pulled the girl onto her lap. "See," she said, stroking her hair. "I told you he lies. It's better not to get your hopes up."

22

Present Day

"Let me in," Wylie cried as she pounded on the back door. The woman with the hatchet had dragged the boy out of sight. The house was completely dark now, all the flashlights turned off, and the fire had died out or had been extinguished. Tas had stopped barking, and the only sounds were Wylie's ragged breathing and the moan of the bitter wind that cut through her clothing like a knife.

She couldn't stay outside much longer, but she had no weapon. Wylie weighed her options. She could make her way back to the barn, search for something to protect herself with, and then return to the house.

Wylie knew there was no time for that. She had to get inside, had to get to the boy. She turned her head, shielded her face, and smashed an elbow into the glass, creating a fine spiderweb of cracks, but still the window held. Knowing that even the roar of the blizzard wouldn't mask the sound of breaking glass, Wylie hit it again, and this time the window shattered, sending shards flying. Holding her breath, Wylie reached through the window and flipped the lock.

She opened the door and stepped into the mudroom, half expecting a hatchet to come swinging toward her head, but no one was there. No ax-waving maniac, no little boy. Not even Tas.

Wylie moved to the kitchen and shut the mudroom door behind her. She quickly groped through the drawers looking for a weapon until she came across a butcher knife buried beneath a jumble of cutlery. The steel blade was nearly eight inches long but dull, blunted by years of use. It would do.

Even in the short time that she'd been outside, the temperature inside the house had plummeted. Using the headlamp to guide her way forward, Wylie inched her way through the kitchen, taking small, hesitant steps. Wylie had one big advantage over the intruder, she knew this house. Knew the layout and knew the deepest recesses and darkest corners. She was halfway through the kitchen when she saw it. So imperceptible, she almost missed it—the basement door. Open just a sliver, barely enough to slide a piece of paper through.

The basement? Wylie wondered. Filled with cardboard boxes and old furniture, there were plenty of hiding spots, but why would an intruder take the boy down there? Wylie shuddered at the thought. She gently closed the door and locked it imprisoning whoever was on the other side.

If the boy and the woman were in the basement, at least she could contain them there for the time being.

On weak legs, Wylie moved down the hallway, through the empty dining room to the living room and paused. The fire was dead; only a few orange embers glowed. Wylie slowly scanned the room, her heart lurching when the headlamp's beam landed on the sofa. There sat the woman cradling the hatchet in her arms.

Barely daring to breathe, Wylie crept forward, eyes fixated on the weapon in the woman's hands. "What do you want?" Wylie asked, knife at the ready.

There was no answer and Wylie raised her eyes to the woman's face.

It was definitely the woman from the crash. She was wearing Wylie's coat and one side of her face was grotesquely swollen and the other side blackened with dried blood. The woman stared back in contempt. Wylie kept the knife raised and the narrow beam of the headlamp pinned on the intruder. It was 2:00 a.m. How had the woman survived all these hours out in the storm? It was impossible.

"Stay away," the woman said swinging the hatchet toward Wylie.

"Jesus," Wylie exclaimed, taking a step backward. "What the hell?" A sizzle of anger ran through her body. The woman had locked Wylie out of the house, would have gladly let her freeze to death, and was now swinging an ax at her head. All Wylie had done was try to help her. What was she up to?

And where was the boy? And Tas? Fear hardened in Wylie's belly.

Behind her, Wylie heard a small grunt. Afraid of what she was going to find, Wylie slowly turned just in time to see the boy, face pale and set with determination, swing the fireplace poker at her head. She managed to sidestep the blow, and the boy laden down by the weight of the poker stumbled to the ground.

"Hey," Wylie cried out. "What are you doing?" The boy looked up at her in defiance. Wylie reached down and easily wrenched the poker from his fingers.

The woman tried to rise from her spot on the couch, but Wylie pushed her back and grabbed the hatchet. The woman gasped in pain and Wylie watched in disbelief as the boy scrambled from the floor and onto the sofa throwing his body across the injured woman.

Wylie's first inclination was to haul the woman out of the house, but she could see fear on the boy's face. It wasn't the woman he was afraid of—it was Wylie.

"I'm not going to hurt you," Wylie said in exasperation. "I'm not going to hurt anyone."

The woman glared at Wylie and the boy buried his face into the woman's chest.

"Jesus," Wylie murmured. "Look at me. Look at me," she said more forcefully. The boy cautiously peeked up at Wylie. "Look, I'm putting these away. See?" Wylie moved, stood on tiptoe, and placed the weapons atop a bookshelf.

Wylie returned and showed her empty hands to the boy and the woman. She still didn't trust the woman but was confident she could overpower her if she tried another attack.

"I see how you are trying to protect her. This is your mom, right?" The boy stared at Wylie for a long moment and then gave a barely perceptible nod.

"Shhh," the woman hissed. "Don't talk."

"You need to shut up," Wylie snapped at the woman. "I don't know who the hell you are and why you felt the need to come at me with an ax, but you're hurt, and you need help. I will help you, but if you pull that crap again, I'll toss you out in a snowbank."

Wylie then spoke to the boy, "Do you want me to help your mother?" This time Wylie didn't wait for him to respond.

"First thing we need to do is get her warmed up. It's freezing in here. Help me cover her up with more blankets."

Wylie took a step toward the sofa and the boy scrambled to his feet, blocking her way. Wylie closed her eyes and mentally counted to ten. When she opened them again, she made sure her voice was calm, measured.

"Haven't I taken good care of you so far?" Wylie asked. "I brought you in from the cold, I've kept you warm, fed you. I'm going to do the same for your mother, I promise."

A flicker of uncertainty flashed in the boy's eyes.

Wylie lifted a flashlight from the end table, flipped it on, and held it out to him, hoping he wouldn't decide to use it as a weapon against her. The boy snatched it from Wylie's hands and held it to his chest.

"You tuck these blankets around her," Wylie said, nodding toward the knot of blankets that had slid to the floor. "I'm going to get some more quilts. We need to get her warmed up as quickly as possible."

Wylie watched for a moment as the boy gently arranged the blankets around his mother. The woman didn't protest but she kept her uninjured eye on Wylie.

Wylie had no clue as to the severity of this woman's injuries. All they could do was try to keep her comfortable and hope that the storm passed soon and that help arrived quickly. "Where's Tas?" Wylie asked, suddenly remembering the dog.

Guiltily, the boy pointed toward the kitchen. Wylie rushed to the basement door, slid open the lock and called down into the dark. "Tas, here! It's okay, you can come up," Wylie coaxed. Tas cautiously ascended the stairs, then went directly to his dog bed and lay down. "He won't hurt her," Wylie assured the boy. "I promise."

Wylie hurried up the stairs and to the bedroom. She didn't know this woman. Couldn't trust her. Wylie felt along the top shelf of the closet until she found her gun, loaded it, and slid into her pocket.

In the hallway she opened the linen closet where stacks of dusty, slightly musty-smelling quilts were stored. She grabbed an armful and returned to the living room where they layered them over the woman until all that showed was her bruised and battered face. The boy snuggled in next to her.

"Who are you?" Wylie asked the woman. "Where were you trying to get to?" The woman stayed resolutely quiet.

"Listen, we're stuck here together until the storm is over, the least you can do is tell me who you are and what you were doing out in the blizzard."

"We'll leave as soon as we can," the woman said thickly.

"And how do you think you're going to do that?" Wylie shot back. "Your truck is totaled, the roads are impassable, and you are hurt."

"We'll manage," the woman said shortly.

"Well, once the phone works again, we'll call 911. They'll get help out here as soon as they can."

"No, no police," the woman said and for the first time Wylie saw true fear on her face. "If you do that, we'll leave. We'll leave right now." The woman pushed the blankets aside and tried to get to her feet but was too weak.

Wylie shook her head in frustration. "Never mind. We can't call anyone right now anyway. We'll worry about that later."

All they could do now was wait out the storm. But in no way did Wylie trust the woman. There were too many unanswered questions. Wylie threw the last remaining scraps of wood into the fireplace and sat on the floor, facing the sofa where the woman and boy were cocooned. She watched over them, hand in her pocket, fingers wrapped around the loaded gun.

23

Three hours after the Blake County Sheriff's Department requested their assistance, Agent Camila Santos sped down the dusty gravel but slammed on the brakes when she crested a hill to find a tree growing in the middle of the road.

"What the hell," Santos exclaimed as her passenger, Agent John Randolph, braced his hands against the dashboard. The black sedan fishtailed and skidded to a stop.

The two Iowa Department of Criminal Investigation agents stared up at the massive tree. "Damn," Randolph said. "That's not something you see every day."

Santos inched the sedan around the scaly gray-green trunk of the eighty-foot tree. "They need a warning sign or something," she agreed.

They crossed a small creek, rounded a corner, and the house

came into view. At first glance, it looked like dozens of other white farmhouses they had seen on their trip from Des Moines to rural Blake County, but the flurry of activity ahead let the agents know they were in the right spot.

Santos slowly drove past dozens of parked vehicles and small teams of searchers wading through the tall grass in the ditches that lined the road. The searchers, grim-faced, paused to watch them creep past. "Hope they didn't trounce all over the crime scene," Randolph worried.

"Double murder, two missing kids, everyone has to be in a panic," Santos said as she pulled up behind a rusty Bonneville parked on the side of the road. "I was assured that the sheriff here has everything under control."

"Why are you stopping here?" Randolph asked, not relishing the long walk up to the crime scene in this heat.

"I want to get the lay of the land," Santos said as she stepped out into the hot glare of the sun and surveyed the surroundings.

The only buildings in sight were the ones on the Doyle property: a house, a silo, a large barn shedding red curls of paint, a few other outbuildings. Surrounded on all sides by mature cornfields. Remote, isolated.

Santos, compact and strong, like a gymnast, was a twenty-year law enforcement veteran who joined the Iowa Department of Criminal Investigation in 1995 after relocating to Des Moines from Kansas City. She quickly rose in the ranks and was the lead investigator on many high-profile cases that included murders or missing persons. This case had both.

Randolph was the younger of the two, wore a suit jacket and red-and-blue-striped tie. His dress shoes were polished to a high sheen that wouldn't last long on these dusty roads.

Randolph was so much taller than his counterpart that the woman had to crane her neck to look up at him. But there was something commanding about the way Agent Santos held herself, the cock of her chin, the set of her mouth. She was clearly in charge.

Crime scenes have a pulse all their own and when managed effectively hum along at an efficient, steady pace. Everyone from deputy to crime scene investigator, to detective, to forensic specialists, to the coroner knew their role.

Santos was assured that the main crime scene—the house, the outbuildings, and the Doyles' cornfield were all secure and being searched only by law enforcement. This was key. But the area outside the crime scene perimeter was important too.

Normally, volunteer searches were not activated so quickly, giving law enforcement more time to get a sense of what happened and keep the distraction of managing those with good intentions at a minimum.

Yes, the locals had organized quickly, but Santos also knew that volunteer searchers could be invaluable in situations like these, especially when the search area was vast and manpower limited. Local folks knew the terrain, knew the nooks and crannies that outsiders wouldn't be familiar with.

Cognizant of the curious eyes that followed their trek toward the house, Santos studied faces, body language. It wasn't unusual for a perpetrator to insert him or herself into the middle of a case in hopes of staying ahead of the investigation.

Men in coveralls and dusty boots stood in clusters shaking their heads. Woman in T-shirts and shorts wore sunglasses to hide their tears. No one appeared overtly suspicious, but that didn't mean he wasn't here, watching.

Santos turned her attention to the farmhouse. It was old, in need of a coat of paint. Already the day's heat pressed down on the purple and white flowers drooping limply in their hanging baskets on the front porch. An eerie lowing sound came from the direction of the barn.

Though the house gave no outward indication that something terrible had occurred here, Santos could feel a sense of dread rising from the earth, shimmering with heat.

Someone was handing out pictures of the missing teens. Agent Santos took a flyer and examined it. The picture of Ethan Doyle was a good one. He smiled brightly and his blue eyes snapped with good-natured mischief.

Santos turned her attention to the picture of Becky Allen. Pretty girl. While most girls this age appeared awkward and hadn't quite settled into their features, Becky conveyed an air of maturity, confidence.

"Hello," the woman handing out the fliers said. "Thank you for coming. If you could please sign in here, we'll…"

"We're with the state police," Santos said.

"Oh," the woman faltered. "I was telling the deputy here that the other night I saw a strange truck parked on the gravel road, right over there." She turned and pointed just beyond the Doyles' cornfield.

"What's your name?" Agent Santos asked.

"Abby Morris. I live out that way," she turned and pointed toward the north.

"I'm Deputy Robbins. I wrote down her account," Levi said, patting a bulge in his shirt pocket where it held a small notebook.

"Make sure we get a copy of it," Santos said. "I'm looking for Sheriff Butler," Santos said.

Levi nodded and said, "It's a bit of a walk."

"Good thing I have my walking shoes on," Santos said. Levi gave a hesitant smile, not sure if he had offended the agent. When she didn't smile back, he let the grin fall away. "He's this way," Levi said and started walking toward the back of the house. "A deputy found it about thirty feet into the cornfield."

"Anyone touch it?" Santos asked.

"They said they didn't. Someone ran to get me and I high-tailed it into the field and cleared everyone out of the area."

"Good," Santos said. The red barn loomed over the property. You could fit three of her house easily inside the sagging building. Santos was a city girl, grew up in Kansas City, and now lived in the heart of downtown Des Moines but knew that zip code was no exemption from violence and death. There was just less concrete and more soil.

As they approached the cornfield, Santos's pulse quickened. She had been in meth houses and down dark alleys, but as they stepped into the corn, the tall stalks towered over her. At the top of each, a spiky tassel poked the sky. In the space of a few steps, the field had swallowed her whole. Santos felt a wave of apprehension.

As they pushed through the corn, Santos could imagine the terror that Josie Doyle must have felt as she hid from her attacker. No matter which direction you looked—left or right— there was another identical stalk in front of you.

Santos lifted her neck and squinted upward. The sky was as vast and endless as the field seemed to be. Insects buzzed past her ears, the sweet smell of corn filled her nose.

Soon the murmur of the breeze through the stalks was replaced with a dry cough. A few steps farther and Sheriff Butler's khaki uniform came into view.

"Sheriff," Agent Santos said by way of greeting. Butler turned toward her and then stepped aside to reveal what had been discovered by the volunteers.

A camo-colored shotgun, muzzle up, leaned against a thick stalk. "Looks like someone just set it there," the deputy observed.

Agent Santos lowered herself into a crouch and examined the butt of the gun that rested atop the dry dirt. "Maybe. Any footprints?"

"Not a one. The ground is too hard-packed," Sheriff Butler said. "But there's a lot of trampled stalks. Squares up with what Josie said about being chased through the field."

Agent Santos lifted a pinch of soil from the ground and rubbed it between her fingers. "Why would he leave the weapon behind."

"Trying to ditch it?" Levi suggested. "He was trying to hide it in a hurry."

"Who is *he*?" Butler asked. "A stranger? Then where are Ethan Doyle and the Allen girl? If he took the two of them with him, wouldn't he need the weapon to help control them? Same case if you think Ethan is the suspect. Wouldn't he need the gun to make Becky comply?"

Agent Santos lithely got to her feet. "We need to get organized. Figure out what we know and need to know. Get a command post. How far is the sheriff's office from here?"

Sheriff Butler shook his head. "It's about thirty miles away. Too far. The department has a remote command post, but it's being used on the far end of the county for a train derailment. I was thinking, how about the old church off Highway 11? It's only a few miles from here."

"Fine," Santos said. "We need to talk to the survivor and the parents of the missing girl."

"We got the basics from Josie Doyle," Butler said. "She mentioned a strange truck hanging around earlier in the day."

"Any names come up?" Randolph asked.

"Nothing that seemed too suspicious—just a few people that the girls came into contact with yesterday," the sheriff said. "Brock Cutter, a local kid. And the Henleys—they live about two miles from here on Oxeye Road."

"Okay," Santos said. "Agent Randolph can help get the command center set up. Sheriff, have someone go talk to the Henleys and this Cutter kid. I'll go meet with the Allens. Once Josie Doyle is given the green light by the docs, we need to interview her more thoroughly. Let's plan on meeting at the church at—" Santos looked at her watch "—4:00 p.m."

Everyone nodded.

"Bag the shotgun and enter it into evidence and go talk to Brock Cutter," Butler ordered Levi, handing him the department's evidence camera.

"Yes, sir," Levi said as Sheriff Butler and the agents disappeared into the stalks.

Levi stayed behind, took several photos of the shotgun and drew a diagram of its position in his small notebook. He slipped on a pair of gloves and carefully picked up the shotgun. He opened the breach, exposing the barrel. The chamber was empty. It wasn't loaded.

Maybe Brock Cutter was a witness to what happened at the Doyle house. Levi remembered the sour smell of sweat emanating off the teenager when he pulled him over. Was it just the heat? Maybe it was fear. And he had let the kid go with barely a second thought.

A current of anger slid through Levi. Had the little fucker lied to him? Maybe he knew something that could break this case wide-open. Holding the weapon off to the side, careful not to smudge any possible fingerprints, Levi began to walk back toward the farm. He needed to find Brock Cutter.

Agent Santos needed to see the bodies. "We okay to go in?" she asked the deputy stationed at the back door of the farmhouse.

The deputy nodded and handed the agents a set of paper booties to place over their shoes. The first thing Santos noticed when she stepped from the mudroom into the kitchen was the oppressive heat. All the windows were shut tight, no fans were running, and the window air conditioners were switched off.

"It has to be a hundred and ten degrees in here," Randolph said, loosening his tie.

"We have to make a note to ask Josie Doyle if the house was shut up this tight last night," Santos said as she moved to the living room. "For how hot it's been all week, I can't imagine they wouldn't have been running the air conditioner or at least had the windows open."

"Maybe the killer was trying to alter the scene," Randolph suggested. "Made sure the windows were shut, turned off the air conditioner so that the bodies decomposed more quickly. That would make it harder for the ME to determine what time they died."

"Could be," Santos said. "Doesn't look like there was forced entry. We'll have to find out if the Doyles kept their doors locked at night." They continued through the house. It looked like a typical, neatly kept home.

"Do we know how many guns were kept in the house?" Santos asked a nearby deputy.

"According to Matthew Ellis, the grandfather, the Doyles had several guns in the house," the deputy said. "Most families around here do. Matthew thought they had three or four."

"Do you know what kind of guns they are?" Agent Randolph asked.

The deputy checked his notepad. "He said he thought they had a pump-action shotgun for deer hunting, a 20 gauge, and a BB gun. Possibly a 12 gauge too."

"Find out if the 20 gauge found in the field belonged to the Doyles," Santos told the deputy.

They slowly made their way up the stairs, careful not

to touch anything. Randolph noted the smudges of blood smeared across the wall next to the staircase. "Could have been left behind by one of the victims or the perpetrator. They also could have been from Josie Doyle's injured arm when she came looking for her family."

Santos and Randolph stepped into the master bedroom. They focused their eyes on Lynne Doyle. The wound to her chest was massive. "Up close and personal," Randolph said.

Sweat dripped down Santos's face but she resisted the urge to shed her suit jacket. It was even hotter in the bedroom than downstairs. "Is the heat on?" Santos asked, moving toward a vent in the floor. Warm air blew lightly on her fingers. "You were right," she told Randolph. "The son of bitch turned on the heat."

They moved on to Josie's bedroom where William Doyle lay in the doorway. "Find anything interesting?" Santos asked a crime scene tech.

"We dusted for prints," the tech said. "Found several different sets. Lots of fibers— won't know if there's anything significant about them for a while."

That wasn't much. "Nothing else?" Randolph asked.

"I was saving the best for last," the tech said with a grin. "We found two different kinds of shells in here. Two shotgun shells from a 20 gauge and one from a 9 mm. We almost missed the shell from the 9 mm."

Santos stood over William Doyle's body and processed this information while Randolph moved on to look at Ethan Doyle's bedroom. Two guns. Did that mean there were two intruders? They would have to wait for the medical examiner's report to see exactly how many gunshots were fired into the Doyles and what kinds of guns were used.

The house wasn't ransacked. It didn't appear that any valuables had been taken in the murders, so robbery wasn't a likely motive.

"Hey," Randolph said, interrupting her thoughts. He handed her a five-by-seven gold picture frame that held a photo of Ethan Doyle standing next to his grandfather. Ethan was proudly holding up a shotgun with a camouflage finish.

Forensics would have to confirm it, but it looked very much like the shotgun found in the cornfield belonged to Ethan Doyle. But where was he now? And what happened to Becky Allen?

24

Wylie kept a flashlight focused on the woman and did her best to assess the woman's injuries as she dozed. One eye was swollen completely shut, her cheek bulged eggplant purple and her lip needed stitches. Her nose was off-center and blisters dotted the tips of her ears. Frostbite. The woman somehow managed to make it to the toolshed and then to the house— that was a good sign, but she needed medical help.

The dark and cold were all-encompassing but the boy wouldn't leave his mother's side. He curled up next to her, once in a while murmuring softly in her ear. So the child could talk, Wylie thought. She had done her best to get more information from the boy by peppering him with questions. *What's your mom's name? What's your name? Are you running from something?*

Wylie aimed the flashlight at her own face. "Look at me," she ordered. "I mean it, look at me." The boy reluctantly lifted his eyes toward Wylie. "Have I hurt you?" He didn't respond. "Even after you pointed a gun at me and hit me with a poker, have I done anything to make you think I was going to hurt you?"

After a moment the boy cautiously shook his head.

"Right," Wylie said. "And I'm not going to hurt your mother either. I promise you."

The boy remained tight-lipped and after a while, Wylie gave up and went to the kitchen. It was freezing. She taped over the broken window with cardboard, and gathered the wood that she had dropped outside. She added several pieces to the fireplace until the flames grew. It would take a while before the room grew warm again. Wylie sat down across from the boy.

Wylie tried to ignore the sharp whistle and pop of the old pipes freezing. The wind continued to scream, rattling the windows.

"I really need your help," Wylie said softly. "You have to tell me who you are, where you've come from."

They sat in silence for a moment, both listening to the woman's ragged breathing and watching the weak puffs of white air appear then fade from her swollen lips.

"If you're running from someone, I can help you—I can help protect you, but you have to talk to me," Wylie begged.

The woman opened her eye. "If you want to talk to someone, talk to me," she said.

"Good idea," Wylie said. "Talk."

The woman stayed silent.

"Fine," Wylie said throwing up her hands. "Hopefully help will come soon and then you won't be my problem anymore."

A ripple of fear crossed the woman's face. "We don't need help."

"Doesn't look that way to me," Wylie said.

"Honey," the woman said to the child. "I'm still cold. Can you go find me another blanket?"

"You know where they are," Wylie said and the boy grabbed a flashlight and hurried up the stairs.

"Listen," the woman said when the boy was out of earshot. "We'll wait out the storm and then be on our way. That's it, then we'll be gone. No more questions. Do you understand?"

"Sorry," Wylie shook her head. "I'm afraid I don't work that way. Besides, the only person I'm concerned about in this scenario is that kid upstairs. And there is no way in hell I'm just going to let you leave here without knowing where you plan on taking him and that he's going to be okay."

The woman glared at Wylie, then glanced up at the staircase. "The man who is after us will do anything to get us back." She sat up a bit straighter and winced at the shift in position. "And I will do anything, and I mean anything," she said in a low, dangerous whisper, "to make sure that doesn't happen. Even if I have to cut straight through you to do it."

A cold current of dread coursed through Wylie and she fingered the gun in her pocket. She believed the woman.

The boy came down the steps, his arms filled with blankets. "Here, Mama," he said proudly. "I brought you two blankets. Will this be enough?"

"Thank you, sweetie," she said, still staring at Wylie. "That is just the perfect amount."

25

August 2000

Margo Allen sat on a chair in her kitchen while her estranged husband, Kevin, paced the floor. The deputy that brought her home had suggested that she call a neighbor to come over and take their younger children while they waited for word. Margo shook her head. There was no way she was going to let her kids out of her sight. Four-year-old Toby was sitting on her lap playing with the silver cross on her necklace while ten-year-old Addie sat across from them, staring intently at her handheld video game.

After seeing the medical examiner pull into the Doyles' drive, Margo nearly passed out. She had never felt such fear before in her life. It was as if someone had reached right down her throat and snatched her breath away. The sheriff wouldn't say who was dead, only that it wasn't Becky. The sheriff murmured a bunch of promises and then handed her off to another deputy, who was little or no help.

When she begged the deputy to take her to Becky, he had to admit that they had no idea where she was, just that everyone was doing everything they could to find her. Margo had lost it then and tried to run into the Doyle house. It took three officers to hold her back. She hadn't meant to cause a scene; she just wanted to see for herself that Becky wasn't in the house.

A deputy drove Margo home while another officer followed behind in Margo's car. By the time they arrived at the small gray house on Laurel Street, it was to find her husband sitting at the kitchen table and the babysitter gone.

"Why haven't we heard anything?" Kevin wanted to know. Like Margo, his eyes were red from crying. Someone was dead, Josie was whisked off to the hospital, and Becky had disappeared.

"I'm sorry, Mr. Allen, I'm sure the sheriff will touch base soon. Are you sure there is no one that you'd like me to call for you? A family member or a friend?"

Margo shook her head. She knew that she should call her parents but they lived in Omaha and would insist on making the four-hour drive. She wasn't ready for that. She willed Becky to come bouncing through the front door, out of breath and apologetic for making them worry. Then Margo could call her mom and complain about how Becky was turning into one of *those* teenagers.

There was a rap at the front door, and Margo quickly stood and then sat back down. Becky wouldn't knock. She stood in the kitchen doorway while Deputy Dahl went to answer the door. He went outside and several minutes later came inside with a woman Margo didn't recognize. She introduced herself as Agent Camila Santos from the Iowa Department of Criminal Investigation.

"Have you found her?" Kevin Allen asked.

"I'm afraid not," Agent Santos said, glancing down at the little boy Margo held on her lap. He kept patting at his mother's face, wiping away the tears. The other child was engrossed in a video game, all the while stealing looks at the adults in the room.

"Ma'am," Agent Santo said gently. "In these situations, we find it vital to have someone here as a support to the families. Is there a family member or friend we can call?" Maybe it was the fact that Agent Santos was a woman, or perhaps because it was her status as an agent that made Margo listen.

Margo nodded and wrote down a phone number and a name on a scrap of paper. Agent Santos handed the slip of paper to the deputy. "Addie, take your brother into our bedroom and turn on the TV."

"Okay, Mommy," Addie said in a small voice and slipped from her chair and grabbed Toby by the hand and led him from the room.

"Oh, my God," Margo rocked back and forth in her seat. "Oh, my God." Agent Santos watched quietly as Kevin went behind her and laid his hands on her shoulders, but she shrugged them away. Margo cleared her throat. "Can you tell me what's going on? The deputy couldn't tell us much."

"Mr. and Mrs. Allen," Agent Santos took the seat across from her. "This is what we know. William and Lynne Doyle were killed last night. Their daughter, Josie, was shot. When law enforcement arrived on the scene, Ethan Doyle and your daughter weren't there."

Margo gripped her hands together tightly, pressing her fingernails into her skin, leaving behind half-moon indentations.

Agent Santos continued. "From what Josie Doyle could tell

us, she lost sight of Becky. We're acting on two possibilities right now. One, Becky ran away and is hiding somewhere, and two, the perpetrator took Becky with him."

Behind Margo, Kevin continued to pace. She wanted to scream at him to hold still, for once in his life to stop moving. Instead, Margo bit the insides of her cheeks until she tasted blood.

"We have an Amber Alert out for a truck that is missing from the scene, and the picture you provided of Becky has gone out to all media outlets. Officers will continue to search the surrounding area and tomorrow, we will bring in search dogs."

"Search dogs?" Kevin stopped in place. "Search dogs are used to find bodies, right? Do you think Becky's dead?" he asked, his voice breaking.

"Shut up, Kevin," Margo said softly.

He started pacing again, walking the length of the narrow galley kitchen, back and forth, back and forth. "That's what dogs are used for. Finding bodies. Is there something you're not telling us? Do you think she's dead?"

"Shut up, Kevin," Margo said again, slapping her hands on the table. The sharp crack filled the room. The sting radiated through her palms and into her wrists. It was a relief to feel the pain in Margo's chest shift to her hands. She slammed them down again and again and again. *Thwack, thwack, thwack.*

She wanted the cheap plywood table to splinter into a million bits but still it held. *Thwack, thwack, thwack.* She curled her hands into fists and tried again. She felt a bone give in her left pinky, but still she pounded on the table. Kevin finally stopped moving and stood, frozen in place, staring at his wife as if she was a stranger. Addie ran into the room to see what was happening, her eyes wide with fear.

Agent Santos, laid her hands atop Margo's so they were pinned to the table. Her skin felt cool against the heat of Margo's. "I know," Agent Santos said in a low voice. "I know."

Margo looked into Agent Santos's dark eyes and Margo knew that this woman had seen things. Terrible things. But there was something else—a tiny glint of hope. Margo latched on to that glimmer and held the agent's gaze. It was going to be okay. It had to be okay.

Back at the sheriff's office, Deputy Levi Robbins entered the shotgun into evidence and put out a *be on the lookout* or BOLO for Ethan Doyle's Datsun truck, but something else was gnawing at his brain.

Brock Cutter and Ethan Doyle were friends. Josie said they had seen Brock earlier that evening. It was after 1:00 a.m. when he pulled Cutter over for speeding, and he was coming from the direction of the Doyle farm. Levi knew he should have spoken up about pulling Brock over but decided to wait until he heard what the kid had to say. Levi hoped he hadn't missed something important.

He headed toward the Cutter farm but lucked out and saw what looked to be Brock's truck parked at the gas station. Levi swung into the lot and pulled into a spot at the far corner. The heat rose from the concrete in waves and had putrefied whatever was in the garbage can so that it emitted a foul smell. Levi leaned against Brock's truck and waited.

Brock exited the gas station with a Gatorade under one arm, sauntered toward his vehicle, and did a double take when he saw Levi. From the way his eyes darted from left to right, Levi thought he might bolt. "Why you so nervous?" Levi asked. "I just want to ask you a few questions."

"About what?" Cutter said suspiciously. He didn't look well. Unkempt and tired. Pretty much how Levi felt himself.

"About the murders at the Doyle farm," Levi said, watching Cutter carefully.

His shoulders sagged. "Yeah, I heard. It's really sad," Cutter said. "Did they find Ethan and that girl yet?"

"So, you know Ethan Doyle?" Levi asked.

"Well, yeah," Cutter said, taking a swig from his bottle of Gatorade. "We go to school together."

"When's the last time you saw him?" Levi asked, rubbing his neck, his hand coming back slick with sweat.

Cutter looked skyward. "Umm, it's been a while. We got in trouble at the beginning of summer for fighting..."

"Against each other?" Levi interrupted.

"No, together. We ran into some jerks, got in a fight. It was nothing." Cutter shook his head regretfully. "Our parents said we couldn't hang out anymore." The kid was lying or Josie Doyle was. Levi couldn't think of a reason why the girl would lie about seeing Brock Cutter on the day her parents were murdered.

Levi wanted to see how far Brock would take the lie.

"But I stopped you not far from his house last night. What were you up to?" Levi asked. "You sure were going fast."

"I told you, I was late coming home. My dad was going to be pissed," Cutter said defensively.

"You were at a movie, right? What movie?" Levi probed.

"*Scary Movie,*" Cutter said. "I went with my cousin, Rick. You can call him."

Levi nodded. "Yeah, I'll do that. So, any ideas where Ethan might be?"

Cutter shook his head. "Nah, man. Like I said, we hadn't seen each other in a long time. Last I heard, he was grounded."

"How 'bout you give me your best guess," Levi pushed.

"I don't know, he liked to go fishing, maybe the pool. He dated Kara Turner for a while, maybe over there," Levi said, then drained the last of his drink. "That's all I can really think of."

"Okay," Levi said, letting Cutter's lie drop for now. He'd get him into the station for a formal interview tomorrow, pin him down then. In the meantime, he'd keep a close eye on Brock, follow him. Maybe he'd lead him right to Ethan Doyle. "If you think of anything else, give me a call, got it?" Levi said pointedly.

"Sure thing," Cutter said, dropping his drink into the garbage can. "I hope you find him."

"Me too," Levi said as Cutter walked away. *The kid is lying,* Levi thought. But why? Was he protecting Ethan Doyle or himself?

Three hundred miles away, not far from Leroy, Nebraska, Nebraska State Trooper Phillip Loeb was traveling west on I-80. He had received an alert to be on the lookout for a 1990 silver Datsun pickup truck and damned if there wasn't one in his rearview mirror. That was some bad business over in Iowa. Two dead, two missing.

Of course, he'd have to get a better look, run the plates. It was probably a false alarm—they usually were.

Loeb slowed his cruiser hoping that the truck would come up beside him to get a look inside, but as he reduced his speed, so did the truck. Several vehicles passed the trooper but the silver truck lagged farther behind. Interesting.

Loeb couldn't get a good look at the occupants in the truck

from his vantage point, but he could see there were two people in the cab. His pulse quickened. He needed to get behind that truck. He called dispatch with his position but the closest trooper was forty miles away. Loeb didn't want to wait that long for backup to arrive but also knew that the lives of two teens could be at stake.

Again, Loeb slowed down, but so did the truck, allowing several vehicles to come between them. The driver was definitely trying to evade him.

Just as Loeb pulled off to the side of the road to let the truck pass him, the driver stomped on the gas. As it roared past the idling cruiser, Loeb got a glimpse of the passenger—a young woman who stared back at him in terror.

Loeb pulled back onto the road and began pursuing the truck, now traveling in excess of eighty miles per hour.

"Dammit," Loeb muttered. He flipped on his siren and lights but had to wait for several vehicles to get out of his way before he could safely return to the road. He accelerated, the red needle on the speedometer hovering around ninety miles per hour.

The cars in front of him were quickly pulling off the road to let him pass until there was only one vehicle between Loeb and the truck. The car, driven by an oblivious young man, wasn't slowing down, wasn't pulling off to the side.

Loeb moved to the left lane to pass the car, and that's when he realized his mistake. The driver of the truck yanked the steering wheel to the right, barely catching the exit.

There was no way Loeb was able to follow suit and he watched helplessly while the exit flew by. Cursing under his breath, Loeb slowed and at the next break in the median made a U-turn.

By the time Loeb made it to the exit ramp, the silver truck was long gone.

★ ★ ★

Agent Santos stood in the middle of Becky Allen's small bedroom and tried to step into the mind of a thirteen-year-old. The room was messy, with an unmade bed and clothes tossed onto the floor. Tacked to the wood-paneled walls were posters of Christina Aguilera, Mandy Moore, and the Backstreet Boys.

She had looked through Becky's drawers, beneath the bed, in the closet—all the obvious spots—but found nothing of particular interest. A new backpack with the tag still on it sat in the corner of the room next to two Walmart bags filled with supplies for the coming school year: notebooks, folders, binders, markers, pens, and pencils.

From what Santos could see, Becky listened to pop music, read books from the Goosebumps and The Baby-Sitters Club series, and from the crumpled-up wrappers beneath her bed, had an affinity for Laffy Taffy and caramel apple suckers. Nothing to indicate that Becky had a secret life. Still, she was missing along with a sixteen-year-old boy. The question was, did she go willingly?

Santos sat on the edge of Becky's bed and lifted one of the Walmart bags from the floor. Inside were notebooks in a variety of colors and a package of fine-tipped markers that had been opened. Santos pulled out the stack of notebooks. She opened the one on top, and sure enough, Becky had written her name on the inside cover using fat, round bubble letters. She flipped through the empty pages until a flash of color caught her eye.

Santos examined the page crammed with doodles of flowers, hearts, stars, and random letters. Among the frenzy of color Santos's eyes landed on a series of letters traced heavily in blue ink. BJA+ED. Becky Jean Allen. Ethan Doyle.

Maybe Becky had left willingly with Ethan. Young love gone rogue? Another Bonnie and Clyde or Charles Starkweather and Caril Fugate? Star-crossed lovers who went on deadly crime sprees. Santos had a few more questions for Margo and Kevin Allen.

Not relishing having this conversation with the Allens, Santos carried the notebook back to the kitchen. Elbows on the table, Margo was resting her head in her hands and Kevin was talking on the phone, his voice breaking with emotion.

Kevin quickly disconnected his call and, wiping his eyes, said, "My sister. I was telling her what was going on."

"We need to keep the lines open," Margo said sharply. "In case Becky calls."

Kevin began to argue, but Santos interjected by holding up Becky's notebook, opened to the page of doodles, then set it on the table in front of Margo. Kevin peered over Margo's shoulder to get a better look.

"What?" Kevin asked. "It's just a bunch of scribbles."

Agent Santos tapped the initials with her finger. "BJA+ED. Did Becky and Ethan have any kind of relationship?" she asked.

"Relationship?" Margo repeated indignantly. "She's barely thirteen! Thirteen-year-olds don't have relationships. They have crushes."

"I'm sorry, I have to ask," Santos said. "Is there any chance that Ethan Doyle may have reciprocated? Felt the same way about Becky?"

"Ethan Doyle is what? Sixteen years old?" Kevin asked with disgust. "What sixteen-year-old wants to hang out with a kid going into the eighth grade?"

"They don't," Margo said, her voice shaking. "Not any normal sixteen-year-old. Are you saying that Ethan Doyle did this? That he murdered his parents and took Becky?"

"I'm not saying that at all," Santos said. "But we have to look at all angles. All possibilities. I need to know if you have any knowledge of a relationship...any connections between Becky and Ethan beyond Ethan being her best friend's brother."

"No, nothing," Kevin said immediately, but Santos was watching Margo. Her expression said something different.

"Mrs. Allen?" Santos prompted, but before she could respond, the deputy came into the room and pulled her aside.

"What?" Margo asked fearfully. "What is it?"

"I have to step out for a moment," Santos said. "I'll be back."

"What happened?" Margo cried. "Did you find her? Oh, my God. Please, I can't take this. You have to tell me." Kevin crouched down next to Margo and put his arms around her. This time she didn't pull away.

"I promise you, as soon as I learn any information that has been confirmed, I will share it with you," Santos told them. "Lots of tips that come in end up being irrelevant. It's our job to sift through them all. I know it's hard, but please be patient. I will keep you informed. I promise."

Agent Santos left the room with Margo Allen's sobs trailing behind her and stepped outside to call Randolph.

"What's going on?" Santos looked around to make sure she was out of earshot.

"Just got word that a truck matching the description of Ethan Doyle's truck was spotted heading west on I-80 over in Nebraska," Randolph said. "Still waiting for confirmation."

"Got it," Santos said. "I just need to ask the Allens a few more questions and then I'll head over to the church."

"This could be it," Randolph said.

"Could be," Santos murmured. "See you soon." Finding the truck would be huge, but who they found inside the truck, that would be key.

Hopefully, Ethan Doyle and Becky Allen would be safe and the perpetrator apprehended. She prayed the two had nothing to do with the murders—Josie Doyle and both families needed a happier ending than that. But Santos knew that crimes as gruesome as this left behind more than just physical carnage. No matter what was found in that truck, the Doyles and the Allens would never be the same.

26

The girl peeked outside and could see the trees swaying in the wind, sweeping the gold and red and yellow leaves from branches. They scuttled across the grass, racing each other until they rested in piles in front of the window.

The room was chilly and the girl was restless. There was nothing on television and she was tired of drawing pictures. She eyed the box of books that sat in the corner next to the bed. She hadn't touched them since the day her father had brought them. She was still angry that he hadn't brought a dog like he promised. But now she was bored, and even a box of old books was better than just looking out her sliver of a window.

Once again, a moldy smell rose from inside the box when she opened it. Though she didn't want to admit it, a flutter of excitement danced in her stomach. The girl liked books. Liked escaping into stories and pictures, and here was an entire box filled with books she'd never seen before. A bit of the iciness she felt toward her father melted.

"We're almost out of food," came her mother's voice from across the room.

The girl continued to sort through the box. There were picture books. One with the illustration of a man holding an umbrella to cover his head while food fell from the sky and one with two hippos named George and Martha.

"This is it," her mother said. "This is all that's left. This and a little bit of peanut butter."

The girl looked up from a book that showed a naughty little boy holding a purple crayon. Her mother held up a can of soup and a sleeve of crackers.

"He'll come soon with more," the little girl said. She wasn't worried. Her father always came with groceries. She didn't always like what he brought home, but they always had something to eat.

For supper they had the soup. Her mother let her open the can using the opener and pour it into the glass bowl and add the water. She even let her press the buttons on the small microwave to heat it up. "We'll save the crackers for later," her mother said.

They ate. The girl went back to the box of books.

The next morning, for breakfast, they each had three crackers. At lunchtime they each ate two with peanut butter. Still, the girl's father didn't come.

"Maybe he's not coming back," the girl said and took another drink of water. Her mother said it would help fill her stomach.

"He'll come back," her mother said but the girl could hear the worry in her voice. "He has to."

For supper the girl ate two crackers with peanut butter and her mother had one. The jar of peanut butter was empty. They drank more water. That night the girl had trouble sleeping. Her stomach rumbled and she kept thinking about the remaining two crackers. What would *they do when there was nothing left? What if her father didn't come back? They would starve to death.*

She crawled from the bed, careful not to wake her mother, and checked to see if the crackers were still there. They were. The girl wanted to snatch them from their plastic wrapper and eat them, but that wouldn't be fair. She went back to bed and tried to sleep.

The next morning, her mother gave her both the crackers. "I'm not hungry," she said. The girl didn't believe her but still ate the crackers in small mouselike nibbles, trying to make them last as long as possible. Lunchtime passed, and so did dinner. Her father didn't come.

The girl grew cranky. Water sloshed around in her empty stomach making her feel sick. "I'm hungry," she complained. "When is Dad coming?" she asked.

"There is no food," her mother finally snapped. "It's all gone. There is nothing left."

"Then you should go out there and get some," the girl shot back. Her mother grew very quiet.

Out There. That's what they called it. Don't go Out There, her mother would say, your father will get mad, it's not safe.

Her father would say, "There are bad people Out There. They will take you away from us, and you'll never see your mother again."

So they never left. They stayed in the basement with its concrete floors and cement walls.

But to her surprise, the girl's mother walked up the stairs and stood at the closed door. She tentatively reached out and gave the doorknob a twist. The door was locked. Her mother came back down the steps and stood in the center of the room.

"What are you doing?" the girl asked, but her mother waved her away.

She stood there for a long time and then told the girl to find her a pen. "A pen?" the girl asked in confusion.

"Get me a pen," her mother ordered sharply. The girl hurried to

her art box, found what she was looking for, and then handed it to her mother. To her surprise, her mother twisted the pen until the outer plastic covering came loose. She tossed this to the table and examined what remained—the pen's sharp tip and the tube filled with ink. Back up the steps her mother went. The girl followed. Her mother crouched down in front of the door and began to press the tip of the pen into the knob.

"What are you doing?" the girl asked, but her mother hushed her and continued to poke at the doorknob. This went on for what felt like an eternity, but suddenly there was a soft click and the door swung open. It happened that quickly, that easily.

Her mother told her to stay put, but the girl didn't listen. Together they both stepped right into the Out There.

The girl marveled at the sight. The kitchen had a large refrigerator, a stove, a microwave, and there was a dishwasher like she had seen on television. There was a round wooden table with four chairs to match and a long row of cupboards above a shiny countertop.

The girl looked to her mother for an explanation. Why did they have to stay in the basement where they ate from a small plastic table and there was no stove and only a small refrigerator that was smaller than she was?

Her mother wasn't looking around the kitchen, though. She started walking, trancelike, through the kitchen and the dining room where there was another table and more chairs. She moved to yet another room. This one had not just one, but two sofas and a chair to match, a television and a tall, slender clock that nearly went to the ceiling. All the windows in this room were covered with heavy shades.

Her mother wasn't looking at all these wonders either. Her focus was on a large door with three square windows near the top. Bright sunshine streamed through the glass, and the two stood in the sunbeam for a moment, feeling the warmth seep into their skin.

Her mother reached for the knob, but the door refused to open. She fingered the brass lock below the knob, then twisted it to the right. She tried the knob again, the door squeaked open.

It was like looking into a picture book. There were so many colors and scents and sights that the little girl had never seen before that she was momentarily stunned. Without thinking, she moved from the house onto the concrete front steps. The air was cool but warmer than the basement. The sky was blue, and the sun was warm and the color of honey. The trees were covered in jewel-colored leaves and all around them were golden fields for as far as she could see. And there was a lane that led from the front of the house all the way up to the road that went somewhere. To the mountains, to the ocean, to the desert—somewhere far from here.

The world outside was quieter than she imagined. There was the soft rustle of the corn stalks as a breeze swept across the fields, the muffled buzz of green grasshoppers, and the whir and warble song from barn swallows. She bent down to pick a pretty yellow flower when she was jerked back by her arm.

She was pulled back into the house and her mother shut the door and twisted the lock. "We can't go out there," her mother said. She looked scared and her breath was fast and shallow.

Holding hands, they moved back through the living room and the dining room and into the kitchen. "I'm really hungry," the girl said, itching to snatch a banana from the countertop. Her mother opened a cupboard filled with cans of soup and beans and corn. She opened another that held boxes of cereal and crackers and cookies.

"We can't take too much," her mother said, scanning the choices. "If he notices anything missing, he'll know that we were up here." She hesitated but settled on two cans of soup and an orange and an apple from the refrigerator.

"Let's go," her mother said. "He could come home at any time." The girl reached for the knob on the basement door but her mother didn't follow. She stopped at the telephone affixed to the kitchen wall.

The girl watched as, with trembling hands, her mother lifted the re-
ceiver, placed it to her ear, and began to press numbers.

The girl wanted to ask who she was calling. They didn't have a
phone downstairs, she had seen one only on television, but her mother
seemed to know what she was doing. A soft trill came from the phone
and then a woman's voice. "Hello?" she said. "Hello?"

A deep sadness settled onto her mother's face and she quietly hung
up the phone. Carrying their small stash of food, they moved through
the basement door, her mother pausing to engage the lock. They walked
downward, and at the bottom, her mother sat on the bottom step and
began to cry. The girl sat at her feet.

When her mother finally stopped weeping, she wiped at her eyes
and said, "Don't tell your dad about this, okay? It will be our little
secret."

The girl liked the idea of having a secret with her mother, so she
nodded, and they pinky promised. But two questions remained on
her tongue, unasked. Why hadn't they ever gone outside before? And
what was stopping them from doing it again?

27

Present Day

So the woman and the boy were running from an abusive man. It made sense. Fleeing in the middle of a blizzard, her desperation to stay hidden, her paranoia. "The police can help you," Wylie said sitting down across from them. "Once the storm stops, we'll go to the sheriff."

"No," the woman said, shifting in her seat painfully. "You don't understand. He's going to come for us. You don't know what he's like."

Wylie couldn't disagree. She didn't know what this woman had gone through, what kind of man she was married to. Her ex, for all his faults, wasn't an abusive man. Just a stubborn, self-absorbed jerk.

Wylie, in the course of researching her books, had come across some of the most possessive, abusive spouses and partners out there. No, Wylie didn't know what this woman had endured in her relationship, but she could empathize.

"Why don't you tell me your names? Tell me his name?" Wylie asked. "So when the storm lets up, I can go with you to the police and they can help keep you safe."

"I can't." The woman shook her head. "I can't say anything. Not until we get far away from here."

"You've got to trust someone, sometime," Wylie said in exasperation. "Why won't you trust me?"

The woman got to her feet. "Come on," she said to her child. "We're going."

Wylie laughed but then saw that the woman was serious. "Where do you think you are going?" Wylie asked incredulously. "Your truck went up in flames, you're injured, and you think you're going to drag your little boy out into this storm? No, way."

"I'm not a boy," came a small, defiant voice.

"What?" Wylie asked, looking at the child. "What did you say?"

"Shhh," the woman said, glaring at the child. "Don't talk."

"I'm a girl," the child repeated more forcefully, running a hand over her shorn head.

Wylie was dumbstruck. She had been working under the assumption that she had found a little boy lying in her front yard.

"What's your name?" Wylie asked. The girl looked about to speak but her mother cut her off.

"Don't tell her. I mean it," the woman said fiercely, tears springing to her eyes.

"I'm sorry," the girl said, leaning into her mother. "I'm sorry."

"Do you see now?" the woman asked. "Do you think I would cut my daughter's hair like that, just because I wanted to leave my husband? Do you think this is just some custody battle that got out of hand?" The woman was yelling now. "If he finds us, he will kill us." She paused, trying to gather herself. "Or worse. He'll take us back home." The woman pulled up the sleeves of her sweatshirt. A wreath of scabs encircled each wrist.

Wylie was at a loss for words. The wounds on the woman's wrists looked like she had been tied up with something—rope or zip ties or handcuffs.

Clearly, the woman and her daughter were desperate and terrified. They were literally running for their lives. Who was Wylie to drag the details from this poor woman?

They'd be safe here. As awful as her husband sounded, Wylie didn't think he would break into a stranger's house to retrieve his wife and child. He couldn't be disturbed enough to do that, could he?

Wylie would give her some space. Let her rest. And when the storm passed, she would put the woman and her daughter in her Bronco and drive them directly to the sheriff's office.

As for the child, her earlier behavior made so much more sense now. Finally, the girl was opening up to Wylie. She was finally trusting her. And maybe, even if her mother wouldn't tell her their names, where they came from, the little girl would eventually share their history.

28

Sheriff Butler parked in front of the Henley residence and examined the weedy yard and the crumbling front steps. The house's gray exterior was pocked and blistered and in need of a coat of new paint. Butler navigated the broken front steps onto the front porch, the rotten wood groaning beneath his feet, and knocked. There was no answer.

He had met June Henley only a few times over the years. He knew that June and her late husband farmed for decades but that June sold the cropland soon after her husband's death several years before. He remembered June as a friendly, sociable woman and didn't relish the thought of having to question her about Josie and Becky visiting their property the day before, but it had to be done.

The couple had one son, Jackson, who was a pretty decent

baseball player back in the day, enlisted in the army after high school and then spent some time in the military. His last stint was during the Gulf War in '90.

When Jackson's tour ended, he came home and started his ragtag salvage business. That's when his many run-ins with law enforcement began—mostly related to his heavy drinking with a few petty crimes thrown in for good measure. It seemed there was also something in Jackson's record that was more serious, but Butler couldn't quite remember what it was.

Butler knocked on the door again. Still no answer. They didn't have time for this. Every minute that passed meant time lost from finding those kids and who murdered the Doyles. He knew he had to talk to June and Jackson Henley, but he'd be more useful doing something else in the meantime. He'd send a deputy back later.

Butler climbed back into his vehicle and drove slowly down the drive to where the lane widened and he could turn the car around. He passed rows of broken-down vehicles and farm equipment piled on top of each other like carcasses. It was downright eerie, Butler thought as he swung the vehicle around and drove around a mountain of black rubber tires baking in the sun.

The house came back into view and Butler saw a white pickup parked in front of the house. Butler pressed on the brakes and squinted through the bright sunshine to see a tall, grizzled man with close-cropped dusty-black hair helping an elderly woman up the porch steps.

June and Jackson Henley.

When Jackson opened the front door, he looked over and spotted the sheriff's car idling in the drive. His eyes widened in alarm.

"Hey, there, Jackson," Butler said casually. "I was hoping you and your mother could help me with something."

Jackson didn't respond and looked at the sheriff with suspicion.

"I'm sure you heard about all the goings-on at the Doyle farm last night. We're trying to re-create a timeline of what Josie Doyle's and Becky Allen's movements were all day yesterday and we know the girls stopped here. It would be mighty helpful if you could tell me about that visit? What time they showed up and what you all talked about."

"I didn't do anything," Jackson said licking his lips nervously. "They were looking for a dog. They didn't find him and went on their way."

"That's what Josie said too," Butler said. He wanted to make sure that Jackson knew the other girl was safe and talking. "I thought you could walk around the property with me, show me where the girls were searching for the dog."

"I don't have to let you on my property," Jackson said inching closer to the truck. "I don't have to talk to you."

"Well, Jackson," Butler said conversationally. "I don't believe this is actually your property. I believe it belongs to your mother."

"You leave my mom alone. She's sick," Jackson said glancing toward the house. "You don't need to bother her with all this."

"But I'm afraid I do," Butler said, his voice filled with regret. "We've got two dead and two missing teens. I have to talk to everyone who saw any of the Doyles or Becky Allen yesterday." Butler tried to give Jackson a friendly smile. "How about it? Let's take a walk around and talk."

Butler saw the indecision on Jackson's face that he'd seen on hundreds of people over the years—should he get back in the truck and take off or stop and wait to see what the sheriff wanted?

Jackson didn't quite do either. He left the truck where it was and took off on foot. Butler watched as the man sprinted behind the house, his boots kicking up thick gray dust in his wake. That was when, in a split second, Jackson Henley went from witness to person of interest.

A buzz of excitement coursed through the sheriff. People ran when they were guilty or scared. Butler maneuvered his vehicle around Henley's truck and parked. He got on his car radio and summoned dispatch. Through the crackling static, Butler told them to have backup on standby and to pull any records they had on Jackson Henley.

Butler knew that he didn't have the legal power to do a search just yet, so he'd have to get permission another way.

Butler exited his car on heightened alert. There were too many unknowns—why Henley had bolted, where he was hiding, what firearms and weapons he had access to.

Hand resting on his sidearm, Butler made his way up the decaying front steps and knocked. June Henley answered the door, her pink hat askew on her head. Butler was struck at how frail the woman looked—as if she could collapse at any moment.

June looked wearily up at Butler. "I imagine you're here to talk about those two girls," she said. "Come on in."

Three hundred miles away, State Trooper Phillip Loeb was still on the hunt for the silver truck. He had taken the exit to McCool Junction, a tiny village about five miles off I-80. Other troopers had also joined the search and were keeping an eye out in case the truck returned to the interstate. But Loeb had a feeling that the driver pulled into McCool to hide. He crept slowly down the quiet streets in search of the truck.

Every other car was a pickup, making his search more difficult. He passed the school, a bank, and a drive-in restaurant.

Loeb took Road 4 out of McCool Junction, came to the
speedway and pulled into the parking lot. And there it was.
The silver truck and its two inhabitants, just sitting there. Loeb
called in his position, pulled out his sidearm, and cautiously
exited his car, taking cover behind the cruiser.

There were no plates on the truck, sending up another red
flag. This was it. He could feel it. "Hands on the steering
wheel," Loeb shouted. "Hands on the dashboard!" He half
expected for the driver to take off, but the truck stayed put.

Within minutes, two more state troopers arrived, as did
three deputies from the York County Sheriff's Department.
Using their vehicles as a blockade, they boxed the truck in.
There was no escape. The law enforcement officers exited
their cars, guns drawn.

"Driver," Loeb shouted. "Open your door." The driver's
side door swung open. "Show me your hands, show me your
hands!" A pair of trembling hands appeared. "Driver, step
slowly from the vehicle," Loeb ordered. One tennis shoe and
then another touched the concrete, and a tall figure unfolded
himself from the truck.

It was a young man, his eyes wild with terror.

"I'm sorry," he stammered. "I'm sorry."

"Get on the ground," another trooper shouted, and the boy
lowered himself to the concrete, hands stretched out. Then
the officers were upon him, guns pointed at his head, pulling
his wrists behind his back.

Loeb turned his attention to the truck's passenger. "Passenger, open the door, hands up!" A petite figure lowered herself
from the truck, hands above her head.

"Are you injured?" Loeb asked. "Did he hurt you?" The sobbing girl shook her head.

"Becky Allen?" he asked. "Are you Becky Allen?"

She looked at the trooper in confusion. "No," she shook her head. "My name is Christina."

Sheriff Butler took off his hat as he stepped into June Henley's living room. The air was cool and smelled of eucalyptus, the hot sun kept out by heavy drapes. The room was sparsely furnished, tidy, and clean. An end table was covered in pill bottles, neatly lined up next to a glass of water. A television tuned to a soap opera sat in a corner. "Yes, ma'am," he said. "I'm here about the two girls."

June settled her thin frame into a chair upholstered in a fabric covered with faded pink cabbage roses. Butler sat across from her on the matching love seat.

"It was reported that Josie Doyle and Becky Allen were here last night," Butler said, getting right to the point.

"They were," June said. "I talked to them around seven o'clock or so. They were looking for a dog. I told them they could go and look for it on the property." She picked up a pill bottle from the table next to her and struggled with the lid.

Sheriff Butler held out his hand and June handed him the bottle. "How long were they here?" Butler asked, twisting the lid open.

"Not long," June said. "Thank you," she said gratefully when Butler handed her the open bottle. "Twenty minutes? Maybe less. They waved goodbye when they left."

"Do you know if your son had any interaction with the girls?" Butler asked.

June tapped two pills into her palm, put them in her mouth,

and took a drink from the glass next to her. "Not that I know of," June said after swallowing. "He didn't mention it."

"Can you think of any reason Jackson would take off when he saw me?" he asked.

"What do you mean?" June asked warily.

"He saw me after he dropped you off at the door and then rushed off. Now, why would he do that?" Butler asked.

June waved Butler's concern away. "Last time he talked to one of you, he was arrested. Can't blame him for being a little reluctant."

Sheriff Butler suddenly remembered the incident June was speaking about. About six months before, Jackson had been picked up after a woman from Burden called saying a man had walked into her house drunker than a skunk and tried to climb into bed with her.

Jackson ended up spending a few nights in the county jail and pleading guilty to public intoxication and trespassing.

"Who was driving the truck that brought you home today?" the sheriff asked.

June's eyes narrowed. "I did," she said firmly. "Jackson came with me to my chemo appointment, but I drove."

Sheriff Butler nodded but had his doubts. Jackson lost his driver's license due to his drinking a long time ago but was most likely still driving all over the county when he had the chance.

"Would you mind if I looked around the property a bit?" Butler asked. "You know we don't have any time to waste. We need to find those kids."

"Then you better not waste your time looking here," June said sharply. She struggled out of the chair and to her feet. "I told you that the girls were here looking for a dog. They looked and they left. That's all we know."

By the time June reached the front door, she was out of breath. Butler followed. "Now, Mrs. Henley, you know we need to do all we can to find those girls. Can you please tell Jackson that I need to talk to him?"

June opened her mouth to argue, but Butler held up a finger. "Just to talk. I know Jackson is skittish around law enforcement, and I have no reason to think that he knows what happened to Becky Allen after she left your property, but she was here, and I need to talk to everyone who came into contact with her. You can understand that, can't you?"

June pressed her thin lips together and nodded. "I'll tell him you want to talk to him, but he won't be able to tell you any more than I did."

Butler stepped from the coolness of the house into the heavy, oppressive heat. He had made a mistake by putting June Henley on the defensive. He'd be back, though, and if Jackson refused to speak to him, he'd come armed with a search warrant. Maybe they could get some answers that way.

29

The girl's father did show up, though it would take three more days. He came through the door carrying a bucket of chicken and a plastic bag filled with containers of mashed potatoes, corn, coleslaw, and gravy.

The smell of the food made the girl dizzy. She was so hungry. She looked to her mother to see if it was okay to go to her father, but her mother's face was hard. Angry. So she stayed put. Her mother got shakily to her feet and stood in front of him, hands on hips. "You left us," she said. "You left us with no food. We haven't eaten in three days."

"Well, you have food now," he brushed past her and set the food on the table.

Her mother followed him. "You can't do that," she grabbed his arm. "You can't leave us like that." Her father turned and glowered down at her mother. She released her grip on his elbow but boldly stared back at him.

The blow came without warning. His fist struck the solar plexus *forcing the air from her mother's lungs. Her legs buckled and she fell to her knees, gasping for breath. The girl moved to go to her mother's side, but she stopped when her father raised one finger.*

"Go sit down," he said, pointing at a chair. The girl took a seat at the table. Her mother remained on her knees, still fighting for air. Her father pulled two plates out of a cupboard and fished silverware from the drawer. He lifted the lids from each of the cartons and began to pile food on her plate and then on his own. Crispy fried chicken, mounds of potatoes and corn, rich brown gravy.

"Eat," he ordered and sat down in a chair across from her.

The girl snuck a look at her mother, who was now curled up in a ball on the floor. "Don't look at her," her father said through a mouth filled with biscuit. "Eat."

The girl picked up a piece of chicken and took a bite. Though the food was cold, it was delicious. She felt terrible for eating in front of her mother but could not stop. Across from her, the girl's father spooned the food into his mouth with exaggerated relish. "So good," he said through a mouthful of mashed potatoes. After picking all the meat from a piece of chicken, he dropped the bones with a clatter to the floor next to her mother.

The girl hated him, but still she ate. The food disappeared from her plate, even the coleslaw, which she thought tasted bitter. Her stomach felt stretched and full, but still she couldn't stop. She ate one biscuit, then two, and didn't complain when her father refilled her plate. When her father wasn't looking, she hid bits of food in her lap beneath the table.

Finally, she laid down her fork and shame, hot and sour, filled her throat. Her fingers were slick with grease and oily crumbs clung to the front of her shirt. Her father laughed. "Good, right?"

It was all the girl could do to keep the food in her stomach. Her mother was cowered on the floor, weak with hunger and fear, and she had eaten without her. She felt disloyal, wicked.

Her father pushed back from the table, stood, and began clearing the nearly empty cartons from the table. Instead of storing the leftovers in the small refrigerator, he made a show of shoving them into the garbage can.

"What do you say, peanut?" her father asked.

"Thank you," the girl said in a small voice.

He stood over her mother, looking down on her with disgust. Her mother braced for another blow. The girl dared not move for fear of spilling the food she had hidden in her lap to the floor. "Grat-i-tude," he said, drawing the word out. "A little bit would be nice, now and then." He waited but her mother remained curled up on the floor. He drew his foot back as if to kick her mother and the girl let out a whimper. Instead, he lightly tapped her with his toe. "What do you say?" he asked as if talking to a child.

"Thank you," her mother said, but she didn't sound thankful at all. Those two words had something new in them. A touch of steel that was never there before.

"You're welcome," he said lightly and then stepped over her. The girl held her breath until he was across the room, up the steps, and out the door.

She waited a few beats longer and then picked the scraps of food from her lap and set them on the table before going to her mother's side. "I'm sorry," she whispered in her ear. "I'm sorry. I shouldn't have eaten without you."

Her mother smiled up at her. "It's okay. I'm glad you got to eat."

"I saved you some," the girl said. "Do you want me to bring it to you?"

Her mother shook her head, her arms wrapped protectively around her midsection. "I think I'm just going to lie here for a few more minutes," she said, her voice tight with pain. The girl went to the bed to get a pillow and tucked it beneath her mother's head.

Her stomach roiled and churned. She felt sick, but she didn't want *to throw up. She never wanted to feel that hungry ever again. She went to the garbage can and began pulling out the discarded cartons of food. Using a spoon, she scraped the remnants, no matter how small, onto a plate.*

When she finished, there was a meager amount of chicken, biscuits, potatoes, and coleslaw. The girl carried the plate to her mother and sat on the floor next to her. "Here, Mama, you have to eat this." Her mother shook her head. "No, you eat."

"I did," the girl insisted. "I'm full. This is for you. Please eat it."

Wincing in pain, her mother pushed herself up from the concrete floor and sat cross-legged, her back against the cold wall. The girl pressed the plate into her hands. "Just one bite," she urged. Her mother lifted the fork to her lips and with tears streaming down her face, began to eat.

30

August 2000

At 4:00 p.m. Agent Santos pulled into the parking lot of St. Mary's Church. Many unique locales had been used for command centers over the years, but a church was something new.

Santos stepped through the main doors into the entryway and was met with the familiar scent of the churches from her childhood. The woodsy, smoky smell of frankincense and myrrh resin that had permeated the red carpet and the stone walls.

Instead of crossing into the nave, Santos took the steps that led down to the basement. In just a few hours, Randolph had managed to set up quite an impressive command post: computers, printers, phones, radios, and local maps.

Sheriff Butler and several deputies sat in folding chairs at a table that had been set up in front of a whiteboard. Agent

Randolph stood, dry-erase marker in hand, jotting down notes in his neat print.

"What have we got?" Santos asked, pulling up a chair. "What happened with the possible sighting in Nebraska?"

"Dead end," Randolph said, shaking his head. "Two teens. Kid swiped his parents' truck to take his girlfriend to Lincoln for the day. He panicked when he saw the state trooper and took off. There have been no other sightings of the truck," Randolph added.

"Okay. What else do we have?" Santos asked.

A deputy named Foster spoke up. "Backgrounds on Kevin and Margo Allen came up clean. Mom said she was home with her two younger kids during the murders, and the dad said he was at his house with his girlfriend. The girlfriend confirmed this."

"No custody dispute in the divorce?" Randolph asked.

Foster shook her head.

"Both parents did seem genuinely distraught," Santos agreed. "And they are being fully cooperative. What else?"

"We've run a list of local sex offenders, and two deputies are running them down," Randolph said. "We also have several officers going door-to-door in the vicinity of the Doyle home and interviewing the residents to see if they heard or saw anything."

"How about you, Sheriff?" Santos asked.

Sheriff Butler described his conversation with June Henley and Jackson's curious behavior. "I think it's worth a follow-up, but Jackson Henley is just a messy drunk. I don't see him getting violent, and to my knowledge, he hasn't had any kind of conflict with the Doyles."

"That brings us back to the two missing teens," Santos said.

"What do we know about Ethan Doyle? What was his relationship like with his parents?"

"We've never had any domestic calls out to their home," Butler said, "but Ethan did get questioned by the police concerning a fight he got into with some other teens."

"And there was that call from Kurt Turner about Ethan stalking his daughter," Foster added.

"Yeah, that's right," Butler said. "Dad was mad because Ethan wouldn't stay away from his daughter. He kept showing up at the house, calling. A deputy was sent over to talk to Ethan about keeping his distance. No charges were ever filed."

Santos shared what she found in Becky Allen's bedroom. "It could just be a schoolgirl crush, but Becky did have some kind of feelings for Ethan. Could they have run off together?"

"Josie Doyle hasn't said much yet," Sheriff Butler relayed. "She's still at the hospital getting checked out. But from what she told us at the scene—Becky Allen was just as frightened as she was. They were both running toward the cornfield when they were separated."

The group heard footsteps and turned to see Deputy Levi Robbins walking toward them. "Sorry I'm late," he murmured, taking a seat.

"So maybe Ethan Doyle and his parents fought," Randolph suggested. "He killed them, shot his sister, and then either killed the Allen girl, or took her with him."

"I'd hate for that to be true, but it sounds plausible," the sheriff said. "What did you find out from the Cutter boy?" he asked Levi.

Levi shook his head. "We need to bring him in and conduct a formal interview." Levi explained how he had pulled Brock over not far from the Doyle home around 1:00 a.m.

"He said he was at a movie with his cousin," Levi said.

"I tracked down the cousin, and at first, his story matched Brock's, but when I pressed him for details, it all fell apart. He didn't see Brock at all last night. The kid lied."

"Could be he's protecting his friend," Sheriff Butler said, rubbing his eyes wearily.

"I don't want to get tunnel vision here," Santos said, pushing her chair away from the table. "But it's looking like Ethan Doyle is at the top of our suspect list. Levi, keep an eye on Brock Cutter, see if he leads us to anything."

She turned to Sheriff Butler. "We need to follow up on Jackson Henley but in the meantime you can introduce me to Josie Doyle. See if she has anything new to add."

The door opened, and Dr. Lopez stepped into the room with Sheriff Butler and two strangers.

"Josie," Dr. Lopez said, "how are you doing?"

"Okay," Josie said, looking uncertainly at the man and the woman with Sheriff Butler.

"Your arm will be sore for a while. We'll give you some pain medication and you should be sure to keep the wound dry. But the good news is that you don't have to spend the night here. You can go home with your grandmother in just a little while."

Josie looked at her grandmother, startled. They were going back to the house? She didn't know if she could ever go back there. Josie thought of her bedroom and all her prized possessions. Her Discman and CDs. Her 4-H medals and collection of glass animal figurines that sat on the windowsill. An image of her father lying on her bedroom floor, face gone, flashed behind her eyes. Miserably, she looked to her grandmother.

Caroline patted Josie's hand as if reading her mind. "You're going to our house," she said.

Josie nodded, taking this in. Of course, she wouldn't be going back to the house. Her parents were dead. She and Ethan couldn't live in their home by themselves—they were orphans.

The sheriff cleared his throat and removed his stiff brown hat. He looked at Josie over his hawkish nose. "Josie, glad to see you are doing okay," he said. "This is Agent Santos and Agent Randolph from the DCI in Des Moines. They're investigating the…what happened at your house last night. They'd like to talk to you for a few minutes."

To Josie, they didn't look like police officers. They weren't wearing uniforms. The woman wore black pants and a matching jacket.

Josie looked to her grandmother, who nodded her approval. "Okay," Josie said, shifting in the hospital bed.

Dr. Lopez took her leave, and Agent Santos pulled up a chair and sat down next to the bed so close that Josie could smell the oil used to clean her sidearm. Sheriff Butler and the other agent stood with their backs against the wall to observe. Caroline stayed where she was, next to her granddaughter.

"I know you've been through a lot, Josie," Agent Santos said kindly. "And we wouldn't be here if it wasn't important. I just have a few questions for you right now, okay?"

Josie nodded.

"Tell me about your brother, Josie," she said.

"Ethan?" Josie asked in surprise. "Do you know where he is?"

"No, I'm afraid not," Agent Santos said, tucking a wayward strand of hair behind her ear. "But that's where we need your help."

"Me?" Josie asked. "I don't know where he is. Maybe he got scared and hid like I did. My grandma said people are looking in the cornfield."

"Yes, yes, they are," Agent Santos said. "We've got people out looking, but we want to make sure that we don't miss a spot that Ethan might be. Where are some of his favorite places to go?"

"I don't know," Josie shrugged. "He spends a lot of time in his bedroom."

"Anywhere else?" Agent Randolph asked from his position by the door. "A certain friend's house? A girlfriend, maybe?"

"Ethan doesn't have a girlfriend," Josie said automatically, leaving out Kara Turner. That hadn't ended well.

"We already know about Kara," Santos said, and Josie blushed at getting caught in a lie. "Where does Ethan spend his time?"

"He likes to go fishing at Grandpa's pond and at the creek," Josie said. "He does that most days." Agent Santos wrote this down in a little notebook she produced from her pocket. "Any friends he spends time with?"

"Cutter," Josie said. "He hangs out with him sometimes."

"Ethan and Brock are good friends?" Agent Santos asked.

"Kind of," Josie said. "My mom and dad don't like Ethan hanging out with Cutter. He's kind of wild."

"Wild in what way?" Agent Santos asked.

Josie lifted her shoulders. "He skips school, and he drinks a lot, I think," she explained. "He's kind of creepy."

"Creepy how?" Agent Santos asked.

Josie chewed on a thumbnail. The way Cutter looked at Becky, the way he touched her. It was hard to put into words. "He kept touching Becky, trying to get close to her. She didn't like it."

"She told you that?" Santos asked.

"Not really. But I could tell," Josie said.

"I heard Becky had a bit of a crush on Ethan," Santos said.

"No," Josie said automatically. "I don't think so. She never said anything to me."

"You're doing great, Josie," Santos said. "Just a few more questions for right now. Can you think of anyone who might be angry with your parents? Want to hurt them?"

Josie's first thought was no. Everyone liked her mom and dad. She'd never heard her mother share a cross word and her father made people smile with his gentle teasing. Agent Santos's direct stare made Josie squirm in the hospital bed.

Josie could really only think of one person who had been so angry, so enraged with her parents, but she couldn't say Ethan's name out loud.

"My dad didn't like Brock Cutter's dad," Josie said abruptly.

"Because of the trouble Brock and Ethan got into?" Santos asked.

Josie nodded. "And they just didn't like each other." She didn't quite know how to explain it. Josie wanted her mother. Her mom would know what to do, help Josie find the right words. Sensing her distress, Josie's grandmother jumped in.

"Randy Cutter was quite angry with my daughter and her husband over a parcel of land," Caroline explained. "It got pretty ugly at the time. William bought a piece of farmland that Randy thought should have gone to him. It came to blows, lawyers got involved. When several of their livestock were found dead, William was sure Randy Cutter had something to do with it. Could never prove it, though. Things seemed to have calmed down over the past few years, but things haven't been the same between them since."

"And this was over land?" Santos asked.

"We don't get many homicides around here," Sheriff Butler said, "but when we do, they can usually be traced back to one of two things—infidelity or land disputes."

This was interesting, Santos thought. The Cutter name was coming up again and again.

"We found your brother's gun in the cornfield this morning, Josie," Santos said in a low, serious voice. "Not far from where you said you were hiding." Josie looked down at her bandaged arm. "Can you think why his shotgun would be there?"

Josie shrugged.

"Josie, I know this is hard," Santos said. "But is there any chance that your brother was the one who could have hurt your parents and chased you into the field?"

"No," Josie exclaimed, her eyes filling with tears. "He wouldn't do that, he wouldn't."

"We have tests to show whether a gun has been fired recently. What do you think that test is going to tell us about Ethan's gun?"

"He didn't mean it," Josie cried. "He wasn't aiming at us. He shot into the air."

Agent Santos and Agent Randolph exchanged glances. "You saw your brother shoot his gun yesterday?" Randolph asked.

"Yes, but he wasn't shooting at anyone," Josie insisted. "My arm hurts," she said, looking at her grandmother for help.

"That's enough for now," Caroline said firmly. "The doctor said Josie could go home."

"We'll talk more later," Agent Santos said. "Get some rest, Josie."

Santos and Randolph stepped into the hallway to find Sheriff Butler waiting for them.

"Two dead parents, a girl with a shotgun wound and the boy's missing along with his truck and a thirteen-year-old girl," Santos stated. "It's not looking good for Ethan Doyle."

Sheriff Butler shook his head. "I've known that family for

a long time and I know how it looks, but I'm having a hard time believing Ethan did this."

"How many murders did you say you deal with in a year?" Agent Randolph asked. There was no rancor in his voice, but Butler knew when he was being talked down to.

With the lowest murder rate in the state of Iowa, his county had little experience in dealing with crimes of the nature that took place the night before, but his department worked hard and did their jobs.

"Not many, but I do know the people in this county, and I don't peg Ethan Doyle as a murderer," Butler said. He rubbed his eyes as they walked toward the hospital exit. Agent Randolph went to get the car while Santos lagged behind.

"You okay?" Santos asked as they stood in the blinding sun.

"Yeah," Butler said. "It's not like we don't see bad shit around here, but when kids are involved..." he trailed off.

"I understand," Santos said. "If Ethan Doyle did this—this community will never be the same."

The radio on Butler's hip squawked. He toggled his microphone, "This is Butler, go ahead." A muffled voice came through the speaker, but the message was clear.

"Sheriff," the voice said. "Just got a report from the Allen house. Margo Allen said they received a phone call from someone claiming to be the one who has their daughter."

Butler looked to Santos. "We'll get someone over there right away to see if we can trace the number in case they call back," she said. "Do the same for Josie's grandparents."

Butler relayed the message to dispatch while Santos called for more tech help.

"Could be pranksters," Butler said as Randolph pulled up with the car.

"Yeah, but we can't take that chance," Santos said. "If it isn't the killer, at least we'll catch the sick asshole playing games with the family."

Butler checked his watch. "Ethan and Becky have been gone for about eighteen hours now."

"We'll find them," Santos said. "I just hope they're alive."

"What's next?" Butler asked.

"We keep searching, asking questions, following up on any tips that come in," Santos said. "And tomorrow, we bring in the dogs."

Josie's ride from the hospital to her grandparents' house was made in silence. Her arm ached and her stomach churned. Images of her mother's and father's bodies flashed behind her eyes. They came to her in snapshots, brief but vivid. In Technicolor. Josie begged her grandmother to pull the car over and Caroline swung the car to the side of the road.

Josie opened the car door, gingerly stepped across the gravel to the edge of the ditch, and stood cradling her injured arm. She took big swallows of air until the nausea passed. The Queen Anne's lace bobbed their white heads, and Josie snapped one from its hairy stem, rubbed it between her fingers, and pressed the tiny crushed flowers to her nose. They smelled like the carrots that grew in her mother's garden.

Josie got back in the car, and her grandmother dug into her purse until she found a small wrapped disk of peppermint candy. She handed it to Josie and then went in search of another one. "It helps with upset stomachs," she said. Together they unwrapped the red-and-white candies and slid them between their lips. The crinkle of cellophane and soft sucking sounds filled the car. After a few minutes, Caroline pulled back onto the road. She was right; the candy did help, but only a little.

By the time they got to the house, it was nearing 8:00 p.m., and the sun was melting into the horizon. Orange sherbet sunsets, Josie's mother had called them. Just one mile down the road was her own house, so close, yet she knew that it would never be home to her again.

Night came flooding in so quickly and the house was dark and still. Caroline came to the car's passenger side, opened the door, and held out her hand. Josie took it gratefully. Together they went through the back door and into the mudroom. Matthew's shoes and boots were lined up in a neat row atop a rubber mat and brass hooks on the wall held his barn jacket and an oversized cardigan that Caroline wore on cool summer nights.

A wave of despair settled over her and she began to cry. Great, gulping sobs that came from an unnamed place deep within. Startled, Caroline pulled Josie onto her lap, though she was much too big. Josie pressed her face into her shoulder and cried. They sat there for a long time, Caroline rocking Josie back and forth on her lap like she did for Lynne when she was a little girl.

When Josie stopped crying, Caroline wearily led her up the steps. "We'll have you sleep in here," she said, opening up the door. It was a cozy room, recently painted a soft sage color, outfitted with a twin bed and a table with Caroline's sewing machine atop it.

Gauzy white curtains framed the window, and Caroline went over to pull down the plastic shade, but not before Josie saw a strange car sitting in front of the house.

"Who's that?" Josie asked.

"Just a deputy. He's going to sit outside the house tonight," Caroline said offhandedly as she began to fuss with the bedcovers.

"Just as a precaution, honey. They do that sometimes."

"But why? Are they afraid the bad guy is coming back? Why would he come here?" Josie asked, pulling aside the shade to take another look.

When her grandmother didn't answer, Josie turned from the window. When she saw the look on her face, Josie understood. The deputy was there for her. They were worried that whoever killed her parents was going to come for Josie.

"Don't worry, you're safe here," Caroline said.

Josie climbed into the bed. The sheets smelled of bleach and were cool to the touch. They felt good against her sore feet.

Josie's mind wandered then to dark and lonely places. Her parents were dead. What could they be thinking? Were they happy she was safe at her grandparents' house or did they think she should have done more to try and save them? Did they think she should be with Ethan and Becky, wherever they were?

Then it struck her. Josie's parents, from here on out, for the rest of her life would be looking down on her. They would know her every move, each thought. They knew what she was thinking at that very instant—that she was glad that the deputy was sitting outside in the dark. That a small voice in Josie's head kept whispering, *Ethan did it.* That she thought her own brother had murdered her parents and probably Becky because of something as stupid as being grounded. That Josie would be dead, too, if she hadn't been a step faster than Becky and made it to the field.

Josie opened her eyes. Black shadows danced across the ceiling, and she listened to the unfamiliar creaks and groans of the house settling in for the night as she waited for sleep. It didn't come. Josie heard the squeak of the door as her grandparents peeked in on her. And later, she thought she heard the soft cries of someone weeping but it could have been the hot wind blowing through the fields.

After a while, Josie slipped from the bed and peeked out the window. The deputy was still there. But there was something else. She stared hard into the dark. What was it? A flicker of light? A shift in the shadows?

It was in the dark, Josie thought, where bad things happened.

She turned on the small lamp next to the bed and crawled back beneath the covers. Sleep came for her then, uneasy and fraught with nightmares.

31

August 2000

Agent Santos knocked on Randolph's motel room door just before dawn on the morning of Sunday, August 13. She and Agent Randolph were staying at the Burden Inn, a low-rise motor lodge that was as grim as its name. It was clean at least.

He answered, ready for the day, wearing his suit jacket and tie.

Santos stepped into the room and was met with stale, hot air. The room was like an oven. "Shit," Santos hissed. "Is your air conditioner not working."

"No," Randolph said, but he wasn't even breaking a sweat.

"I got a message to call the medical examiner at the state lab. I'm hoping she's got some results for us." Santos sat at a small desk and reached for the phone while Randolph tried to coax the air conditioner into operation.

"Yes, this is Camila Santos. Dr. Foster, please," she said. "I'm returning her call."

The air conditioner shook and rattled but whatever Randolph did to it seemed to be working. Semicool air breezed across her forehead. Santos sat up when she heard a voice on the other side of the line and Randolph looked on as she listened and jotted a few notes.

"You're sure?" Santos asked, setting down the pen. "Why would someone do that?" At the response, she gave a little chuckle. "No, I think that's why they pay *you* the big bucks. Thanks for letting us know—we'll add this to the list of things that don't make sense about this case."

Santos hung up the phone and looked up at Randolph who was watching her expectantly.

"The Doyles were shot with more than one gun," Santos said, getting to her feet.

"We did find two types of shell casings at the scene, so that's no surprise," Randolph said. "So we've got two shooters and two guns."

"Or one shooter, two guns," Santos suggested. "Where the Doyles were shot, that's what's interesting," Santos explained. "William Doyle was shot in the throat with a 9 mm and again in the exact same spot with a shotgun. Same with Lynne Doyle, except in the chest."

"Maybe to conceal the type of firearm used," Randolph mused. "We know Ethan Doyle had access to a shotgun, did he have a handgun too?" Randolph asked. "But they had to know that eventually we'd find out what kind of weapons were used. Seems pretty calculated for a sixteen-year-old."

"I agree," Santos said, "but it's possible. If we're looking at a Bonnie and Clyde crime scene, maybe Ethan and Becky both shot the Doyles. Kind of like a pact—I'll do it if you do it kind of thing."

"Maybe, but if that's not the case, why?" Randolph asked.

Santos thought about this a minute. "If I killed someone with my 9 mm, it might be beneficial if someone thought a shotgun did the deed. It makes a bigger hole, does more damage. It would buy me some time at least."

"Shotgun beats 9 mm," Randolph said, heading to the door.

"Every single time," Santos agreed.

Farmwork didn't end with death. Matthew Ellis needed to care for the animals at his daughter and son-in-law's farm. Though Caroline and Matthew were hesitant to let Josie come along, she begged to. She didn't want to go anywhere near the house but wanted to visit the goats and see if Roscoe had come home.

Though it was early, and the sun was just rising, the heat was going to be as unrelenting as the day before. Temperatures were forecast to hit a hundred and four degrees with the heat index.

They made the short drive to the house without seeing any other vehicles. No volunteer searchers had yet arrived, and only one deputy was stationed at the top of the lane.

When Matthew slowed his truck to pull into the drive, the deputy waved at him to keep moving. "Hey," he said, "you can't come in here."

In the passenger's seat, Caroline straightened her spine. "This is my daughter's house," she said through the open window. "I want to talk to who's in charge."

"Yes, of course," the deputy apologized. "I'm sorry for your loss. Go on through. You can pull right into the drive. Another deputy will meet you down there."

Matthew parked in front of the house and they stepped from the truck. Josie looked up at the house. Homes were supposed to be safe havens, meant to protect. It was supposed to be a shelter from the elements, a fortress to keep out evil, and her home had betrayed Josie in the worst possible way.

"We'll go and tend to the animals," Matthew said. "Are you sure you want to go in the house?" he asked Caroline.

"I'll be fine," she said stoically. "I'm just going to get a few things for Josie."

Matthew and Josie watched as Caroline and the deputy made their way into the house.

Josie imagined her grandmother having to walk through the house, up the stairs, past the room where her daughter died, then having to step across the bloodstained carpet in her room. Josie didn't know how she could do it, knowing what had happened to them. Josie vowed to never step foot in that house ever again.

From behind them came the sound of footsteps. They turned to see Margo Allen coming toward them.

Matthew was surprised. After what had happened the day before, he wasn't expecting Margo to come back to the house, but he understood it. This was where her daughter was last seen. When she dropped Becky off, she had been healthy, happy, safe. And now she was gone.

He reached out his hand to her, but she let it hang in the air.

Despite the heat, Margo wore an oversized sweatshirt and jeans. Her eyes were puffy and her skin mottled from crying. Josie wondered if she looked like that. As if one wrong word, one wrong look would shatter her into a million pieces.

"I just wanted to talk to Josie for a minute," Margo said,

her lips trembling. "Will that be okay? If we just talk for a minute?"

"I don't know." Matthew hesitated, looking around for someone to tell him what to do.

"I just want to know what happened," Margo said. "The police won't tell me anything." She turned to Josie, took her hand in her own. Josie wanted to pull free, but Margo held tight. "I just want to know how you were able to get away and Becky wasn't."

Josie looked to her grandfather. "Now, Mrs. Allen," he began.

Margo focused her attention on Josie. "No, no, it's okay. I'm glad you're safe. You got outside, right? They said you were outside, but where was Becky? Was she in the house?" Margo's voice rose. "Did you leave her in the house with him or did she get out too? I'm just not sure why they won't tell me anything. But you'll tell me, won't you? You'll tell me what happened."

"I'm so sorry about Becky," Matthew said. "Everyone's doing all they can to help find her."

"Not everyone," Margo said shrilly. "Not me. They said I shouldn't. They said it would be better if I stayed home and waited. But I can't wait. I need to know what happened."

Matthew looked around desperately for someone to help him comfort the poor woman, but there was no one.

"They think that maybe Becky had a crush on Ethan," Margo said, squeezing Josie's hand even more tightly. "Do you think he might have taken her?"

"No!" Josie exclaimed. "He wouldn't," she said, trying to wrench her hand free.

"She's only thirteen," Margo said plaintively. "Why would he be interested in a thirteen-year-old? She's just a baby," Margo said, her face pale and desperate with grief.

"Hey, now," Matthew said sharply. "Ethan didn't do anything. He's missing too. Let her go," he said, peeling Margo's fingers from Josie's. Margo finally released them, leaving behind half-moon indentations on Josie's skin.

"I just want to know where my daughter is!" Margo cried out. "We're getting calls," she said, tears streaming down her face. "Did you know that? We're getting calls from someone saying he's Ethan and that he has Becky. Do you know what that's like? Do you?"

"My grandson would never do that," Matthew said, his voice choked with emotion. "It's someone else. Now, I have to ask you to leave. I'm sorry, but you shouldn't be here."

The raised voices carried, and the deputy and Caroline came hurrying from the house. "Ma'am," the deputy said, "Step over here and we'll talk."

"I want to know where my daughter is," Margo begged. "Please." Her eyes searched Josie's. "Please, they won't tell us anything. Please, Josie, you're Becky's best friend, don't you want to help her?"

Josie couldn't answer. Caroline held her arms out as if trying to be a barrier between Josie and Margo. The deputy gently tried to lead Margo away.

Margo stepped around Caroline and gripped the wrist of her injured arm. Josie cried out in pain. "Your brother did this, didn't he?" Margo said between clenched teeth. "Why? Why would he take my baby?"

The deputy stepped in then and pried Margo's fingers from Josie's wrist. "Stop. You're hurting her," he said in a low, firm voice.

"I just want to talk to Josie for a minute. Please," Margo said. "I need her to tell me what happened."

The deputy who was posted at the top of the lane came

trotting toward them. "Ma'am, you can't be here." He stepped between Margo and Josie while the other deputy whisked Josie quickly away. The next thing she knew, she was sitting in the back of a deputy's vehicle parked next to the tent.

"You'll be fine in here," the deputy said, turning on the car and cranking the air-conditioning so that lukewarm air puffed from the vents. "She doesn't mean anything by it," he said. "She just wants to find their daughter."

Josie knew this was true. She wanted to find Becky and her brother too, despite the suspicions that kept creeping into her thoughts.

Josie watched as the deputies spoke with Margo and her grandmother, their voices growing louder, more frustrated.

Finally, Margo threw her hand up in the air and rushed toward the deputy's car.

"Josie, where is Becky?" she called out as she tried unsuccessfully to wrench open the car door. She pressed her hands against the window. "Open the door, Josie," she ordered.

"Where. Is. My. Daughter!" Margo pounded out each word and the glass quivered beneath her fist. Josie slid to the car floor and covered her head with her arms.

"Ma'am, come away from the car," the deputy said. There was quiet for a moment, then a wounded shriek that sent a spasm of dread down Josie's spine.

I want to die, Josie thought as Margo Allen's cries grew fainter. But if she couldn't die, this was where she belonged, on the floor of a deputy's car, her face pressed to the floor mat, gritty with dirt from criminals and drunks and bad people.

Deputy Levi Robbins tapped his steering wheel impatiently. He was agitated. He couldn't shake the feeling that Brock Cutter knew a hell of a lot more than he was letting on.

It was looking more and more like Ethan Doyle killed his parents and took the Allen girl with him. Or maybe he killed her too, dumped her body, and took off. The evidence was mounting against him: the tension with his family, the alleged harassment of the ex-girlfriend, the shotgun found in the field. And now he learned that the Allen family was receiving phone calls from someone claiming to be Ethan Doyle.

And as the case against Ethan was growing, so was his suspicion of Cutter. He was with Ethan Doyle the day of the murders, was near the scene of the crime soon after, and was trying to cover his own ass by lying to law enforcement.

He didn't have high hopes of finding him at home. Brock wouldn't be eager to talk now that he'd been found to be lying about his whereabouts the night of the murders.

He was so tired. Dirt tired, as his grandpa used to say. If he was smart, he would go home and get a few hours of sleep, but with every second that passed, chances of finding Becky Allen alive were getting less likely.

On his drive to the Cutter house, he passed three roadblocks and what looked like a pair of search dogs and their handler. The state police were pulling out all the stops. Excitement bloomed in Levi's belly. He was onto something with Brock Cutter; he knew it.

The Cutters lived a mile from the Doyle farm and Levi knew there was bad blood between the two families. He had even been called out to deal with a few of their disagreements over the years: a fertilizer spill, damaged crops, a few missing animals. Nothing ever came of the reports, just more resentment. This was one of the reasons that Levi was surprised that Brock and Ethan were supposedly friends. This wouldn't have gone over well with the parents.

Levi drove down the Cutter lane and parked in front of

the sprawling rust-colored brick ranch home surrounded by three hundred acres of corn and soybeans. Beef cattle grazed in a far-off field.

Before Levi even stepped from the car, Deb Cutter was at the front door. "Hello," she called out. "Is everything okay?"

"All's well, ma'am," Levi said, keeping his voice light, conversational. "You heard about what happened over at the Doyle farm the other night?"

"Of course, everyone's heard about that," Deb answered, twisting a dishrag in her hands. "Another deputy was out here yesterday. I told them I thought I heard the shots."

"What time was that?" Levi asked.

"Around midnight or a bit later," Deb said. "I didn't realize what it was until I heard the news. Terrible, just terrible."

"It is," Levi agreed. "And that's why I'm here. I've been sent out to talk to Ethan Doyle's friends. See if they had any insights as to where he might be."

"Brock and Ethan are not friends," Deb said sourly. "We told those two boys to stay away from each other. Nothing good ever came out of those two boys being in the same space with one another."

"I understand, ma'am, but you know boys." He leaned in conspiratorially. "Sometimes they don't do what we know is best for them, right?"

Deb gave a little smile as if she knew exactly what Levi was talking about. "Maybe come back later, when my husband is home," she suggested.

"Sure, but the thing is," Levi said, running a hand through his hair. "We're running out of time. The longer it takes to find those two kids, the less likely we're going to be able to. And as a mom, I think if the shoe was on the other foot, and

Brock had gone missing, you'd sure appreciate any and all the help someone could give."

Deb considered this. "Brock's not home, but I can have him call you when I see him."

"Any spots you can think of that he might be right now? Any bit of information can help. Brock probably might not even be aware that he knows something." Levi waited while Deb Cutter mulled this over, then added, "After two days, chances are we won't find Ethan and Becky alive."

Deb shook her head at the tragedy of it all. She couldn't imagine losing her son. Brock was wild, but he always came home. What if one day he didn't? She would be heartsick. Terrified. "You might try the old Richter farm. Randy's setting up a hog confinement over there. Brock's been helping out."

"Thank you, Mrs. Cutter," Levi said, "and if you can think of anything else, don't hesitate to call."

"Of course," Deb said. "I'll do anything I can to help."

Levi climbed back into his car and cranked the air. The Richter farm was only a few miles away, but he felt like he was going on a wild-goose chase. He would talk to the Cutter kid even if he had to chase him across all of Blake County.

The old Richter place was exactly how it sounded. Broken down and desolate. The farmhouse was crumbling and all that remained of most of the outbuildings were piles of barn boards. It smelled even worse. A combination of decomposed swine fecal matter and urine, creating a thick stink that made Levi's eyes water.

Levi stepped from the car and examined the landscape. No vehicles were parked nearby, and except for the snuffle and grunt of the hogs locked away in the confine, the place appeared to be deserted.

Levi made his way around the house. The gray paint had

faded, bleached by the sun and scoured by the elements. It was uninhabitable, the windows and doors covered with plywood, the guts shucked down to the studs. Levi remembered hearing something about a farm auction after the death of Leland Richter, the eighty-six-year-old man who insisted on staying in his home until his death a few months ago. Randy Cutter must have had the winning bid, though it didn't look like he won much of anything.

A flash of movement caught his attention, and Levi eyed the long metal building that held the pigs. Something or someone had moved around the corner and out of sight.

Jesus, now he'd have to go check out the confine. Hogs gave him the willies. They could be mean sons of bitches with their tiny black eyes and flat, snuffling snouts. They ate just about anything you put in front of them, including flesh.

Levi strode toward the confine and when he turned the corner Brock Cutter was sitting in the bed of his truck, taking a swig from a bottle in a brown paper bag.

"Hey, Brock," Levi called out. "I've been looking for you." In surprise, Cutter fumbled the bottle and it fell to the ground, the dry soil quickly sucking up the liquid.

"Jesus, you scared me," Cutter said, scrambling from the back of the truck.

"I scared you, huh?" Levi asked as he approached Cutter. "Let me tell you who is probably scared out of her mind right now—Becky Allen."

"I don't know anything about that," Cutter said, kicking at a clod of dirt.

"You sure about that, Brock?" Levi asked, inching closer, forcing Cutter to move backward. "Didn't your truck have a cover on it the last time I saw you? When was that? Oh, yeah, the night William and Lynne Doyle were murdered and Ethan Doyle and Becky Allen disappeared."

"I wasn't there. I don't know what happened," Cutter said, cocking his chin defiantly.

"But you were nearby," Levi said, poking a finger at Cutter's chest. "I pulled you over, remember? You were driving like a madman and sweating like a pig when I stopped you." Levi gave a little chuckle at his own joke. "You told me some bullshit about being at a movie with your cousin. And you had a cover over the bed of your truck. Why'd you take it off?"

"I just did," Cutter said. "And it's none of your business. I can do whatever I want. It's my truck."

"Looks pretty clean," Levi said, eyeing the truck up and down. "Looks like it's been recently scrubbed out. What'd you do that for, Brock?" he asked. "Trying to get rid of some evidence, maybe?"

"No!" Cutter protested. "I keep my truck clean. I like it clean."

"And the cover?" Levi pushed.

"My dad wants me to move some of these barn boards." Cutter gestured toward a pile of lumber. "People pay money for crap like that. I needed to take the cover off so I could load the truck."

"What do you think we'd find if we got a forensics team out here to check things out?" Levi asked.

"Nothing! You won't find anything," Cutter said, his face red with heat and indignation. He tried to move past Levi, who sidestepped right along with him.

"You're probably right." Levi sighed. "If I wanted to get rid of evidence, I'd probably toss it in with the hogs." Levi reached over Cutter's shoulder and pounded on the confinement building. Startled by the sound, inside the pigs squealed and snorted and jostled for position. "Let's go take a look." Levi grabbed Cutter by the elbow and frog-marched him to the doors of the hog house.

"Hey, hey!" Cutter cried. "You can't do this—let me go."

"I tried to be nice to you, Brock. You were speeding, probably drunk or high, but I gave you the benefit of the doubt the other night because I grew up with your cousin, who happens to be a nice guy. You, on the other hand, are a little shit.

"Then the next time I see you, you lie to me and say you hadn't seen Ethan or Josie or Becky at all the day of the murders. Come to find out that you had seen them and proceeded to feel up a thirteen-year-old girl."

"I nev..." Cutter began, but Levi shook him into silence.

"Are you calling Josie Doyle a liar, Brock?" Levi asked. He knew he was on the edge of losing control, but he was so tired and time was running out. They had search dogs and roadblocks and hundreds of people looking for Ethan Doyle and Becky Allen and had come up with nothing.

Levi would bet his badge that Cutter knew something, probably more than something. He probably knew a lot, and neither of them was leaving this godforsaken cesspool of pig shit until Levi knew what it was.

Levi yanked the door to the hog barn open and shoved Cutter inside. The smell was overwhelming and Levi swallowed back the urge to gag. "Hogs eat everything you put in front of them, but I bet you already know that, don't you?"

"Let me go, man, you're crazy," Cutter tried to squirm away, but Levi held tight.

"Now, Brock, if you have any information about what happened to the Doyles and where Ethan and Becky Allen are at, you need to tell me right now."

"Fuck you," Cutter spat.

In one swift move, Levi kicked Cutter's feet out from beneath him so that he fell to the ground, his fingers landing just inches from the hogs rooting along the edges of their pen.

Cutter tried to pull his hand back but, Levi lowered the heel of his shoe atop Cutter's wrist, pinning it into place. Levi watched as the hogs' fleshy, leathery snouts snuffled at Cutter's fingers, their sharp canines grazing across his knuckles.

"Okay, okay!" Cutter cried out. "Ethan had a thing for that Allen kid. He was all over her that day."

Levi removed his foot from Cutter's wrist and pulled him up by the collar of his shirt.

"You can't do that shit," Cutter exclaimed, his eyes wide. "You're not supposed to do that!"

"What else?" Levi asked, ignoring Cutter's protests.

"Ethan hated his parents. Hated them. Said he wished they were dead," Cutter said, sliding his arm across his dripping nose.

"So Ethan said he wanted his parents dead?" Levi asked. "He told you that?"

Cutter nodded. "He couldn't stand it in that house. He couldn't wait to be rid of them. He told me."

"You better not be lying to me, Brock," Levi said as he pulled him from the hog barn.

"I'm not. I promise," Cutter insisted.

"When was the last time you saw Ethan, Josie, and Becky?" Levi asked.

"I don't know, after dinner. Around six or so. We went shooting," Cutter said.

"Shooting?" Levi asked. This was the first he heard of this.

"Yeah, just at targets, though. It was nothing. We shot a few rounds and I went home."

"But you were driving around after midnight, why?" Levi asked.

"I don't know, I was just bored," Cutter said. Levi grabbed him by the scruff of the neck and started dragging him back toward the hog barn. "Okay, okay," Cutter said, twisting away from his grasp. "After Ethan's dad made him walk home for not handing over the shotgun, I met up with him. We drove around, went to Burden because Ethan wanted to talk to that old girlfriend of his."

"Kara Turner?" Levi clarified.

"Yeah. We stopped to see Kara and her dad was pissed. Then we drove around for a while, shot a few more shells, then I dropped him off at the top of the lane and left."

"What time was this?" Levi asked as they moved into the shade of a gnarled crab apple tree. The fallen ones squished beneath their feet, emitting a smell more like rotten cabbage than apples.

Cutter gnawed at his lip. "I don't know, around eleven, I guess. I'm not sure."

"I stopped you at about one, Brock," Levi reminded him. "What were you doing for the next two hours?"

Cutter's shoulders sagged. He knew he was caught. Levi crossed his arms and waited.

"I wasn't ready to go home yet, so I drove around some more and then parked." Cutter reached up and plucked a crab apple from the limb above him, rolled it around in his fingers. "I smoked a little bit. Listened to music." Levi didn't ask him what he was smoking.

"Where'd you park?" Levi asked, swiping the apple from Cutter's fingers.

"I don't know, some gravel road," Cutter said. "Can I go now?"

"No," Levi said shortly. "You can tell me what you saw

while you were sitting on that gravel road. What you saw that made you tear down the road at ninety miles an hour."

"I didn't see anything, I swear," Cutter insisted. Levi stared him down. "I heard the shots, okay," Cutter said, his voice thick with emotion. "A bunch of them. And I thought, *he did it, he really did it*. Then I sat there for a long time, trying to tell myself that I was wrong, but then I heard more shots and got scared and left. I drove around some more completely freaked out and then you stopped me."

"Okay, good," Levi said, clapping Cutter on the shoulder. "Now, don't you feel better telling me the truth?" Cutter looked like he didn't but nodded.

"Now what?" Cutter asked. "Can I go now?"

"Sorry," Levi said, tossing the apple to the ground. "Now you get to tell me the whole story all over again. From the beginning."

Josie heard the click of the car door opening and peeked up from her spot on the floor to see a deputy and her grandfather. "It's safe to come out now. She's gone."

Josie didn't want to get out of the car. The world outside was too hard, too painful. She turned her head away.

"Come on, now, Shoo," he said wearily. "You're too big for me to carry you. Get on up and walk."

Josie had always thought of her grandfather as old, but at that moment, the man standing before her looked ancient. His skin was pulled tight against his skull and purple veins mapped his forehead. His eyes were red rimmed and the skin beneath deeply creviced.

Josie stepped from the car, looked around for any sign of Becky's parents. "The sheriff took her away," Matthew explained.

Josie's eyes widened. "They took her to jail?" she asked in disbelief.

"No, no," Matthew said, putting an arm around his granddaughter and leading her past the tent and toward the house. "They took her to a quiet place where they could talk. She's pretty upset, Shoo. Their little girl is missing. Don't be too hard on her."

"But they think Ethan killed Mom and Dad and took Becky," Josie cried, unable to stave back the tears.

"People don't think straight when they're scared," Matthew explained. Josie leaned into his thin frame as they walked. "And you're probably going to hear people say a lot of bad things about Ethan. They're looking for someone to blame and Ethan's that person right now. But we know better, don't we? We know Ethan couldn't hurt anyone, right?"

"Right," Josie sniffled. But she wasn't sure if she believed it. She saw the look on Ethan's face after he fired the gun into the air. She heard the anger in his voice when he was arguing with her father. "They're going to take Ethan to jail when they find him, aren't they?"

"We don't know anything for sure," Matthew said. "We just have to be patient until all this gets sorted out. And whatever happens, we'll be okay."

Josie wanted to believe her grandfather.

Ignoring the spasms of pain in her arm, Josie ran across the yard to the barn, eager to see the goats. Once inside, she looked up at the rustic beams that ran the length of the ceiling like the ribs of a great, benevolent beast and breathed in the scent of the fresh straw her grandfather must have spread out for the goats in the feed bunks, several eight-foot long, three-foot deep trenches that ran down the center of the barn.

Out of the corner of her eye, Josie saw a figure step into the barn. At first, she thought it was her grandfather coming to collect her, but this person was too tall and broad shouldered, too sure-footed to be Matthew Ellis. As he came closer, Josie could see it was Randy Cutter, Brock's father.

Randy didn't seem to know that Josie was sitting just a few yards away from him. There was something cold, calculating in the expression on Randy Cutter's face. Something that made her want to stay hidden, unseen even in her own barn.

Josie eyed the distance from the pen to the barn door. It wasn't far, but with her injured arm, she wouldn't be able to run very fast. She had no specific reason to be afraid of Randy, but she knew her parents didn't like him.

Josie thought of Agent Santos's question about whether her parents had any conflicts with anyone. Josie's father wasn't a great fan of Randy Cutter or his father, a blustering, red-faced man who was slowly gobbling up all the farmland that came for sale. *He won't stop until he gets a thousand acres*, William observed.

But Randy Cutter hadn't been able to get his hands on the farmland that William and Lynne Doyle had their hearts set on though he tried mightily.

The feud, if that was what you could call it, lasted for years and bled into their day-to-day lives. There were fences that William Doyle was sure Randy Cutter had damaged and calls to the sheriff about wayward cattle. And there was Ethan's friendship with Randy's son, Brock. That didn't sit well with either family.

Randy stood in the center of the barn and slowly turned in a circle, his eyes scanning the great expanse. *He shouldn't be here*, Josie thought. People didn't just walk into another person's barn. Not without permission. He continued his slow spin until he was facing Josie. Their eyes locked for a moment, and then he looked down as if embarrassed for getting caught.

"Sorry," he said. "I didn't mean to scare you. I was looking for your grandpa," Randy said, pulling his red McDonough Feed and Seed cap from his head and kneading it between his large fingers.

"Josie," came Matthew's raspy voice. "Time to go." Then seeing Randy, his face changed, his eyes narrowing suspiciously. "Can I help you?" he asked Randy.

"No, no," Randy said in a rush. "I was just stopping in to see if there was anything I can do to help out. See if you needed any help with chores and such. I'm so sorry about what happened. Man," he shook his head, "I just can't imagine."

After Matthew sent Randy Cutter on his way, Josie stayed close to her grandfather as they did the chores. He milked the nannies while Josie watered and fed the goats. Flies buzzed about Josie's head as she scooped grain into the feed bunks and then added fresh hay atop the loose hay that was already there.

Josie got to the final bunker and started pouring in the grain when a putrid odor filled her nose. She covered her face with her hand. Goats had a strong scent, especially the billy goats, but that wasn't what she smelled.

It was a distinctive odor. Animals were always dying on the farm. Whether it be a goat, chicken, or a nighttime visitor like a possum or raccoon, animals died, and their stink was unmistakable. Josie knew that she couldn't let the goats feed from bunks that contained a carcass. She was carefully pawing through the three feet of hay that lined the bottom of the bunk in search of the animal when she saw it. The deep indigo of denim. Josie paused. It was so out of place, so foreign a sight, it took a moment for her to register what she was seeing.

Josie tugged on the fabric, but it resisted. She brushed away more hay and more denim appeared. A shudder crept up her spine as the smell grew stronger. Josie knew she should stop and get her grandfather, but still, she swept aside the hay, slowly working her way up the length of the bunk until the dark blue turned pale, not much lighter than the hay it was sitting in.

Still not sure what she was seeing, Josie leaned in more closely to get a better look. It was a hand, palm facing upward. Cupped as if ready to receive something, a coin or communion. Then Josie saw them. The scars. He had gotten them when he fell into a barbwire fence when he was fourteen. Tore the flesh clean across his palm in a ragged X.

It was Ethan.

32

When the snows first came, the girl would stand on her chair beneath the window and watch the dancing flakes fall to the ground. She longed to reach through the glass and catch the white crystals in the palm of her hand. They looked like glittering stars.

All the lights were to be turned off when the sun went down, so darkness came early. The little girl and her mother spent much of their time listening for her father's footsteps above and huddled near the space heater to keep warm.

The girl's father consistently brought them food now, even including treats like snack cakes and small plastic containers of pudding. Still, her mother didn't trust him. She rationed their meals, always making sure they had enough cans of chicken noodle soup and ravioli, jars of peanut butter, and tins of tuna fish in case he decided to stay away for an extended time again.

Though her mother always gave her a larger portion at mealtime, there was always a gnawing in the girl's stomach, an emptiness that was never quite filled.

Her mother was quiet and often lost in thought. The girl had to repeat things two or three times before she would answer. Her mother paced, often stopping at the bottom of the stairs to look up at the locked door. The girl was left to read and color and amuse herself on her own.

One day, her mother climbed a few of the steps but then quickly came back down. The next day, she went one step higher. This went on for days. Up four steps, up five steps, up six, until she finally reached the top. The girl held her breath. Would she open the door? Her father would be so angry. Her mother stood there for a long time but in the end, came back down.

One evening, her father came bursting through the door carrying a plastic bag. "I'm having a few people over tonight," he said. No one ever came to the house, at least no one that the girl knew about. "Who?" the girl asked, but her father silenced her with a sharp look.

"You have to be quiet, I mean it. Not a sound," he said. "They'll be here in a little bit." He reached into the plastic bag. The girl was hoping it was a carton of strawberries—they were her favorite. Instead, he pulled out a round silver roll of tape.

Next to the girl, her mother stiffened. "What's that for?" she asked warily.

"It's only for a little while," her father explained as he tore a six-inch length of tape with his teeth.

"No," her mother said, shaking her head. "You don't need to do that. We'll be quiet."

"Can't take any chances," her father said regretfully. "Come here, peanut."

"No," her mother repeated. "She's quiet. She's always quiet."

"Now you know that's not true," her father said, and the girl's face burned with shame.

"Come here," he ordered. The girl stepped toward him and he

smoothed the duct tape over her lips. Immediately, her lungs tightened, the room seemed to close in around her.

"She was little," her mother argued. "She couldn't help it."

The girl's fingers moved to her mouth and began peeling away the tape. Her father slapped at her hands. "Stop," he said. She dropped her fingers to her sides and struggled to breathe.

Then he turned to the girl's mother. "Come here," he ordered. She shook her head, tears streaming down her face. "Please, no. I'll be good," she cried. He yanked her toward him, ripped another piece of tape from the roll, and pressed it to her mouth.

Tears filled the girl's eyes, and she watched as he dragged her mother over to the bed and handcuffed her to the headboard. Her mother didn't resist. She knew if she fought back, things would be worse.

"Go sit down," he told the girl and pointed to the metal pipe that rose up from the concrete floor and joined the circuit of cobwebbed pipes above them. The girl shook her head. She knew what was coming next. He snatched her into his arms and the girl bucked and writhed as he carried her over to the pipe. "Stay still," he growled as he tossed her to the ground. Again, he tore a strip of tape from the roll and lashed her hands behind her back and her ankle to the pole.

Breathing heavily, her father took a look at his handiwork. Satisfied that they weren't going anywhere and would make no noise, he went up the stairs. "Be good now," he called down just before closing and locking the door.

The girl lay facedown on the cold concrete, mouth covered, arms tied behind her back, one ankle affixed to the pipe. She couldn't catch her breath, couldn't see her mother. Tears rolled down her face and her nose filled with mucous, making it even harder to breathe.

Above her, she heard her father's heavy footsteps and several lighter ones. She heard the tinkle of laughter, the chatter of unfamiliar voices, the cheerful chords of Jingle Bells. She closed her eyes to sleep, but the tape bit deeply into her skin and her muscles ached.

She imagined what it would be like to be upstairs sitting in the big living room singing Christmas carols. She would be dressed in pretty clothes, eating cookies in the shape of bells and reindeer and elves. She would be counting her wrapped presents beneath the tree.

The girl opened her eyes. She looked to her window. Through the gap in the curtain, snow was falling. She imagined what it would be like to feel snow on her face, to taste it on her tongue.

33

August 2000

The sound of screams filled the barn and Matthew came running, his eyes darting in search of the source of Josie's distress.

"Josie, what is it?" he shouted. All she could do was point to the feed bunk. Matthew's eyes followed her finger and landed on Ethan's body. He fell to his knees in front of the bunk. "Ethan," he said in disbelief. The mournful bleats of the goats rose up around them.

"Is he dead?" Josie asked, though she already knew the answer.

"Come away from there. Don't touch anything," came Matthew's strangled reply. He struggled back to his feet, avoiding using the edge of the bunk to pull himself up.

Josie moved backward, but already denial was overtaking rational thought. "Maybe it's not him," she said. But she had seen the scars on the palm of his hand. The body in the bunk was her brother. The goats cried out as Matthew led Josie from the barn as if begging them to come back.

"I'm going to be sick, Grandpa," Josie said apologetically and then veered away from him and vomited into the grass.

"It's okay," Matthew said, holding Josie's hair away from her face until her stomach was empty and the dry heaves had passed. When she finally stood upright, he reached into his pocket and pulled out a clean handkerchief and wiped Josie's mouth.

Matthew hurried to the house for help and returned with the deputy and Caroline. Josie stood beneath the maple tree, its broad leaves shading her from the relentless sun. Josie couldn't stand the thought of her brother, dead, lying all alone in a feed bunk covered in hay. She couldn't bring herself to even look toward the barn.

She never wanted to set foot on this farm again. Her family's blood now coursed through its soil. She imagined the corn and alfalfa rising from the earth stunted and black with rot.

The deputy called for more help and secured the barn while Matthew, Caroline, and Josie huddled together beneath the tree.

The ambulance was the first to arrive, speeding down the gravel road, siren blasting, dust rising around the rig in a gritty mist.

Next came the sheriff in his cruiser and then Agents Santos and Randolph who drove up in their black sedan.

"I'm sorry, Josie," Santos stopped to say. "You've lost more than a person should have to."

Josie didn't know how to respond, so she said nothing. She sat on the grass and leaned her back against the trunk of the tree and covered her face. Caroline sat down next to Josie, pulled her close and they cried together.

The EMTs came out of the barn, their stretcher empty. "Aren't you going to take him with you?" Josie cried, feeling hysteria bubbling inside her chest. They couldn't just leave Ethan in the feed bunk, covered in straw.

"No, I'm sorry," the paramedic said apologetically. "The sheriff and the police have to do their investigation. Someone else will come for your brother. But when they do, they'll take good care of him, I promise."

Josie wanted to believe him, but so many people had been telling her how everything was going to be okay. Nothing was okay, would never be okay again.

"Agent Santos will want to talk to us again," Matthew said, rubbing his hand across his face. "When will this end?" he pleaded.

Agent Santos made her way toward them. She had removed her black suit jacket and was sweating through her cobalt blue blouse. "We'll have the crime scene techs go over everything, collect evidence. But it does appear…" She stopped speaking as if suddenly remembering Josie was only twelve.

"Go on," Matthew urged. "Josie has the right to know."

"It does appear as if it's another homicide," Agent Santos said, wiping the perspiration from her forehead with the back of her hand.

Though Matthew had prayed that Ethan would be found safe there was a part of him who knew his grandson was already dead. He knew Ethan wasn't capable of what people were whispering about. Though the medical examiner would make the final determination, it looked like Ethan had been beaten and strangled to death before being hidden in the feed bunk beneath a blanket of hay by the monster who had killed Lynne and William.

Ethan had been here the entire time, right beneath their noses.

Matthew clutched Josie's hand and watched as deputies clustered around Agent Santos. "We need to regroup," Santos said. "Any word on the phone calls to the Allen house? The calls were obviously not made by Ethan. We have to find out who's behind them."

"Not yet. I'll check on it," Randolph said.

"Let's gather everyone together. See where we are with the sex offenders in the area. And we need to find Ethan's truck. If we find that truck, I think we'll find the girl."

Matthew hoped they would find the Allen girl but feared she met the same fate as the others. There was just Josie left, Matthew realized. She was all they had left. They were all she had.

Search and rescue volunteer Sylvia Lee brought the T-shirt close to the dog's nose, and Jupiter, her one-hundred-and-ten-pound bloodhound, snuffled at the fabric.

"Go find," she ordered, and Jupiter lifted his long, wrinkled face and sniffed the air. Jupiter focused his attention on the trampoline near where the missing thirteen-year-old girl was last seen. He circled the trampoline and then turned back toward the house stopping at the barn and lingering momentarily.

He lowered his snout and trotted toward the cornfield. Sylvia held tightly to the long rope that connected to the dog's harness as Jupiter pulled her along. Though it was still early, Sylvia was already sweating, and the cuffs of her pants were drenched with morning dew.

Jupiter stopped just short of the corn but once again changed course and headed past the house, up the lane, and toward the road.

As soon as he stepped onto the gravel, Jupiter paused momentarily, his nose testing the air. He was a dignified-looking

dog with a wrinkled face and solemn brown eyes. He seemed
to understand the gravity of his work, understood that people
depended on him to bring their loved ones home. He took
his job very seriously.

Jupiter hesitated. He took a few steps toward the west,
stopped, and then looked to the east. Sylvia was patient. If
the girl had come this way, Jupiter would find the scent. Back
and forth, Jupiter paced. He seemed intent on a spot just off
to the west but then quickly lost interest. This could mean
many things: the scent could be fading, the girl could have
gotten into a vehicle and driven off, or she didn't move in
that direction.

The loose skin around his jowls swayed as Jupiter looked
from left to right. And coming to a decision, he headed east.
Jupiter was onto something now, and Sylvia had to trot to
keep up with his pace. They moved down the road at a quick
clip; gray dust collected on Sylvia's shoes and Jupiter's paws.
His long, droopy ears turned ashy as they brushed across the
ground.

Sylvia could feel Jupiter's excitement through the length of
rope. He had picked up the girl's scent. They moved farther
from the Doyle home but Jupiter stayed primarily on the road.
Every few hundred yards or so he would veer off into the tall
grass or down into a ditch. When this happened, Sylvia's pulse
would quicken. Though she wanted to find the missing child,
she didn't want to find her lying among the switchgrass and
chicory at the side of the road.

Periodically, a vehicle drove slowly past, the driver lifting one finger from the steering wheel as greeting. The tires
kicked up dust and the minuscule scent particles that Jupiter
was tracking.

Gravel dust clung to Sylvia's sweaty skin and coated her lips.

She unhooked the water bottle strapped to her belt and took a long swallow. Up ahead was a farm. Or what used to be one. It looked like a salvage yard. A large barn listed dangerously to one side, and rows of farm equipment and broken-down vehicles filled the yard. A wall of tires blocked Sylvia's view of the rest of the property and a burnt rubber smell permeated the air.

Jupiter suddenly yanked the leash to the left, nearly lifting Sylvia off her feet, and disappeared into a ditch thick with prairie grass, pulling Sylvia down with him. The grass came up past her waist and the dry, rough leaves rasped against her skin.

Suddenly, the leash went slack. The only way Jupiter would stop was if he found what he was looking for.

Sylvia cautiously moved forward, using her arms to part the vast green sea of prairie grass. Flies buzzed noisily around her head, and as she followed the limp length of rope, she knew Jupiter had a hit.

Sylvia found him waiting for her, sitting at attention. His eyes mournful. Lying on the ground next to Jupiter was a rag, stiff with what Sylvia knew was dried blood.

She patted Jupiter and fished out a treat from her pocket and offered it to him. "Good boy, good boy," she said, then pulled out her radio to call for help.

34

Present Day

It was nearing 4:00 a.m., and Wylie was running on fumes, but she couldn't rest. The woman and girl sat next to one another on the sofa, while Wylie used the fire's light to read through the manuscript.

The book was finished. There was little left to add. She considered adding a *Where Are They Now* section that explained what happened to the major players in the story, but there really wasn't too much to say there. Everyone was either dead, impossible to locate, or simply wished to remain in the shadows, limping along in their broken lives.

Once this nightmare was over, after the storm ended and after she made sure the woman and her daughter were safe, Wylie would get the hell out of Blake County and go home.

She would deliver her manuscript to her publisher and try

and repair her relationship with Seth. She'd even try a little harder to get along with Seth's father.

Wylie looked up to find the little girl staring at her from her spot on the sofa. The girl's mother was curled up so that the uninjured side of her face rested on the pillow, the quilt pulled up to her chin.

"How did you get your name?" the little girl asked.

Wylie was surprised that of all the things the girl wanted to talk about, it was her name. She was used to it. Upon learning her unusual name, everyone wanted to know how she got it. "It's a family name," Wylie said simply.

"What's your name?" Wylie tried, hoping the girl would let it slip.

"My mom says I can't tell you," she answered, slipping out from beneath the covers and coming to sit on the floor by Wylie.

The light from the fire illuminated the girl's face—her large brown eyes, the grimy residue left behind on her face by the duct tape that had been used to cover her mouth. Wylie couldn't fathom what the girl had been through.

"How about your last name?" Wylie asked. "Mine is Lark. What's yours?"

"I don't think we have one," the girl answered as if considering this for the first time.

Well, that wasn't possible.

"What's your dad's name?" Wylie kept pressing.

The girl's forehead creased with worry and she stayed quiet. "It's okay," Wylie said, glancing at the sleeping woman. "You can tell me."

"He's just Dad," the girl whispered.

"Okay," Wylie said in resignation. "Oh, hey, I meant to give something back to you earlier after I washed your clothes."

Wylie got to her feet and went through the darkened kitchen to retrieve the toy she found in the girl's pocket hours earlier.

Wylie shivered when she left the relative warmth of the living room and, using her flashlight, scanned the countertops until she found it.

Wylie took a closer look at the toy. It was a figurine of one of the lesser-known action heroes. His green mask was nearly worn away, his white gloves were now a dingy gray, and the plastic exterior was scratched and dented from years of play.

Wylie hadn't seen one of these in years. A wave of nostalgia swept over her, but she quickly brushed it away.

"Here you go," Wylie said, returning to the living room and handing the toy to the girl. Wylie smiled at the way the little girl's face lit up, the way her eyes snapped with joy at being reunited with her toy. Then Wylie's smile faded. She stood there for a moment, trying to think.

"Thank you," the girl said, holding the toy tightly in her grasp, and she climbed back onto the sofa and beneath the covers next to her mother.

Wylie reached for a flashlight that sat dormant on the end table and flipped the switch. She did the same with another flashlight and another and another until the room was filled with light. Wylie took a seat opposite the woman and child at a loss for words. The fire popped and crackled ineffectually; Tas snuffled.

Wylie moved to the kitchen and returned with two bottles of water. "Here, you need to drink." Holding the lantern, Wylie went to the woman's side and knelt so that she was looking down on her.

The woman, now awake, squinted painfully against the glare and held up a hand, fingers slightly black at the tips from necrosis.

"I brought you some aspirin," Wylie said. "It might help a bit with your pain. I don't want to give you anything stronger in case you have a concussion."

Wylie broke the pill in half and laid the pieces in the woman's open palm and that's when she saw the horseshoe-shaped scar. Instinctively, Wylie grabbed the woman's hand knocking the pills to the floor.

"Ouch," the woman said, pulling away.

"Sorry." Flustered, Wylie bent down to retrieve the aspirin. "Here you go," she said handing the woman the pills again.

The woman looked at Wylie suspiciously, but placed the pills on her tongue and grimaced at the bitter taste.

"You need to take a drink," Wylie said softly and carefully tipped the bottle to the woman's lips spilling water into her mouth.

Wylie stared down at the woman's battered face. One mistrustful brown eye looked back at her. Wylie looked down at her own hand, where a matching horseshoe-shaped scar, though less pronounced, marred her palm.

35

At night the girl dreamed she was drowning, of her nose and mouth and lungs being filled with dank, dark water. She'd wake up gasping for air. Her mother would hold her close and tell her that it was going to be okay. But it wasn't.

The basement was so cold that the space heater couldn't keep up. She ate her soup, she colored her pictures, and she watched television with the sound on low.

She never knew what to expect when her father came down the steps. Sometimes he had a roll of duct tape in his hand; sometimes he brought cupcakes with pink fluffy frosting or pizza in a box.

But even on the days he brought treats and touched the girl's hair and told her she was pretty, he was quicker to slap and push and pinch.

It was worse for her mother.

One morning the girl woke to find that her mother wasn't next to her in the bed. She rubbed her eyes and looked around the room. It was *empty. She crawled from the bed and pushed on the bathroom door. It was empty too. There wasn't a closet door or furniture to hide behind. Despair poured over her. She was all alone. Her mother had left her. She heard the shuffle of feet overhead. Her father was coming. He would want to know what happened to her mother. What would she say to him? The door creaked open and the girl scurried back to the bed, pressed her soft, worn blanket to her cheek, and slid her thumb in her mouth.*

The footsteps came closer and the girl's heart beat so loud she was sure her father could hear it.

"Sweetie," came her mother's voice. "It's time to get up."

The girl was bursting with questions. Where had she gone? What did she do? Why had she gone up the stairs?

Her mother just pressed a finger to her lips and said, "Shhh. Remember our little secret." She had brought down a plastic bag filled with all kinds of things. There was an apple, a few dollar bills, and a pile of quarters, dimes, and nickels that jangled together in the bottom of the bag.

Her mother handed her the apple and then tied the plastic bag handles together and hid it at the bottom of the garbage can. The girl gnawed on the apple while her mother paced around the room.

The day crept by slowly. Her mother was preoccupied. Nervous. The girl asked what was wrong, but her mother just smiled and said everything was just fine. A sliver of worry pricked her chest, and she ran to the cupboard to see how much food they had left. She sighed with relief. There was plenty.

"Do you think he will come tonight?" the girl asked.

"I don't know," her mother said, staring up at the door. "I hope not."

Her father did come that night and he was in a foul mood. He told the girl to go to the bathroom, and she did so reluctantly. She knew it was going to be bad. She picked a book from the shelf and closed the bathroom door behind her. She couldn't see what was going on, but she could hear everything. The bed squeaked violently and her mother cried out with such pain the girl had to cover her ears until it was over.

For the next three days, the girl awoke to find her mother gone, but she always returned, each time with an item to add to the bag hidden at the bottom of the garbage—a pair of sharp scissors, an electric razor, two bottles of water, two keys.

"Aren't you afraid he's going to come back?" the girl asked.

Her mother shook her head. "He's always leaving at six. He goes into town for coffee and a donut," she said. "He's always back by eight. I love you," her mother murmured out of the blue. The girl smiled, but an uneasiness settled in her chest because the way she said the words sounded a lot like goodbye.

Later, the girl's mother shook her from her sleep. "Wake up," she said. The girl rose to her elbow and looked blearily back at her.

"What time is it?" the girl asked.

"Just get up and do what I say—we have to hurry," her mother said, pulling a red sweatshirt over her head. "Get dressed and go to the bathroom."

The girl did as she was told. The room was dark except for the flickering light from the television. A weather anchor was taking about sleet and snow and gusts of wind. She went to the bathroom and pulled on her jeans, a gray sweatshirt, and a pair of tennis shoes.

"What's going on?" she asked. "Is he coming?"

Her mother shook her head. "No. Now listen, we're going to do something scary, but you need to trust me. Do you trust me?"

The little girl nodded. Her mother went to the garbage can and pulled out the plastic bag. She untied the handles, reached inside, and brought out the pair of scissors and the electric razor. The girl looked at her in confusion. There was nothing scary about a pair of scissors, though these were much sharper and the blades longer than the pair she had in her art box.

"Come here, sweetie," her mother said. "I'm going to cut your hair."

"*Why?*" the girl asked.

"*Do you trust me?*" her mother asked again, staring directly into her eyes.

"*Yes,*" the girl said in a small voice.

Her mother lifted a section of the girl's hair and, using the scissors, began to snip. Long dark curls fell to the floor. The girl gasped, and her hand flew to her head.

"*Don't worry, it will grow back. I promise,*" her mother said and kept on cutting, and she didn't stop until there was a thick mound of black hair on the floor. She plugged in the electric razor and it came to life with a low buzz. Her mother pressed the razor to the girl's scalp and the remaining bits of fine hair floated around her head.

Finally, her mother let out a long breath. "*Okay, I'm done.*"

"*Can I go look?*" the girl asked, and her mother reluctantly nodded.

She hurried to the bathroom and stood in front of the cracked mirror. She looked awful. Not like herself at all. She was practically bald and her neck and ears felt naked, exposed.

"*Please don't cry,*" her mother said, her voice thick with her own tears. "*I need you to be brave.*" The girl tried, but she couldn't stop the tears from falling. "*We're going to be different people for a while. I had to cut your hair, and I'm going to cut mine and change the color after we leave. Can you pretend to be a boy? Do you think you can do that just for a little while?*"

The girl nodded.

"*Good,*" her mother said. "*We're leaving now and we're never going to come back.*"

"*Won't he be mad?*" the girl asked through her tears.

"*Yes, and that's why we need to hurry,*" her mother said and began snipping at her own nearly waist length hair, cutting it to just above her shoulders. "*The calendar he has upstairs said cattle auction, Burell, Nebraska, under today's date. But we have to go—we have to*

*leave now. Go pick out one special thing to bring with you and I'll
unlock the door."*

*They were leaving. They were actually going to walk up the stairs
and out the door. A shiver of excitement went through the girl. They
were going to the* Out There. *She knew exactly what she was going to
bring. Her little white blanket with the bunnies on it. It was a blanket
she'd had since she was born. She wished she could bring some books
and her art box, but her mother told her to choose just one thing, and
she couldn't leave without her blanket. Then her eyes landed on the
plastic figure of a man dressed in green. Her mother had given it to
her when she was little, said she had it for a long time. The girl almost had forgotten about it—she spent most of her time coloring and
reading books these days. The girl slid the figurine into her pocket.
She'd bring both of them. Her mother wouldn't mind.*

*"No, no, no," came her mother's voice from the top of the stairs.
The girl heard the rattle of the doorknob, the pounding of fists on
wood. "It doesn't work," she said, coming down and sitting on the
bottom step in defeat. "He must have added another lock. It won't
open. He'll know we were up to something. He's going to kill me for
cutting your hair," she said, lowering her face into her hands.*

*"He doesn't have to know," the girl said, squeezing onto the step
next to her. "We'll tell him I did it. We can pinky promise."*

*"He'll know," she said, shaking her head. "He'll find out I got
out and took the keys and money and the razor. I'm so, so sorry," she
cried. "I promised you everything was going to be okay, and it won't."*

*They sat that way for a long time. The little girl rubbed her mother's
back with one hand and her shorn head with the other. She looked around
their small room. It wasn't so bad. She had the bed and the television and
the bookshelf and the window.*

*"Mama," the girl said, sitting up a little straighter and pulling on her
mother's arm. She pointed, and her mother followed her finger's path.
"We don't have to use the door," she said. "We can use the window."*

36

It couldn't be, Wylie thought. It wasn't possible. Becky was dead. Had died years ago. She was certain of it.

But what if that wasn't the case? What if Becky had been hidden away for all these years? What if she'd had a child with the man who took her?

A surge of guilt crashed over her. Wylie's mind flashed back to the night of the murders when she and Becky were in her bedroom, the moonlight splashing through the window. Just a short time later, Becky was gone.

Becky wouldn't have even been at the house if it hadn't been for Wylie.

A little voice in her head nagged and poked at her. The horseshoe-shaped scar on the woman's hand, a twin to her own.

Wylie blinked and gave a small shake of her head. It was impossible. Becky Allen was dead.

For years, Wylie ran from her past, from this house, from that deadly night, from the man who had stolen her entire family from her.

Not long after her parents were murdered, Wylie moved with her grandparents two hundred miles from Burden to begin a new life, to get a fresh start, to escape the reminders of all that they lost. And to get away from the man that everyone knew killed them.

Her grandparents tried to create a new life for her, but her past haunted her no matter where she went. She was always Josie Doyle—the girl whose family was murdered, whose best friend vanished without a trace. So when she was old enough and she knew she couldn't be Josie Doyle any longer, she took the *W* from William, the *L* from Lynne, the *E* from Ethan, and her grandmother's maiden name and had become Wylie Lark.

Then she began to write books about terrible crimes. Why? She never tried to analyze it too closely, but it made sense. The murder of her family and the kidnapping of her friend had never been officially solved so she would chronicle the tragedies of others.

Until now. Now she was writing her own story. Josie Doyle's story for the entire world to read and to examine.

No. Wylie shut the folder and stood. It was crazy—Becky was dead. She was determined to push the thought from her head when she heard a faint rumbling sound coming from outside.

"What is it?" the woman asked fearfully.

The little girl ran to the front window and pulled back the

curtain. "I can see a light," she exclaimed. "It's way up on the road."

"Come here," her mother ordered. "Get away from there." Guiltily, the girl returned to her mother's side.

"I think it's the snowplow," Wylie said with relief.

They paused to listen to the grumble of an engine and the unmistakable scrape of snow being pushed aside. Seeing the alarmed expression on the woman's face, Wylie spoke. "This is a good thing. It means the storm is winding down. They'll get the power going soon and we'll have electricity and heat." The woman didn't look convinced.

The engine suddenly went silent. "Is it gone?" the girl asked. "Are they all done?"

"Maybe, but they'll be back to clear the other side of the road," Wylie explained.

The girl left her mother's side and returned to the window. "How come I still see a light?" she asked. Wylie joined her and the woman even eased from her spot on the couch to see. "Maybe he's stuck," the girl offered.

"More likely he saw your overturned truck and stopped," Wylie said. "I'm going to go check it out, talk to him."

"Please don't," the woman said. "Stay here."

"I'll be gone for only a minute. Don't worry. He'll have a radio on the plow. He can help us," Wylie said.

Ignoring the woman's protests, Wylie grabbed her coat from the back of the sofa and a flashlight and moved to the mud-room. She shoved her feet into her boots and tucked her hair beneath a stocking cap. She had to catch the snowplow driver before he left. In the very least he could radio for help, let the authorities know they needed medical attention.

Wylie threw open the door and came face-to-face with a man dressed in winter gear. Startled, she dropped the flashlight and it fell to the ground with a clatter and rolled away. They both bent over to retrieve it.

Wylie got to the flashlight first. "Oh, God, you scared me," she laughed nervously. "I was just coming out to try and catch you."

"I didn't mean to frighten you," the man said as they both stood upright.

"No, no," Wylie said turning the flashlight toward the man, "I'm glad you're here. We need..." And that's when she recognized him. It was Jackson Henley, the man who murdered her family. The man who took Becky.

37

Things were moving fast. Agent Santos got the call that the search and rescue dog got a hit right on the edge of the Henley property. Thankfully, it wasn't a body. But a bloody rag with Becky Allen's scent on it was bad enough.

While she waited to hear if their request for a search warrant was approved, she discovered a few more unsettling details about Jackson Henley. He was part of the ground offensive that liberated Kuwait during Operation Desert Sabre, but beyond this, his military record was marred by several run-ins with his superiors. Jackson Henley did not like to follow orders, liked to drink, and to harass his female soldier counterparts.

One woman reported that Henley, along with a group of other male soldiers, mentally and sexually harassed her to the point of a near breakdown. Another woman accused him of false imprisonment after he purportedly refused to let her leave after the two spent a night together. The charges were eventually dropped, but it appeared that even as a young soldier, Henley liked to keep his girlfriends all to himself.

There was more, most dealing with his apparent battle with alcohol, and in 1992, Jackson came home to Blake County a shell of the person he was before he left.

Santos knew that one bloody cloth didn't mean that Jackson Henley was guilty of anything, but it didn't look good. They couldn't even be sure that it was Becky's blood. She may have touched or held the rag in her hands, transferring her scent to it, but the blood could belong to someone else.

It took precious minutes trying to secure a search warrant for the Henley property. A piece of evidence on the edge of a property didn't mean that a judge would automatically grant a search. Still, Jackson's skittish behavior and his past legal issues went a long way in getting the judge to agree to sign off on the warrant. They were good to go.

Now all they could do was hope that it wasn't too late for Becky.

Santos pulled up to the Henley property and her nose was immediately assaulted with the noxious smell of burning rubber. Now why would anyone be burning anything on a hot day like this? she wondered. Sheriff Butler had the same thought. When Santos stepped from her car, Butler was shaking his head and coming toward her.

"Son of a bitch is burning something," Butler said, his face flushed with anger. "I should have made him talk to me yesterday."

"Well, we're going to talk to him now," Santos said. "But first we have to find him. We'll serve the warrant and talk to

Mrs. Henley, and then you head toward the burn pile and try to make sure he's not trying to torch any evidence."

"Be careful," Butler said. "If Jackson is in the house and drunk, he can be pretty unpredictable."

"Got it," Santos said as she and two other deputies approached the house. She saw movement behind the heavy curtains that covered the window. "See that?" Santos asked. The deputy leading the way nodded and her hand moved to her sidearm. On high alert, they picked their way up the broken steps to the front porch.

Santos rapped on the door and identified herself as law enforcement. "Mrs. Henley," she called out, "we have a warrant to search your property. Please open the door."

The door opened a crack, and a rheumy blue eye looked back at them. "What's going on?" June Henley asked.

"Ma'am, I'm Detective Camila Santos of the Iowa Department of Criminal Investigation, and we have a warrant to search your premises and the adjoining property. Please open the door." Santos and the other officers waited tensely as June decided what to do.

Detective Levi Robbins was interviewing known sex offenders in the area when he learned two pieces of information that led to the end of his career in law enforcement and a civil lawsuit against the Blake County Sheriff's Department.

The first was that the body of sixteen-year-old Ethan Doyle had been found buried in a feed bunk in his family's barn.

"Don't leave town," Levi told the scumbag he was questioning.

Levi jumped into his cruiser and headed toward the Doyle farm. *That poor family*, Levi thought. The only consolation was that Ethan hadn't been the one to kill his parents and kidnap

Becky. But that didn't change the fact that three-fourths of the Doyle family had been wiped out, and a thirteen-year-old girl was still missing.

Levi's mind was buzzing with questions when the second piece of information reached him. The state police had worked quickly and were able to trace the number tied to the cruel calls that were made to the Allen family. Tied to the caller who claimed to be Ethan Doyle. The Cutter residence.

Levi's gut told him to find Brock Cutter. Goddamn Cutter. He had fed them the information that Ethan was homicidal—wanted to kill his parents, that Ethan had something going with the Allen girl. It was all a load of bullshit. So, what did he do? Go to the scene or go after Cutter? Just as he was going to turn off onto the road that led to the Doyle home, Levi decided to go straight toward the Cutter farm. He was going to get some answers.

In the distance, Levi saw a vehicle approaching at a high rate of speed. He tapped his brake and locked eyes with the driver. Cutter. Levi slammed on his brakes, his tires screeching across the pavement, leaving a wake of acrid smoke and skid marks. He made a sharp U-turn, flipped on his lights and sirens, and pressed on the gas.

In front of him, Cutter was speeding up. What the hell? Levi thought.

Levi floored it, and the cruiser screamed forward until he was just behind Cutter's truck. Why wouldn't the kid just pull over? Cutter made a quick right onto a gravel road and Levi nearly missed the turn. "Son of a bitch," Levi cried out as his car nearly went off the road and into a cornfield. He wrenched the steering wheel to the left, and the car straightened out. Still Cutter sped forward. Dust billowed and enveloped both vehicles in a gray cloud. He couldn't see what was in front of him, beside him, behind him. Chalky dust covered the windshield.

He needed to slow down, but it was too late. The cruiser slammed into the back of Brock Cutter's truck. The crunch of metal filled his ears and Levi felt his legs snap, felt his torso strain against the strap of the seat belt. He howled in pain, felt his stomach lurch as the car spun round and round until it came to a stop. When Levi opened his eyes, the cruiser's front was smashed, pinning his legs beneath the steering wheel. Strangely, he didn't feel much pain, just a heavy pressure on his chest.

He cautiously turned his neck from left to right. At least his neck worked. Next, he tried his toes. He thought they were moving. He wasn't sure. Slowly the dust cloud around him settled and gradually the world outside the car came into focus. In the bright beam of his headlights, he saw it. Cutter's truck was nearly split in half by a telephone pole. And there was Brock Cutter, half hanging out of the driver's side door, knuckles scraping the gravel road, a gaping wound at his neck. He wasn't moving. How could he? There was so much blood.

Levi closed his eyes. He'd only wanted answers. Only wanted to find out what happened to the Doyles, to that little girl. It was the right thing to go after Brock Cutter, wasn't it? He was only doing his job.

38

"Keep back," her mother said. She was standing on a chair beneath the window, holding the porcelain lid that covered the toilet tank. She closed her eyes and rammed it into the window, raining glass to the floor. She tossed the lid to the ground, and the girl flinched as it cracked against the concrete. "Hand me the towel," she ordered.

The girl handed her mother the towel, she wrapped it around her hand and began clearing the window of the remaining broken glass. A wall of hard-packed snow stared back at them. She tried to dig the snow out with her fingers, and when that didn't work, she told the girl to hand her the space heater.

The girl did as she was told and her mother held the small space heater just in front of the snow. "Pull another chair over and grab a spoon," her mother said. The girl found a spoon and dragged the other folding chair next to where her mother stood and climbed up. "Now hold the heater, and I'll dig," she said.

They made fast work of it, and within ten minutes, her mother's arms were wet from the melted snow. A bitter wind blew through the window and took the girl's breath away.

"Okay," her mother said. "It's going to be cold and we have to hurry. Hand me the plastic bag and get your blanket." The girl hopped off the chair, the glass crunching beneath her feet, ran to the table and retrieved the items, then returned to her mother's side.

"I'm going to help you through first, and then I'll climb out," her mother said. "Don't cut yourself." She hoisted the girl up, and she easily slid through the window. Next came her blanket and the plastic bag. The girl stood back and waited for her mother. It was sleeting. Icy rain slid down her neck and the sharp wind cut through her sweatshirt and jeans.

It took several attempts before her mother was able to pull herself up far enough to get her shoulders over the threshold of the broken window. The little girl grabbed onto her outstretched arms and pulled. With a groan, her mother heaved her body the rest of the way through and collapsed atop the snow.

She quickly got to her feet and looked around, trying to get her bearings. "This way," she said, squinting as icy pellets struck their faces. Holding hands, mother and daughter picked their way across the slippery yard until they came to the front of the house and stood on the front porch to get out of the rain.

"What now?" the girl asked. She shivered and pressed herself close to her mother. The night was dark and wet and cold and looked bigger than she imagined it would.

Her mother opened the plastic bag and pulled out the set of keys she had placed there days before. "I know one of these keys is to a truck," she said. "I hope one of them opens the front door, or we'll have to walk."

She tried the first key in the front door. It didn't fit. Then the second and third. Finally, the fourth key slid in easily, and the door swung open. Once inside, they crossed the darkened room into the kitchen. Her mother paused at the basement door. "That's why it didn't open," she said softly and pulled the slide lock at the top of the door to the left. "He used both locks." She slid the lock back into place.

"Come on," her mother said and guided her to another door. This one opened to a dark, windowless space. She felt along the wall and light flooded the room. It was a garage. One stall was empty. In the other sat another vehicle covered with a tarp.

The woman pulled the tarp away to reveal an old black truck that was rusty and scratched. This was the truck that he said he didn't drive often, but he had no intention of ever getting rid of it. He liked to sit in it sometimes, he told her, and remember.

Her mother ran her hand across the cold metal. Bits of black paint stuck to her fingers. "Get in," her mother said, opening the door for her, "and buckle up."

The girl didn't know what that meant.

Her mother climbed up behind her, shut the door, and fumbled with the keys until she found the one that fit the ignition. She then reached over and pulled a strap that fit over the girl's lap and chest and clicked it into place.

"How do we get out?" the girl asked, staring at the lowered garage door.

"Like this," her mother said and then reached above her head and pushed a black button. With a loud rumble, the garage door began to slowly rise. Her mother put her hands on the steering wheel and studied what was in front of her. She turned the key and the truck's engine came to life. "Here we go," her mother said, giving her a frightened smile.

The truck lurched forward and onto the glazed driveway. The tail end shimmied left, then right, and then straightened out. Her mother pressed lightly on the gas, then the brake, and slowly inched forward.

"Where are we going?" the girl asked as they moved slowly up the long driveway.

"Shhh, I need to focus," her mother said. The rain was coming down in icy slashes and a murky fog covered the windshield. She found the headlights and the windshield wipers and that helped a bit. At the top of the drive, she had to make a decision. Turn right or turn left. She had no idea where she was or where to go. She took a deep breath and turned the truck to the right.

The truck kept jerking and sliding and stopping so that the girl's stomach began to churn. She held tightly to her blanket and hoped she wouldn't throw up.

Finally, her mother seemed to get the hang of it, and they drove slowly down the road. "Whatever happens," her mother began, "I want you to keep going. If he shows up, keep running. If we get separated, keep running. Do you understand?" Her mother took another right. The wheels seemed to catch the road easier here, and her mother pressed down on the accelerator. The truck sped up. She glanced over at the girl. "Find somewhere safe. Don't tell anyone anything. Not your name, my name, not anything until you know you are in a safe place."

"How will I know if it's safe?" the girl asked.

"You'll know," her mother said. "You'll know."

The girl wasn't so sure. She looked at the road in front of them. They could go anywhere, be anyone they wanted to. Through the headlights, the girl saw a tree. A tree growing right up through the middle of the road. "Mama," she cried out.

Her mother tried to swing the steering wheel to the right, but the truck still glanced the side of the tree. The girl heard the crunch of metal and the crack of wood, and then the road wasn't there anymore. Her stomach swayed and the truck bounced and bucked, and suddenly the girl was upside down. She bit her tongue, and blood pooled into her mouth. Her head struck something hard and the truck spun and slid until it came to an abrupt stop.

The girl was upside down in her seat. Her mother was gone. She touched her fingers to her head and they came away red with blood. "Mama?" she called out. There was no response. The windshield was shattered, and through the prism, all the girl could see was white. The air grew colder. With aching fingers, she was able to release her seat belt and she tumbled down with a painful thump. She was sitting where the ceiling should have been. She cried out again for her mother, but all she could hear was the wind crying back at her.

She didn't know what to do. The pain in her head was nauseating and her fingers and toes burned with cold. Her mother told her to keep going, so that was what she would do. No matter what. One of the truck doors was wedged open and she dizzily crawled through it. All around her were broken pieces of the truck, but her mother was nowhere to be seen. "Mama, where are you?" she called out, but her words were swallowed up by the snow that was falling furiously now.

Tears gathered in her eyes and spilled out onto her cold cheeks. Keep going, she told herself. She stepped forward and immediately slipped to the ground. She crawled on hands and knees until she was atop a little hill. Squinting through the storm, she saw it. Pale and weak, but it was there. She got to her feet, and moving slowly, steadily, the girl headed toward the star.

39

August 2000

The front door slowly opened and Agent Santos assessed the woman standing in front of her. She was as thin as a skeleton; her face was pale and pinched. She looked two steps from death.

"He said you'd be coming," June said in a raspy voice.

"Where's Jackson?" Santos asked, her eyes darting around the room.

June sat down wearily in a chair. "He's my son. I love him," she said simply.

Santos knew they weren't getting any help from Jackson Henley's mother. "You stay with her," Santos ordered a deputy.

Santos and her team began with a cursory search of the house. Everything was as neat as a pin. Even the basement with its concrete walls and floor was swept clean. There was no sign of Jackson Henley or Becky Allen. Santos returned to the living room where June Henley sat, watching them warily.

The house, so far, was ordinary—it looked like the home of an elderly woman who had married and raised a son there. There were pictures of Jackson at various ages, of June and her husband on their wedding day. But something was missing.

Then it came to Santos. The house looked like it belonged to an ill, elderly woman, not a woman who lived with her adult son. There was no sign that Jackson slept in the house. No closet filled with his clothes or personal items.

Jackson, for all intents and purposes, did not live in the house. He had another spot, somewhere on the property where he spent his time.

Santos went to the front window and pulled aside the curtain. Outside, Sheriff Butler and his crew were searching the property and the outbuildings. Off in the distance, thick black smoke rose from the burn pile, and along with it, a sick feeling settled in Santos's stomach.

Burning tires weren't like burning fallen tree limbs or yard refuse. It was illegal. Had been since '91. Jackson would know this but apparently didn't care. Setting tires on fire wasn't easy. They burned hot, and once ignited, they were hard to extinguish. And the smoke from tire fires was filled with noxious chemicals like cyanide and carbon monoxide.

June said Jackson knew law enforcement was coming. Being arrested for illegal tire burning would be worth it if any evidence connecting Jackson to the Doyle murders and the disappearance of Becky Allen was destroyed.

They had to put out that fire.

"Call the nearest fire department, and get them out here," Santos ordered. "Tell them we've got a tire fire."

She turned to June Henley. "Ma'am, it's not safe for you

to be here. The smoke and fumes from the burning tires will make you sick. We need to take you away from the area."

June's shoulders sagged in resignation, but she got unsteadily to her feet. "You're wrong about this," June said. "Jackson didn't kill that family or take that girl."

"I hope so, ma'am," Santos said as a deputy escorted June from the house.

A sound of a gunshot cracked through the air and Santos rushed outside. The air was thick with rolling black smoke and the smell of burning rubber filled her nose and burned her eyes. She covered her mouth with her elbow and went toward the sound of the gunshot.

The fire was about a hundred yards from the house where the rubber tires were stacked. As Santos came closer, deputies, coughing and wheezing, rushed past her in the opposite direction.

Santos snagged an officer as he ran by. "What's happening?" she asked.

"The guy's guarding the fire with a shotgun. Won't let anyone come near him," he said. His eyes were red and irritated from the smoke. "We caught him tossing some guns into the fire. He's got a shitload of them. An arsenal."

"What about the gunshot?" Santos asked. "Anyone hurt?"

"I couldn't see. The smoke is too thick." The deputy bent over, hands on his knees, and coughed and gagged.

"You go," Santos said. "Make sure everyone is well away from the property. Call in backup." The deputy nodded and disappeared into a black cloud.

Santos knew she should retreat and go to safety too, but the sheriff hadn't emerged from the smoke and she couldn't leave him behind. Shrugging out of her suit jacket, Santos used it to cover her face and went deeper into the smoke.

The pyre of rubber tires was fully engulfed in fire, and Jackson Henley, brandishing a shotgun, was standing in front of it, his eyes as wild as the flames behind him. Several gas cans lay at his feet.

Santos tossed aside her jacket and raised her sidearm.

The sheriff, overcome with toxic fumes, was on his knees, struggling for air. "Jackson Henley," Santos called through the smoke. "Put your weapon down."

"I knew you would come," Jackson slurred. He was drunk, Santos thought, making him more dangerous and unpredictable. His face was black with soot, and his pale blue eyes sparked with anger. "I tried to help that girl. She was bleeding and all I wanted to do was help her. Now you think I took her."

The black smoke was hardening like cement in her lungs. She needed to get Butler out of there; she needed to get out of there.

She considered shooting Henley. It would be the fastest resolution. Santos knew she'd be justified—he was waving a shotgun around. It was almost as if he was begging to be shot. But there were so many unanswered questions that she needed to know the answers to, the number one being the whereabouts of Becky Allen. If he died, Becky Allen could die with him.

Santos made a decision. It was a risky one, but it could be their only chance to learn the truth. She lowered her gun knowing that her fellow officers had her covered.

"Come on, Jackson," Santos said. "Let's talk about this. I want to hear what you have to say, just not this way. Not here. Let's go somewhere safe."

Henley shook his head. "You won't believe me. No one ever believes me."

"That's not true," Santos said in a rush. "Your mother believes you, I believe you."

Henley gave a bitter laugh and kicked over a nearby gas can and it exploded with a loud pop. Jackson Henley watched, mesmerized, as the fire rushed toward him. The flames, following a frenetic path across the ground, coiled their way around his ankle like fiery snakes and slithered up his leg.

Agent Santos tossed her gun aside and rushed toward Henley. Using her jacket, she tried to smother the flames that covered Jackson's leg and had jumped to his arms.

A rush of firefighters in protective gear came toward them. Someone pressed an oxygen mask to her face and she was lifted to her feet.

Anguished screams filled her ears. Jackson Henley was alive, and he would tell them what happened to Becky Allen.

40

Present Day

Training her flashlight on the man, Wylie examined his face more closely. He was twenty-two years older, of course, and his hair had receded, exposing a broad, heavily creased forehead with a sparse whorl of gray hair. But there was no denying who it was—she could see the thick, rough scars just below his jawline. She had seen his picture a thousand times on the news, in the newspaper clippings she kept over the years. This was Jackson Henley, the man who murdered her family, had taken Becky, and now he was back to claim her.

Wylie fought the urge to smash him in the face with her flashlight. To kick and beat him until he was as bloody and broken as her parents and brother were. She wanted him dead. But she had to hold her fury in check, at least for now. She needed to make sure he didn't come inside the house.

"I saw the wreck and thought someone might need some help down here. I was just getting ready to knock."

"No, we're fine," Wylie managed to say, then mentally kicked herself for signaling that she wasn't there alone. "My husband and I are just fine," she lied hoping that would do the trick and he'd just leave.

"That must have been one hell of a crash," Jackson said. "I saw some lights. I thought any survivors might have come here to get out of the storm. It's the closest house to the wreck. I didn't think anyone was living here right now," he said, removing his stocking cap from his head.

Jackson didn't recognize who she was or at least made a good show of pretending not to know her. Wylie and her grandparents had left the area soon after the funerals. She'd been gone for over twenty years, and no one here knew that Josie Doyle had come back to town as Wylie Lark.

But Wylie had been watching Jackson Henley. She drove past his home—the same one that he'd lived in with his mother. He had cleaned up most of the junk—the tires, the farm equipment—all gone. All that remained were a few vehicles parked in his yard. What she hadn't known was that he was a snowplow driver.

"Anyone from the crash show up?" Jackson asked.

Wylie paused before speaking. If Jackson had been watching her as closely as she had been watching him, he'd know that she didn't have a husband, that she was here all alone. She had been so careful though not to have any interactions with the locals. All her interviews for the book had been done months ago by phone. She hadn't wanted anyone to know who she really was.

"No," Wylie said as casually as she could. "I checked and it looks like help got to them before I got there. It was really nice of you to stop by." She had to find a way to get him out of here.

"My name is Jack—I live just a mile down the road," he explained. "I didn't know anyone was renting this place. Like I said, I saw the wreck and just wanted to check on things."

"I'm Wylie," she said, and Jackson didn't flinch. "My husband and I are renting the house." Maybe he really didn't have any idea he was standing in front of the woman whose life he ruined, but Wylie was sure that he knew that Becky and her child were in the other room.

"Actually, I could use your help," Wylie said. "We're out of wood and I don't want to wake my husband up to help me bring it in. Maybe you could carry in a few armfuls?" she asked, hopeful that her voice sounded natural.

"Sure thing," Jackson said. "Just point me in the right direction."

"It's in the toolshed over there. Come on, I'll show you." Holding her breath, Wylie led Jackson through the storm to the old toolshed, a small sturdy building between the house and the barn. She had no idea if her plan would work but it was all she had.

She opened the door to the toolshed and over the wail of the wind she shouted, "The wood is in there. We can both grab an armful and that should keep us going through the night."

Jackson nodded and they both stepped into the dark outbuilding. "It's back there," Wylie said briefly lighting up a far corner with her flashlight. She then used the light to scan the space for a slim, sturdy tool. Her eyes landed on screwdriver and she snatched it from the wall.

"I don't see it," Jackson said. "Can you shine that light back this way again?"

This was when Wylie made her move. She gave Jackson a

quick shove from behind causing him to stumble and fall to his knees.

"Hey," Jackson cried out in surprise.

Wylie turned and ran, heart pounding. She thought she heard his footsteps behind her, his hot breath on her neck, and for a moment, she was back in the cornfield, trying to outrun a killer. Wylie didn't pause, didn't look back to see how far behind her he was.

She slammed the door behind her, flipped the hasp and frantically slid the screwdriver in place, locking the door just as his body thudded into it.

"Hey," Jackson yelled and pounded on the door. "Let me out!"

Wylie pressed her back against the door as Jackson threw his body into the heavy wooden door. The door vibrated but her makeshift lock was strong. It would hold, at least for now.

From within the shed came a guttural scream and the sound of footsteps and the crash of his shoulder striking the wood. Then came the bumps and grunts of someone falling to the ground.

Then there was nothing. No sound. No movement on the other side of the door.

She had to find her gun, had to find a way to keep Jackson locked in the shed and out of the house. She would keep Becky and her daughter safe and she would kill Jackson Henley if she had to.

41

Wylie had been gone a long time. The girl slid from her spot on the sofa next to her mother, who was rocking back and forth and moaning, "He's coming, he's coming."

Was her mother right? Had her father found them? If so, he would kill them all. Maybe, she thought, if she talked to her father, Wylie could get away. Find help. Carrying her flashlight, the girl slipped from the sofa and tiptoed to the kitchen just as Wylie flew through the back door, slammed it shut, and pressed her back against it as if trying to keep it closed.

"Is it my dad?" the girl asked.

"Yes," Wylie said. "It's him. Grab a chair from over there." She nodded toward the kitchen table.

Josie dragged the chair over to Wylie and watched as she tipped the chair on two legs and slid the top rail beneath the doorknob.

Her father was somewhere outside, the girl thought. Only a few inches of wood stood between them.

"He'll get in," the girl said resignedly. "He'll get in."

"No," Wylie told her breathing heavily. "I won't let him. And if he gets through the door, he won't get past me. I won't let him hurt you anymore."

Then there was silence. They stood there for a long time, listening, waiting. Nothing came.

Wylie turned toward the girl. "Your mom's name is Becky, isn't it?"

The girl froze. Did she trust Wylie? You'll know, *her mother had told her.* You'll know.

"Please," Wylie said. "I have to know. Is her name Becky?"

The little girl nodded and Wylie covered her eyes and wept.

42

Present Day

Embarrassed by her rare outburst of emotion, Wylie quickly dried her eyes and stared at the little girl in disbelief. The woman in the other room was Becky. This was Becky's daughter. The girl that everyone thought was dead was alive. And the man that killed Wylie's family and kept Becky a prisoner was locked in the toolshed.

Wylie pressed her face to the window and looked toward the shed for any sign of movement from Jackson. All was quiet. Maybe he had hurt himself trying to break down the door. Or maybe he was just waiting for Wylie to let down her guard.

They would just have to stay alert and wait. Wylie was good at waiting. All those years ago, she had waited for someone to come into the cornfield to save her, waited for someone to save her parents, her brother, Becky. She waited for Jackson

Henley to be put in prison for murdering her family. But none of those things came to be until now. Becky had come home.

Wylie could wait Jackson Henley out. She had been doing it for twenty-two years; what was one more day?

Taking the little girl by the hand, Wylie led her to the living room. Becky was gone from the sofa. Wylie pulled the missing person's flyer from the file folder.

She heard soft crying coming from the closet and slowly opened the door. The woman, Becky, was sitting on the floor, trembling. Wylie lowered herself to the ground and climbed in next to Becky, setting the flashlight on the floor in front of them. The girl stood just outside the closet door, listening.

"He's out there, isn't he?" the woman asked, her voice shaking with fear. "He's come for us."

Wylie tried to smooth the edges of the creased photograph and then handed it to Becky. She stared at it for a long time as if trying to place the person in the photo. Though she wasn't looking at Wylie, the woman was listening so intently she was barely breathing.

"Becky," Wylie said softly. "It's me. It's Josie."

The woman lowered her head and shook it from side to side in disbelief. Tears streaked down her face leaving a ragged path through the dried blood.

Wylie reached for the woman's hand and she flinched as if burned. Wylie kept a gentle grip on her hand and turned it over, palm up. She traced the horseshoe-shaped scar with her finger. "I have one too," Wylie said trying to keep her voice even and calm. The knowledge that Jackson Henley was locked in the toolshed would keep but not for long. But first, Wylie had to make Becky understand who she was.

"We were ten, I think," Wylie said. "We got the idea that we should be blood sisters. We used my mother's paring knife.

You were braver than I was and made a deeper cut. That's why you have such a noticeable scar. But I have one too, see?"

Wylie held out her hand and the woman's eyes flicked toward it and then away. "Sisters forever," the woman murmured.

The girl, seeing her mother's distress, climbed into the closet with them.

Wylie waited for the woman to speak, to say something, anything. But there was only silence, and for a moment, Wylie thought she had gotten it all wrong. This wasn't Becky—only a scared, lost stranger looking for safety in a storm. Wylie suddenly felt foolish. After all these years, she had forgotten how to hope and understood why. It was too painful. She pulled her hand away.

Finally, the woman spoke. "I'd forgotten what you looked like. I mean, if I closed my eyes really tight, I'd get little flashes."

Becky looked up at Wylie, her eyes shining with tears, and then she smiled, and there she was. The Becky Wylie remembered.

"I thought you were dead," Wylie said. "We all did, except for your mother. She never gave up looking for you."

Becky wiped her eyes. "I thought she was dead. He told me she was dead. That no one was looking for me anymore, that no one cared."

"We all cared, everyone cared," Wylie tried to assure her. "Agent Santos did everything she could to try and get Jackson Henley convicted."

"Jackson?" Becky asked, her forehead furrowed in confusion.

Wylie nodded. "Yes, Jackson Henley. There just wasn't enough evidence to arrest him for killing my family and your disappearance. They couldn't find the gun he used or my brother's missing truck. They couldn't find you. But don't worry. He's caught now. I locked him in the toolshed. He'll never hurt you again."

43

Wylie and her mother were sitting in the closet, whispering. She squeezed into the space between them and rested her head on her mother's lap. Tas, not wanting to be left out, lay down in front of the open closet door.

Wylie talked while her mother and the girl listened. She told them about when she and her mother were young. Talked about school and overnights and birthday parties with cake and ice cream and balloons and long afternoons at the pool. Things that the girl didn't even know were possible.

Wylie and her mother had known each other before. Before her father, before the room in the basement, before her.

Wylie also talked about how she had moved far away when she was twelve, became a writer, got married too young, and had a baby named Seth. "I never thought I'd get married," Wylie said. "Or have children." She glanced over at the girl, then said, "I didn't think I *deserved it after what had happened. But I miss my son. I miss Seth very much."*

Wylie crawled from the closet and came back a moment later with a picture. "This is Seth, this is my son."

The girl wanted to know what she meant. Wanted to know what Wylie did that was so bad that she didn't deserve a nice husband and a son with laughing dark eyes and deep dimples, but she didn't want Wylie to stop talking. She liked the sound of her voice, wanted to know more.

For a while, her mother didn't say a word. She just listened and stroked the girl's head. The girl felt an ache in her chest that she couldn't quite name. It wasn't sadness or anger. It felt more like hope.

"I thought if I wrote everything down," Wylie said, "I might be able to move on. Live my life, be a good mom. Instead, I've been hiding out here, trying to write a book about what happened but not really wanting to face it."

The girl's eyes grew heavy. She was warm and safe and with her mother. Everything was okay. She could sleep now if she wanted, and all would be well.

"Your mother still works at the grocery store," Wylie said, and the girl's eyes opened. A small sound escaped her mother's lips. Her mother rarely talked about once having a mother. It made her too sad.

"I haven't talked to her since I've been back," Wylie went on. "I was too much of a coward. I haven't talked to anyone."

Her mother lowered her head. Tears spilled from her cheeks to the girl's, but she didn't move.

Finally, her mother spoke. "He told me she was dead. He told me that you were all dead—your family, your dog—and it was all my fault. But I snuck out of the basement and I called home. And she answered. My mother. She wasn't dead. But I couldn't say anything. I just hung up." Her mother wiped at her eyes. "But your parents? Your brother?"

"Yes," Wylie said. "He killed them."

Her mother's shoulders sagged. "I thought so," she said in a soft voice. "He put me in your brother's truck and told me he would kill me too."

"My parents must have gone to get Ethan's truck from the gravel road and brought it home that night," Wylie murmured.

"He hid the truck in his garage all these years," Becky went on. "It's the one we took when we ran. He painted it black, but I knew it was Ethan's. We had to get out of there. I didn't know how to drive but it was our only choice. With all the snow and ice—" she shook her head regretfully "—I couldn't stay on the road. I lost control and crashed. I'm so sorry."

Wylie reached for her mother's hand and held it gently in her own. They sat like that for a long time, waiting. For what? The man in the shed to come for them or someone else?

It didn't matter. For the first time in a long time, the girl felt like things just might be okay.

44

Present Day

There was a knock at the door, and Wylie and Becky went silent. The girl looked up at them anxiously.

"Please don't answer it," Becky begged. "Please. It's him—he has so many friends. He always told us no matter how far we ran, he'd find a way to get us back."

"You're safe. I locked him in the shed. I think I should answer it," Wylie said, getting to her feet. "I know you're scared but we need to get the police here, and we need to get you to a hospital. We can't stay here any longer. We need to leave."

There was more knocking on the door. "Hey," a voice called out. "Everything okay in there?"

"It's him," Becky said, holding her daughter close and pulling her as far back into the closet as she could. "He's come for us."

"Stay here, I'll go check," Wylie said.

"No, no, don't leave us," Becky begged.

"I'm not going anywhere. Just hold on," Wylie went to the front window and pulled aside the curtains. "It's Randy Cutter again," she said with relief, letting the curtain drop. "He was here earlier. He said he would come back. He can help us."

"No, it's him," Becky whispered. "He's the one. It's Randy."

"Randy Cutter?" Wylie asked in confusion. "It can't be. I told you, it's Jackson Henley. All they really had on him was the cloth with your blood on it. But it wasn't enough."

"Blood?" Becky asked. "What blood?"

"A search dog found a rag covered in your blood near the Henley property, but it just wasn't enough. But don't worry, he'll never hurt you again."

"I know who took me," Becky insisted, panic rising in her voice. "Josie, it was Randy Cutter."

For a moment, Wylie couldn't speak. No one had called her Josie in years. "But it had to be Jackson," Wylie said. Her grandparents had told her that a few days after the murder, Jackson Henley had been arrested on weapons charges. She had confirmed it when she was researching the book. He had been badly burned during the arrest and spent several months in a burn unit in Des Moines, and when he was well enough he was sent to the men's prison in Anamosa for eighteen months.

"The man who took you, he has burns over a good part of his body, right? His leg and arms and neck?" Wylie asked still not ready to give up the idea that Becky's kidnapper was Jackson.

"No," Becky shook her head. "You need to listen to me. It's Randy Cutter." She looked at Wylie, terror in her eyes. "He's outside right now. I know him. I know his voice, dammit, I've heard it nearly every day for the last twenty years."

Wylie stared at Becky and then looked to the little girl for confirmation. She nodded.

"Jesus," Wylie breathed. Randy Cutter? It didn't make any sense.

"Hello," Randy called out. "I came out to check on you and I saw a man creeping around the house."

Jackson Henley. Oh, God, she had locked him in the toolshed. How had she been so wrong about him? How had everyone been so wrong?

"Maybe he'll go away," Wylie whispered.

"He won't leave," Becky said dully. "He'll never let us go."

"Hey, you're making me nervous," Randy called through the door. "I'm worried about you. I'm coming in, okay?" The doorknob rattled and Becky emitted a small squeak of fear.

Wylie felt in her coat pocket for her gun. It wasn't there. She scanned the floor, searched the couch cushions. Where had it gone? They would be dead without that gun.

They had to arm themselves with something. Wylie thought of the knife and hatchet sitting on the shelf above them. She grabbed them and pressed the knife into Becky's hands. "It's all we have right now," she said.

To the little girl she said, "If I tell you to run, you go out to the barn and hide. It will be cold, but there are lots of hiding spots. I'll come find you when it's safe."

The girl nodded, her face pale. Wylie handed each of them a flashlight. "Keep them off unless you really need it. We don't want him to know where we are."

Wylie tiptoed around and turned off each of the flashlights illuminating the room until all that was left was the glow from the fireplace. Wondering if she had just sealed their fate, Wylie poured water over the fire. It hissed and spit, and the room went black.

She checked her watch. It was still an hour until dawn.

"It's going to be okay," Wylie whispered. To that, Becky said, "I can't run. I won't be able to keep up with you. Please, just take care of my daughter."

"I'll take care of both of you," Wylie promised, clutching Becky's hand.

"What should we do?" Becky asked.

"We have to separate. Hide in different spots. Remember the little crawl space in my old bedroom?" Wylie asked Becky. "Take her and hide up there. He'll have a hard time finding you. I'll stay down here and hide. If he breaks in I'll be ready."

"What about Tas?" the girl asked.

"He'll be okay," Wylie assured her. He had settled into his dog bed. She didn't think he would give away her location and considered locking him in the bathroom but decided against it. Maybe Tas would be inspired to protect her if it came to it. "And remember to keep your flashlights off," Wylie whispered as Becky and the girl rushed up the stairs.

She tried to think of the best spot to hide. Wylie needed to be able to react quickly if Randy broke his way into the house. She wished she had time to search for her gun, but she didn't dare turn on a flashlight for fear of giving away her location.

Finally, Wylie sat on the floor behind the sofa with the hatchet and waited. She would hear Randy enter the house. She would know where he was; he would have no idea where she was.

The air was bitterly cold and deathly quiet. There was no crackle of flames in the fireplace; the wind outside had died down. Wylie hoped that Jackson Henley was okay and hadn't frozen to death in the toolshed. She had been terribly wrong about him. The eerie stillness grew up around her like a cocoon.

The minutes ticked by. Wylie counted the seconds in her

head. Maybe Randy had given up and just left. He couldn't stay outside for very long. It was too cold. Wylie quickly dismissed this thought. If Randy Cutter was the one who murdered her family and kidnapped Becky, then he had everything to lose. Becky was right. He would stop at nothing.

How had she not known? Randy Cutter had shot her, chased her into the cornfield, stalked her, and still, Wylie didn't know who it was. She had doubted her own brother—thought he was capable of slaughtering their parents. *I was twelve years old*, Wylie reminded herself. But still, anger and guilt swirled through her.

The room was growing colder with each passing moment. Her fingers stiffened, and she released the hatchet to rub her hands together to try and warm them up.

Wylie cocked her ear. Had she heard something? A soft shuffling sound?

She waited to see if the sound came again and relaxed when it didn't.

That's when a terrible thought struck Wylie. The broken window in the back door. He could easily remove the cardboard and reach inside and unlock the door.

Wylie sensed Randy's presence before hearing or seeing him. She froze in her spot behind the couch and tightened her fingers around the shaft of the hatchet. She held her breath knowing that he was only a few steps away from her.

There was a soft click, and suddenly the room was cast in a ghostly light.

"Josie, Becky," Randy sing-songed. "I know you're in here."

Wylie pressed her fingers to her mouth to hold back the scream that rose in her throat.

His shadow crawled across the wall. He was getting closer.

"Come on," he called out. "Did you really think I would let you leave? You know better than that. You belong to me."

Then he was standing over her, staring down. He raised the shotgun and pointed it directly at Wylie's head. "And you," he said ruefully. "I wish I would have done this the last time I tried," he said and pulled the trigger.

Nothing happened. He looked down at his weapon, perplexed, and Wylie leaped up, swinging the hatchet. She struck him on the shoulder, his thick parka taking the brunt of the blow. It was enough to throw him off balance and the shotgun tumbled from his hands, striking the floor.

The hatchet slipped from Wylie's fingers and skidded across the floor and out of sight. As Randy and Wylie fought to find the weapons, there was the thunderous sound of footsteps on the stairs, and Becky stepped into the beam of light. She pounced on the shotgun, picked it up, and aimed it at Wylie and Randy as they struggled on the floor.

"Stop," Becky screamed. "Stop!" Randy released Wylie and they both staggered to their feet.

"Run," Wylie said to the little girl. "Run and hide. Now." The girl didn't move.

"Go now," Wylie said.

The girl shook her head defiantly. Wylie and Becky exchanged a look. "Run," Becky said. "Go now."

"Chamber's jammed," Randy said with confidence. "Nothing will happen if you pull the trigger."

"You don't know that," Wylie said. She moved slowly toward the girl while Becky kept the shotgun trained on Randy. Wylie snatched the girl into her arms, carried her across the floor, and opened the front door. Tas slipped past them and out the door as Wylie set the girl on the front porch. "Do what I told you, now. Run and hide. It's going to be okay, I promise." Wylie closed the door hoping the girl would run to the barn and take cover.

Becky kept the shotgun pinned on Randy Cutter, who was slowly inching toward her. "Stay put," Becky ordered, and Randy froze.

Wylie couldn't make any sense of what was happening. Over the years, she had made an uneasy peace with the truth. Knowing that Jackson Henley had killed her family, had taken Becky, and had gotten away with it. Now the real killer was standing right in front of her. Wylie remembered the day after the murders when Randy Cutter had walked into the barn. The slick knot of fear that had filled her chest.

"Give me the gun, Becky," Randy said in a low, soothing voice. "I know you don't want to hurt me. I love you."

Becky's hands were shaking so hard she could barely hold on to the shotgun.

"Hand me the gun," Wylie said. "I can do it."

"Don't listen to her, Becky," Randy said. "Who's taken care of you all this time? Who gave you a baby? I did. No one else was there for you. Just me. No one even cared that you were gone."

Becky's face went slack. *She's giving up*, Wylie thought. *She's going to give him the gun.*

"Don't listen to him, Becky," Wylie snapped. "He doesn't love you. He killed my parents and my brother. He shot me. He stole you. Everyone looked for you. The entire town. For years. Your mom has never given up. Never."

"Becky, honey," Randy said, taking a small step toward her.

Becky pulled the trigger. The wall behind Randy exploded, sending shards of plaster in the air. Becky pulled the trigger again, this time striking the ceiling. Both Randy and Wylie shielded their heads from the falling debris. Becky pulled the trigger again and again until the chamber was empty.

45

Once Wylie shut the door, the girl immediately got to her feet and began pounding on the front door. She tried the knob. It was locked. The cold wind bit at her exposed skin. "Mama," she shouted, slapping at the door. "Mama, let me in."

The cold seeped through her body. She wanted to go back to her little room with her bed and her books and her television and her small window. But she wanted her mother even more.

They were shouting inside the house. The girl squinched her eyes tightly shut. Then she heard the bangs. With each blast, she cried out.

The girl had known Wylie for such a short time, but it felt like much longer. Did she trust her? She didn't know. She felt a nudge at her knees. It was Tas looking up at her with his amber eyes.

Wylie told her to hide. She would hide.

She ran to the barn with Tas at her side. She tried not to think of her mother back in the house with her father and the sound of the gun. *Wylie told her to run. She would run. The cold bit at her face and her fingers, and every few yards, she would fall through the snow up to her waist, but still, she forged forward.*

She slipped into the barn with Tas right behind her and scanned the dark space for somewhere to hide. Her eyes settled on the ladder and the hayloft, and she began to climb.

46

Becky dropped the shotgun as if it burned her fingers and cowered in a corner.

Randy and Wylie reached for the weapons at the same time. Wylie grabbed the hatchet, Randy the shotgun. They both brandished their weapons—each waiting for the other to make the first move.

"You killed my parents." Wylie's voice shook so hard she thought she might crack into a thousand pieces. "You beat my brother, strangled him, and hid his body in the barn. You tried to frame him and you kidnapped my best friend. You shot me. Why? I don't understand."

Randy just laughed. Wylie wanted to throw herself at him. Wanted to dig her fingernails into his eyes, to scratch that smug, superior look from his face.

"We're leaving," Wylie said. To Randy, she said, "If you let us leave, we won't hurt you."

Randy turned toward Wylie. She was ready. She wasn't going down without a fight. She thought of Seth, of Becky, and the little girl. She had too much to live for.

She swung the hatchet but only managed to send a glancing blow off Randy's shoulder. He tried to wrench the weapon from Wylie's hands, but she held tight. He let go and she stumbled backward, striking her head against the floor. Dazed, she dizzily tried to get to her feet.

She prepared herself for another attack, but he stepped right past her toward Becky.

Wylie reached for him but missed, instead knocking over the woodpile so that the kindling scattered across the floor. Randy stood in front of Becky as she cowered before him, and then he slammed her into the wall behind her. She crumpled at his feet.

Wylie jumped atop Randy, but he shrugged her away and she hit the floor hard.

Groaning, Wylie pulled herself into a fetal position, trying to protect her head from further attack. She could hear Randy's heavy breaths as he stood over her, deciding what to do next.

He lowered himself down so that he was kneeling beside her. "Relax," he whispered. "It's all going to be over soon." With that, he grabbed a fistful of her hair, lifting her head from the ground and slamming it to the floor. Stars exploded behind her eyes, the pain white-hot and searing.

Wylie felt the world fall away from her, and everything went to black.

Minutes passed or perhaps hours. Wylie forced herself back from the brink. It was like swimming through black tar, but she knew if she didn't stay conscious, she would die. Becky and the little girl would die.

Pain radiated through her skull. Wylie swallowed back the vomit that crept into her throat and concentrated on keeping her breath slow and regular. She didn't need to appear dead, just unconscious. Once she got her bearings, she could fight back.

Wylie hoped that the little girl had made it to the barn, found a hiding place that would buy her some time.

This would be the time to make her move, Wylie thought. To get up and fight back.

Wylie heard footsteps, and then she felt Randy standing over her.

He bent over her, and Wylie could feel the heat of his breath on her face. She tried not to wince at the foul odor. He smelled of garlic and onions and something else. Fear, Wylie decided. Randy was afraid. His perfectly created world had been disrupted. Becky and the girl almost made it out.

Now Wylie was the only one who could help give Becky what she wanted for her daughter. Freedom.

Randy slid his arms beneath her armpits and began to drag her across the floor. He paused to open the door, and the blast of cold air almost made Wylie gasp, but she managed to remain still. He pulled her down the front steps, then he paused.

Wylie knew what was going through his mind. He was going to let her freeze to death out here. He didn't want to waste any more time with her. He wanted the girl. And where was Becky? And Jackson Henley? Had Randy killed them? Had Wylie found her friend only to lose her again?

Randy released her arms and scooped her up against his shoulder as one would a baby. She let her head loll against his neck, trying to make contact with any exposed part of his body. DNA, she kept thinking. Collect as much hair, sweat, cells that she could.

Randy tossed her face-first into the snow, and the shock from the pain nearly caused her to cry out. He came to her side, bent over, and arranged her head so that the side he slammed against the floor was down. The cold was a welcome balm against the fiery pain that radiated through her head.

Wylie didn't know how long he stood there staring down at her, but it seemed to be forever.

Wylie held perfectly still, and finally, Randy stepped away from her, his heavy boots crunching through the crusty snow. He was looking for the girl now. She waited until she heard the creak of the barn door before she stirred. Wylie's head felt like lead. When she staggered to her feet, she looked down on the imprint she left behind—a bloodied halo atop a snow angel.

She zigzagged toward the barn, willing herself to stay on her feet. She had to find a way to overpower Randy, but the world kept tilting. When her hand finally touched the rough wood of the barn, Wylie bent over and vomited. Terrified that Randy heard her retching, Wylie pressed herself against the side of the barn, willing her stomach to settle and the spinning to stop. She had only one chance to get this right.

She peeked through the narrow opening in the barn door and scanned the dark interior for any sign of the girl or Randy. The storm was dying. The wind had calmed, and night was beginning to fray at the edges. It would be light soon. Did she go inside and confront him? Or should she wait until he came back outside with the girl? No, that was too risky. If she was going to act, it would have to be now.

Wylie crouched down and slipped into the barn, careful not to touch the squeaky door and alert Randy of her presence. From her vantage point, she couldn't see him, but she heard his lumbering footsteps and heavy breathing as he rummaged behind stacks of boxes, searching for the girl.

Wylie ducked down at the rear of the Bronco and looked around for a weapon. Hanging on a hook against the barn wall were a number of lethal-looking tools—lawn rakes, heavy-headed shovels, and bedding forks. All had long handles and could be cumbersome to wield as a weapon. Instead, she set her sights on a warren hoe with a sharp V-shaped blade. Long enough to keep Randy out of arms reach but not so heavy that Wylie couldn't wield it. To reach it, Wylie would have to come out into the open and would most assuredly be spotted by Randy. She'd just have to be faster, smarter.

Before she could move, Randy came into view. He looked upward toward the hayloft. Wylie's heart dropped. If the girl was hiding up there, she was a sitting duck. There was only one way up and one way down. Wylie watched helplessly as Randy made his ascent up the ladder that led to the loft. She prayed that the brittle wooden rungs would snap beneath his weight and send him tumbling to the ground, but they held fast.

Taking a deep breath, Wylie lunged toward the barn wall and reached for the warren hoe. The garden tools clattered together like wind chimes. She half expected him to come back down the ladder, but he continued upward.

God, she wished she had her gun.

Wylie hurried to the ladder. Above her, Wylie could hear the swish and rasp of Randy rustling through the straw. "Come on out now, pumpkin," he said kindly. "Come to Dad. I'm here to help you. I'm going to take you and your mom home now. And you aren't going to believe what's there waiting for you. It was going to be a surprise, but I got you a puppy. Don't you want to go home and see it?"

With the hoe in one hand, Wylie put her foot on the lower rung of the ladder, reached for the rung just above her head, and then hesitated.

One way up, one way down, Wylie thought again. Wylie began the climb upward, trying to move silently, but her boots scraped against the weathered rungs, and her ragged breathing raced up the ladder in front of her.

As she approached the top, Wylie peeked over the landing, expecting to find Randy standing there, waiting. Instead, he was facing away from her, still kicking at the thick straw. He was moving methodically as if walking the grid of a crime scene.

Wylie eased herself over the edge and crept slowly up behind him, raising the hoe above her shoulder as if holding a baseball bat. Just as she was going to swing, Randy's toe connected with something solid. A loud gasp followed, and the girl scrambled out from the straw.

"There you are," Randy said, holding on to his fatherly tone. "What'd your mom do to your hair? You two trying to run away from me? You know better than that. It's time to go home, honey."

Bits of hay clung to the girl's shorn scalp, and her eyes went back and forth between her father and Wylie, who was still behind him. Wylie put one finger to her lips and waved her hand as if to tell her to move away.

The girl slowly crab-walked backward, putting distance between Randy, until she bumped into the broad side of the barn, below the sharp widow's peak, where the loft doors, when released, swung outward. The only thing holding them shut was a simple slide lock.

"I know you're behind me," Randy said, not bothering with a backward glance. He had no fear. Wylie was nothing but an inconvenience, a gnat to flick aside. "You're not making this easy. I have to give you credit for that. You always were a survivor."

The rage that coiled in her chest began to build. Wylie wanted to beat his skull in, wanted to feel the vibration of metal on bone, wanted him to cry out for mercy like she imagined her family had, the way Becky had, but she had to choose the right moment. Instead, she directed her attention to the little girl.

"Stand up," she told the girl. "I want you to go down the ladder. Once you're down, go inside the house and lock the door. Make sure your mom is okay." The girl looked up, fear etched across her face. "Don't worry, I'll be there in a few minutes. I promise." The girl slowly got to her feet.

"Stay put," Randy countered, and she froze. He turned to face Wylie.

Wylie knew that Randy expected her to swing high with the hoe—to aim at his head. Instead, she set her sights low.

"Go now!" Wylie shouted and swung. With a hiss, the metal rod sliced through the icy air and connected with Randy's knee. With a cry, his legs buckled and he dropped to the ground.

Wylie felt the girl brush by her, but she knew that her work wasn't done yet. As long as Randy was moving, they were both in danger.

"So Jackson Henley was innocent all along?" Wylie said, trying to keep his attention away from the girl. "All these years, everyone called him a monster, but it was you. Only you."

Randy gave a little shrug and staggered to his feet. "It was a happy accident that you two happened to show up on his property and when the dog found the rag with Becky's blood on it. Well, that was just perfect."

"But you had a family. You had a wife and a son. Where did you keep her? How did you keep her hidden for all these years?" Wylie shook her head. "It was a miracle that you pulled it off."

Randy scoffed. "My marriage was over, thank God. And my son hated me. I had plenty of time to plan and prepare the old Richter house. I set up the hog confine there and started fixing up the house and its basement. And with everyone pointing fingers at Jackson Henley, I was in the clear."

"You're sick," Wylie said with disgust. "Evil and sick. And now you plan on killing us all. Finish what you started."

Randy gave a sly smile. "Just you and Henley. The police will think he killed you to finish what he started, and Jackson, well, he'll just disappear. I'm good at that. Making people disappear."

Wylie thought about what might happen to Becky and her daughter if she let Randy walk out of the barn alive. With a guttural scream, she struck Randy again. This time she thrust the sharp, pointed blade forward, slicing through his thick parka and piercing his shoulder.

Randy roared with pain and grasped the shaft of the warren hoe, and for a moment, they were lodged in a surreal game of tug-of-war. It didn't last long. Despite the injury to his shoulder, Randy was bigger and stronger than Wylie and easily pulled it from her grasp.

Relieved of her only weapon, Wylie knew she had to get out of there. The girl was gone and hopefully made it to the house. She glanced at the hayloft door. As children, Wylie and Ethan had spent countless hours swinging from the door's rope to the ground below. She mentally measured the distance to the door and, in a split second, knew that she'd never get past Randy. Her only way out was down the ladder.

Wylie scrambled toward the ladder, her feet slipping on the slick straw but managed to swing her legs over the hayloft ledge. With shaking limbs, she skirted down the first few rungs and jumped to the barn floor below. She landed with a bone-rattling crash. From the hayloft, Randy loomed above her, the shadow monster of her childhood, now flesh and blood.

Outside the barn doors was a snowy wasteland. Icy despair flowed over her. She hadn't been able to save her parents or her brother.

But now there was Becky and her daughter. This was her chance to make up for what she couldn't do all those years ago.

"Give it up," Randy called down to her.

Wylie staggered to her feet. Blood flowed down her temple from the gash in her head. Then a thought came to her. The Bronco. It was at the far end of the barn. Wylie started to run toward the vehicle. She leaned against the car and scanned the barn in search of a weapon. At least she could go down fighting, shed as much of Randy's blood as possible. She waited until Randy turned his back in order to begin his descent down the hayloft ladder and then sprang into action. She yanked open the Bronco's door and quickly shut it behind her as she slid into the driver's seat.

She reached into her pants pocket in search of her car keys, all the while watching Randy descend. From the glove box she grabbed a flashlight and set it on the seat next to her.

With shaking hands, she tried to insert the key into the ignition but fumbled and dropped the key ring. "Dammit," she muttered, snaking her hand between the seats, feeling around frantically until her fingers landed on the cold metal.

Wylie took a deep breath and willed her trembling hands to still. She slid the key into the ignition and forced herself to wait. The timing had to be perfect. She clicked her seat belt into place, counted to three, and turned the key. She flipped on the headlights and Randy looked over his shoulder when he heard the roar of the engine coming to life.

Wylie threw the car into gear and stomped on the accelerator. The Bronco surged forward. The scream of metal on metal filled her ears as the speeding vehicle grazed the riding lawn mower pushing the Bronco too far right. Wylie swung the steering wheel to the left and back on course.

Through the windshield, Wylie could see Randy clinging to the ladder trying to decide what to do. He hesitated a split second too long. And for one brief moment, their eyes locked, and Wylie saw the fear in Randy's eyes.

She imagined it was the same terror that her mother and father felt before he shot and killed them. The terror that Ethan felt when Randy wrapped his gloved hands around his neck and squeezed, the terror that thirteen-year-old Becky felt when he stole her away from her family and subjected her to the unspeakable. And the terror the girl felt growing up with a monster.

Wylie gripped the steering wheel more tightly, preparing for impact. The Bronco struck Randy squarely in the legs and he screamed. Later, Wylie would wonder if it was the snap of the ladder or Randy's legs that she heard just before he flipped over the hood and bounced across the roof of the car.

Wylie slammed on the brakes, but it was too late. She careened into the barn wall. The crack of splintering wood filled her ears, the crunch of metal and the shatter of glass as she came face-to-face with a wall of white.

47

When Wylie told the girl to run, she scrambled down the hayloft ladder through the barn and across the yard to the house. Tas was sitting by the door looking cold and despondent. Once inside, she slammed the door shut and turned the lock.

Heart slamming against her chest, she ran to the living room where her mother stood, still holding the shotgun.

"Mama?" she asked.

"Where are they?" her mother asked.

"In the barn," the girl said, eyeing her mother nervously. "Wylie said she'd be back. But I think he's going to kill her."

"Josie," her mother said. "Her name was Josie. She was my best friend."

"Josie?" the girl asked in confusion. Her mother was scaring her.

"Go hide, sweetie," her mother said. "I won't let him hurt you. Go hide where no one can find you."

"*Okay, Mama,*" *the girl said. Instead of hiding, she went to a window at the back of the house where she could see the barn. "Hurry up, hurry up," she whispered, begging Wylie—Josie—to return. What if her father came back and Wylie didn't? What would she do? She'd have to listen to him, he was her father, but she knew he was a bad man.*

From the direction of the barn, the girl heard the rev of an engine and then the splinter of wood as a car crashed through the wall of the barn and came to a jolting stop. Wood and debris showered atop the car and tumbled to the ground.

The girl hurried back to the living room, dropped to the floor, and slid her hand beneath the sofa. Her fingers brushing across thick dust until she found what she was looking for and got to her feet. Wylie needed her help.

48

Wylie mentally scanned her body for any injuries. Her chest ached from being held back by the seat belt, and she knew she was going to have a hell of a sore neck the next day, but everything else seemed to be in one piece. She opened her eyes. The front windshield looked like an intricate spider's web. She had driven right through the barn wall.

With a moan, Wylie released her seat belt and tried the driver's side door, but it was blocked by a snowdrift. She crawled over the gearshift and tested the passenger door, and it swung open just wide enough that she was able to get out. Wylie's legs felt rubbery as she stepped out of the Bronco and into the dark, her only light coming from the nearly full moon.

The back half of the vehicle was still inside the barn, and the wooden planks above the hole sighed and swayed. Afraid that the barn's remaining section was going to come tumbling down, Wylie picked her way around the rubble to a safe distance away. Her first instinct was to hurry back outside to make sure that the girl and Becky were okay. But before she did that, Wylie knew she had to look for Randy and make sure that he was incapacitated or dead.

With heavy legs, Wylie stepped through the debris and back inside the barn. She scanned the floor for Randy. He should have been somewhere nearby, but there was no sign of him except for a streak of blood on the ground.

The hair on the back of Wylie's neck stood up. She couldn't imagine anyone surviving the impact. Wylie reached for a hammer sitting in a jumble of tools and followed the bloody path as it wound its way around old furniture and broken-down farm equipment.

She held her breath as she turned each corner, expecting Randy to be there, ready to pounce. Instead, she found him on his stomach, trying to army crawl across the floor, his right leg bent, bloodied, and dragging uselessly behind him.

"There's nowhere to run, Randy," Wylie said, echoing the same warning he had given her. He turned his face to the sound of her voice, and Wylie bit back a gasp of revulsion. The right side of his face was shredded, his nose bent at an unnatural angle.

He opened his mouth to speak, but all that came out was a gurgle as blood bubbled from his lips. He tried to drag himself forward, his hands scrabbling at the ground in front of him, but didn't have the strength.

Wylie looked at the hammer she held in her hands. It would be so easy. One swing and it would be over. For all of them. She raised the hammer above her head, her tired muscles and sore chest protesting. The little girl and Becky would be free from their captor. And so would Wylie. She would be free from the black shadow that she had been trying to outrun, the shadow that haunted her for years.

Randy's breathing was shallow, and his face was tight with pain, but he watched Wylie warily as she spread the hay over his body. "What's her name?" Wylie asked. "Becky's daughter, what's her name?"

Randy looked at her, his eyes narrow slits, and his mouth curled into a mean smile. Wylie turned to leave, but Randy called out to her, and she stopped.

"It was supposed to be you all along," Randy said, his voice weak but taunting. "Just you. But your family got in the way and Becky didn't run as fast as you did."

Wylie wanted to throw up. Not only had she let go of her best friend's hand when it mattered most, Wylie was the intended victim from the beginning.

She tried to shake the thought away. For decades she wanted to confront the person responsible for the destruction of her family. "You turned off the air-conditioning after you shot them. Why? To make it harder for the police to figure out time of death? Well, they figured that out. And you tried to make everyone think it was my brother," Wylie said angrily. "You shot my parents with your gun and then when my brother confronted you, you killed him then took his shotgun and shot my parents again to try and throw the police off. They figured that out too. You weren't as smart as you thought you were."

"I guess it worked," Randy rasped. "No one ever tied the crime to me. I was very careful but I watched you," he said. Wylie froze. His words hit her chest like daggers. "Even afterward. I still watched you, and you never knew. I thought about taking you, too, but your grandparents moved you out of town. Too bad. It would have been fun."

She turned her back to him, refusing to give him the reaction he wanted. "We're leaving, and the police are going to come for you."

"Well, let's both hope I die before then," Randy gave a little laugh. "We all know where I'm going either way."

"Straight to hell," Wylie said with satisfaction.

As she turned to go, Randy's hand shot out from beneath the straw and grabbed her ankle. Caught off balance, Wylie crashed to the ground, the air forced from her lungs. Pain reverberated through her body.

She'd let her guard down, Wylie thought as she tried to harness her breath. She tried to crawl out of his reach, but with a grunt, he latched onto her waistband and began to drag her toward him. His strength surprised her. She should have known he wouldn't give up so easily. Wylie tried to fight back but his grip was like a vise. She had nowhere to go.

Randy flipped Wylie onto her back and pinned her arms above her head. Wylie stared up at his mangled face. Why wasn't he dead? The car should have killed him. Wylie writhed beneath his weight.

"No," she cried out over and over. Things weren't going to end this way. She managed to free one hand and raked her fingers down the injured side of his face. He howled in pain but was able to snag her wrist and force it to the ground.

"No!" Wylie screamed again on a continuous loop.

"Shut up," Randy panted, stuffing a wad of straw into Wylie's open mouth. She tried to spit it out but the dry, prickly hay filled her cheeks and her throat, instantly cutting off her supply of air. She kicked out in panic, but Randy's weight was too much for her.

It would be so easy to let go, to just die. She would be able to be with her mother and father again. She could almost feel her father's hand on her head, could practically hear her mother's voice. *Smile big.* Her grandparents would be there too. *Time to come home, Shoo,* her grandpa would say. Her grandmother, stoic as always, would just nod her approval. And Ethan. She would finally be able to apologize to Ethan for not believing in him. *It's okay, little sister,* he would say. *I always believed in you.*

Randy's hands were around her throat now, squeezing. It wouldn't be long now. Little snaps of light floated above Wylie's face—almost close enough to touch.

But there was Becky and her daughter. An image of thirteen-year-old Becky with the wild tangle of curly black hair and the quick smile appeared as she floated in and out of consciousness. They needed her. She couldn't leave them behind. Not again.

A fistful of stars, Becky whispered and reached out for her hand and Wylie smiled.

49

The girl knew that she wasn't strong enough to fight her father, and she knew that Wylie wasn't strong enough either, but if you had a gun, it wouldn't matter. She would get the gun to Wylie, and she would make her father leave them alone, make him go away forever.

The snow had stopped, and in the beam of her flashlight, the world looked magical. Part of her wanted to pause and stare at the prettiness of it all, but she knew she had to keep moving. When the girl made it to the barn, she could hear the clatter of a struggle, the flailing of limbs, and a strange gasping sound. Except for the narrow beam from her flashlight, the barn was black. I'm not afraid of the dark, *the girl reminded herself. With trembling hands, she moved in the direction of the raspy breaths to find her father. His face was covered in blood, but beneath it, the girl saw his all too familiar rage. He was on top of Wylie with his hands around her neck.*

He was killing her. He always threatened to kill them, but he said it so often, she stopped believing it. But here he was, squeezing Wylie's neck so that her face was turning purple.

"Let her go, Daddy," the girl said, her voice small and timid. He didn't even acknowledge she was there. "I mean it," she said, this time more loudly, with more confidence.

This caused her father to look in his daughter's direction, but instead of being frightened, he laughed. Shame spread throughout her body. He never listened to her. Ever. She rushed forward until she was standing behind him. "I mean it, let her go," the girl said, raising the gun she found beneath the sofa after it fell from Wylie's pocket.

He swung back his hand, striking the girl across the face, sending the gun and the flashlight sliding across the barn floor. In doing so, he released one hand from Wylie's throat, giving her a chance to fight back. Wylie squirmed out from beneath Randy and wrapped her fingers around the first thing she could lay her hands on, the hammer.

Gasping for breath Wylie managed to get to her knees and swung her arm with all her remaining strength, striking Randy across the shoulder with the claw end of the hammer. He swore and dove toward Wylie. Again, he was on top of her, hands around Wylie's neck.

"Daddy," the little girl said from her spot on the barn floor. She had gained purchase on the flashlight and aimed the beam directly in his eyes so that he raised one hand to block the glare.

"Stay out of this," he said. "Stay back and shut up."

Wylie had stopped moving. Stopped fighting back.

The girl lowered the flashlight and scanned the floor and spotted the gun. Her father blinked rapidly and reached for the claw hammer that lay in Wylie's limp fingers. "Close your eyes, peanut," he said. "You don't want to see this."

He rose up, hammer lifted above his head, poised to strike when he felt the cold metal barrel of the gun pressed against the back of his head.

The girl closed her eyes and pulled the trigger.

50

Holding hands, Wylie and the girl lurched to the house; the gash in her temple throbbed. She felt sick, dizzy, and most assuredly had a concussion. The girl kept looking back toward the barn in search of her father. "Don't worry," Wylie said, squeezing her hand. "He's not coming."

They stumbled through the front door to find Becky still sitting there, the empty shotgun aimed at them.

"Becky," Wylie said in alarm. "It's okay. It's over."

"He told me he had friends everywhere, and if we tried to get away, they would take us back," she said shakily.

It took a moment for Wylie to figure out what Becky was saying. "Randy lied to you," she said. "He told you those things to scare you. He took you all by himself. No one helped him. Randy was the monster. The only monster. And now he's dead."

Becky allowed her grip on the shotgun to relax. "He's dead?" she asked breathlessly.

"Yeah," Wylie said. She didn't mention that it was her daughter who pulled the trigger. There would be time enough for all of that. "He can't hurt either of you ever again. I promise."

Slowly, Becky lowered the shotgun and began to cry. The little girl went to her. "It's okay, Mama," she whispered. "It's okay."

Wylie opened the shades so they could see better. The sun was just beginning to rise.

"We have to get out of here," Wylie said. "We need to get you to the hospital. We're out of wood, and God knows if the storm is going to start up again."

"How?" Becky asked through her tears.

"Randy's truck. I got his keys," Wylie said pulling them from her pocket. "He's probably got chains on his tires."

"Okay," Becky said in a small voice. "What about the man in the toolshed?"

Jackson Henley. She had been so wrong about him—they all had been. That poor man had been accused of the most heinous crimes, and he was innocent. He may not have been sent to prison, but he had been tried and convicted by his community. Jackson was a victim too.

"I unlocked the shed and let him out. I tried to explain, but don't worry about him right now. He's fine," Wylie said. "You'll be able to go home—see your mom and dad, your brother and sister."

"I don't believe it," Becky said, settling gingerly onto the sofa. "It doesn't seem real."

Wylie led the little girl to the kitchen. "Are you okay?"

Wylie asked, getting a good look at the girl's clothing, hands, face—all splattered with her father's blood.

The girl nodded, her eyes blank. Wylie feared she was going into shock.

"Everything is going to be fine," Wylie said, guiding the girl over to the sink and pouring bottled water over her bloody hands. "We're all safe now. We're leaving here, and he will never be able to hurt you again."

The girl's chin trembled. "I picked up the gun. I saw it fall out of your pocket. I know I wasn't supposed to touch it, but when you didn't come back, I got scared. Then I saw the car come through the barn. I thought you were dead," she said tearfully. "I didn't know what I was supposed to do. So I came to find you."

"You sure did," Wylie said, gently wiping a damp cloth across the girl's face.

The girl gave her a wisp of a smile, and then it fell away. "I shot my dad." The girl's voice broke. "I'm sorry."

"You had to." Wylie tried to assure her. "You saved my life. You saved your mother's life. Thank you." Wylie reached out her arms. After a moment's hesitation, the girl walked into them, and Wylie pulled the girl into an embrace. They stood there for a long time, the girl's tears dampening the front of Wylie's coat. For Wylie, there were no tears. Not yet. She would save them for later.

Wylie grabbed an armful of coats and hats and moved to the living room.

Wylie dressed Becky and the girl in layers of clothing to keep them adequately warm for their journey. Becky seemed to be in a daze. Shock probably. Wylie pulled wool socks over the girl's hands, a stocking cap over her ears, and wrapped a scarf around her neck so that only her eyes were showing.

"Do you trust me?" Wylie asked. The girl nodded. Together they helped Becky toward the door, Tas at their heels. "Are you ready?" Wylie asked.

"Yes," came the girl's muffled reply. Through the opened door, the wind had stilled, and the snowy landscape glittered like diamonds.

"Wylie," the little girl said shyly. "My name is Josie." And they stepped out into the brittle sunshine.

15 MONTHS LATER

Libraries, no matter what state or city Wylie visited, had the same comforting smell, and the Spirit Lake Public Library in Iowa was no different. The books, paper, glue, and ink—all in various stages of disintegration—had a musty, vanilla-like scent that eased her anxiety.

Wylie looked out over the crowd of fifty eagerly waiting for her to read from *The Overnight Guest*. A year after finishing the final edits, the book was out in the world and Wylie was on tour, making her way across the United States, inching her way toward Burden. Tomorrow she would leave Spirit Lake and drive thirty miles to the tiny library in her former hometown. Wylie was nervous about it. She hadn't been back for over a year.

After Becky and Josie's escape in the middle of a snowstorm and the events at the farmhouse that led to the death of Randy Cutter, they found themselves in the spotlight along with the small Iowa town. After speaking with law enforcement and making sure that Becky and Josie were safe and reunited with family, Wylie went home. Went back to Oregon, back to her son. She had a lot to make up for and she spent every minute of the past year doing just that.

Speaking in front of groups of people, large or small, never got easier, but libraries and bookstores did their best to make her feel comfortable, at home, and this library was no exception. All the folding chairs were filled, and more people lined up against the back wall.

As the library director introduced Wylie, she searched the crowd for Seth who had reluctantly agreed to come on tour with her. Now fifteen, Seth had a summer job and a boyfriend.

Wylie understood his reluctance. "I want to show you where I grew up," she told him. "I want you to see where my story took place. Why I'm the way I am."

Seth had grown quiet. "Okay," he finally agreed. "But can we please go see the Dodgers when they play in Boston?"

Wylie laughed. Seth loved baseball as much as she did. "It's a deal," she promised.

And there he was, sitting in the back row, head bent over his cell phone. He glanced up, saw Wylie looking at him and gave her his thousand-watt smile. They'd come a long way in the last year.

As the library director finished her introduction, the room filled with polite applause and Wylie stepped to the podium.

"Good evening," she began. "It's such a joy to be back in my home state of Iowa, to be here talking with you tonight. As a true crime writer, I'm used to writing about other people's lives. I write about regular, everyday people who have unimaginable things happen to them. I write about the impact it has on families, on communities, on those left behind.

I also write about the perpetrators—try to delve into their backgrounds, their upbringing, their psyches in order to try and comprehend why they commit the terrible acts they do. *The Overnight Guest* was a very different project for me. It was personal."

This was where Wylie read from the book. She always chose the first few pages.

At first, twelve-year-old Josie Doyle and her best friend, Becky Allen, ran toward the loud bangs. It only made sense to go to the house—that's where her mother and father and Ethan were. They would be safe. But by the time Josie and Becky discovered their mistake, it was too late.

They turned away from the sound and, hand in hand, ran through the dark farmyard toward the cornfield—its stalks, a tall, spindly forest, their only portal to safety.

Josie was sure she heard the pounding of footsteps behind them, and she turned to see what was hunting them. There was nothing, no one—just the house bathed in nighttime shadows.

"Hurry," Josie gasped, tugging on Becky's hand and urging her forward. Breathing heavily, they ran. They were almost there. Becky stumbled. Crying out, her hand slipped from Josie's. Her legs buckled, and she fell to her knees.

Here, Wylie's voice always broke. Every single time. This was her biggest regret—not getting Becky into the cornfield and to safety.

Wylie lifted her eyes. Two women and a young girl stepped into the meeting room. Wylie immediately recognized Margo

Allen, Becky's mother. She hadn't seen Margo since Becky and her mother had been reunited at the hospital after they had escaped the farmhouse.

When Margo had been escorted into the hospital room where Becky, Josie, and Wylie were being tended to, at first she didn't believe the emaciated woman with the bruised and swollen face was her daughter.

Wylie had felt like an intruder, an interloper. Margo, once the shock of having her daughter back and discovering that she had a granddaughter had settled in, regarded Wylie coolly. Wylie felt that Margo had never quite forgiven her. Becky had been abducted at her home, on her parents' watch, and Wylie had walked away while her daughter had not.

And now standing next to Margo were Becky and Josie. Wylie faltered. She hadn't expected them to show up here. She wasn't prepared to read these words in front of Becky. It felt wrong.

Becky gave her an encouraging smile and Wylie swallowed back her tears and continued to read.

"Get up, get up," Josie begged, pulling on Becky's arm. "Please." Once again, she dared to look behind her. A shard of moonlight briefly revealed a shape stepping out from behind the barn. In horror, Josie watched as the figure raised his hands and took aim. She dropped Becky's arm, turned, and ran. Just a little bit farther—she was almost there.

Josie crossed into the cornfield just as another shot rang out. Searing pain ripped through her arm, stripping her breath from her lungs. Josie didn't pause, didn't slow down, and with hot blood dripping onto the hard-packed soil, Josie kept running.

Wylie lowered the book and looked out over the crowd who stared back at her with rapt attention. Most knew by now that Wylie was Josie Doyle and that Becky and her daughter had miraculously survived after years of being locked in a basement, but still it was a shocking story.

Margo Allen dabbed her eyes with a tissue, Josie rifled through her grandmother's purse, and Becky looked down at the floor.

Hands shot up and Wylie began fielding questions. *When did you decide to become a writer? Why true crime? Why did you decide to write your own story? How does Becky Allen feel about the book? Are you still in contact with Becky and her daughter?*

"Becky Allen and her daughter," Wylie said, "are the bravest, strongest people I've ever known. I hope the world will let them have their privacy."

"But you wrote a book about her tragedy. How does Becky feel about it?" a woman in the crowd asked.

Before the book went to print, Wylie offered to send the manuscript to Becky so she could read it, so she could share her input. Wylie told her, unequivocally, that she would pull the plug on the book if Becky wanted her to.

"I don't need to read it," Becky had said. "I trust you."

Wylie looked to the back of the room for the final confirmation and Becky gave her a sad smile and nodded.

"Becky gave her approval," Wylie told the audience. "I wouldn't have finished the book—I wouldn't have released it without her blessing. It was our tragedy, both of ours. Over the years we shared this nightmare in different places and different ways, but we shared it." Wylie bit back her tears. "And we came out on the other side. I'm so grateful to have my friend back."

The room filled with applause.

An hour later, once the last book was signed, the last picture taken, Wylie thanked the library director and she and Seth made their way toward the exit where Becky, Josie, and Margo were waiting just outside.

"I can't believe you made the drive over here," Wylie exclaimed.

"It wasn't far and we wanted to surprise you," Becky said with a grin. She looked completely different than the last time Wylie had seen her. The swelling in her face and the bruises were gone and were replaced with the features Wylie remembered most about her friend. Her dimples and bright smile. But still, scars remained some visible, some less so.

"Hi, Wylie," Josie said shyly. Josie, too, had changed. Her shorn hair now fell below her chin in a mass of wild dark curls. She had grown a few inches taller, and her thin, emaciated frame had filled out some.

"Look at you," Wylie said pulling Josie into a tight hug. "You've grown a foot. And you," Wylie said grabbing Becky's hand, "you look amazing."

Becky and Josie did look better but there was a wariness in their eyes, a haunted look that made Wylie want to cry. Instead, she looked around for Seth. "And this is my son. Come here, Seth."

"Hi, Seth," Becky said. "It's great to finally meet you."

"You too," Seth nodded. Becky began peppering Seth with questions about his summer plans and Margo drew Wylie aside.

"Becky and Josie told me everything you did to help them," Margo said, squeezing Wylie's hand. "I know I wasn't kind to you..."

"It's okay," Wylie said shaking her head. "I understand—I

really do. And as much as Becky and Josie say I helped them, they saved me too."

Margo's eyes glittered with tears. "Thank you. Thank you for bringing them back to me."

Wylie didn't know what else to say and was grateful when the moment was interrupted. "Anyone hungry?" Becky asked. "There's a little bar and grill just around the corner. Do you have time to grab a bite?" she asked Wylie.

Wylie looked to Seth who nodded. "I'm starved," he said.

The group began walking and Wylie and Becky lagged a bit behind and watched as Seth entertained Josie and Margo with funny stories of their time on the road.

"We have great kids," Becky said. She lifted her face to the evening sun, basking at the feel of it on her skin. Wylie did the same. Since the snowstorm, she had tried not to take small, ordinary moments for granted.

"Yes, we do," Wylie agreed, then hesitated before asking the question she had been wanting to ask Becky for a long time. "Are you really planning on staying in Burden? Isn't it hard? I couldn't wait to get far away from there."

Becky shook her head. "My mom's there. And my dad. My brother and sister aren't far. I can't leave. I just got back."

Wylie tried to understand. "Don't you worry about Josie growing up in a place where everyone knows what happened? Doesn't she have nightmares? Don't you? I know Randy Cutter is dead, but you and Josie could come and stay with us in Oregon."

The more Wylie said it out loud, the more it sounded like a good idea. There was nothing in Burden anymore for Becky and Josie—nothing but bad memories. "You could get a job when you're ready and there's a great elementary school for Josie right near my house. Your family could come visit you there anytime. They'd understand. How could they not understand?"

Becky stopped walking. "It is hard being there, but I think it would be hard anywhere. We both have nightmares. More than nightmares," Becky amended. "I dream that we're back there, in that basement. I can actually feel the concrete beneath my feet, can smell him. And Josie, well… We're both talking to a counselor. It helps some." When Wylie didn't look convinced, Becky took a breath and tried again.

"You lost your parents and brother there, in your childhood home. I know how hard it was for you to go back there and work on the book—but if you hadn't been there, Josie would have died and I would have too. Or maybe Randy would have found us and brought us back home."

"That wasn't your home," Wylie interrupted angrily. "It was a prison."

"Yes," Becky agreed. "It was a prison. But Josie was there with me. And because of you, I was lucky enough to go back to my true home. The house where I grew up. A place where I felt safe and loved every single day of my life. I'm sleeping in my old bedroom, in my old bed and my mother is right down the hall."

"But…" Wylie began.

"And that's all I've wanted since that night Randy Cutter took me," Becky continued, "to go home. And now I'm home with my little girl. I know that things aren't going to be perfect, that I've got a long road ahead of me and Josie probably has a longer one. But we're home and that's enough for now."

Becky reached for Wylie's hand. "Think about it. What's the safest place you know?"

Wylie wanted to say she didn't have a true home. It was one

of many things that Randy Cutter had stolen from her. She was still always looking over her shoulder. She had no safe place.

Wylie looked down the sidewalk where Seth, Josie, and Margo were waiting for them at the corner. Seth raised his hand and waved.

And then it came to her. Her son. No matter where she went, no matter the number of miles between them, he was her true north. He was her home.

Wylie smiled, waved back, and then turned to Becky. "Everything is actually going to be okay, isn't it?" she asked.

They stood there, watching for a moment as Seth, Josie, and Margo laughed and called out to them, "Hurry up!"

"I think it is," Becky said. "But listen, I know you still blame yourself for what happened to me. I saw how you reacted when you read from that part of the book."

Wylie shook her head. She didn't want to talk about this anymore.

"No, wait," Becky said standing in front of Wylie so she had to look her in the eye. "Sometimes letting go is a good thing. Sometimes it's the only thing left to do."

Wylie bit the insides of her cheeks, trying not to cry, but still the tears came.

"It wasn't your fault," Becky said. "It was Randy Cutter's fault—his alone. Let go of it," Becky begged. "I never blamed you, not even once, so please stop blaming yourself."

Becky took Wylie's hand in her own. "Sisters forever, right?"

"Sisters forever," Wylie whispered.

★ ★ ★ ★ ★

ACKNOWLEDGMENTS

Even though this novel was written and rewritten during the pandemic, I never felt alone along the way and there are so many people to thank for this.

Thank you to Marianne Merola, my dear agent, who continues to be a great source of wisdom, friendship, and support throughout my career. Thanks also to everyone at Brandt & Hochman Literary Agents Inc. for all their work on my behalf.

Many thanks to my favorite plot puzzle solving partner and editor, Erika Imranyi—I love our phone calls talking through those sticky plot points—it's always an adventure. Emer Flounders, PR guru extraordinaire, works tirelessly to spread the word about my books and for that I am so grateful. Thanks also to everyone at Park Row, HarperCollins, and Harlequin including the amazingly talented marketing, sales, art, and production teams who support me and my books in too many ways to count.

Several early readers offered priceless feedback on *The Overnight Guest* including Jane Augspurger, Molly Lugar, Amy Feld, and Lenora Vinckier. Thank you.

Big-time thanks go to Mark Dalsing, Dr. Emily Gudenkauf, and John Conway for their expertise. I can always count on them when I need guidance when it comes to law enforcement, the medical field, and farm life.

My sweet family continues to be my greatest supporters. Much gratitude goes to my parents, Milton and Patricia Schmida, and to my brothers and sisters. And as always, thank you to Scott, Alex, Annie & RJ, and Gracie—I love you and couldn't do it without you.

QUESTIONS FOR DISCUSSION

1. With Wylie's tragic history, why do you think she would choose to be a true crime writer where she is continually faced with the brutal realities of violence and its impact on victims and their families? Why do you think Wylie felt the need to return to Burden and her childhood home in order to write her book?

2. Discuss the rural setting of the novel. How do you think living in Burden shaped the characters? How would the story be different if it was set in a large city?

3. The child says, "It isn't the dark you should be afraid of... It's the monsters who step out into the light that you need to fear." What do you think they meant by this?

4. Wylie and Becky vowed to be "sisters forever." After all that they've been through, what do you think their friendship will look like? Will it last? Why or why not?

5. *The Overnight Guest* is set in a blizzard and in the scorching heat of summer. What role does weather play in the story, both literally and metaphorically?

6. The child says there are three kinds of dark. What is the relationship that each of the characters have to darkness? How does it change throughout the novel?

7. Parenthood is a common theme throughout the story. How does it manifest itself throughout the story? How did each of the characters step into that role?

8. Wylie, Becky, and Josie have been through so much. Where do you see them a year from now? Five years? Twenty?

9. Discuss the ways in which the idea of being a prisoner is explored throughout the story for each of the characters.

10. By the end of the novel, we learn secrets that change the way we think about certain characters and the way the characters see one another. What character do you think changed the most over the course of the book? How did your opinions of the characters change throughout the story?

Read ahead for a bonus excerpt of Heather Gudenkauf's gripping thriller Not a Sound.

PROLOGUE

I find her sitting all by herself in the emergency waiting room,
her lovely features distorted from the swelling and bruising.
Only a few patients remain, unusual for a Friday night and a
full moon. Sitting across from her, an elderly woman coughs
wetly into a handkerchief while her husband, arms folded
across his chest and head tilted back, snores gently. Another
man with no discernible ailment stares blankly up at the television mounted on the wall. Canned laughter fills the room.

I'm surprised she's still here. We treated her hours ago. Her
clothing was gathered, I examined her from head to toe, all
the while explaining what I was doing step-by-step. She lay on
her back while I swabbed, scraped and searched for evidence.
I collected bodily fluids and hairs that were not her own. I
took pictures. Close-ups of abrasions and bruises. I stood close
by while the police officer interviewed her and asked deeply

personal private questions. I offered her emergency contra-
ceptives and the phone number for a domestic abuse shelter.
She didn't cry once during the entire process. But now the
tears are falling freely, dampening the clean scrubs I gave her
to change into.

"Stacey?" I sit down next to her. "Is someone coming to
get you?" I ask. I offered to call someone on her behalf but
she refused, saying that she could take care of it. I pray to God
that she didn't call her husband, the man who did this to her.
I hope that the police had already picked him up.

She shakes her head. "I have my car."

"I don't think you should be driving. Please let me call
someone," I urge. "Or you can change your mind and we can
admit you for the night. You'll be safe. You can get some rest."

"No, I'm okay," she says. But she is far from okay. I tried to
clean her up as best I could but already her newly stitched lip
is oozing blood, the bruises blooming purple across her skin.

"At least let me walk you to your car," I offer. I'm eager to
get home to my husband and stepdaughter but they are long
asleep. A few more minutes won't matter.

She agrees and stands, cradling her newly casted arm. We
walk out into the humid August night. The full moon, wide
faced and as pale as winter wheat lights our way. Katydids
call back and forth to one another and white-winged moths
throw themselves at the illuminated sign that reads Queen of
Peace Emergency.

"Where are you staying tonight? You're not going home,
are you?"

"No," she says but doesn't elaborate more. "I had to park
over on Birch," she says dully. Queen of Peace's lot has been
under construction for the better part of a month so parking
is a challenge. It makes me sad to think that not only did this

poor woman, beaten and raped by her estranged husband, have to drive herself to the emergency room, there wasn't even a decent place for her to park. Now there are five open parking spaces. What a difference a few hours can make in the harried, unpredictable world of emergency room care.

We walk past sawhorse barriers and orange construction cones to a quiet, residential street lined with sweetly pungent linden trees. Off in the distance a car engines roars to life, a dog barks, a siren howls. Another patient for the ER.

"My car is just up here," Stacey says and points to a small, white four-door sedan hidden in the shadows cast by the heart-shaped leaves of the lindens. We cross the street and I wait as Stacey digs around in her purse for her keys. A mosquito buzzes past my ear and I wave it away.

I hear the scream of tires first. The high-pitched squeal of rubber on asphalt. Stacey and I turn toward the noise at the same time. Blinding high beams come barreling toward us. There is nowhere to go. If we step away from Stacey's car we will be directly in its path. I push Stacey against her car door and press as close to her as I can, trying to make ourselves as small as possible.

I'm unable to pull my eyes away from bright light and I keep thinking that the careless driver will surely correct the steering wheel and narrowly miss us. But that doesn't happen. There is no screech of brakes, the car does not slow and the last sound I hear is the dull, sickening thud of metal on bone.

1

Two Years Later…

Nearly every day for the past year I have paddle boarded, kayaked, run or hiked around the sinuous circuit that is Five Mines River, Stitch at my side. We begin our journey each day just a dozen yards from my front door, board and oar hoisted above my head, and move cautiously down the sloping, rocky bank to the water's edge. I lower my stand-up paddleboard, the cheapest one I could find, into the water, mindfully avoiding the jagged rocks that could damage my board. I wade out into the shallows, flinching at the bite of cold water against my skin, and steady it so Stitch can climb on. I hoist myself up onto my knees behind him and paddle out to the center of the river.

With long even strokes I pull the oar through the murky river. The newly risen sun, intermittently peeking through heavy, slow-moving gray clouds, reflects off droplets of water kicked up like sparks. The late-October morning air is bracing and smells of decaying leaves. I revel in the sights and feel of the river, but I can't hear the slap of my oar against the water, can't hear the cry of the seagulls overhead, can't hear Stitch's playful yips. I'm still trying to come to terms with this.

The temperature is forecast to dip just below freezing soon and when it does I will reluctantly stow my board in the storage shed, next to my kayak until spring. In front of me, like a nautical figurehead carved into the prow of a sailing vessel, sits Stitch. His bristled coat is the same color as the underside of a silver maple leaf in summer, giving him a distinguished air. He is three years old and fifty-five pounds of muscle and sinew but often gets distracted and forgets that he has a job to do.

Normally, when I go paddling, I travel an hour and a half north to where Five Mines abruptly opens into a gaping mouth at least a mile wide. There the riverside is suddenly lined with glass-sided hotels, fancy restaurants, church spires and a bread factory that fills the air with a scent that reminds me of my mother's kitchen. Joggers and young mothers with strollers move leisurely along the impressive brick-lined river walk and the old train bridge that my brother and I played on as kids looms in the distance—out of place and damaged beyond repair. Kind of like me.

Once I catch sight of the train bridge or smell the yeasty scent of freshly baked bread I know it's time to turn around. I much prefer the narrow, isolated inlets and sloughs south of Mathias, the river town I grew up in.

This morning there's only time for a short trek. I have an interview with oncologist and hematologist Dr. Joseph Huntley, the director of the Five Mines Regional Cancer Center in Mathias, at ten. Five Mines provides comprehensive health care and resources to cancer patients in the tristate area. Dr. Huntley is also on staff at Queen of Peace Hospital with my soon-to-be ex-husband, David. He is the head of obstetrics and gynecology at Q & P and isn't thrilled that I might be working with his old friend. It was actually Dr. Huntley who called me to see if I was interested. The center is going to update their paper files to electronic files and need someone to enter data.

Dr. Huntley, whom I met on a few occasions years ago through David, must have heard that I've been actively search-ing for work with little luck. David, despite his grumblings, hasn't sabotaged me. I'll be lucky if he can muster together any kind words about me. It's a long, complicated story filled with heartache and alcohol. Lots of alcohol. David could only take so much and one day I found myself all alone.

I come upon what is normally my favorite part of Five Mines, a constricted slice of river only about fifteen yards wide and at least twenty feet at its deepest. The western bank is a wall of craggy limestone topped by white pines and brawny chinquapin oaks whose branches extend out over the bluff in a rich bronze canopy of leaves. Today the river is unusually slow and sluggish as if it is thick with silt and mud. The air is too heavy, too still. On the other bank the lacy-leaf tendrils of black willows dangle in the water like limp fingers.

Stitch's ears twitch. Something off in the distance has caught his attention. My board rocks slowly at first, a gentle undulation that quickly becomes jarring. Cold water splashes across my ankles and I nearly tumble into the river. Instead I fall to my knees, striking them sharply against my board. Somehow I manage to avoid tumbling in myself but lose my paddle and my dog to the river. Stitch doesn't appear to mind the unexpected bath and is paddling his way to the shore. Up-

river, some asshole in a motorboat must have revved his engine, causing the tumultuous wake.

I wait on hands and knees, my insides swaying with the
river until the waves settle. My paddle bobs on the surface of
the water just a few feet out of my reach. I cup one hand to
use as an oar and guide my board until I can grab the paddle.
Maybe it's my nervousness about my upcoming interview, but
I'm anxious to turn around and go back home. Something
feels off, skewed. Stitch is oblivious. This is the spot where
we usually take a break, giving me a chance to stretch my legs
and giving Stitch a few minutes to play. I check my watch. It's
only seven thirty, plenty of time for Stitch to romp around
in the water for a bit. Stitch with only his coarse, silver head
visible makes a beeline for land. I resituate myself into a sitting position and lay the paddle across my lap. Above me, two
turkey vultures circle in wide, wobbly loops. The clouds off
in the distance are the color of bruised flesh.

Stitch emerges from the river and onto the muddy embank-
ment and gives himself a vigorous shake, water dripping from
his beard and mustache or what his trainer described as *facial
furnishings*, common to Slovakian rough-haired pointers. He
lopes off and begins to explore the shoreline by sniffing and
snuffling around each tree trunk and fallen log. I close my
eyes, tilt my face up toward the sky and the outside world completely disappears. I smell rain off in the distance. A rain that
I know will wash away what's left of fall. It's Halloween and
I hope that the storm will hold off until the trick-or-treaters
have finished their begging.

Stitch has picked up a stick and, instead of settling down
to chew on it like most dogs, he tosses it from his mouth into
the air, watches it tumble into the water and then pounces.
My stepdaughter, Nora, loves Stitch. I think if it weren't for

Stitch, Nora wouldn't be quite as excited to spend time with me. Not that I can blame her. I really screwed up and I'm not the easiest person in the world to communicate with.

I'm debating whether or not to bring Stitch into the interview with me. Legally I have the right. I have all the paperwork and if Dr. Huntley can't be accommodating, I'm not sure I want to work for him. Plus, Stitch is such a sweet, loving dog, I'm sure the cancer patients that come into the center would find his presence comforting.

My stomach twists at the thought of having to try and sell myself as a qualified, highly capable office worker in just a few short hours. There was a time not that long ago when I was a highly regarded, sought-after nurse. Not anymore.

Stitch has wandered over to where the earth juts out causing a crooked bend in the river, a spot that, lacking a better word, I call the elbow. I catch sight of Stitch facing away from me, frozen in place, right paw raised, tail extended, eyes staring intently at something. Probably a squirrel or chipmunk. He creeps forward two steps and I know that once the animal takes off so will Stitch. While nine times out of ten he'll come back when I summon him, he's been known to run and I don't have time this morning to spend a half an hour searching for him.

I snap my fingers twice, our signal for Stitch to come. He ignores me. I row closer. "Stitch, *ke mne!*" I call. *Come.* His floppy ears twitch but still he remains fixated on whatever has caught his eye. Something has changed in his stance. His back is rounded until he's almost crouching, his tail is tucked between his legs and his ears are flat against his head. He's scared.

My first thought is he's happened upon a skunk. My second thought is one of amusement given that, for the moment, our roles have reversed—I'm trying to gain his attention rather than the other way around. I snap my fingers again, hoping to break the spell. The last thing I need is to walk into my new job smelling like roadkill. Stitch doesn't even glance my way.

I scoot off my board into knee-deep water, my neoprene shoes sinking into the mud. I wrestle my board far enough onto land so it won't drift away. Maybe Stitch has cornered a snake. Not too many poisonous snakes around here. Brown spotted massasauga and black banded timber rattlers are rare but not unheard of. I pick my way upward through snarls of dead weeds and step over rotting logs until I'm just a few yards behind Stitch. He is perched atop a rocky incline that sits about five feet above the water. Slowly, so as to not startle Stitch or whatever has him mesmerized, I inch my way forward, craning my neck to get a better look.

Laying a hand on Stitch's rough coat, damp from his swim, I feel him tremble beneath my fingers. I follow his gaze and find myself staring down to where a thick layer of fallen leaves carpets the surface of the water. A vibrant mosaic of yellow, red and brown. "There's nothing there," I tell him, running my hand over his ears and beneath his chin. His vocal chords vibrate in short, staccato bursts, alerting me to his whimpering.

I lean forward, my toes dangerously close to the muddy ridge. One misstep and I'll tumble in.

It takes a moment for my brain to register what I'm seeing and I think someone has discarded an old mannequin into the river. Then I realize this is no figure molded from fiberglass or plastic. This is no Halloween prank. I see her exposed breast, pale white against a tapestry of fall colors. With my heart slamming into my chest, I stumble backward. Though I try to break the fall with my hands, I hit the ground hard, my head striking the muddy earth, my teeth gnashing together, leaving me momentarily stunned. I blink up at the sky, trying to get my bearings, and in slow motion, a great blue heron with a wingspan the length of a grown man glides over me, casting a brief shadow. Slowly, I sit up, dazed, and my hands go to my scalp. When I pull my fingers away they are bloody.

Dizzily, I stagger to my feet. I cannot pass out here, I tell myself. No one will know where to find me. Blood pools in my mouth from where I've bitten my tongue and I spit, trying to get rid of the coppery taste. I wipe my hands on my pants and gingerly touch the back of my head again. There's a small bump but no open wound that I can feel. I look at my hands and see the source of the blood. The thin, delicate skin of my palms is shredded and embedded with small pebbles.

The forest feels like it is closing in all around me and I want to run, to get as far away from here as possible. But maybe I was mistaken. Maybe what I thought I saw was a trick of light, a play of shadows. I force myself back toward the ridge and try to summon the cool, clinical stance that I was known for when I was an emergency room nurse. I peer down, and staring up at me is the naked body of a woman floating just beneath the surface of the water. Though I can't see any discernible injuries on her, I'm sure there is no way she happened to end up here by accident. I take in a pair of blue lips parted in surprise, an upturned nose, blank eyes wide-open; tendrils of blond hair tangled tightly into a snarl of half-submerged brambles keeps her from drifting away.

Pinpricks of light dance in front of my eyes and for a moment I'm blinded with shock, fear, dread. Then I do something I have never done, not even once at the sight of a dead body. I bend over and vomit. Great, violent heaves that leave my stomach hollow and my legs shaky. I wipe my mouth with the back of my hand. I know her. Knew her. The dead woman is Gwen Locke and at one time we were friends.